D0548463

My Other Life

My Other Life

A NOVEL

PAUL THEROUX

HAMISH HAMILTON · LONDON

To Jonathan Raban

HAMISH HAMILTON LTD

Published by the Penguin Group
Penguin Books Ltd, 27 Wrights Lane, London w8 5tz, England
Penguin Books USA Inc., 375 Hudson Street, New York, New York 10014, USA
Penguin Books Australia Ltd, Ringwood, Victoria, Australia
Penguin Books Canada Ltd, 10 Alcorn Avenue, Toronto, Ontario, Canada m4v 3b2
Penguin Books (NZ) Ltd, 182–190 Wairau Road, Auckland 10, New Zealand

Penguin Books Ltd, Registered Offices: Harmondsworth, Middlesex, England

First published 1996
1 3 5 7 9 10 8 6 4 2

Set in 11.5/13.5pt Monotype Sabon
Typeset by Datix International Limited, Bungay, Suffolk
Printed in England by Clays Ltd, St Ives plc

A CIP catalogue record for this book is available from the British Library

ISBN 0-241-13503-6

Trade paperback ISBN 0-241-13601-6

Author's Note

This is the story of a life I could have lived had things been different; an imaginary memoir. The fact that there are limits to serious travesty and that memory matters means that even an imagined life resembles one that was lived; yet in this I was entirely driven by my alter ego's murmur of 'What if?'

These characters do not exist outside this intentionally tall story, the cities are pretty lofty too, and the action of the narrative is vagrant in every sense. There are some names you know – Anthony Burgess, Nathan Leopold, Queen Elizabeth II, and more, but they too are alter egos, other hes and other shes. As for the other I, the Paul Theroux who looks like me – he is just a fellow wearing a mask. It is the writer's privilege to keep some façades intact and use his own face in the masquerade. It was the only area in which I took no liberties. The man is fiction, but the mask is real.

P.T.

I do not know which of us has written this page.

Jorge Luis Borges, 'Borges and I'

ONE

PROLOGUE
Uncle Hal's Other Life

When people say of someone, 'You'll either love him or hate him,' I always have the feeling I'll hate him. Then I remember my Uncle Hal and I know better.

Uncle Hal seldom spoke to us except to tease or criticize, but once he told me that his mother – Grandma – had never picked him up when he cried in his crib. She simply let him lie there and scream – didn't touch him, didn't talk to him, didn't feed him until a specific minute on the clock. He must have been forty-something when he confided this, and he looked at me and added, 'Imagine what that can do to a person, Paulie.'

He was unshaven and his whiskers were grayer than they should have been. He was always clawing his hair. I never saw him sit down at his table to eat a meal. He stood up, looking out of the kitchen window, forking tuna fish out of an open can, then he threw the can away and wiped his hands on his shirt. He drank out of bottles – even milk bottles, even milk cartons that had spouts that missed his lips. He put his mouth under the faucet. He hated the way that other people ate – sitting down, taking their time. Just a small amount of sitting down made him jump up and rage. 'We're wasting time! I've got so much to do! I've been sitting down all day!'

His house needed painting, he said; his grass had to be cut. He needed something at the hardware store – and it might be a hinge that he would fasten by banging screws through the holes as though they were nails, he was so impatient to get the thing hung. And the way he used a hammer made you think of a murderer.

'I'm going off-Cape,' he would say, whether his destination was Boston to the dentist's or to Mexico, where he claimed he hunted giant lizards.

I went one hundred and forty miles with him in his old Ford, on a winter day. He owned a pony then, and his blue jeans were stiff with

I

pony shit. The car windows were shut tight and his heater was on. 'I never got carsick when I was your age,' he said, as I held my face miserably in my hands.

'It's his fault that I'm late,' he said to the salesman when we got to the shop, which was outside Bridgeport. He scrubbed at my scalp with his knuckles and said, 'He's on medication. It's given him an unbelievable case of the squitters. We've stopped at every filling station between here and the Cape.'

It was an astonishing three-part lie, but the man accepted it, smiling pityingly at me.

This place looked like another hardware store or junk shop, but Uncle Hal came out with a book. He let me glance at it – gold stamped leather and tissuey pages. He put it into a brown paper bag and I never saw it again. He kept such treasures in a trunk in his attic, or in drawers. If he opened a drawer and you looked in you would see glints of gold, daggers, chains, dented goblets, silver plates, carvings; and then he shut it and complained. 'I have nothing,' he said. 'No wife, no money, no children, nothing.'

His closets were full of fine clothes, but the clothes he wore were always torn. He wore everything until it was in tatters and then he threw it away – wore his shoes until they were cracked and broken, wore his sweaters until they were frayed and pilled. And I have already mentioned his pony-shit trousers.

I never saw him in clean clothes, and while from a distance in these torn things he looked like a carefree boy, up close he looked like an old tramp, and he smelled.

'You're wasting water, Paulie!' he screamed at me one time when I was letting the water run from his faucet. Was that it? That he felt that by not washing he was saving water and money too? Certainly he was frugal. He ate alone, he slept alone in a narrow bed, and if you asked him whether he had seen a particular movie he would say, 'Two bucks! I'm not paying two bucks to see their movie. I wouldn't give them the satisfaction.'

'They' and 'them' were words he frequently used. 'You know what they're doing to the interstate? They're widening it!' 'They always say "Happy Holidays" and never "Merry Christmas" at this time of year. I hate it when they do that.' 'They're building another supermarket!' 'They're the kind of people who, if you ain't talking about them, ain't listening.'

Uncle Hal was the sort of person who, if you didn't see him for a while, you might think had killed himself, or gone to Alaska, and then, when you saw him again, you realized that he would probably never die, not in the normal way, nor would he go anywhere at all. When he did go outside the house strange things happened. People drove more slowly and always in front of his car, and he yelled at them, his spit flecking his windshield; and red lights came on suddenly and made him stop and curse some more; and the sky grew cloudier. The sun dimmed, dusk came, it rained, the wind sprang up, leaves were beaten from the trees, and Uncle Hal would say, 'I could have told you this would happen. I left my windows open!'

When Uncle Hal went out the world stopped being simple. It filled with obstacles, accidents happened, and my uncle tripped or banged his head or caught his finger in the slamming door or spilled his coffee – and he raged. Just being with him could make you very tired.

His silences were worse than his shouts. Sometimes he stared and said nothing, and you wanted to run. When he was silent his face was darker, his movements much slower, his clothes dirtier and more rumpled. He would not linger – he fell silent and a moment later he was gone. He would stay away for months or more. One entire year we did not see him, though we saw his car flash past. He reappeared and when we told him we had seen him he said, 'That wasn't me. I was making an assault on Kanchenjunga – rushing the summit. Without oxygen.'

And a moment later he was complaining about the price of paper – so many dollars for a ream. After he told me what a ream was I wondered why he needed all that paper. He made no mention of what he had done in the year that he had vanished. And then his real reason for showing up after all that time came out. 'Listen, Paulie, I need a hand moving a ladder. If you don't want to do it just say so.'

Though Uncle Hal was famous for saying no, no one ever said no to Uncle Hal.

It was a big ladder, splashed with paint, and carrying it through his cellar I saw a number of shadowy objects. Some I could not make out, but others I clearly recognized – a spinning wheel, a cider press, a musket, a brass telescope, a copper basin, a thunder jug, an ornate spittoon, a samovar, a marble-topped table, a pair of deer antlers, a walking stick with a bird's beak for a handle, a toothy pair of fish jaws, a Chinese lantern, and something that looked very much like a human skull, the color of old meerschaum. Just as he kept treasures – daggers, chains, silver coins – in trunks and drawers, he kept larger objects here in his cellar. It was all hidden here, but why?

'That looks like part of a skeleton,' I said, because I was too timid to admit that I saw a human skull resting on top of a wind-up Victrola.

Instead of replying he began to rant.

'Everyone's got a big American flag flapping in front of his store or gas station or whatever,' he said. 'Ever notice that? I've got a theory that they're meant to attract attention. It's not patriotism – it's a kind of advertising.'

But I was glancing back at the spittoon and the skull and the musket, and I lost control of the ladder.

'Why don't you drop it? Why don't you hit something with it, like the door frame? Chip some paint off. Why not?'

I had just done that very thing.

'Why not make it hard for me? I like that! I want to spend the rest of the afternoon fixing the door you just scratched –'

He stopped when he saw that I was crying, but after we put the ladder against the house he simply climbed it and slung a bucket on a hook and started working some white paint into the eaves with a stiff brush. I knew that it was time for me to go and that I would not see him for a long time.

Perhaps he went away. If he was planning to travel a long distance, he rose at four in the morning in order to beat the traffic, and he set off in the dark. 'They're always crowding the roads and they can't drive for beans.' But he was an early riser. That meant that he was tired by early evening. He was usually in bed by eight or so, which was why he never went to dinners or to parties. 'I'm tired!' he shouted, if you called him at six-thirty or seven. But he also said that he never slept through the night, and sometimes at odd hours the blue light of the television upstairs would flicker through the darkness.

He yelled at the television too.

We were watching a program once, and an elderly man came on smiling and talking about politics.

Uncle Hal laughed out loud and said, 'That's Walter Cronkite. He hates me.'

He was sitting in a battered chair, wearing a Thrift Shop T-shirt and torn jeans and mud-caked shoes. His baseball hat was on backwards, the fits-all-sizes adjustable band clamped against his forehead. There were green stains on his jeans, the smears of a whole day's grass cutting, and small green clippings clung to his face and arms. And this Walter Cronkite, looking like a college professor, was smiling in a television studio almost two thousand miles away in another time zone in Chicago. What was the connection?

'I wrote him a letter,' Uncle Hal said. 'I set him straight.' He chuckled to himself. It gave him pleasure to see this man on television, as though the man was looking through the window of the TV screen and recognized Uncle Hal in his baseball cap.

'I reminded him that "Cronkite" in German means "sickness".'

Eventually he told me everything, because he was proud of what he had done. He had written letters to the Governor (about the condition of the roads), the Pope (because of his stand on birth control in India), the Prime Minister of Canada (acid rain), and not the President of the United States but his wife, the First Lady, because of something she said, a careless remark about someone in the British Royal Family – their eating habits, I think. And there were more letters – to movie actors and famous sportsmen and millionaires – especially millionaires. He had, he said, sent detailed letters of advice to football coaches and city planners. He scolded celebrities. *You have all the qualities of Hitler except his vegetarianism*, went one of his letters, so he said.

He was proud of them, and proudest of all when he got a reply, no matter how baffled or hurt it was. A nasty reply excited him into writing another stinging letter, and he would keep it up until he had the last word. His letters all said, more or less, *I'm watching you*. When he was sitting in front of a television he imagined that these people were looking back at him – specifically him: they knew he was watching them.

But that mention of letter-writing had made me pause, because I had always assumed that Uncle Hal was a handyman as well as being the blackest of the family sheep. And it can be rather alarming when someone you consider to be eccentric says they have written something. It is a reckless confession that an act of writing has been committed, and it quickly converts an odd person into a lunatic. I guessed that it was another example of something Uncle Hal said to shock people. It was not the end. Many times after that when we were together someone's name would come up, someone in the news – Fidel Castro, Joe DiMaggio, the Emperor of Japan, and, 'I wrote him a letter,' Uncle Hal would say. I was always startled, which I think was Uncle Hal's intention.

'"I think my private parts are beautiful,"' he said once. '"I have black tarry bowel movements. Answer true or false." Those are two of the questions I was asked in an exam once at graduate school.' I had not realized he had ever been to graduate school, and if so what had he studied?

'I originally wanted to go to West Point,' Uncle Hal said. 'Did you know that in 1957 you could be refused entry to West Point for' – and here he made a horrible face – ' "excessive ugliness?"'

He could get angry in seconds if you said the wrong word.

'People who said "preppy" are preppies,' he snarled. 'People who use the word "yuppy" are yuppies.'

He screamed at the word 'hopefully,' but he smiled at 'wing nuts,' or 'pebble dash' or 'fish fingers,' or 'griddle iron.' He laughed out loud when he heard someone like an old carpenter look up at his house and say, 'The cheeks of that dormer are out of whack,' and once when I said 'shitsy' he wrote it down.

I said, 'Why did you do that, Uncle Hal?'

He said, 'I didn't do anything. I didn't write anything. What are you talking about?'

Had I even mentioned writing? But there was the pen in his pocket, and the little notebook. He saw me looking. 'That's my wallet,' he said. 'I use it as a wallet. Don't you know that it's rude to stare? A gentleman never stares.'

But I could not help it and that made him madder.

'Paulie, are you one of these people who has all the qualities of a dog except fidelity?'

'Sorry.'

'A gentleman is always correct in his demeanor!'

He was wearing a stretched Red Sox T-shirt, a ski hat with a bobble on top, a pair of army pants with big deep pockets at thigh level, and string instead of laces in his shoes.

People thought he was half-Indian – he had that look, dark and

6

unpredictable, as though he would fly into a fit of sudden anger or else stalk away. He didn't look like anyone else in the family. Uncle Hal's appearance convinced me that a person's disposition gives them certain features and changes them physically for life. He was big and shaggy and fierce, and if he was invited for lunch he probably would not come, but if he did he would show up late in his ragged clothes, stinking of his stables, and his expression and the look in his eyes challenged you to make a comment. *I dare you to mention my clothes.*

If you did he would not say anything, though he would hesitate, as though pronouncing a curse on you, and wiggles of steam would start from his body. Next he would vanish and someone would say, 'Where's Hal?' and someone else would say, 'He was here just a minute ago.'

Eventually you would get a letter – a horrible corrosive letter, one of his worst, *You have all the qualities of a maggot except vitality*, and no one would see him for months.

But when you saw him again he might be wearing Mickey Mouse ears and singing, 'My name is Annette Funicello,' or else doing the bunny hop across Route 28, down by the mini-golf, to make the traffic stop and to amuse the person he was with, probably a young woman, giggling with bewilderment.

He did not drink alcohol. He stopped smoking through 'sheer willpower' and then he gained forty-five pounds. He cried bitterly when his cat Dedalus died. He was always to be avoided when the Boston Celtics lost a game.

A lunch party he was invited to might result in much worse than his disappearance. What if there was someone present he instinctively disliked, such as one of the celebrities or millionaires he had sent a poison pen letter? What if it was someone to do with literature?

'Lecheracha – litracha – letterachore – I can't even say the word!'

He seemed to develop an instant hatred for anyone who wrote or published or sold books, and his hostility could be baffling. It often took the form of fooling questions, and the people didn't know whether they were being mocked. Maybe Uncle Hal was just being friendly, they thought. But I knew better.

'Spell "minuscule,"' he would say to these book people, and most of them thought the word began m-i-n-i-. Or Uncle Hal would chant at them, 'Harry Martinson! Odysseus Elytis! Rudolf Eucken! Karl Gjellerup! Verner von Heidenstam!' – and sometimes more names; and when he had the attention of the whole room he would ask, 'Who are they?'

None of the book people knew until Uncle Hal laughingly told them that these men had all won the Nobel prize for 'lechera-chore – excuse me!'

With the other party guests he took a different line. If they talked about art, he changed the subject and complained about the high price of cat litter, or claimed he had never missed a single episode of *The Howdy Doody Show*, or wasn't it time we espoused a keener interest in the future of the Kurds?

'I didn't hear your poem,' he said, tottering like a bear with his cheeks blown out, and facing the man who had just recited the poem, 'because I had a mouthful of crackers and I like to hear them crunching loud in my ears as I chew.'

They were Uneeda Biscuits, he said. Weed Wacker, Beard Buster, Froot Loops, Panty Shields, Odor Eaters, Sno-Pake and Duck Tape were other names he liked saying.

The Duck Tape he used for mending his glasses, and there was so much it made them lopsided. He squirted oil on his shoes, and boasted about how cheap it was, until his shoes caught fire when someone accidentally threw a match. He bought two-gallon jars of mayonnaise that were labeled 'For Restaurants and Institutions.' One Christmas he gave my forty-three-year-old aunt a baby doll with a crack through its wooden head and told her it was very valuable.

That same year he gave me a pair of nutcrackers. They were rusty, but Uncle Hal said, 'Made in Germany. The finest nutcrackers are made in Germany.'

For three years, Uncle Hal wore nothing but black clothes and – someone said – a cape. I never saw the cape. He was expert at table tennis, pool, basketball and chess. He claimed to know the obscure rules of various card games. He was unbeatable at checkers and tic-tac-toe. He said he had once eaten kangaroo meat, smoke-dried, on the Gulf of Carpentaria, in Australia. You would have to marvel at this, because if you doubted it he would go silent and vanish again.

He could not swim, and once, out quahogging, he stepped in a mudhole and almost drowned. 'Quicksand!' he said afterward. He was afraid of spiders and loud noises – thunder in particular – and said he was disgusted by the sight of other people's feet. He hated high winds and after a whole summer of wind he climbed on his roof and fired his shotgun into the gusts. Ice cream, he said, was his weakness. He would drive fifteen miles to a place that sold frozen pudding flavor. ('Howard Hughes was addicted to chocolate chip,' he said, 'which is another difference between us.') He had a fondness also for pumpkins, lobsters and pistachios ('It means "grinning" in Farsi, as you know'). He often snacked on dog biscuits.

He had a habit of leaving notes for you – stuck in the window or shoved under the door or squeezed beneath the windshield wiper. The messages said *I totally disagree with you*, or *Do not make any attempt to communicate with me*, or *I will be unavailable until November*. The simple message was hurtful enough, and then you realized that in order for him to get the message to you in this way he had to sneak to your house in the darkness, sometime between two o'clock and five o'clock that morning.

'I'm busy! I've got a million things to do!' he would shriek just before he left us. He had no wife, he had no children, he had no job, he lived alone, he never traveled. We could not imagine what he was busy doing. *Don't put Uncle Hal on the spot* was a family caution.

On one occasion Uncle Hal began to reminisce, to an Irishman, about Dublin, Ireland. He named specific streets and pubs where he had drunk pints of ale, and churches where he had prayed. He lamented that it was all gone – replaced by cheapness and fakery.

Afterwards it gave me a pang to recall the look on that Irishman's face as he listened. But some years later I discovered that Uncle Hal had never been to Ireland, nor had he been to Australia. He said he could speak Swahili, but since no one else in the family knew how, there was no way of verifying it. 'Conversational Latin' was how he described another language he knew.

He liked telling the story of how he had had an appointment with a billionaire ('There are only thirty-six in the entire world, and I know five of them'). This was to have taken place at the Ritz-Carlton in Boston, but Uncle Hal had been turned away by the doorman for not wearing a tie – he was wearing a war-surplus sailor suit and rubbers. The billionaire had to meet him at the Shamrock Luncheonette. The business was unspecified.

9

He had been bitten on the thigh by a rat, he said. 'This was in the market in Antsirabe, in Madagascar. Oh, years ago.'

He owned a pair of wooden skis, a wooden tennis racket, a leather hat, a manual typewriter of cast-iron, clamp-on roller skates, and a bike with no gears. He claimed he used them all the time. I never saw him use any of them.

After he stopped visiting us, Uncle Hal was seen playing with the neighborhood children who regularly came to his house. He gave them candy, he showed them his Japanese sword, he taught them how to do the bunny hop, he played tag with them, he encouraged them to tell him about their fears and hopes. At Halloween, he put on a mask and led them around the neighborhood. He was Santa Claus at Christmas, he was the Easter bunny, and on the Fourth of July he let off fireworks in his orchard.

While these small children boldly went upstairs and demanded candy, we hung back – too afraid to approach, afraid he would angrily send us home. We stood at the margins of his yard and saw him playing – running, screeching, his gray hair twisted, his shirttails flying. 'You can't catch me!'

People saw him at the playground, the beach, the schoolyard, the swings.

I was at college then. One weekend, returning from Boston – this was the spring I graduated – I bumped into Uncle Hal at the post office. He was sending a large parcel and being very mysterious about it, concealing the address from me. I never knew what sort of welcome I would get from him and so I gave him the most tentative greeting. He surprised me by saying how glad he was to see me. 'Want to see something? Huh? Something really amazing?'

He pushed the parcel across the counter and then he was breathless, he was flying. His shirt was inside out, he was wearing striped pants and high-top sneakers. He hurried me to his house and pulled out a drawer – one of his treasure drawers. He took out a toy rifle – an air-rifle, but an old one.

'It's a bee-bee gun – the original. I had that very model when I was ten years old. See the Red Ryder insignia on the stock? Listen, it's in perfect working order.'

He aimed it and went pah! pah! pah! 'I've been looking for one of these for years.'

There was more in the drawer. A green plastic water pistol. A pack of bubble gum wrapped in colored waxed paper and containing two baseball cards. A Sky King ring, with a secret compartment. A copy of *Tales from the Crypt* comic book. A hat – but no ordinary hat. He put it on.

'We used to call this a beanie,' Uncle Hal said. There was a propeller on top. He spun the propeller with his finger and said in a small boy's quavering, stuttering voice, 'I got an idea! Let's go down to Billy's house and play marbles. Hey, I got my bag of aggies. These are good shooters.' He swung a little clinking bag out of the drawer. 'This one's a real pisser. Hey, what's wrong, Paulie, don't you want to come?'

He took me by the arm. The propeller on his beanie was still slowly turning. Was he defying me to make a remark?

I clutched the books I had brought him to study for the weekend, for the paper I had to write.

'Malinowski makes the point,' Uncle Hal said – but how had he seen the small printed name on the spine of the book – 'that in the Trobriand Islands, the relationship between a woman's brother and her son is stronger than between the boy and his father. In other words, the uncle and nephew – because there is a definite proof of a blood relationship and there is always an element of doubt about the true paternity of a child. And similarly in *Beowulf* you see the same affinity, and a specific Anglo-Saxon word for the relationship – the uncle and nephew usually fighting together in battle.'

As he spoke, the propeller on his beanie still spun.

'Paulie, don't you see that I am showing you how to fight,' he said, 'and how to live?'

The propeller slowed as he stared at me. I was too afraid to say anything.

'What are your plans?'

'I joined the Peace Corps. I'm going to Africa. Nyasaland.'

'Capital, Zomba,' Uncle Hal said. Jerking his head in a nod of self-congratulation, he got the propeller going again.

He went to a bookshelf and hunted for a moment, then found what he was looking for, a bulky biography entitled *Rimbaud*. He opened it and with the propeller on his beanie still slowly turning, he read, 'I am obliged to chatter their gibberish, to eat their filthy messes, to endure a thousand and one annoyances that come from their idleness, their treachery, and their stupidity. But that is not the worst. The worst is the fear of becoming doltish oneself, isolated as one is, and cut off from any intellectual companionship.'

Listening, but also watching the propeller on his beanie, I was too distracted to reply.

'Am I keeping you?' he asked in a voice as dry as paper.

He's a terrible enemy, people used to say; *but he can be much worse as a friend*.

We saw less and less of him. He stopped phoning. He didn't even call us when he wanted to move a ladder or push his car. Instead, we heard stories about him. His name would come up, and someone in the room would say softly in a wounded voice, 'I once got a letter from Hal,' and would turn pale and serious, remembering. You would not want to hear any more.

Or someone would tell how Uncle Hal had been very ill, and had spent a month in the hospital. We would feel ashamed that we had not known; but then the stories would come out – how he insisted on wearing his bobble-hat while being X-rayed; how he had accused a distinguished surgeon of stealing his old pocket watch; how he had run up an enormous phone bill by making repeated calls to London, England; how he had begged his nurse to marry him and then changed his mind when he discovered that she had been recently divorced. 'Damaged goods,' was all he said. After he was discharged from the hospital the telephone in his room was missing, and an armchair, and a gallon jar ('For Institutional Use') of aspirin.

Another story began circulating, that he had been seeing a psychiatrist for some time, that he had told this man about his childhood, and how his mother, my grandmother, had never picked him up when he had cried in his crib. And that was not all. There were childhood humiliations, episodes of loneliness and rejection and total isolation, and stories of his imaginary friend 'Robin' who was sometimes a boy and sometimes a girl, his nightmares and his rituals about opening jars and crossing streets.

In this story about Uncle Hal and the psychiatrist, the analysis went on for about a year, and then after listening to so many of these sad strange tales, the psychiatrist became depressed, canceled the remainder of the sessions, and killed himself.

Uncle Hal vanished so completely we thought that he had died. People wondered about him, and then even the stories stopped. We moved. There was no word of him. Better not to ask, we said. We got on with our lives, feeling steadier and more certain now that he was gone.

He was not dead. How silly of us not to have realized what he had been doing all this time.

When Uncle Hal's novel was published it was praised for its humanity, its luminous subtlety, its sense of fun, its quiet wisdom. It was, everyone agreed, a masterpiece of sanity and elegance.

TWO

The Lepers of Moyo

I

Boarding the train in the African darkness just before dawn was like climbing into the body of a huge, dusty monster. I rejoiced in the strangeness of entering it, and I felt safe and happy inside, curled up half-asleep on a wooden bench. After sunup it did not seem so huge. And in harsh daylight, the dirty walls confined me, the bars on the windows became black and apparent, and my coach began to stink in the heat. I had a book on my lap, a new translation of Kafka's *Diaries*. I read only a few pages, in the way you nibble a sandwich, knowing it will have to last; and then I glanced around.

The unpainted seats had been brought to a rich mellow shine, the wood buffed by years of ragged bottoms. The whistle blew, we started to move, and on the first bend I saw the gasping boiler of the black steam engine, the locomotive drooling oil and water – looking wounded. It was just another old colonial train.

Once we were out of town, ten minutes or less, the huts beside the tracks were poorer – thatched roofs instead of tin, and clusters of them, the simplest villages, showing their skeletal framework of sticks through the mud and daub like the bones of their occupants, who squatted near them, watching us pass by. When I caught their eye they looked fearful and apologetic.

The trees along the tracks were thin, the soil was poor, and this stony land became flatter and drier as the train labored north, snorting. When the sun was above those spindly branches, slanting into the gaping windows of the train, it heated the rusty bars and the battered interior, and the coach became very hot. And now I could see the peanut shells, the orange peels, the spat-out mass of bitten and chewed sugar-cane stalks on the floor. A woman in the next seat was nursing a child, but the child was seven or older and so this act

of suckling seemed like incest, awkwardly sexual instead of mater-
nal, because she was young and small and the child was large and
greedy.

Dust stirred by the locomotive and the front coaches floated
through the windows with sticky smoke clouds, reeking of burned
coal. The locomotive dated from the British period – the war perhaps. This thick engine smoke left a layer of soot and greasy smuts
everywhere, and it soon blackened my bare arms. I sweated and
smeared it. I had not thought to bring food. I had nothing to drink.
And I was alone on this first day of October, known in Malawi as
'the suicide month,' because of the intense heat.

This trip should have been miserable. It was magic.

It was my first taste of freedom in Africa; it was drama, it was romance, too. I had the sense that I had successfully escaped in this big
clumsy train. Although I had not published any of the poems I had
written, this trip made me feel like a writer. It was something about
the risk I was taking – into the unknown – but it was also the sense
that I was making discoveries. The train was carrying me away from
the only Africa I knew, a demoralized place of bungalows and
shanty settlements, the white club, the black slums, the Indian
shops, a town that was no more than one wide street. I had come to
dislike Blantyre for its being ordinary. I needed something darker,
stranger; I needed risk – danger, even.

For almost a year I had been teaching at a small school just outside the town and the more time I spent at the school the more tame
it had seemed. I had grown used to it, but I had wanted more. All
this time I had wanted to travel in the bush. Now was my chance.

'Going up-country?' my friend Mark had asked the day before I
left. He was English, from Southern Rhodesia.

'Up-country' said it all.

This was my vacation work. We Peace Corps teachers were told
to get jobs or to do something useful in the African school holidays.
I could have stayed at my school and catalogued books, or led a
team of brush-cutters for the new sports field. I could have invented
a job, or made any excuse to stay at the school. Then one of my students mentioned that he was from Central Province, near the lake
shore. He told me the name of his village and said it was on the way
to the mission hospital, Moyo.

'The leprosarium,' he said.

I had never heard this English word before and I was bewitched by it and grateful to the student who taught it to me.

My student went on to say that at this mission the priests and nuns were *mzungus*, like me.

I wrote to the Father Superior and said that I wanted to visit during the long school holiday. I could teach English, I said. Father DeVoss replied saying that I would be welcome. For the next few weeks I thought of nothing else.

Everything about the trip excited me. I would be traveling by steam train to a remote part of the country, I would be in the bush – alone, in a leper colony. I would be leaving behind politics and order and dullness. It was what I craved, a place in Africa that was wild. Wilderness was paradise, where you could begin again.

'Leprosarium' was a fascinating word. I was tantalized by the name of the disease, by the remoteness of the place. It was not just unusual, I felt; it verged on the bizarre. Leprosy was a primitive and dark disease, like an ancient curse. It suggested the unclean, it called to mind outcasts. There was something forbidden about it. It was an aspect of old unsubtle Africa. Leper, leper, leper. I was sick of metaphors. I wanted words to have unambiguous meanings: leper, wilderness, poverty, heat.

These were my thoughts. The tropical sky was vast and pale. I liked the heat. I was grubby and comfortable, buying food from old women at the stations where we stopped, and sitting in the sooty coach, peeling oranges, eating peanuts, like the rest of the passengers.

Such a journey had been my object in coming to Africa. I was twenty-three years old. I wanted to make my living as a writer. I yearned to know the inside of the continent – its secrets. I was disappointed in my town, Blantyre. I hated its muddy main street. These towns in central Africa had been laid out by the British, and they had the look of garrisons. There were bars and there was a movie theater and a fish and chip shop. But I had not come to Africa to drink beer and go to the movies. There were girls who hung around the bars and they went home with anyone and never asked for money. Prostitution and political tyranny were in the future. These were years of innocence in Africa.

I looked up from my book and out the window of the train and saw that we were penetrating the bush. I was happy. Besides Kafka's *Diaries* in two volumes, which had recently been sent to me, I had my own writing, a folder of poems, my notebooks. I planned to work in the daytime and be a poet at night, the way I lived at my school. This was like a voyage. I had prepared for it as though I was going to sea, and that was how the bush seemed to me, like an ocean.

I had never been in a train that moved so slowly. It made the trip especially strange, this ponderous movement. After three hours the train seemed – not clumsy and old anymore, but venerable and important, and the image of the bush as an ocean that had come to me earlier was part of it, the train like an old vessel plowing this ocean. It stopped often and everywhere, not always at a station or a platform but in the middle of nowhere, in the yellow bush, the spindly tree limbs stuck against the window, and the wall of foliage so close that the locomotive's racket echoed against it. There seemed no point in these stops, fifteen or twenty of them before noon, and several times the train hesitated, rolled backwards for half a minute, lurched, and then started up again. I was not dismayed. Like the slow speed, the sudden stops and reverses made the whole business odd and agreeable.

This African train, burning wood and coal in its firebox, clattered deeper into Africa. The children in the coach stared at me. The older people were polite, even a bit fearful. I dozed, I was wakened at one of the stops by the anvil clang of the coupling – and I smiled when I looked out at my black arms, from the soot and smuts settling on my skin.

I compared arms with the small boy next to me.

'Mine is blacker than yours.'

'My arm is not black,' he said.

At one that afternoon we came to the town of Balaka, where dogs slept in the middle of the street. Balaka, a railway junction (another line went to Fort Johnston and Monkey Bay), was hotter and flatter than any place I had ever seen. Walking along the platform to ask the conductor what time we were leaving ('Not before tree,' he said), I saw that one of the forward coaches had a good paint job and shuttered windows. A shutter rose as I watched and a small blue-eyed child looked out – it could only have been a missionary's child – and I realized that I was looking at a first-class passenger. I had not known about first, the one good coach on the train, shutters down, doors locked.

I had no desire to hide in there and travel with my fellow mzungus, first class on soft seats. I did not want to listen to them complain. 'Shocking train,' they would say. 'Filthy weather . . .' 'Bloody Africans . . .'

That was expatriate life in Blantyre. I wanted wooden seats and strangeness. I imagined the mzungus behind the locked doors of their first-class coach, grumbling, hiding, killing time by reading the yellow-bound copies of the *Daily Mirror*, months old, that were sent sea mail to Malawi from London.

There was an African restaurant behind the goods shed at Balaka Station, and for four shillings and a tickey – threepence – I was given a chipped enamel bowl of chicken and rice. Afterwards I sat in the shade of the verandah, watching the hot street and the white sky, the earth like pale powder, and everything still except the insects. I walked into the sun and immediately felt the weight of it on the top of my head. I stood alone in the middle of the street on the small black island of my shadow, and thought: I am where I want to be.

The whistle blew at about two-thirty and after some hesitation – shunting in the Balaka tracks – the train set off again, north, through the dusty landscape of yellow bush and low skinny trees and the elephant grass that was taller than the Africans. On this blazing October afternoon there was no movement – nothing stirred, no birds, no people, nor any animals. The bush was dead still and looked stifled of air. The train was the only moving thing in that whole hot world. We raised dust and smoke and noise, but after we passed – I could see out of the back window of the rear coach – our commotion subsided and all was still again.

No animals, no people, not even any gardens or huts. Just miles of sunburned bush – 'miles and miles of bloody Africa,' the mzungus said. And the howl of insects, like a fever; a high temperature, going higher.

The sun had made an arc over the train, rising above the windowsill on the right when we left Blantyre, drumming on the metal roof of the coach at noon, and now it had slipped sideways again and was shining through the windows on the left-hand side. I nodded and dozed to the clanking of the wheels on the long, straight rails, hammering more insistently where the rails butted, and at each stop there was the clutch and clawing sound of the brakes, the screech of metal against metal.

I had never been on a train like it, and it did not seem to me like a train at all. My earlier impressions of it as a vessel were truer. But not a ship, it was more like a paddle steamer with its gasps and its shrill whistle, rattling along a coast and then penetrating the land by plunging up a narrow river that led sinuously through the bush. Here and there a station or a siding appeared, like a man-made feature on a jungly riverbank.

Most stations were wooden sheds with tin roofs and no sign giving their name. On their dirt platforms, packed hard by all the tramping feet, women and small girls sold greasy dough cakes and bananas and peanuts, carrying them in tin basins on their heads. They were skinny, ragged, barefoot, and the farther north we went the nakeder the women were. Now most of them were bare-breasted on this hot lakeshore plain. It was the Africa of my imagination, at last.

I sat at the window, squinting through the coal smoke at Africa and waited and watched and went deeper. Through the late afternoon I saw shadows rippling in the trees like phantoms, Africans whispering, watching the train, and I knew they had seen my white face. They were like glimpses of strangeness. On a passing embankment I saw a funeral, a mass of chanting people marching behind a wooden coffin. I saw naked children. I saw two people, a man and woman, rolling on the ground in panic away from the train, startled in the act of love.

Now the sun was below the tattered trees and dusk was gathering in shadows under a briefly bluer sky.

'Ntakataka,' an African said to me.

That was the station for Moyo.

It was almost six. I had been traveling in a state of great happiness for over twelve hours.

Father DeVoss met me. He was tall and gaunt, and although he was not old he was gray. He wore a dusty white cassock and looked at me – fondly I thought – with a sad smile.

'Good to see you,' he said. 'You play cards?'

2

The dark house on the only high ground here looked haunted, one of its windows lit by an overbright pressure lamp, the rest of the windows shuttered or in darkness. Its shadows and its size and its crumbling stucco gave it a ghostly wolfish look. But I soon realized that was misleading. The house was mostly empty, a relic of an earlier time, when the mission had been much bigger and there had been more lepers and more priests. It was like the rubbly ruin – of a fort or a palace – that lay neglected and overgrown in the African bush. Inside, the priests' house seemed forlorn.

We had passed through the village below it, which was a place of fires and wood smoke and voices and yapping dogs. Because of the crude lamps flaring inside the huts, all the shadows were active and black. There was a smell, too, human, sweetish, like decay – the smell of illness and death.

An old priest came fussing forward on the stone stairs. He managed to snatch my bag over my protests, and he passed it to an African in khaki shorts and a white shirt, an African servant's basic uniform. Another priest, much younger, stared at me from behind the fussing priest, who was speaking in Chinyanja and who I now realized was talking to me, not to the African, slapping at my bag.

'*Moni, bambo, muli bwanji?* – *eh, nyerere! Eh, mpemvu! Pepani, palibe mphepo. . .*' Hello, how are you? What's that? An ant! A roach! Sorry, there's no breeze here . . .

The old priest went on jabbering and sweeping away the insects from my bag, and it was clear to me that he did not speak English and, as I did not speak Dutch, this would be our way of communicating. But he tended to use very precise words when he was speaking the language, such as *majiga* for railway station – most Africans just mangled the English word station. And that very night he taught me the word *mberetemberete*, when I glanced down at the village at the lamps showing through the ragged curtains of the mud huts. It meant 'shining faintly through,' like a woman in a loose dress with a light behind her, a sight that made me pause many African nights.

'*Dzina lanu ndani?*' I said, asking him his name.

His reply sounded like 'Fonderpilt,' but when he added in English, 'The poor ones, not the rich American ones,' I understood that his name was van der Bilt. To everyone he was Brother Piet.

The younger priest was Father Touchette, newly arrived from Canada, still sallow from the trip and rather confused by this torrent of Chinyanja. The African, Simon, put my bag in the corner and then returned, and dished up some food. Father DeVoss sat and simply watched and listened. He was tall and had an air of gentle authority. He seemed at once kindly and remote. He had a melancholy smile.

I was thinking how white their cassocks had seemed when I had approached the men on the verandah, and how dusty and stained and torn they were when I saw them up close.

Washing my hands at the sink in the kitchen, I glanced at my face in the mirror and hardly recognized myself – my sooty hair and skin, my sunburned nose, my exhausted bloodshot eyes. Brother Piet sat me down and gave me the food that Simon had prepared – beans and boiled greens and boiled peanuts and roasted corn and a lump of steamed dough they called *nsima*: African food.

Brother Piet asked me about the train. He traveled on it now and then, he said, to get to the market in Balaka.

'I always go second class,' he said. 'Then I have someone to talk to.'

'But Holland is your home,' I said in Chinyanja.

'*Pepani!* Sorry!' he said. 'The noise of Amsterdam! The tram-cars! The crowds of people! It hurts my ears. *Chinthunthumira! Misala! . . .*'

'He shivers,' Simon explained. 'It is madness.'

'. . . Sorry. I stay here where it is peaceful.' Brother Piet repeated the African word, *mtendere*.

He was seventy-four and had last been on leave in Holland in 1951.

'When did you come to Africa?'

'So long ago' – and the phrase he used, *za kale*, meant in ancient times – 'that I traveled down the Nile River from Cairo to Juba. Yes! And I drank the water of the Nile!'

I went on eating, scooping it with my hands, using a ball of *nsima*, in the African way.

'When I die, maybe,' he said, and laughed, 'they send me back to Amsterdam. Then I won't mind the noise! I am dead, eh?'

I liked his humor and oddity, speaking Chinyanja in his boisterous way, and occasionally throwing in an English word.

Father Touchette did not have much conversation. He was new, fearful, with the tense demeanor of a strict believer; no jokes – pious perhaps because he was afraid. He clutched his breviary as though it was a brick he wanted to throw at a sinner.

He seemed to be listening at the window, one ear cocked in the direction of the African shouts and laughter, and the random dribbling sound of the drums.

'And how did you happen to come here to Moyo?' I asked.

'I was sent here,' Father Touchette said sternly, as though it had been a punishment.

'It is his good luck,' Father DeVoss said in a cheery voice, and it seemed to me that he had detected a grievance in what Father Touchette had said and was trying to make light of it.

'I am happy to be here,' I said, truthfully, and I had the sense that they were glad to have a visitor. My smile revealed my weariness – I was tired from the trip, and from the hot meal in that humid room, all the dark heat of the night hanging like black curtains at the windows.

'Does Paul know where his room is?' Father DeVoss said, seeing that I was tired.

I said goodnight and with a candle in a dish Simon led me down a long hallway and showed me to my room.

'This is a good place,' I said.

'Yes,' he said.

'But some people are sick.'

'This is where they are cured,' Simon said. 'That is why it is a good place.'

He had put the candle down and was throwing open the shutters.

'In the villages' – he meant everywhere else – 'people are sick, but they stay that way.'

After he slipped away into the darkness I lay on the hard bed with dust in my nostrils, in the cool room, the candle flame making shadows twitch on the plaster wall. It was like being in the antechamber of a castle – strange and spooky.

I had been reading Kafka. But it was more than Kafka's imagery that inspired this feeling. It was the experience of the train trip, and the heat and the dry yellow landscape and the black night and the smell of poverty and illness.

The next morning everything was different. In darkness Africa seemed enchanted. In daylight it was hot and pitiless. Most of the trees were so wraithlike, their leaves so slender, there was no shade under them.

The light at Moyo was more intense than where I lived in the south of the country. Was it some effect of the lake near here, the surface flashing it back? But the lake was twenty miles away. Perhaps it was the flatness of the land, the high clouds, the thin bush, or perhaps the time of year. Whatever, it was something that made for glaring leaves and a shine on some rocks and pale soil and white skies. It made for nakedness.

It was scorching light that exposed everything so completely it even burned shadows away. It was not sunshine, not warm and bright, but a fiery African light that swelled in the sky and seemed to drum against the land. It came rattling straight through the threadbare curtains into my room, waking me like a blade piercing my eyes. I saw that the walls were cracked plaster and dusty whitewash, with a wooden crucifix of a skinny, suffering Jesus over my bed. The floor was dusty, the wood doorjamb was pitted with termite holes and the whole place smelled of ants. It had seemed so substantial last night, the whole building on its hill, but in this harsh, truthful light the structure was frail and elderly.

In the kitchen, Simon poured me a cup of milky tea. The large screened-in box that looked like an animal cage was, I knew, a meat safe, and its contents – plates of chicken – were going rancid. That was the smell that hung in the room, dead meat. On the table, the bread, the papaya, the margarine and the jam all smelled of the meat safe.

'Where is Father DeVoss?'

'He is saying mass.'

So I sat at the worn table in the blinding light, with my bottle of Koo Ketchup and dish of Springbok margarine.

'Are there nuns here, too?'

'Yes, there are three,' Simon said.

'What do they do?'

'The nuns take care of our bodies. The priests take care of our souls,' he said, with the sententiousness of a convert. 'And one American mzungu.'

'What is the American's name?'

'I don't know. But they call her Birdie.' He pronounced it in the African way, 'Buddy.'

'Like "bird"? *Mbalame?*'

'Yes. She is a sister.'

It was British usage – a sister also meant nursing sister, a nurse.

'Is the convent nearby?'

'It is near to the hospital.'

'How long has the woman Birdie been here?'

'She was coming this side in July.'

Three months ago.

'What about Father Touchette?'

'He was coming this side in April.'

I asked no more questions, yet Simon sensed unspoken ones and told me that the old priest, Brother Piet, had helped build the church at Moyo, and that Father Touchette did not like to hear the drumming from the village, and that when Father DeVoss first came to Moyo, Simon had been a small child, and Simon's father had pointed him out and told him not to be afraid.

'We thought that white people were ghosts who would eat us. But my father said, "No, he is a good man."'

'What was your father doing here?'

'He was sick with *mkhate*.'

A leper.

Father DeVoss appeared soon after that. His look of distraction, a dreamy vagueness and inattention made him seem kind and gentle and a little sad.

'Did you have a full house?'

'Attendance at mass is not so good.'

'Maybe I should go.'

'If you wish,' he said, as though he hardly cared.

'I was about to prepare some lessons. I thought I might start my English classes soon.'

'That is a good idea,' Father DeVoss said. 'But there is no hurry.' He was smiling sadly out of the window. 'Would you like to see the church?'

I said yes, because I suspected that he wanted to show me. It was a short walk from the priests' house, on the other side of that same low hill, and it was large and dusty, smelling of lighted candles – the tallow, the flames, the burned wicks. Some of the windows were stained glass, and the Stations of the Cross were African carvings.

'Some of the lepers made them. They are not bad, eh? They are crude, but they have emotion.'

He looked around the church with a crooked smile that seemed like skepticism, as though he only half believed what all this represented. He pointed to a plaster statue.

'Saint Roche. You know about him?'

'No,' I said.

Father DeVoss smiled, he said nothing more. There were other plaster statues, and plastic flowers, and small gilt ornaments, but even so, from the light alone, streaming through the cracked windows, the church had an odor of sanctity.

'What about the hospital?'

'If you want to see it,' Father DeVoss said, as though surprised by my interest.

Ever since I had arrived the night before, the leper village had been audible. It smoldered and crackled beneath the trees at the foot of the priests' hill. There were always voices and shouts and laughter, the continual cockcrows the Africans called *tambala*, and the thump of the pounding of the pestles in the mortars as the women made *ufa*, the corn flour that was one of their staple foods. The village was also the smell of wood smoke and that other obscurer odor, of decay, of human bodies, the smell of disease and frailty and death, which was also the smell of dirt.

Father DeVoss was offhand introducing me to the nuns, like a man bringing a stranger to meet a wife or close relation. He hardly looked at them, and he did not tell me their names, but only who I was.

'Paul insisted on seeing the hospital,' he said. 'As you know, this is all strange to me.'

He laughed softly and then left, to return to the priests' house.

In his self-conscious way he made me understand that the hospital was not his operation, but theirs, a clumsier cruder business than saying mass perhaps, the inexact science of doctoring in the bush – knives and sutures and purple disinfectant, and lepers always in line, waiting for bandages or pills.

This central building with the tin roof and the verandah was the dispensary, the oldest nun said. There were several other buildings, lined with cots, for seriously ill people, or disabled ones, who had no families. But most of the lepers lived at home, in their huts, and were looked after by their relatives. Their bandages were changed in the afternoon, they picked up their medicine in the morning, and except for the severe cases who were bedridden, the lepers lived at home in their nearby village.

The nun was still explaining as she led me around. But I was thinking of the strangeness of the place, and the word, leper. Leper, leper, leper.

At the second building I saw the woman whom Simon had told me about, the mzungu nursing sister he had called Birdie. She was bandaging a leper's foot, wrapping it like a package. A cheap clock with a stained face of tin ticked on the wall.

The woman was older than me, perhaps thirty, thin, with a sallow complexion, a yellowish pallor that serious mzungus acquired in the African bush. It was only the fools who sat in the sun; the rest stayed indoors or under cover, like this woman, and they worked at their jobs.

I smiled while she wrapped the rag-like bandage. She said nothing, she did not smile back, as though she resented the nun showing me around the hospital and interrupting the daily routine. A kind of pointless strictness was another characteristic of people in bush posts, as though such punctuality gave the day a shape and a meaning.

It was unusual in the Africa I knew for strangers not to introduce themselves so I said, 'Hello, I'm Paul.'

'Linda,' she said. 'They call me Birdie.'

'That's pretty.'

'It's short for Birdsall. Everyone in my family gets it,' she said. 'Have you just arrived?'

'I came on the train yesterday.'

'That train is scary.'

'I liked it. I guess I don't scare easily.'

'Then you came to the right place,' she said. 'Wouldn't you say so, Sister?'

The nun smiled, but grimly. She had parchment-like skin, very white and wrinkled, as insubstantial as tissue, and a bristly mustache, and wore rubber gloves.

I hated myself for being a spectator here among these women who did this every day.

Birdie was still holding the leper's bandaged foot, snipping and trimming the twisted ends of the knot she had fastened. A man in the next cot groaned. His hands and feet had been bandaged with strips of cloth. But his bandages were dirty and stained and some foul colored liquid had leaked through and darkened his instep.

'What will you be doing here?' Birdie asked.

'Teaching English for anyone who wants to learn.'

Without replying, Birdie went to the next cot, where the leper was softly complaining. She took up one of his legs and began scissoring away his dirty bandages. Her silence made me think I had said something silly.

The nun went to work on another man's bandages and said, 'I'm sure your class will be very popular.'

Yet just the mention of an English class among this bandaging made it seem utterly frivolous. Birdie was cutting efficiently through the soiled bandages, using her sharp knife like a letter opener.

'They make baskets,' she said. 'They color the fibers with ink from old smashed ballpoints. The baskets are very ugly.'

'Years ago they mixed their own colors from berries,' the nun said. 'They were so lovely we used them at the church.'

'It seems such a busy place,' I said.

The nun said, 'We have about 400 lepers and with their families there are about 2,000 people altogether. Quite a number, and from all over the country. We have Tumbuka people from the north, Angonis from nearby, Sena people from the Lower River. Even some Yao Muslims from Fort Johnston.'

'You look after all of them?'

'Oh, yes,' she said, flinging the cut and stained bandages into a bucket. 'Their villages turned them out. There is so much superstition and prejudice connected with this disease. Because for so many years there was no cure. People simply suffered and were treated horribly.'

'But it's not very contagious and it's simple to cure,' Birdie said.

She too was discarding bandages and revealing a man's foot pitted with sores. 'There's no chance of any of us catching it. Yet very few of these people will ever go back to their own villages, because they're scarred. A person with toes missing looks like he still has the disease.'

She held the evidence in her hand, but seemed unconcerned as she

27

swabbed it with a damp piece of cotton. I wanted to ask her what had impelled her to do this.

'This is the last illness in Africa,' she said, as though reading my thoughts. 'It's all curable, and when it's gone the curse will be lifted and there will be no other disease as bad.'

'I like Birdie's spirit,' the nun said.

'But you have them for life,' I said.

'More or less. Some are useful,' the nun said. 'The ones that are cured help us give out medicine and do the bandaging.'

'That guy looks really sick,' I said. It was a skeletal man, with no flesh, only blotchy skin hanging loose on his bones and his knobby joints, his cheeks sunken, his eyes glazed and popping. He turned his face on me with that accusatory look that very sick people often wear when they stare at healthy ones.

'Poor Malinki,' the nun said. 'He had all the symptoms of TB, and so we treated him for that. But he did not improve. We ran all the tests. He gets thinner and thinner. He can't hold his food. And his family doesn't want him.'

'So what are you giving him?'

'Prayers.'

Birdie had moved to a different patient, whose leg was swollen like a club and was grayish and as rough as the bark of a tree.

'This is snakebite.'

'*Mamba akudya?*' I asked him, mentioning the cobra whose bite was so venomous, the black mamba. He was clutching a porcupine quill.

'*Kasongo,*' he said softly, correcting me, with a strange pedantry for a man in his condition.

He had not been bitten by a mamba but by another black snake, as deadly as the cobra, but with a red crest. The hot regions of Malawi were full of huge poisonous snakes, and they were so feared that if a snake crossed your path it was a bad omen and if you did not manage to kill the snake you were to return home at once and stay there until the following day.

'His leg looks horrible.'

'Snake venom has an enzyme in it that helps the snake digest its food. That's what meat looks like when it's swallowed. A *mganga* sold him the quill – it's good *mankhwala*. Glad you came?'

'What about that guy?'

It was another man, with bandaged arms and head.

'He was hacked by his neighbor. An argument over a woman.'

Men and women were staring at us through the window.

'They are lepers. They're supposed to be working. They don't care.'

Another nun came into the ward, carrying scissors and a knife, looking businesslike.

'This is the new English teacher,' Birdie said, and it sounded like sarcasm.

After I left the hospital I cut through the village, aware that I was being stared at by everyone, and went back to the priests' house and prepared my English lessons.

The evening meal was the same, *nsima* and beans and boiled, spinachy leaves. I asked Brother Piet more questions about Amsterdam, but his answers were the same as those he had given me last night. Father Touchette glowered by the window, listening to the racket from the village.

'Deal the cards,' Father DeVoss said at last, and Brother Piet obeyed, chattering in Chinyanja.

Father DeVoss was my partner, Simon was Brother Piet's; Father Touchette clutched his breviary and suffered, looking vindictive. We played six hands of whist and then went to our separate rooms. I read Kafka's *Diaries* by candlelight, no longer rationing them, for now they seemed self-pitying and faintly ridiculous, like the whining of a high-strung child. It was another language, another world, remote from this one at Moyo.

3

'You can use the old bandaging room in the leprosarium for your English class,' Father DeVoss said, and I thought how striking the remark would have been as the first line of a poem. 'It's just a *banda*, but it's got tables,' he added.

Where the lepers used to lie, I thought, my students would now sit.

But there were no hidden meanings for these priests and nuns. This leper colony was not a metaphor to them, not a microcosm of the human condition. It was reality, a community of Africans, some sick, some well. It was not subtle. It led nowhere. It was a beginning and an end. It was their life – the lepers and their families, the priests, the nuns. When Father Piet said he never wanted to go back to Amsterdam it was his way of explaining that he intended to die here at Moyo. They would all die here.

This was the whole of their reality, their entire world. The leper colony did not lead anywhere else. No one, not even the priests, expected more than this. Their house – and most of the buildings – were bare: no books on shelves, no pictures on the walls, nothing except the simplest chairs and tables. Except for the hymns in the church, and the drumming in the leper village, which began after dark and continued until eleven or so, there was no music. In this atmosphere, Father DeVoss's deck of playing cards, especially the picture cards, seemed highly colored and evocative, and I found myself lingering and discerning expressions on the faces of the Jack, Queen and King – mockery, haughtiness, defiance.

The games of whist were to pass the time. At Moyo, there were no other games of any kind, no exploitation, no work, no play. There was what you saw and nothing more. No wanting, no desire. The melancholy of it, I thought; but that was my feeling not theirs. It was not heaven, not hell, but earth as limbo for those who believed in limbo.

There was no talk of the past in the priests' house. The other world was so remote in time and space that it had no features. The leper colony had replaced all other realities, and so no one reminisced. The talk was of practical matters in the present. And though Africa was their reality, neither African politics nor African culture interested them much. Everyone spoke Chinyanja except Father Touchette. They had no vanity and yet they were inward, even a bit shy. When they were not being silly – in front of me they always talked in a jokey way – they were solemn. They did not talk about the future, though they occasionally mentioned death, or eternity.

Their clothes were dusty and dirty, but even so that did not make them seem poor. On the contrary, it gave them a sense of serenity, made them seem indifferent and unworldly and spiritual.

One night while I was making notes for my class, sitting at the dining table, where the only Tilly Lamp stood, its brightness making me see double, Father DeVoss walked behind me, hesitated, picked up the English textbook, *Foundation Secondary English*, then examined it – looked it over rather than read it – and set it down. He did the same with Kafka's *Diaries*, which was also in the stack. He might have been picking up a pair of shoes, to look at the soles and the stitches. There was nothing inside these books for him. He was utterly uninterested, as though the books were mute objects without any function, like worn-out shoes – and this was, I was beginning to think, precisely what they were: dead weight.

I felt the priests were humoring me about the English class. They were going along with it. I was not dismayed by their low expectations. That they helped me in spite of their lack of faith meant they liked me, and that pleased me. I found them congenial, even nervous Father Touchette, who always winced when the drumming started in the leper village.

The two worst fears of an expatriate going to a new place in the African bush were that the weather might be awful and the local people unfriendly. This was a manner of speaking. 'Awful weather' might mean deadly ninety-five-in-the-shade days and suffocating nights; 'unfriendly' might mean murderous. It was hot here in Moyo, but bearable; and all the people I had met were friendly, the priests, the nuns, the lepers, the woman named Birdie. I was glad that I had come and for the first time since arriving in Africa I did not want to be anywhere else.

*

I had put up a sign on the dispensary wall, where medical calls and bandaging times were announced. My note, lettered in Chinyanja, said there would be an English class on Wednesday afternoon at five. It seemed to me an appropriate time. The lepers spent the morning lining up for medicine and bandages. It was too hot after lunch for a class. Life in the leprosarium resumed when the sun dipped below the treetops, and the shadows lengthened. In the hottest brightest part of the day, when the sun was overhead, life came to a stop, and there was no one to be seen. People withdrew into their huts, where the dirt was damp and cool.

Wednesday came. At breakfast, Father DeVoss said, 'You don't have to hold your class today. If it doesn't work out, there's always Friday, or next week.'

Time has little meaning here, he meant. But it was for my sake that I needed to make my English class seem urgent; otherwise, I would lose interest in it. I had been in Africa long enough to understand that to survive I had to impose a shape on the long day – break it into three parts – even if it was all a pretense.

So I needed the class. I needed the certainty of the old bandaging room. The priests had their rituals, to deliver them from the days of harsh light and the nights of drumming and darkness.

The bandaging room was a large, open-sided shed with a sloping tin roof and a large water butt at one outside corner under a rusty down spout. At one time, this water butt must have been important, perhaps a source of water for drinking or washing. But there were standpipes in the leper village now and so this big barrel, murky, and haunted by breeding mosquitoes was unused.

Some men were waiting for me at five. I knew they were lepers from their walking sticks and their bandages. Seeing me approach, some other men got up from under a tree and came over. That made eight. Then an old woman shuffled in, guided by a young girl. It was clear that the old woman was blind, one eye looked as though it was badly sewn shut – an illusion of the lashes – and the other distorted and as glazed and marbled as an agate. This old blind woman and the young girl were the only females in the class. The girl was in her teens, barefoot, wearing a wrap-around and a purple scarf on her head that made her seem exotic. She led the blind woman to a bench, then sat beside her and whispered, while the blind woman made passes in the air with her damaged hand like a clumsy blessing.

'Please write your names on this piece of paper,' I said.

This caused a commotion. Some of them understood, others didn't. Three of them could not write, and these did not include the blind woman, whose presence baffled me.

One man with a full set of teeth and scars on his forehead that seemed more an accident than a design rattled the paper and began to laugh.

'Do you want to learn English?'

He paid no attention.

'That man is sick in his head,' a man in the back said.

The other men laughed at this. They had big, misshapen feet and bruised legs and had brought into the room that earthen odor of sickness and dead flesh.

I ignored them and said to the man, 'My name is Paul. What is your name?'

'Name,' he said. There was a dribble of spittle in the corner of his mouth. He seemed very innocent and helpless, almost childlike in the way his face was about to crumple, either into laughter or tears.

Some of the others laughed, and the man in the back laughed the hardest, commanding attention.

'Why are you laughing?'

'Because he is foolish,' the loud man said.

'Please stand up.'

He did so.

'What is your name?'

'You can read it for yourself on the paper, Father.'

'But I want you to tell me,' I said.

'My name is Johnson Magondwe and I am very well, thank you.'

'You may sit down.'

'What is your name, Father?' he said, folding his arms and still standing, as though defying me.

'I've already told you that.'

'No. You were telling that foolish man your name, but you were not telling us.'

He grunted 'eh, eh,' and looked around at the others in the room in triumph, believing that he had been superbly witty.

'My name is Paul. Please sit down.'

'I am having one more question, Father.'

'You can ask it later.'

But he kept his arms folded and set his jaw at me, and I saw that the other men around him were giggling with a sort of submissive fear.

I turned my back on them and spoke to another silent man in the first row, hoping that he was not the simpleton he seemed.

'Hello. How are you?'

He looked terrified. He sucked on his tongue and said nothing.

'He is not understanding, Father.'

'*Moni, bambo,*' I said.

'He is deaf in his ears, Father.'

'*Muli bwanji?*' I said.

'And foolish, Father.'

That was Johnson Magondwe, calling out from the back of the room. I ignored him, but I felt weary in anticipation. So far, one woman was blind, one man was crazy, and another deaf. Several others obviously spoke no English at all. And Johnson was a bore and a bully.

The young girl in the colorful turban was twisting her fingers, looking anxious.

'Do you speak English?'

'Yes, I do speak,' she said almost in a whisper, lowering her eyes.

'Who is this old woman?'

'She is my granny.'

'What is your name?'

'My name is Amina.'

Then she bowed her head, but even so I could see her long lashes and clear skin, and her shoulders shining. She was thin, but sturdy. Her neck was long, her fingers slender. She had full lips and large eyes. I loved her for my being able to see the suggestions of her bones beneath her flesh, in her face and her hands, her shoulders. She was young though not so young in African terms. Many girls her age – sixteen or seventeen – already had several children.

The men in the room were surprised that she spoke English. Of the dozen Africans in the room only five spoke English. I wrote some lines of dialogue in chalk, on a smooth plank that was painted black. Johnson, and the man next to him, Phiri, could read it easily, and so could Amina; with my coaching, two of the others learned it. While this went on, the blind woman grunted, the simpleton drooled, the deaf man rocked back and forth.

I was tired yet they seemed oddly rested and calm. They were not eager, but curious, watching me, waiting for me to teach them, the way they stood at the dispensary with their hands out, empty palms upward, expecting me to pass them medicine.

'Repeat after me,' I said. 'It's a dog.'

I chose them at random.

'Is a dock.'

'It's a dog,' I said. 'You.'

'Is a dock.'

'But this is a duck.'

'Thees a dock.'

'A duck,' I said. 'You.'

'A dock.'

'A dog,' I said.

'A dock.'

While they repeated these words, saying them with little com-
prehension, I could hear the clank of pots, the murmur of voices,
the whack of wood being chopped, the timid complaining of
chickens and dogs.

'It's a dog.'

'Is a dock.'

The cooking fires were all alight; each hut had its own fire in
front, filling the clearing with a stink of burning and a low crackle.
The heavy wood smoke rose so slowly that it became tangled in the
jutting bunches of thatch, and hung there, disentangling itself, and
seeping upward into the somnolent air in blue rags of smoke. This
atmosphere was everlasting; such villages had always sounded and
smelled this way. It was not a sleepy village – it was the opposite, a
place of continuous activity, but the idea of all that toil, had a
fatiguing effect on me. Its simplicity overwhelmed me and made
me tired.

'That's all for today,' I said.

'It is not yet six o'clock,' Johnson said, in a challenging tone,
rising to his feet at the back of the room.

I smiled defiantly at him.

'A class last for one hour. I am knowing that from English lessons. I have been schooling in my district.'

The way he stood, in a domineering posture, his hands on his
hips, taking up more space than he needed, seemed to indicate that
he was speaking on behalf of the others, or at least trying to. I was
already sick of him. I would have preferred a room full of Africans
who spoke no English at all; beginning with a blank slate and bringing them along.

'This is American English,' I said. 'The class lasts forty-five minutes. We will meet again on Friday.'

Just saying that, anticipating the day, wearied me. The class was
silent, attentive in the failing light. They were not looking at me but
rather at the side of the shed where one of the nuns stood, her white
robes luminous in the dusk.

'This man is in the wrong place,' she said.

It was Birdie, in a nun's habit, wearing the starched bonnet that doubled as a sun hat.

'His family is looking all over for him.'

She extended her hand to the silent man in the front row and helping him up seemed to frighten him. He allowed himself to be tugged along, and went with her, with a stiffness that looked like resistance. He was obedient but his eyes were filled with terror.

I dismissed the class and joined Birdie and the man, and said, 'I hadn't realized you were a nun.'

'I'm not,' she said. 'It's just that I get more respect dressed this way.' She smiled, she was friendlier than when I had first met her in the dispensary. 'And this stuff's cooler.'

Just her face was visible, framed by the bonnet that looked as though it was made out of brilliant white cardboard, a prettier face than the one from the other day.

'I mean, I'm naked underneath,' she said.

Without knowing why – perhaps it was my confusion – I looked at the African, his glassy eyes, his fists at his side, his rigid way of walking. Birdie laughed at me and steered the clumsy African towards his hut.

For a long time afterwards I could not think of anything else. I was dizzy with the words *I'm naked underneath*. Her saying that stunned me, had a physical effect on me, made me slightly deaf and near-sighted and stupid. She must have known that, from the way she laughed. Over cards that night, and in the darkness of my room, and the dusty heat the next day and especially during meals, while I was swallowing something, I thought of what she had said, and went stupid again.

On Friday there was another class, again a dozen Africans, big and small, sick and well. The simpleton was not there, and some of the others had not come back. But Johnson was in his same seat, and Amina and her blind granny were there. Two other young women were also there, and from the undercurrent, the whispers and the gestures of the men, I could see a sort of courtship going on, as the class progressed. At the end, they paired up and sneaked into the bush.

I was almost fearful that Birdie might show up as she had on Wednesday, but she was nowhere to be seen. It was one of the characteristics of the leprosarium that people kept to themselves, each person to his portion of the place, the priests in their house, the nuns in the convent, the lepers in their village. I realized that one of my reasons for missing mass on Sunday was the thought that I might run into Birdie. Her laughter had excited and disturbed me. I needed to be calm, and so I avoided her. It was not difficult. In fact, the whole of Moyo seemed to contain separate kinds of solitude.

The Monday class was a smaller group than Friday's; Amina and her granny were missing, and of the others, the same two young women, fewer men. They giggled among themselves. They were in-attentive. I was sure the class was now simply a pretext for a liaison in the bush later on. Aware that no one was listening to me, I became tired and hoarse.

I wondered why Amina had dropped out. When she did not show up at the next class, I took it as a rejection of me, taught for half an hour and then disgustedly sent them all home.

4

The leper village was active, it had an air of being industrious, and yet none of this work seemed to change it. Was there something African in the way all this energy and motion left no trace behind? It reminded me of the riverbeds I had seen in the southern region – flooded, brimming, bearing whole trees and logs and huts in its torrent one day; dry as a bone the next, just dusty gullies. The fury came and went, and there was no visible memory of it.

Moyo was like that. Women carried firewood, big girls carried small children or else buckets of water, boys played or hoed the rows of corn, men squatted in groups, muttering and smoking pipes. Some were lepers, others relatives. Food was grown and cooked and eaten. Firewood was burned. The buckets of water were emptied. So the people were sustained, the achievement of the work was that life continued. It was the meaning of subsistence, an active way of marking time. The reason for all this effort was to hang on to life and to remain the same.

At midday a stillness settled over the place and only then was it apparent that something had been happening – this sudden stillness was the proof that work had been going on, but it was only noticeable when it stopped, like a hum that goes dead, or a clock that stops ticking, and the silence is shattering. At noon on Saturdays the silence was more obvious. It was a large hole in the day and nothing followed it. The shop closed, the dispensary was locked, gardening ceased, the market emptied, and the women who sold bananas and peanuts and boiled potatoes and the black bony smoked fish that looked like shingles in stacks – these market women drifted away. Then the leprosarium, the village of pale mud huts, lay silently baking in the sun, and the only sounds were barks or cockcrows; no voices. Behind it all, like vibrant wires, the howl of locusts. Saturday was like a day of mourning.

I sat on the verandah of the priests' house. Nearer the rail, Father Touchette read his breviary, turning the pages with clean white fingers. Brother Piet dozed, his hands clasped over his stomach. His snoring was like an obvious form of boasting. Father DeVoss had gone to the lake shore on his motorcycle to say a Saturday mass at a village church where he went once a month.

I unbuckled the belts on my leather satchel and slipped out a cheap Chinese-made notebook, its spine covered in red cloth. I wrote, *11 Oct., 1964, Moyo Leprosarium, Ntakataka, Central Province*, and then I looked up, beyond the tin roofs to the thatched roofs, to the treetops, smoke mingling with dusty sunlight, and the Africans looking as upright as exclamation marks. I thought that, but I did not write it into my notebook. Writing seemed irrelevant.

My poems, about a dozen of them, I had copied carefully into the back. I turned to them and read some lines, and then I began to skip. They were lifeless, they seemed trivial, I hated and was bored by the repetition of the word 'black.' My eye fell on the words 'pulpous,' and 'gorgeous,' and 'taut.' I disliked them too, and I shut the notebook, because I was tempted to tear them out.

There was no point in a letter home. I seldom wrote anyway, and they might be alarmed by this one. They might misunderstand and pity me. I had no way to describe this place. The danger in writing about it was in making it seem worse than it was. Yet leprosy was accepted, snakebite was normal, work changed nothing. Everyone except the foreigners was either a leper or else a relative of a leper. I did not know how to write about this without embellishing it, and I knew that it would be a mistake. It was as far from my notion of literature as it could be. I was reminded of the cassava and how it looked when it was dug out of the ground, just a rough hairy root covered with reddish dirt. You would never think that it was edible. And yet we ate them every day, peeled and boiled. They were a little stringy but after you had been eating them for a year you noticed that their taste was almost delicate.

Moyo – the leper colony, the mission, all the people and their simple buildings – was a little world of illness. Yet it was more real to me than the colonial town I had left behind in the south, the main street and its look of feeble mimicry. I had had no trouble writing poems about Blantyre, because it had once seemed real. The trip to Moyo showed me that I had been mistaken.

The reality here was that no one was sentimental. They came here ill; they declined; they died. No one advanced or prospered. It was a small world in which no one had the illusion of making choices. And no one minded that. I did not know why this was so, though I suspected that it was because the people here were always in the presence of death.

My poems were pointless and trivial. The very word 'poems' irritated me, because they were made of artifice and self-consciousness. 'Look at me,' all poems said. They called attention to themselves rather than their subject. I wanted to throw them away, but paper was such a luxury here that someone was bound to retrieve them from the barrel and I would be ashamed. So I hid them and vowed to destroy them in my own secret way.

I turned to the Kafka *Diaries*, and read some pages and found them gloomy and tormented and filled with morbid self-pity. The worst of it was Kafka's hypochondria. Reading it in sight of the leper village, I almost laughed at Kafka's repeated expressions of anxiety and the minutiae of his exaggerated ill health. *Sleeping badly*, he wrote. *Shortness of breath and a tightness in my chest*, he wrote. And then my eye fell on the word leper in one entry. *Sometimes I feel like a leper*. But he had no idea how a leper felt, or what it meant to be a leper. I could not read anymore.

I thought: You could stay here and learn to hate all written words, and despise literature most of all. I decided to find a shovel and dig a hole and bury my notebooks of poems and my Kafka book.

Father Touchette did not stir when I got out of my creaking chair to creep off the verandah. Though he looked as though he were meditating on his breviary in a posture of great piety, he was asleep. He was not ecstatic, simply napping.

I got up and walked along the path to the edge of the village where I had seen a beehive of smoking bricks and some shovels. They made bricks the old way here, digging a hole in clayey earth and dumping in water and straw and then tramping in it until it was mixed. Then they crammed it into a mold and stacked the bricks and baked them.

I wanted to dig a hole here. It would give this day a meaning – but more than that, anything buried here would (to use a word from one of my poems) become friable – crumble to dust, and one day, wetted and molded and baked, be turned into bricks for a latrine, a fitting end for these paltry poems.

The earth was dry. It seemed hard at first, but it cracked and gave and came apart and soon, digging with a rusty shovel, I had a deep enough hole to bury the Kafka and my notebooks. I flung them in casually, raising dust, liking the way they plopped into their pauper's grave, and then I covered them with dirt.

'Great,' I said loudly.

In that same moment I heard a startled yelp and looked up. A little distance off I saw a woman running away and a man hitching his shorts up and dusting off his knees, slapping at them. He coughed loudly, glanced in the direction the woman had gone, and then hunkered down, elbows on his knees and stared at me.

'Are you looking at me, Father?' he said in Chinyanja.

He was as black as the shadow of the mango tree in which he crouched.

'These bricks' – I was mounding the dirt over the corpses of my papers -'are they yours?'

Now I saw his sweating face and bandaged feet, smeared with dust.

'They belong to the hospital,' he said, using the word *chipatala*. The sick ones called it a hospital, the healthy ones referred to it as a village or a mission.

I walked nearer to him. He was wrinkled and black. Like many other Africans I had seen he looked as though he had been worn down by the weather. His skin was roughened by wind and sun like a tree stump or a fence post.

'They are for the kitchen,' he said.

I could see a partly made wall, the mortar hardened as it had oozed out from between the bricks. This was perhaps the foundation, the outline of fireplaces that were like a row of barbecue pits. It was to be a communal kitchen.

'Is it your kitchen?'

'It is anyone's kitchen.'

He seemed bored but it was the way most of the lepers talked to mzungus – offhand, faintly jeering, because this was a world the lepers could not leave. And why should they care, when they had the mzungus to worry about them?

'Are you working on it?'

In the same bored tone, now sounding haughty and indignant, he said, 'No, I am sick.'

He held up his bandaged hands.

'I thought maybe your woman was helping you.'

'Not to work, but to play.' He laughed in a rumbling way, and coughed and then spat, and all of that too was like a pronouncement.

'I just buried some rubbish,' I said, realizing that he might have seen me. In Chinyanja the word rubbish suggested something that was contaminated and unclean. I did not want him to become curious and dig it up, as a scavenging African might.

'If I work on the kitchen, will you help me?'

'How much will you pay me?'

'Nothing.'

'Then I will not work.'

It was a leper's response and it verged on insolence. He was frank, he was not afraid, he was blunt. In Blantyre, an African would have humored me and still not done any work.

'Why should I?' the man said, because I had not replied to him.

I thought of Franz Kafka in Prague confiding to his diary, *I feel like a leper*. The book belonged in the ground with my bad poems. Kafka was not a leper. He was a middle-class insurance clerk with a batlike face, pathologically timid and paranoid and guilt-ridden, developing various personal myths as he wrote long, fussy letters to lonely women desperate for the chance to love him.

This was a leper: guiltless, maimed, seeping into his bandages. He had just copulated under a tree with a leper woman, and he was now staring me down. In many ways he was healthy – certainly healthier than Franz Kafka. Reading meant nothing to him; a book was a mute object. He was patient and contemptuous because he was powerless and he knew it. Perhaps he knew that nothing would change for him, nor would he change anything. He had no illusions, and so he was fully alive every waking moment, looking for food or water, looking for shade, looking for a woman.

'What is your name?'

'Wilson. And yours?'

'Paul.'

'From England?'

'America.'

'Americans have so much money.'

'I don't have any.'

He laughed at me and hobbled away before I could say anything else. One of his feet was bandaged, the other was big and yellow and cracked, with twisted toes. He wore a ragged shirt and tattered shorts. His hands were bandaged like mittens.

That night I remembered his confident mocking laugh and I was ashamed of what I had told him. Did the disease make them frank because it made them clear-sighted? Of all the people I had met in my life they had the least to lose.

One morning I went to mass. I had not been to mass for six or seven years, and I entered the church wincing and a little apprehensive, the way I had come home after a long absence without a good excuse. And yet I need not have worried. The church was large and sunny and forgiving. One pew was taken up by lepers, about six men, and there were several pews of women, some with crying babies, the others suckling infants. There were nuns in the front pew, and Linda – Birdie – wearing a white dress. Standing at the back of the church was the pretty young girl, Amina, and her blind granny.

I felt friendly towards these people, and as mass began and progressed I thought of how my feelings of pity and my sentimentality had influenced so many of my friendships. And I knew self-pity, too, and the busy, domineering feelings that came from pity, saving myself by pretending to save other people. Here, in the place most likely to arouse such feelings, I was detached – not indifferent – and free to examine how I felt. Not pitying any of them I felt lost and a little disoriented, but freer than ever.

Kneeling at the consecration, I found myself staring at Amina. She was not kneeling – because she was a Muslim, obviously – but she was steadying her granny, who was murmuring and motioning, making the sign of the cross; and I admired the young girl for doing this, being dutiful.

The mass was hot and solemn, all mumbled, with the cocks crowing just outside.

That night, during a lull in the game of whist I said to Father DeVoss, 'I'm giving up the English class.'

'That's a good idea.'

They had been his exact words when I told him I was planning to start the class.

'I think I'll work on the bricks at the outdoor kitchen instead.'

'If you like, yes,' he said. He smiled, but he might have been smiling at his hand of cards. 'That's a good idea.'

'Maybe Father Touchette will help me.'

Father Touchette fumbled with his breviary, looking startled.

'I am busy with baptisms,' he said. 'So many of them these days.'

'I suppose the lepers might help me.'

'*Pepani, bambo!*' Brother Piet exclaimed. Sorry, Dad!

'You really can't do anything,' Father DeVoss said. But he was speaking of the game. He collected the last trick and then began counting the cards stacked in front of him. His satisfaction and his remoteness touched me. Nothing of what I had said really mattered to him. He was very happy.

'The kitchen and the bricks were Father LeGrande's idea,' he said, smiling again. 'He is now in Basutoland.'

*

There were no Africans at the outdoor kitchen the next morning. In the mottled shade of the scrawny trees the half-built kitchen looked like an old ruin, one of those useless walls or battlements the British had left behind. I carried and piled bricks for an hour or so, and then as I mixed some mortar in a pit I looked up and saw some Africans staring at me. I had not seen their approach – they simply materialized, squatting, three ragged men.

They muttered, but none spoke to me as I continued the wall, scraping mortar and setting the bricks in place.

'Do you want to help?'

I used the plural, but there was no reply. I said it again in a matey way, using the word *iwe* – eeway – the bluntest 'you' in the language.

They laughed and grunted as though I had nudged them with my elbow.

'Pay us some money,' one said in English.

'*Ndalama*,' another said. Cash.

I ignored them and went on laying bricks. They were still talking softly among themselves, and I had the impression that they were debating the issue of whether to help me.

'It is your kitchen – not mine,' I said.

'Then why are you working on it?'

'To help you.'

'It is your choice,' the English-speaking one said.

'Mzungus like to help,' the third one, an old man, said.

They left soon after, crept silently away, leaving patches of shadow, deep black in the white dust, where they had been.

Feeling angry, I stayed there, laying bricks, wanting to be stubborn. I worked through the lunch bell and I was pleased when Birdie came over with a plate of *nsima* and beans, and a cup of tea. I needed her as a witness.

'Father LeGrande would be happy to see you working here,' she said. She was wearing a long blue skirt and a floppy hat.

'I wish I had some help.'

She was smiling at the leper village. 'They're lazy,' she said. 'They just don't want to work. They don't care whether it's done or not. We do everything for them.'

I was shocked by the casual brutality in her tone, and by her healthy, confident face.

'They pretend to be sick,' she said. 'They laugh at us behind our back. And they're bloody rude. If we went away, they'd die or kill each other. They can't go home – they don't fit in.'

She was smiling – she wanted to shock me.

'I'll send someone for the bowl and the cup,' she said, and gathered her skirt so it wouldn't drag in the dust and headed for the dispensary, leaving me flustered.

What she had said made her physically repulsive to me. I repeated it in a whisper to myself and, watching her making her way down the path, I found fault with the way she walked, her ridiculous hat, her raised elbows, the jumping of her skirt.

The Africans did not come back that day. I worked until dusk, when the mosquitoes came out, and then I headed for the priests' house for dinner. I was too tired to play cards, or read, and the priests were still awake when I went to my room.

I did the same the next day. Birdie brought me food, and again she said, 'And where are they? Sleeping in their huts while you work.'

'I am doing this for myself,' I said. 'This is my idea, not theirs.'

I ate the food, while she watched, standing over me.

'Why don't you sit down?'

'Dust,' she said, and smiled.

'Have you stopped wearing your nun's outfit?'

'I'll start wearing it again if you want.'

She went away laughing, and I thought: Do I dislike her because she says what I secretly think? I knew that I had begun to resent the Africans at Moyo for just the reasons she said.

But I kept at it the following days, always starting just after breakfast and working through lunch until Birdie showed up with a plate of *nsima* and beans, heading home at dusk and arriving at the priests' house in the dark, when the path had been swallowed by night, and guiding myself by the pressure lamps blazing at the windows.

I like this place because no one knows me, I thought.

On the Friday of that week, I was walking through the leper village in the falling darkness, which was night mingled with dust and the smell of dirt and lamp oil. I heard a shriek, and a gasp, and a groan – the sounds of suffering coming out of the open window of a mud hut. I suspected that it was a woman being beaten, or perhaps suffocated by her husband. That kind of random domestic violence was fairly routine. This sudden brutality seemed like another aspect of the sexuality of the leper village.

I went to the door of the hut, but seeing two women, one of them a nun, kneeling beside a mat on the floor, and the other lying on the mat and gasping, I hesitated. A kerosene lamp lit only the room and the women; it distorted everything else, and outside the shadows were dark enough so that I could hover without being seen.

The woman on the mat called out again and I could tell from the way she gasped, and the naked heap of her belly, that she was in the throes of childbirth.

The white nun and the African woman spoke to her gently, and the nun held the woman's legs, bracing her. The African chafed the woman's hand to comfort her, and I could see that the woman about to give birth had a hollow between her thumb and forefinger – the tiger's mouth – and the fingers themselves were mangled: a leper.

Childbirth scenes in movies, my only experience of a woman giving birth, I had always found excruciating: the screams, the hysteria, the upraised knees, the parted legs, the contorted face of the mother. But this was different, no more than muttering now, a labored breathing, a kind of sighing, as the midwives encouraged her. After another grunt the child was lifted into the yellow lamplight.

'*Mwana*,' the nun said. It's a boy.

It was a perfect child, pinky gray with a full head of hair, all his fingers and toes intact. He dripped for a moment and then pissed – a narrow stream in the air – while he howled, growing pinker, as the women laughed in relief.

When I got up to go, I staggered and almost fell, and wondered why. My eyes hardly focused. I seemed to see a small group of people, gathered in the shadow just beyond the reach of the lamplight. Was one of them Amina? I saw the smooth face and bright eyes and blue turban. I had the sense that she was looking at me and not at the hut, where the women were rejoicing. Then I was groping on the path in the darkness, and I thought of the man beneath the tree telling me, 'I'm sick.'

5

'I think I'll lie down,' I said as I entered the priests' house. My voice was quacky and echoey in my ears, and I felt terrible, though I pretended to be well – just tired, as I had been each evening on returning from the kitchen outside the leper village. Tonight I tottered like a drunk trying to pass for someone sober.

As soon as I reached my room I collapsed, my head aching, all my bone joints cracking. In seconds my skin was on fire and every sound was a howl in my head. It was as though I had been flayed alive, my skin peeled from my flesh to expose the naked white threads of my nerves.

I lay in the hot darkness, with dust in my nose, dying. The fever took hold. I felt I was in the grip of a fatal illness, and I was sure of it when bony fingers squeezed my flesh, wickedly, like pincers in torture. Those skeletal fingers were the fever. I was too sick to be able to tell anyone. I could hear the clatter of plates; they had finished dinner, Simon was gathering the dishes, Father DeVoss snapping the playing cards, Brother Piet humming as he sewed, Father Touchette clutching his breviary. I groaned and could not get up from my bed. I regretted that I had shut and bolted the bedroom door.

The overloud voices in the next room sounded in my dream. They were rough, indifferent men in stained robes, laughing as they played cards. They gambled while I lay dying. Each time I woke, greasy with my sweat, I felt frailer and more fearful.

Help me.

But the moan stayed in my mouth because I was too weak to cry out.

I thought: They could come in here, any of them, and they could help me. They don't care!

I shivered, I sweated. My heart drummed. The laughter – was it Brother Piet? – was sudden and explosive and the racket of it tore into my head.

A shadow rattled against my eyes. It was a bat, flying back and forth in the room, the way I had once seen one flap in a barn. This fever bat was cut by the stripes of light from the cracks in the door frame. I watched the creature seeming to crackle in the broken light. I was not afraid, but I was helpless. The pain in my head and my bones paralyzed me, and my sense of powerlessness frightened me. I sensed the thing swoop near my face, beating its skinny wings, and I got a whiff of its stink. The bat bothered me less than the intimation that I was dying, yet it seemed part of the paraphernalia of my death, like a funeral prop, a candle or an owl.

I implored the darkness for one of the priests to look up from his hand of cards and think of me and show concern and break the door down. Then I would have a chance. But I was alone and I was trapped in this room. I was lost. They would not miss me until tomorrow, noon at the earliest, and by then I would be dead.

This terrified me and made me so sad I began to cry again, like a child, not sobbing but whimpering and squeaking as I cowered.

Then I was dreaming of enormous women, Birdie and others,

with green skin and stupendous breasts and hot, scorching mouths, laughing at me and biting me, wrestling joyously with each other and casting me aside. Quite near me a leper woman with stumps where her limbs should have been, turned away, and I realized that I was even uglier than she. Laughing at me she twisted her nose off – it was like the damp prune of a dog's nose – and she reached for me.

That woke me, but moments later I was in another dream. Every dream was a dream of enemies – of my weakness. I was overwhelmed and mocked and intimidated. Occasionally a giantess would throttle me while I tried to summon the strength to plead for my life.

I was washed ashore on to a beach of broken bones, a foreshore crisscrossed by bird prints, spirals of their tracks which were neat and simple, like new letters of the alphabet. It was stony, with broken shells and pockmarked rocks and fragments of white wave-smoothed stones that gave the beach its look of doom, a place of dry bones and skull fragments. There were human footprints but no one in sight. All I saw was an expanse of white sand. At first I felt the heat on my face, but hurrying across the sand I burned my feet. In the distance the sea was a deep blue, but brown against the shore, under a pale sky. The sun was directly overhead and blazing down upon me. I struggled on scorched feet to the edge of the sea and then tipped myself into the water and was scalded by the heat of a wave. The sea was simmering and close up it was a foul stew of bubbles and weeds.

I was jerked from this awful dream by the sound of drumming.- Like the voices that had jarred me earlier I had a hallucinatory sense of pain, my eyeballs aching, my ears ringing, not knowing whether I was asleep or awake. The priests were asleep – must have been. But the absence of their voices seemed only to make the drumming louder. It tumbled in a cascade of thumping, and it shivered and stopped before starting again, faster and louder.

And I imagined I could see the dancers – toothy, grinning villagers, lepers and their families, ugly and stubborn, showing aggression, snatching at each other. Other shadows rutted under the dusty trees. The priests stood by saying nothing, their arms folded, while over the drumbeats I tried to call out, '*Save me!*'

There was drumming in my dreams and when I woke the drumming continued outside the window, and I hated them – the dancers, the drummers, the priests especially, because they did nothing to stop it or help me.

So the night went on. Was it one night? But the bat was real, and so was the laughter and the drumming. I was not imagining these things. I could have endured the dream, though. What was real frightened me: the pain in my head and the knowledge that I was small and sweaty and weak and sick, and that I would die before dawn. Knowing that was an agony.

Without making a sound, I wept. Tears streamed down my cheeks. I was afraid of death but after all those dark hours I wanted to die – to be rid of this pain.

That was before dawn. Then I slept and dreamed in sunlight, which gave my dreams the bright colors of a crackling fire. The cockcrows reassured me, and when I woke at last to knocking on the door, I struggled out of bed and slid the bolt and collapsed. And then Brother Piet was kneeling near my bed and murmuring, 'Pepani, pepani' – Sorry, sorry – and fumbling with a thermometer.

My temperature was 103. I thought: I know something I did not know before, but I could not remember what it was.

I lay there too weak to raise my head, yet I was glad that I had been found. It had been a long, painful night, at the edge of death. I had sensed myself slipping away, unable to call out. Now I had a chance.

Father DeVoss visited me, his hands behind his back. He said, 'It's lucky you decided to spend your holiday at a hospital.'

I had not thought of Moyo as only a hospital. It was everything – a mission, a church, a village, a leper colony. It was for castaways – lepers and syphilitics and snakebite victims, with extravagantly ugly afflictions; and they lay disfigured and hopeless, because they had been cast out of their own villages. Not a hospital, but a refuge for desperate people. They were not sick, they were cursed.

A fever was something else, a ragged pain that droned like a buzz-saw in my head and throughout my body. I was not like those other people. There was no cure for me – I knew that much. You lived with it and you suffered and in a week or so you either got better or steadily worse, and even if you got better you were never the same again, because the fever killed something inside you. That was what Africans said of fevers; and now I knew enough of fevers to believe it.

'It could be malaria,' Father DeVoss said, lightly speculating. He did not seem concerned, and he stood to one side as Brother Piet set down a tray.

'You drink this while it is hot and then I give you *mankhwala*,' Brother Piet said. The seriousness of the occasion inspired more English words than I had so far heard him use. He offered me a cup of sweet, steaming tea. He dosed me with chloroquine, six tablets now, six more at noon, and paracetamol, to bring my temperature down.

'Or blackwater fever. Even cholera. Or one of the fevers that doesn't have a name,' Father DeVoss said. 'But we'll treat you for malaria first, because we have the *mankhwala* for that.'

Drenched in sweat and gasping, I nodded and tried to smile and thanked them both in a croaky voice, glad that I had survived the night and that I had witnesses now to my fever.

'I think Paul is feeling better already,' Father DeVoss said.

It had been an awful night. But now the attention of these kind men had raised my hopes and dulled my pain. I felt looked-after and I was reassured by Brother Piet's fussing. He carefully changed my sheets and at once in dry sheets I felt calmer.

Father DeVoss still smiled at me but in such a melancholy and benign way I felt he was blessing me. His forgiving eyes seemed to bestow grace. He was looking beyond my fever and my frailty to my soul, while Brother Piet was tending to my body.

All that day Brother Piet and Simon the cook served me tea and made me gulp chloroquine tablets. When I grew feverish again in the early evening, Simon folded wet towels on my head to cool me and bring my temperature down. In the darkness of the night I still burned with fever, but I was less afraid. I prayed that I was on the mend, and when morning came – with the first light – I was more hopeful. I had made it through another night. Then it was hot tea and sour quinine and watery chicken soup that Simon made. As each day waned my temperature went up, my skin burned, my nerves ached, my eyes began to boil in their sockets. And I was afraid again, that I might falter in the darkness and die.

The drumming continued, carrying through the trees and up the slope from the leper village. I could smell the sharpness of the dust that was raised by the stamping feet of the dancers. I easily imagined them, dancing, bringing their feet down as though they were killing the fat, white worms they called *mphutsis*. My fever intensified with the drumbeats and the darkness, giving me a kind of night vision that was also hallucinatory, and I saw them, the dancers – many of them naked, their gleaming bodies lit by flames, their black shadows jumping in my room.

Through burning eyes I saw the young girl Amina flinging herself into the jostling mob of dancers, working her thin arms and legs, thrilled by the drums, her face streaming with sweat, her small breasts reddened by the firelight, her eyes rolled up so that only the whites showed. And then her cloth wrap-around slipped and was trampled. She was entranced and did not notice, only became more sinuous, and brighter, her body like a single flame, while her granny stared with blind eyes, hearing the drums, perhaps wondering where the girl had gone.

In her room in the convent, Birdie also heard the drumming. She too imagined the black, sweating bodies, the crackling fire, the yodeling women. The village which slumbered in the dust all day came alive at night. Nothing in daylight mattered. I tried to think about what Birdie felt when she heard it – was she aroused or disgusted? She was excited, of course, but appalled at her excitement, and so she would pretend to disapprove.

My fever helped me see it all clearly, not just the drumming and dancing, but the girl Amina, and Birdie, the nuns, the priests, sweating in their upper rooms, some of them praying. My illness fed me visions and made these people familiar. I knew them all better in my fever.

And then I began to think that it was my lesson. I had to be sick and feverish and lying on my back, unable to form a word with my scummy tongue, to realize that any effort here seemed pointless.

Simon went through the motions of bringing me wet towels and tea and soup and medicine. But neither he nor any of the priests seemed unduly alarmed. They did their duty and they were watchful. But their attitude was as fatalistic as the lepers'. How in this world of lepers could I expect sympathy for my fever? In spite of what they said, they looked upon me as someone who might die.

'There was drumming again last night,' I said to Simon, stating the obvious, just to hear my voice.

'There is drumming every night.'

'And dancing?'

'Yes, Father.'

I was sure it was as I imagined it, the lepers naked and stamping, Amina twitching before her blind granny.

'Is it some sort of harvest festival?'

'But we have no harvest, Father,' he said. 'We work in our gardens all the year.'

'Then what is the *chamba* about?' I asked, using the word that meant dancing generally.

'It is not *chamba* but *zinyao*.'

I did not know the word, and so I asked him to explain it. Simon shook his head, as though he could not disclose the secret.

'Perhaps you will see it sometime when you get well.'

I had begun to sit up, to sleep better; and my head ached less. My fever was intermittent. I still swallowed many bitter-tasting tablets and six or eight aspirin a day. I felt better – not stronger, but less feverish. And then I began to eat more, a slice or two of Simon's crumbly bread with the soup.

More eating did not make me well or even strong. It simply gave me diarrhea. So instead of using the chamber pot, I had to hobble to the latrine. I had always used the one outside the kitchen. But there was one in an overgrown part of the garden, all mossy bricks and weeds, just outside my room. It was as old as the house itself. It was a nightmare but it was near.

This shed – mud walls, thatched roof, sagging door, spider webs – was built on to a back entryway near my part of the corridor. Now and then I heard it used because its door hinges squeaked, sometimes at the oddest hours of the day. It had been part of my feverish hallucination, this squeaking in the dark hours of the morning.

I was surprised to find that there were no door hinges. I stood dizzy from being upright and saw that the door was fixed with loops of knotted rope. But I had not imagined the rusty scrape of metal – I heard it again as I stood in the sun, just outside this old latrine. The squeaking was louder inside. When my eyes grew accustomed to the dark, I saw that bats – three or four rat-sized ones – had attached themselves with dirty claws to the rough edge of the wooden seat hole. I banged the seat with my fist and they took off, dropped into the pit, where they flew in fluttering batty circles. Still they flapped and squeaked under me while I sat wincing, trying to hurry the business.

A week of this: sleep, fever, dysentery; and Brother Piet. *'Pepani.'* Sorry. Most nights, the drumming. My fever subsided, and one day I woke without a headache. My eyes did not hurt. The day was fresh, and the film of moisture on the leaves and darkening the dust under the trees with dew, gave the illusion that it had rained during the night. I marveled at the sky which was an ocean of light and for the first time I felt hungry and wanted to eat, and I thought, I'm alive.

'What was wrong with me?'

'A fever,' Father DeVoss said.

'What kind?'

'In Africa most fevers have no names,' he said. 'But what does it matter? You've pulled through.'

6

And only then, more than three weeks after I had arrived at Moyo, did I understand the leper colony. Now, bleary-eyed, I saw it as it was. I was groping towards recovery, taking slow steps with Brother Piet's carved walking stick. The effects of the fever were settling within me. Light-headed and weak and trembly, I was still hungry but could eat very little. My heart was fluttering, my hands unsteady; a walk to the bat-haunted latrine left me breathless, and a trip to the dispensary took all morning. I had survived the fever but I had not fully recovered.

In this watchful, passive state of convalescence I saw the leprosarium's indifference to the world. No one could explain exactly what it was. On my arrival I had accepted what they had said about the disease, but you had to be ill in that place to know where you were. It hardly mattered what your illness was. Any high fever that was potentially fatal sufficed to put you in touch. My nameless fever had done it. They were naked, and now I was naked too.

Naked here meant no clothes; it was not a figure of speech. That kind of talk was unknown. Words here had definite meanings. There were no metaphors, no symbols; nothing poetic or literary.

Sick meant leprosy, fever meant a week of suffering, hot meant this pitiless sun, dust this sour powder that covered the ground and was the grit in every mouthful of food. And desire – I had seen it enough times – was a man kneeling against a woman in the dust, behind a blind of crackling corn shucks at the edge of the village, pumping while she thrashed, and it was brief and brutal.

This was the bush, and had its own bush rules. The leper colony was an oversize village. It was foolish of me to think that I could come here to teach English. And it was ludicrous for me to think of the outdoor kitchen in terms of a deadline. No one cared. Anyway, the leper village of the day was just subsistence and struggle: staying alive. The leper village of the night was pleasure. While the rest of us were sleeping, the leper village was alive, even frenzied. It had nothing to do with us.

But both day and night were outside time, because time had no meaning. Today was like yesterday or tomorrow, like forty years ago; and forty years from now, there would be the same dust and drums and hunger. There were no expectations, there was only resignation. Used to their illness and grateful for their blessings, they embraced life, they were roused by sex, they shrugged at sickness, they accepted death.

Moyo was a complete world, simple enough to see, all on the surface, all visible. It was changeless. It made no allowance for ambition or alteration. A casual visitor might see it as a prison, but it was more like a home – an enormous family, with a few easily breakable rules. Apart from gardening and a little basket-weaving there was no work. Everyone was either sick or else related to a patient; everyone had an excuse. There was a church but few people attended services. Sex was almost constant, and often in view, the man and woman glimpsed, she on her back, he kneeling; and small mimicking boys were always chasing girls. It was the leper life, leper sex, leper idleness, a whole life of it in one place, and then they died. It now made sense to me.

I understood the meaning of words I had not known until then. And still feeling brain sick and lame I saw people clearly. They took me more seriously too – the lepers, their families, the nuns, Birdie. Amina now said hello to me – slyly murmuring and waving while her granny, hearing her, demanded, 'Who is that?'

The priests and Brother Piet were, as before, somewhat remote, on their low scrubby hill, concerned with the spiritual side, as Father DeVoss put it, saying mass, which was an unchanging duty. Because so few Africans went to mass it was like a private ritual, a daylit European version of the nighttime drumming.

The priests had sympathized with me in my fever but, believing in the afterlife, they were calm in the presence of any illness. I knew that from the way they spoke of the young man, Malinki, whom I had seen that first day. Still he lay without moving in a corner of the men's ward wasted like a castaway – yellow eyes, his tongue swollen, struggling to breathe. Never mind his collapsing body, and all his leaks. His soul was their mission. It was almost as though, trapped by his unknown illness, unable to move, he could be claimed: they'd snatch his soul while he was flat on his back.

We had resumed our after dinner card game. Playing one night, just after we lost a trick, I asked how Malinki was. For my own morale in my period of convalescence I wanted to hear stories of recovery.

'He's very ill,' Father DeVoss said, picking up his hand, and concentrating on each card as he arranged them in a fan.

The next night, during the whist game – as though a lost trick were the reminder – Father DeVoss turned to me and said, 'That young fellow didn't make it.'

'*Pepani!*' Brother Piet said.

'We have the funeral tomorrow,' Father Touchette said from across the room. He was not playing whist tonight. Simon had taken his place. Simon played without speaking, with a kind of anxious caution that made him lose.

'What would you have done if I had been as sick as that African?'

'We would have taken care of you,' Father DeVoss said, surprising me with his vagueness.

'I'm talking about an emergency,' I said. 'Who would you have called?'

'We have no telephone.'

'And there is no one to listen!' Brother Piet said bluntly in Chinyanja. *Palibe anthu senga!* And the card game resumed.

Few of the lepers ever attended morning mass, but when they were ill they were given the Last Rites – Extreme Unction. And when they died they had a funeral, with a mass, and were buried in the cemetery surrounded by the stone wall, in the shade of the mango tree, where I sometimes saw a man and woman coupling.

'Maybe Paul will be our altar boy.'

'All right,' I said.

It was years since I had been an altar boy serving at mass, but with a little prompting I remembered the responses, from '*Introibo ad altare Dei*,' I will go up to the altar of God, to thanking the priest when he said '*Ite, missa est*,' Go, the mass is ended.

The Africans at Malinki's funeral sang in a moaning harmony, the men groaned, the women shrieked, they all wept. And they carried Malinki's corpse in a battered coffin that would be reused after they dumped him out and buried him in a burlap sack.

Later, in the sacristy, Father DeVoss said, 'That soutane looks good on you.'

He stood and admired the white cassock that I had started to unbutton.

'You don't have to take it off. You'll find it very cool to wear, because it's loose. Better than your heavy trousers. Go on, try it.'

I wondered whether I ought to. I knew I was too weak to work. Anyway, I had abandoned my English class and was sick of laying bricks in the outdoor kitchen. So I kept the cassock on, and I walked down to the dispensary. I needed more aspirin, but I also wanted to walk among the Africans while I was dressed as a priest, in this White Fathers' gown.

'Hello, Father,' Africans said, as I passed by. That was a usual greeting: '*Moni, bambo*.' *Bwana* – master – was more respectful; *achimwene*, brother, was more intimate. I thought 'Father' was about right, even though I had only just turned twenty-three. Yet when they said it they hung back, bowed and clapped their hands, and some women and most children dropped to their knees.

Seeing me approach the dispensary, the nuns smiled, knowing that I was an impostor; nevertheless, they regarded me as an ally. And Birdie, who was doling out white tablets in paper cups to a long line of lepers, laughed out loud, as though seeing an old friend.

'Yes!' she called out.

She let her African assistant take over the pill pushing and hurried towards me, smiling.

'It gives you a feeling of power, right?' she asked, and touched my sleeve.

'It's just cooler, wearing it.'

'Oh, sure.'

And I remembered how I had seen her in her nun's outfit and her saying I'm naked underneath, and her watching my reaction.

Now there was a different look on her face – more sympathetic and animated, quicker to respond, brighter and kinder. Even the way she touched my sleeve seemed like a gesture of affection.

She said, 'I'm glad you're feeling better.'

'So am I.'

'I was starting to miss you,' she said. And perhaps detecting skepticism on my face, she added, 'There are so few people here.'

'Two thousand is a lot.'

'I mean mzungus.'

All this time she was glancing at my white cassock. Her scrutiny had started to make me feel uncomfortable, because she was looking at my clothes and not at me. I wanted to change the subject.

'Are these people getting their medicine?'

'The second batch,' she said. 'We give them a hundred milligrams a day, half in the morning, half in the afternoon.'

'What is it?'

'Dapsone. It's a sulfa drug. We're getting low – not that the lepers care,' she said. 'We do their worrying for them.'

'You don't look very worried.'

'Does it matter?' She gestured to the line of men and women who were waiting to receive their Dapsone tablets. There were some children, too. All this patience and submission. Towards the end of the line I saw Amina and her granny.

'Some of these people don't look like lepers.'

'Looks are deceiving. A child may have leprosy but won't know it until he or she is an adult.'

Seeing her staring at them, some youngsters in the line lowered their eyes.

'A bunch of these older people are almost cured,' Birdie said. 'But they have to go on taking medicine for ten years to be completely clear.'

As she spoke, she glanced at me and saw that I was smiling at Amina. Birdie turned towards Amina and gave her a swift, pitiless look, as though sizing up a rival, and reached over and lifted up Amina's slender arm and pinched her skin and held it between her fingers.

'You see this hard, dry spot? It is dead. That's the body's reaction to the bacillus. It's like a wall, sealing off the germs. That helps, but it also makes parts of the body die.'

Yet Amina was lovely – she was murmuring to her old blind granny who had asked, '*Ciani?*' What is it? I had not known until Birdie had pointed it out that Amina was a leper. I had thought she was there only to help the old woman.

'Arms and legs can become useless,' Birdie said, still watching Amina closely. Was I imagining that she sounded triumphant? 'It can turn the hand into a claw.'

Amina touched the spot on her arm and seemed to shrink back into the line of lepers waiting for medicine, as her granny groped for her shoulder.

'It cuts off the nerves.' She indicated a man whose hand had become cup-shaped as it had withered. 'He feels no pain.'

But I was looking back at Amina. 'I don't get it. I thought leprosy disfigured people.'

Amina was standing shyly among the lepers, a turban wound around her head, her face so sweet and smooth, her hands clasped, her cloth wrapped around her, so that she seemed like an upright bundle, very slender and straight. And just behind her the old blind woman, now gripping her shoulder with a diseased hand, to guide herself.

'On some people it doesn't show for years. And it's not the lep-rosy that disfigures, but the body's reaction to it. By fighting the bacillus the body destroys its own tissues. It starves and hardens them.'

'Is that how their fingers and toes fall off?'

'That's a myth. We amputate them when they harden and become useless.'

I saw Wilson, the African man who had refused to help me with the kitchen. I saw Simon the cook, and Johnson Magondwe, and the rest of the people from my English class, including the deaf man and the feeble-minded man, some of them twisted and limping on bandaged feet, others looking perfectly all right. A few seemed much healthier than me.

'That disfigurement is its success. It stops the bacilli.' Birdie turned away from the line of people. 'It stops the body too.'

The lepers were moving past a barred window which was like a ticket window, and each of them took a paper cup of tablets from Birdie's assistant. They swallowed the tablets or held them into their mouth while a nun filled the paper cup with water which they drank. Then they went outside.

'That girl you were staring at. She has a nodule on her arm. A lot of these people have nodules. That's why it's called tuberculoid leprosy.'

The nun with the pitcher said, 'But it's not all like that.' And pouring water into a man's paper cup, she went on, 'This man Yatuta is lepromatous.'

He had a heavy face and a shriveled nose and thick, bunched-up skin that was as coarse as the bark of a tree. The nun explained that the cells in this type of leprosy did not fight the disease, which was a slow destruction of the body, and the collapse of the extremities – nose, fingers, toes.

'It's terrible,' I whispered, as the man gulped the pills with the water and moved slowly outside, stabbing his walking stick into the dirt floor.

Birdie was smiling at me, as though to ridicule my sympathy.

'These people aren't dying,' she said.

I turned sharply at her, disliking the expression on her face and hating her dismissive tone. But what did I know?

'You don't die of leprosy,' she said. 'You shrink and become crippled. You live out your life. But you're disfigured and covered with scars.'

I felt self-conscious talking about the lepers in their own presence, as they moved in the long line and took their medicine. They were glancing up at us and looking helpless, as though they knew they were being discussed. But Birdie went on chattering. In a hospital everyone was naked, and this leper colony was an extreme example of nakedness.

'That fever you had was much more dangerous,' Birdie said.

I wondered whether she knew how sick I had been; and if so, who had told her?

'A fever's not contagious, though.'

'This disease will be completely cured,' she said, belittling leprosy the way she had seemed to belittle me. 'But there are other diseases. Some of them aren't in the medical books. People are brought in ill. We think they have TB – they have all the symptoms. But they don't respond to treatment. They waste away, they die. We stand and watch and then we bury them, like that young guy Malinki. We never found out what was wrong with him.'

The nun with the water pitcher said, 'But we have a good idea of how leprosy is spread. Probably from mucus, probably from running sores.' She shrugged and filled another paper cup.

'That's why we keep the wounds clean,' Birdie said. She was standing very close to me, and still smiling, and her smile seemed to have nothing to do with what she was saying to me. 'All this bandaging.'

'If you have friends in America who can send us bandages or old bed sheets,' the nun asked, 'we'd be happy to receive them.'

'What about these children?' I asked, seeing some small boys and girls in the medicine line clinging to their mothers. 'Do they have it?'

'We don't know. But if a child is born to a leper woman, it's almost certain the kid will get leprosy.'

I recalled the birth I had witnessed, just before I fell ill. It had appeared in my feverish dreams: the leper woman, the perfect child. It had seemed miraculous.

'Do you separate them?'

'No. The mothers won't let us. We give them *mankhwala*.'

The nun said, 'We had leprosy in Holland once, long ago. Europe was full of lepers. That was when Europe was poor and people lived in dirty conditions. Now the dirty conditions are in the tropics – Africa especially. That is why leprosy is here. It is a disease of dirt – of people living and breathing in one hut.'

Another nun folding bandages said, 'When I came here in 1946 we treated people with oil. That was the old remedy for leprosy.'

'Did you say oil?'

'Chaulmoogra oil. It worked!' she said. 'But now we use the sulfa drugs. They are better and stronger. This disease will be gone some day.'

The other nun frowned. 'Europe was full of huts once,' she said. 'Little dirty huts.'

I was on the path walking back to the priests' house thinking that Birdie and these nuns were admirable, when I heard footsteps behind me. I turned to see Birdie hurrying. Such a rare sight, someone running here in the heat of this slow-motion world.

'Almost forgot,' she said. 'Here's your aspirin, Father.'

'That's not funny.'

'I mean it, Father.'

She glanced around, as though to make certain that no one was watching. She seemed hesitant and self-conscious. In such a frank and wide-open place any hesitation seemed obvious, even furtive.

'Have you been to the lake, Father?'

'Stop saying that.'

'You're wearing a cassock – I can't help it,' she said. 'What about a picnic at the lake?'

I had nothing – no work, no reading, no writing. I had time to fill with whatever I wished to do.

'How would we get there?'

'Father DeVoss will let you use his motorcycle.'

I had started again to walk along the path, thinking that she would accompany me. But she did not move.

'Aren't you coming this way?'

'Yes, but . . .' She smiled instead of finishing the sentence.

'What's wrong?'

'It's not a good idea for us to be seen alone together here,' she said. 'That's another reason to head for the lake.'

Only when she said that did I realize that the whole time we had been discussing leprosy she had been flirting with me.

7

The longer I stayed at Moyo the clearer it was to me that Father DeVoss was not very religious. I suspected him of being an atheist. His title was Father Superior, and I knew he took it seriously from the way he mocked it. His spiritual presence made religion irrelevant. He said mass in a bored and sometimes impatient way, muttering, hesitating, seeming to forget some prayers, leaning with his elbows on the altar as though it were a card table. He was careless with communion wafers, poking and sorting them as though they were Malawi sixpences. He seemed bored when he was saying mass, but it was the intense reflection of a scientist sweeping a laboratory floor. His face was blank but a pitiless light burned behind his eyes. He believed in himself; therefore he did not need to believe in God. Father DeVoss framed all the rules, and he was kind, and when he was in a good mood the whole of Moyo glowed with his benevolence.

God's grace is like a weather system, I thought: sunny, or cloudy, sometimes stormy, or an eerie emptiness that might be a prelude to anything, an uncertainty that tests faith. It was obvious when Father DeVoss was happy, because it showed on everyone's face. It was yet another instance of his power, that his spirit was felt throughout the leprosarium.

Tonight the sky was gray. I sensed over dinner that Father DeVoss was displeased.

'Why did you take your soutane off?' he said. Calling it a soutane seemed to make the thing even more exotic. 'It looked right on you.'

This pronouncement, spoken with Father DeVoss's lofty simplicity, was like Holy Orders, as though detecting a latent vocation in me he had taken the authority to make me a priest, much as God might choose me.

'I don't want to mislead anyone,' I said.

'Perhaps you would be telling them the truth by wearing it.'

So I had guessed right. He was ordaining me in his forthright way, with a word and a wave of the hand, because he was God here.

'It will be very useful to you on your trip to the lake,' he said. 'Believe me, it's wise to wear it on the bush roads these days.'

I had asked him before dinner about using his motorcycle. It was another aspect of his complexity that he was able to convey his displeasure about the cassock while at the same time saying that he was delighted to loan me his motorcycle. It was the first favor I had asked of him. I knew he had been aloof. He was solitary, and I suspected him of being lonely. His granting me the favor brought me closer to the community. He wanted me to depend on him, because he was generous, and asking him for something was a way of making him powerful.

'Some of these boys in the bush can be difficult.'

'*Chipongwe*,' Brother Piet said. '*Kwambiri*.'

Very insolent, he was saying, but making it sound comic, as this old Dutch man did when he was speaking Chinyanja.

'And they'll respect my robes, is that right?'

It was what Birdie had said.

'More than you might imagine,' Father DeVoss said, lifting his arms to allow Simon to collect the dirty plates.

'I will deal the cards,' Brother Piet said.

Father DeVoss touched my shoulder. There was gentle pressure in his fingers. He said in an affectionate way, 'Have faith.'

I wanted to say that I had faith in him – more than I had ever felt for anyone, more than I had been able to muster for God. I liked this for being a house without books, not even religious books. Except for the simple crucifixes it was a house without pictures either. I had faith in Father DeVoss's patience, and doubt, and humanity; his spirit, his compassion, his detachment. I had faith in Father De-Voss's lack of belief.

'If you have faith in God you will have eternal life,' Father Touchette said.

Father DeVoss smiled his melancholy smile and said, 'I simply meant to trust the soutane, because of the roadblocks.'

But I decided to reply to Father Touchette. 'How can I believe in something I can't see?'

'People practice faith all the time,' Father Touchette said. 'They do it in order to be strong.' He was pale, he was agitated, he looked haunted.

'Not me,' I said.

'You should do it most of all,' he said. 'We are talking about the spirit and the soul. You are not a savage.'

'I think I am a savage,' Father DeVoss said, seeming jauntier, as though my argument with Father Touchette was lifting his mood. 'Yes, I am a savage.'

It was possible to tell how long a person had been in Africa by the way they used the word 'savage'. For Father Touchette a savage was an ignorant enemy, and hardly human. For Father DeVoss it was simply another harmless group of people, not enemies but allies, like unpredictable younger brothers.

'You mean savages don't have faith?' I asked the young priest.

'They have trouble with it,' he said.

'I don't agree. So-called savages are famous for being afraid of things they can't see. Most of their world is invisible and taken on faith.'

'Paul is right,' Father DeVoss said. 'The Africans here are afraid of *mfiti*, invisible witches, who summon corpses from their graves and then eat them. They dream of *mzimu*, the spirit of the dead, who can take hold of their mind and rave and babble and utter oracles.'

'*Bwebweta*,' Brother Piet said, and motioned with his hands, indicating that it was the word for babbling. He was clowning again with the language, but Father Touchette looked terrified.

Father DeVoss smiled and went on, 'That's why you have so many baptisms, Father.'

It occurred to me then that Father DeVoss never performed baptisms. I said, 'Having faith isn't a mark of civilization.'

Father Touchette's eyes glistened as he said, 'You are talking about superstition, not faith. One is false, the other is God's truth.'

'I need to see things. I need to ask questions. I want to know more.'

'Then you're in danger. You're looking in the wrong place. I pity you.'

'Please,' Father DeVoss said, with a gentle smile. But he was not protesting. He seemed to be enjoying the argument.

'Don't I get credit for asking questions?'

'No,' Father Touchette said. 'You are turning your back on Almighty God.'

'You're going to say, "The answer is within you."'

'Yes.'

'I think the answer is probably out there.'

I gestured towards the leper village. As always at this time of night the drumming was a muffled pandemonium, mingled voices and shrieks, and the knock of clubs against the scooped-out logs they used as drums.

'*Sewerendo masewera a ng'oma*,' Brother Piet said: They are dancing the dance with drums. He touched with his fingertips the cards he had dealt, and he went on speaking. '*Wopusa n'goma*.'

'What's that?'

'A proverb. "The idiot beats the drum. The clever one dances,"' Father DeVoss said. 'Now let's play cards.'

'What is the answer, then?' I asked Father Touchette.

He stared at me and clutched the black brick of his breviary, and his look was so sad, so much deeper than anger or insult it might have been despair.

'He has forgotten the question,' Father DeVoss said, and though his face was solemn there was laughter in his voice, and it was like wisdom.

Again it struck me that Father DeVoss's melancholy humor seemed to indicate a lack of religious belief. It was spiritual, though – quiet, serene, a bit spooky, like the Africans' wary reverence. They did not discuss or elaborate their fears of witches. You knew what they feared by their conspicuous silence.

As we began to play whist – tonight my partner was Simon – a child's sudden whimper just behind me made me jump. It was Father Touchette, crying in his chair. Father DeVoss raised his eyes from the card he was about to play and his eyes found the younger priest and silenced him.

*

'I love it,' Birdie said.

'So do I,' and I gunned the engine.

Father DeVoss's motorcycle was a black, older model Norton, with fluted plates on its twin-cylinder heads and two wide, dishlike seats. Its fenders curled front and rear like the brims of Spanish helmets, and it had roomy leather saddlebags. Like every other material thing in the priests' lives, it was simple and practical and well-cared-for.

'Not the bike,' Birdie said. 'The outfit.'

My white cassock, she meant. But wearing it, I felt more like a choir boy than a priest.

'It was Father DeVoss's idea.'

Smirking, as though she did not believe me, Birdie got on to the rear seat. She was wearing Bermuda shorts and a loose blouse and kneesocks. She clung to me instead of to the leather loops, and I could sense a nervous impatience in the way she held me.

It was two in the afternoon – a late start because of extra bandaging. At this dizzy time of day, the sun at its hottest, the village was empty and not even the small boys were outside.

We passed the dispensary, the hospital, the village, and then we were out of the leprosarium, jouncing on the rutted road through the stands of thin yellow trees. I slowed down for the railway tracks.

Beyond them, there were no huts, no people, no dogs, no gardens, only baked earth and dusty sunlight and the narrow road. I settled the bike into a wheel rut and took off.

I had done this before in the south of the country, traveled fast on a motorcycle in the groove at the side of the road, but after so many weeks of following the routine of the leprosarium there was something unreal about this. It was not just the speed; it was that I was hurrying away from an existence I had begun to understand.

So, on the road with Birdie, I felt uneasy and somewhat unsafe – insecure, anyway. I had no desire to see the lake or the roadblocks Father DeVoss had warned me about. There was also something less definite in my anxiety. Outside of the leprosarium I was in the big, unstable world. It was a mid-afternoon of hot stillness and slanting shadows. Here and there were baobab trees, looking like a child's monstrous version of elephants, distorted and fat and gray. I was already anticipating being late on the return trip. No one traveled in the dark on a bush road in this part of Africa.

Behind me, Birdie was talking excitedly. I could hear the sound of her voice, but the slipstream of rushing wind muffled her words.

I had been put off by Birdie's first reaction to my wearing a cassock. 'I love it.' Farther along, an African woman on the road dropped to her knees when she saw me, and she made the sign of the cross, almost spilling the load of wood on her head. Birdie clutched me tightly and called out in triumph. That repelled me, too.

Soon after, we passed a cluster of mud huts, and at the edge of this small settlement there was a horizontal bar across the road, an iron pipe resting on two oil drums: a bush roadblock. At either side of the road were about eight men and boys, looking hot and bad-tempered, wearing the faded red shirts and smocks of the Malawi Youth League. They held wicked-looking sticks and vicious slashers and crude, lumpy truncheons. Yet seeing how I was dressed, they backed off, seeming sheepish and awkwardly respectful, handling their weapons with obvious embarrassment.

'Good day, Fadda-sah,' one said.

'You can pass this side,' another said, raising the iron pipe.

It was all just as Father DeVoss had said.

They were staring at Birdie now, their mouths slack and hungry.

'What's the problem?' I asked.

'We are assisting wid da security situation, Fadda-sah.'

The man who said this was dressed like the others – faded red shirt, khaki shorts, barefoot – but he was grizzled, with a nasty face; a little old man in a boy's clothes.

Assisting with the security situation was the opposite of what they were doing. They were the paid thugs of the government, obstructing the road in order to intimidate anyone on it into buying (for five shillings) a membership in the Malawi Congress Party. Like other hacks in this one-party state, they were making trouble while pretending to keep the peace. At Moyo I had forgotten the political trouble in the country.

There were two more roadblocks (grubby men, a dusty iron pipe, 'You can pass, Fadda') before we got to the lake. Then Birdie was shouting into my neck. I saw the lake shining through the trees, not cool or blue, but a hard metallic glitter, like tin foil, a great wrinkled expanse of it, and I felt helpless. There was too much of this emptiness, and this was not where I wanted to be. I wanted to ride straight back to Moyo. I said so to Birdie.

'But I brought food,' she said.

Because she had food was I obligated to eat it? I parked the motorcycle but I did not walk far from it.

'I'm not hungry.'

'I am,' she said. 'Very hungry.'

She said this in a good-humored way, paying no attention to my ill temper.

'I hate those roadblocks. I hate those horrible guys and their dirty faces.'

'They respect your cassock, Father. Doesn't that give you a sense of power?'

'No. It's like scaring someone by wearing a mask,' I said.

'They do it all the time.'

'It's cruel.'

'They're cruel.' She said this with a shrug, as she poked in the saddlebags for something to eat.

'I'm thinking about the trip back.'

'I know, Father.' She unwrapped a sandwich and took a bite.

'Stop calling me Father.'

She ignored me and said, 'I sometimes think I don't belong anywhere else.'

As she chewed the bread, she seemed innocent and defenseless, and I thought how a person's character was never more apparent than when they were eating. There seemed to be a brainlessness about eating, too: poor dumb hungry animal.

Perhaps sensing my pity for her and mistaking it for compassion, she swallowed and looked grateful. Then she touched my hand and in the kindest way said, 'What would make you happy?'

I was glad that she had put it that way. It gave me the confidence to say plainly that I was uneasy here on this great sloping shore, among the boulders and the stones and the blowing trees and the splash of the lake. It was almost four-thirty. It would be dark at six or so. Couldn't we just leave?

Birdie said, 'I was imagining a picnic by the lake. But we could have it somewhere else.'

'What about back at Moyo?'

'I have a bottle of cream sherry in my room back at the convent.'

'Let's go home.'

8

This abrupt change of plans was like a reprieve and put me in a good mood. Everything seemed simple now. Instead of killing time at the lake we would forget the picnic and go back. I had not had an alcoholic drink in over a month, and the prospect of it, the novelty, and the way Birdie had tried to please me, made me willing. She said, 'OK, let's go,' and without realizing it I began following her directions – a short-cut back to the mission. I was glad we were together and liked her high spirits and this haphazard outing that had just proven to me that I too felt at home among the lepers of Moyo.

It was growing dark when we got back – dark enough for me to need my headlight. The road and the paths were empty, the whole mission occupied eating their early supper. I drove slowly behind the dispensary and up the hill to the motorcycle shed, which was near the church, and between the priests' house and the convent.

As I cranked out the kickstand with my toe and propped the bike, Birdie said, 'Let me go first, to see if the coast is clear.'

I did not wonder what she meant by that. It seemed just another expression of her unpredictable high spirits.

At this time of day the fading light gave everyone a ghostly appearance, the threadbare look of an apparition that might quicken or fade. Birdie turned and glowed for a few moments and then was gone.

I waited – longer than I expected – wondering what to do. Then I saw a light go on in an upper room of the convent. Birdie came to the window – said nothing, but raised her head, beckoning me.

And I obeyed. I did not question all the randomness that had led me this evening to climb the back stairs of the convent to Birdie's room. I did not take Birdie seriously because I knew that if I did I would have to conclude that I did not like her very much.

She opened and shut the door so quickly that I was inside before I realized that she was dressed as a nun, in the white robe and bonnet of this severe order of the Sisters of the Sacred Heart. Birdie had switched her lamp off. Two candles burned on her dresser giving it the look of an altar and the room itself the feel of a dim chapel.

'Just a joke,' she said.

People said that self-consciously of their most passionate acts. I did not know what to reply.

'Did anyone see you?'

I shrugged – what did it matter whether anyone saw me?

'Because you're not supposed to be here, Father.'

She was whispering, she was barefoot, she had a crazed nun look of sacrilege. She must have put her nun's habit on hurriedly because a lock of her hair was loose at the side of her face, and the gown itself – the robes, the sleeves – was disheveled. I could see her naked breasts through a wide, hitched-up sleeve.

When I turned to push the door open, to leave, she stepped quickly over and held the door shut. This was a nimble move, swift and serious, and when she put her finger to her lips to shush me I heard other voices.

'This box of bandages has to be sorted for size.'

'Did you see this other stack?'

They were nuns outside in the hall, speaking through an open door.

'We can start now or go on with it after dinner.'

Go, I urged with my whole mind.

'I will do some. Sister Rose can wash the vegetables and then you both can come to help.'

Sorting bandages, washing spinach – good plain chores. It was what I wanted, what I valued most in the place, simplicity and completeness. For this I had gladly rejected my writing and buried my books. And this was the reason I was so uncomfortable in Birdie's room, with a bottle of South African sherry, by candlelight, the two of us dressed as priest and nun.

Her tongue was clamped between her teeth, in a parody of concentration. She slid the heavy deadbolt in the door then plucked my sleeve and led me across the room to the only place to sit, the edge of the bed.

The nuns were still fussing, some of them muttering in Dutch.

'I feel sorry for them,' Birdie said. 'But sometimes they're awful.' She thought a moment, biting her lip. 'I'm as bad as they are.'

I did not need to be convinced that it was unwise of me to leave just then, with nuns hurrying back and forth in the hallway. But I realized how great a mistake it was for me to be here with Birdie. What convinced me of my error of judgment was Birdie's energy: my enthusiasm waned as hers rose. She liked this game of dressing up, she in her habit, me in my cassock, nun and priest clinking glasses of sticky South African sherry, sitting side by side in the narrow convent room, the door locked and bolted.

She seemed very excited, as though we shared a terrific secret. But each thing that roused her only made me more gloomy.

I said softly, 'This is ridiculous.'

She opened her mouth eagerly, as though shaping the word yes. It was the absurdity of it that she seemed to like best. She sipped more wine and kissed me, forcing my lips open with her tongue and spat this sip of wine into my mouth. My surprise as I choked and swallowed only thrilled her more.

'Father,' she said, and kissed me, holding my head, searching my mouth with her tongue again. At first I was so startled I began to pull away, but her boldness challenged me. I was astonished at the strength of her hunger.

Outside the room a nun said, 'Twenty-eight. All folded. The rest are stained. We'll have to bleach them. It's never enough.'

Birdie was probing my ear with her tongue. Her breath was hot, and she whispered, 'No, Father. Don't make me. I'm so afraid.'

And still she held me. I was going blind and deaf, fooled with the inklings of desire.

I would have taken my cassock off, but I was stuck in it – it confined me, like a sack around me; and her gown and robe were caught in its folds. So we embraced, pleaded in our different ways, in a great soft knot of white cotton, her gown, my cassock, the starched wings of her bonnet askew, and all her nakedness shifting beneath this tangle of cloth. Trying not to hold her, I trapped my fingers in the plackets of her robe and touched the softness of her warm skin, and, breaking free of her kissing, I dislodged her bonnet with my chin and her hair tumbled between our faces.

'Don't touch me, Father,' she implored, her breath harsh with heat.

Her irrational sincerity scared me, and then her hands were on me, searching through the unbuttoned flap of my cassock. I was confused. I drew back, saying, '*No, wait*,' though I could feel her pleading in the pressure of her fingers.

'Not if you don't think they're clean,' a nun said in the hall.

Birdie took hold of the inert slug of my penis and began pumping it, as though trying to start some odd, primitive engine with a churning, chafing motion of a little handle.

It hurt. I wriggled free, keeping her away by holding her shoulders.

'Don't rape me, Father,' she said, and now her eyes were unfocused and she lay back as though she were my victim.

There was drumming – was it from the village or from the throbbing of my temples? Whatever, it too made me hesitate.

I was overcome with embarrassment and anxiety. Everything that aroused her unnerved me – the clothes, the pretense, the seclusion, the nuns yakking outside, the risk of being caught in the convent room on this hot night. I could not lead her on. My heart was not in it. I had no interest in her – did not even like her much. I was too afraid and self-conscious and too remote from her fantasy to be able to perform in this sad comedy of dressing up.

'Then just hold me,' she said. She was trembling.

I could not even do that simple thing. I was preoccupied with the problem of how to escape from her.

'I have to go,' I whispered, though it probably sounded to her like a wicked hiss.

She said nothing, and then, 'You can go at any time. You don't belong here.'

Her face was in shadow, and she was a rumpled mass of hair and tangled clothes.

I stood up and undid the rest of the buttons on my cassock and took the thing off. I had a T-shirt and bathing suit on underneath. I folded the cassock and sat and put it on my lap. Birdie lay across the bed in a tragic posture, looking grotesque, a mass of shadows, sorrowing.

Nothing, not even laughter, kills sexual desire quicker than tears. The spell was broken. There was no more to be done. I could not determine her mood, whether she was disappointed or embarrassed.

I hugged her and she went rigid against my arm, pretending to be stubborn and unyielding. I imagined her to be very angry.

'This was a bad idea.'

'I don't think so,' she said. 'But if you do . . .'

I held my breath, waiting for her to finish the sentence, because she was on the verge of tears.

'. . . then you're useless.'

She began soundlessly to cry, making a horrible face.

That was not the end of it. I stayed two more hours, until eleven or so, which was after lights-out in the convent. She ate some of her food. I chewed on its tastelessness and found it hard to swallow, because of my mood. The bed creaked and so I lay very still beside Birdie, without touching her, and we talked in whispers about ourselves.

I was young: my story was short. I told it quickly. But she was seven years older than me. She had been sent here on a Catholic church program, as a trained nurse. 'I couldn't go home. I wouldn't fit in.' It was exactly what she had said about the lepers. She was from a small town in southern Indiana. She told me about the town, how the high school kids hung out at the Dairy Den, and celebrated at Punchy's after the Panthers won a game, and how they drove up and down Main Street on Saturday nights, and hung out at Mickey D's and then paired up and went parking at the cemetery.

After that long, unusual day we lay like old friends, listening to the murmuring nuns closing drawers and doors. At last Birdie took a deep breath. When she let it out, all her frustration, all her yearning and humiliation were audible in the sigh.

'I wanted it to happen,' she said. 'Now it will never happen.'

I did not dare to look further into that thought.

'Don't you have any fantasies?' she asked.

'Not here,' I said.

9

It was said at the leprosarium that there were no secrets. No matter what happened in darkness, it was known; no matter how soft your whisper, it was heard. Then everyone knew. That was another aspect of the reality of the place. Nothing was hidden, everything known – no subtlety, no symbols. A leper was a leper, and everything was easily visible. It was like a doctrine. We were naked.

And yet no one seemed to know what happened between me and Birdie in the convent that night. Perhaps it was too absurd, too outlandish – inconceivable in a place that was so lacking in fantasy and pretense. Perhaps it was because this knowledge of secrets did not include mzungus. Perhaps it was because we really had no secrets: the truth was that nothing had happened.

It was not a scandal that I sneaked out of the convent in the dark wearing my cassock. I took the long way back to the priests' house in order to conceal where I had been. By then the priests were asleep. If anyone else saw me, they did not say anything. I crept into bed, hardly believing myself what had happened, and I was so exhausted by the suspense and the fear of being caught in the convent that I went straight to sleep and did not wake until the sun was in my face, blazing into my eyes through my eyelids.

None of the priests mentioned my adventure. Whether they were ignorant or just being tactful I had no way of telling. Still I felt certain the secret was safe, perhaps I felt it most strongly because we had done nothing improper. We had lain in the path of temptation and afterwards gotten up and dusted off our souls, feeling lonelier than before.

'Now it will never happen,' she had said.

She was probably right. And it cured me of dressing up in a cassock – of dressing up at all. It was not that I had been tempered in the fire. I was not stronger for having resisted. It was just that if it had happened as she had wanted, I would have had to leave the next day.

I was not ready, and though I was roused, it was not for her.

Now my days were orderly. I woke squinting and blinking like an animal, and then foraged for my breakfast and kept busy until the next mealtime. When I thought of reading or writing, I felt a giddy thrill knowing that I would do neither. I had that same feeling waking from a dream in which something important and difficult was expected of me, a task that would involve my whole attention and engage my brain – and still I might fail; one of those dreams where the last words I heard were from a large, gray figure insisting that I meet this deadline. I would feel inexpressible relief that I had woken from this demanding dream: and then the whole day stretched ahead of me, all sunlight. The burden of writing had been lifted from me. I was excused from having to notice details; not writing meant not having to remember. I lived now in a luxury of forgetfulness.

I had never known such easy days. Birdie and I greeted each other as friends, and I understood her better. I saw her difference, her weakness. She was like a nun, like a leper – she belonged here, more than I had ever imagined. This interested me, yet I had very little to say to her. Except for being here we had almost nothing in common. And she had never taken much notice of me. It was my cassock that had attracted her, and now I did not wear the thing.

Father DeVoss was the only person who mattered. He said nothing. His mind these days was on more pressing matters.

It had begun that night of Father Touchette's tears, the angry discussion, the sobbing that had followed. There was more sobbing on other days. Father Touchette's crying was like an audible form of bleeding. You could not play cards when he was doing it. It was messy and shocking, it upset anyone who witnessed it, and it seemed to weaken him. And then one morning, after another night of this, I heard Africans grunting and their hard feet scuffing on the cement floor. They were laboriously moving furniture, I thought – no, not furniture. It was a large tin trunk, new enough to be only slightly dented. The three men struggled trying to share the weight.

'*Katundu* of Father Touchette,' Simon said.

I had breakfast alone. I kept out of sight, spent the morning in my new way: cleaned the spark plugs on the Norton, talked to an old man about witches, looked for snakes to kill. On my way back from the withered cornfield I bumped into Father DeVoss.

'Is anything wrong?'

'No,' he said. He glanced aside. The tin trunk rested on the verandah of the dispensary. 'But Father Touchette is leaving us.'

He said it as though it were no great occurrence: it was in the nature of things – not wrong, no one to blame. People came and went. I had asked the wrong question.

'He will be happier somewhere else,' Father DeVoss said.

The old priest did not elaborate, but now I understood Father Touchette's sobs, and the way he had stood trembling at the open windows, glaring at the sound of the drumming at night from the leper village.

*

A solemn White Father, his bulky body obvious under his creamy robes, arrived at Moyo that evening on the train. He was Father Thomas, come to take Father Touchette away. There was no card game after dinner that night. Instead, Father Thomas conferred with Father DeVoss. The next day a high mass was held in the church – because we had an extra priest, Father DeVoss explained. I suspected that the service was being held in order to offer prayers for the troubled soul of Father Touchette, who sat with his hands in his lap in the front pew, looking stunned and shamed, like a fallen angel.

There was singing, there was drumming, there were solos with Angoni finger harps; hearing this, more Africans came from the village and crowded the church. The front pew was all nuns, with Birdie at the end. She did not look at me. I knelt just inside the communion rail while the priests sang the mass, and in between – dressed in black pants and a white shirt – I served as altar boy.

I rang the bell, I genuflected, I uttered the responses. I brought the tray of cruets at the Consecration. I bowed and I gloried in the strangeness of it – the heat, the ceremony, the singing, the drumming that rattled the loose panes of glass in the church windows. No one outside Moyo knew we existed or that this ritual was taking place. As always I had a dusty sense of remoteness here, but I found an intense pleasure in this obscurity, in no one else knowing or caring about us, because I knew this world was real.

The mass was sung in Latin, the hymns in Chinyanja, the drumming too was African – filling the gaps of the ritual. The drumming seemed to unnerve Father Touchette again. His mask of sadness grew tighter on his face as the drumming banged louder, echoing against the walls of whitewashed plaster, while incense rose from the thurible, drifting past the glitter of the monstrance. Then the smoky incense curled as thick as drug fumes in the shafts of sunlight that pierced it.

Amina sat in one of the rear pews with her blind granny. I watched Amina closely, the way she followed the priests with her eyes, the passing back and forth, the sudden chants and sung prayers, my spoken responses, the jostling at communion.

In her eyes this must have seemed strange, even frightening, like a ritual of magic, the kind of sorcery that went on in a village to cast a spell, drive out devils, making a person whole again. In a sense this sort of purification was the aim of the mass – the holy sacrifice of the mass, as I had been taught to call it.

Afterwards I put out the candles and gathered the cruets and tidied the sacristy while Father DeVoss whispered to Father Thomas. And I knew exactly what he was saying – practical things, like the mood of Father Touchette and the time of the train to Balaka and Blantyre.

Lunch was a long silence. We sat eating *nsima* and chicken in the heat while Father Touchette paced the verandah. Then Father Thomas led the weakened priest to the Land Rover, and helped him in, taking him by the arm. Father Touchette climbed in slowly, like someone elderly or ill, and without a word he folded his arms, seeing no one, waiting to go. His eyes were sunken and dark, he looked haunted, his mind was elsewhere. I heard someone in the watching crowd of lepers say the word *mutu*, referring to Father Touchette's head – something wrong with it. Talking louder than the others, Amina's blind granny was asking questions: Who is it? Where is he going? Will someone else come to take his place? Is he sick?

With the old blind woman monopolizing the attention of the crowd, I sidled over to Amina and was glad when she did not move away.

'I saw you in church, Amina.'

'Yes.'

'But you are a Muslim.'

'I went because of my granny. To help her. She is a Christian.'

'Did you see me watching you?'

'Yes.' She sniffed nervously. 'I did not know why.'

'Because looking at you makes me happy.'

She sniffed again, she blinked. What I had said embarrassed her.

'How did you know I was looking at you?'

'Because I was looking at you,' Amina said.

This touched me, and though she spoke with her eyes averted, out of shyness, she was bolder than I had expected. And perhaps she was not looking away out of shyness, for there was confusion in the dusty road, as Father Touchette's big trunk, hoisted by dirty ropes was slung into the back of the Land Rover. Already Father DeVoss was gunning the engine and beside him Father Thomas had the grim resignation and grumpiness of a parent who has been inconvenienced by his son's expulsion from school. Father Touchette was in the rear seat, looking defeated, watched by lepers who seemed stimulated, even thrilled by the sight of this ruined mzungu.

Father DeVoss had tried to play it down, but in a place where very little changed from year to year this departure counted as momentous, an event that would be remembered and distorted in the years to come.

'*Alira*,' someone muttered. He is weeping.

It was so odd to see this grown man sitting in the vehicle with his face in his hands, tears running through his fingers. The crowd of lepers and others simply gaped at him – they were skinny, crippled, crooked, barefoot, ragged. So many of them wore large dirty bandages. They watched impassively, with hardly a murmur. It was the lepers' pitiless curiosity that made Father Touchette especially pathetic.

I had always disliked the way Father Touchette carried his breviary around with him, consulting it and seeming to wrestle with its verses. I resented his saying, 'I have baptisms,' when I needed help carrying bricks. The book seemed like a talisman against his ever having to work. He used it the way the lepers used their mutilation as an excuse. The young priest wore socks with his sandals, which made him look silly. I thought how madness is often a way of dressing.

'He is your friend?' Amina asked.

'No.'

'But he is a mzungu.'

'I would rather talk to you.'

I wanted to tell her that I was glad to see him go. He was a worrier, a baptizer, a converter, a scold. 'That's savage,' he had said of the drumming almost every night. Perhaps I had alarmed Amina by being forthright, for after the Land Rover had driven off she disappeared as the dust settled over us.

The drumming was louder that night, there were shouts and yells, a kind of whooping, like panic. In my fever that same drumming had filled my imagination with vivid images of Amina dancing – her slender body gleaming, her mouth open, her glazed eyes looking drugged.

Desire for me was always the fulfillment of a fantasy – not a surprise or a shock, but something studied in advance, dreamed and premeditated. It was pleasure prepared, the completion of a thought begun in a vision. Desire was familiar and fixed; not something new, but an older, deeper wish, with a history, an embrace that had already shadowed forth in my mind. It was something specific, like a gift I yearned for. And later, when it seemed to be granted – flickering into reality and becoming attainable – I seized it.

I had heard that same drumming many nights before, rattling through the heat to reach me in my bedroom where I lay alone on my cot. It was also the sound the village women made when they pounded corn into flour, thumping a heavy pestle into the mortar. When there was more than one woman pounding, it set up a syncopation in the trees, and a chorus of grunts and thuds.

'No cards tonight,' Father DeVoss said. He did not have to explain that this was out of respect for Father Touchette, who hated our card playing. Among other things, the sight of us flipping cards and collecting tricks had driven him crazy. Never mind, we would play tomorrow.

'No cards,' Brother Piet exclaimed, taking up his sewing. '*Pepani – palibe sewendo!*' Sorry, no games!

It was as though we were respecting the memory of someone who had just died. And leaving Moyo was like death: life outside it bore no resemblance to life here.

'I hope he gets better,' I said.

Guessing what was in my mind, Father DeVoss said, 'He won't come back.'

There was a great cry from the village and a surge of brightness, as though a mass of dry straw or corn shucks had been dumped in the fire and exploded into flames.

'They never come back,' Father DeVoss said.

At just that moment it seemed that the only life in the place was down in the leper village – the drumming like a faulty heart beating; not wood at all, but the racing pulse of the place.

Brother Piet was sewing by the light of the pressure lamp, while Father DeVoss sat near him, with shadows on his face. In any other place they would have been reading, writing a letter, looking at pictures. But this was Moyo, as stark as anything else in the bush. They were like an old married couple.

I said good night and went to my room, where I stood by the window. I was restless, impatient, ready to leap into the darkness. The trees beyond that darkness were lighted by the fire in the village. Because of the flames each branch was distinct and black.

Slipping down the back stairs, I went outside, avoiding the path but following the firelight and the sounds of the drumming.

Though there was a thin circle of spectators, almost the whole village was dancing in the clearing, women on one side, men on the other, shuffling and stamping their feet, nodding their heads, raising their arms, calling out. Their heavy tread echoed in me as though they were moving flatfooted through my body.

The men clapped their hands and the women yodeled in a shrill ululation that was both fearful and triumphant – a sort of war whoop. There were no carved masks, but there were painted faces, none more frightening than the man whose face was dusted with white flour. He was a leper and he was wearing a bed sheet and carrying a crucifix. A woman opposite him was also wrapped in a bed sheet. Priest and nun, writhing in a suggestive dance that was riotous sexual mockery or a ritual, or both.

The lepers danced on their dead feet that were swollen with bandages, making the sound of clubs. Small boys dressed as dogs or monkeys, naked except for the mangy pelts flapping on their backs, moved on all fours through the chanting, stamping crowd.

Another group, entering from the shadows of the huts, lifted an image on a set of poles. It was a small building like a doll's house and I guessed from its cupola, a crude steeple, that it was meant to be the representation of a church. It rested on the middle of a little platform that was set on poles as though they were carrying a stretcher.

I had missed the preliminaries, I knew. The dance had been going on for an hour or more. I had been listening to it throughout dinner and afterwards, while I had sat in silence with the two priests. The dance had now grown to a pitch of excitement that had bystanders jumping in and joining. It was impossible to tell the dancers from the spectators, there was so much movement, the stamping, the drumming, the clapping, the flapping rags.

The man dressed as the priest and the woman as the nun were at the head of a frenzied procession. Just behind them was the fragile little church building made of sticks and paper. This was either exaggerated respect or elaborate mockery.

I recognized many of the dancers as the people I had come to know since my arrival in Moyo. It was strange to see them so active, in motion. The leper dressed as a priest looked like Johnson from my English class. He carried a book – not a Bible nor a breviary, but the message was clear enough. This was Father Touchette and for their own reasons, because he had just left, they were dramatizing what they knew of him. He performed a baptism on one of the dog boys. He read his book with rolling eyes. He pranced, looking haughty. He rebuffed a flirtation from the nun. And the drumming was both music and hoarse, hectic commentary.

Among all the moving bodies it was easy for me to pick out Amina. She stood to one side, in the shadow of a hut's eaves, the firelight on her face, watching while the rest of the leper village worked themselves into a state of hysteria. And her granny seemed to be made of stone, while just in front of her Amina nodded at the dancers and clapped to the stamping rhythm.

The risen dust floated in the firelight and the moving bodies cast shadows in the trees that were broken and made more frantic by the picked-out branches. Some of the dancers looked tearful, almost tormented, with heavy faces. I saw how the lepers' dance was not many individuals but a mass of people that had one will and one shape, a swelling organism. This trembling creature filled the clearing.

Amina remained apart. If she had been among the dancers I would not have been able to get near her. But because she was next to the hut, watching – nodding to the beat of the drums – I approached her. I touched her arm. All the physicality of the dance seemed to make this touching permissible. Amina did not draw away. That meant a great deal.

'I want to visit you at your hut.'

She faced the throng of dancers, the dust, the lighted smoke, the dog children, the dirty feet, the drummers beating on logs and skins, the swaying image of the church. She was too demure to speak the word. Her silence meant yes, all right.

'But what will your granny say when she sees me?'

'She will not see you,' Amina said. 'She is blind.'

10

Now there was so much noise that I could not hear Amina clearly. I had been hearing those drums since the night of my arrival, when I had lain awake in my bare, whitewashed room, wondering why I had come here and what would happen to me. The drums had been part of my fever, they had been a feature of our card games, always pulsing in the background. I was certain that they had driven Father Touchette out of his mind.

That was understandable. The drums of Moyo had penetrated me too, but they had energized me. It was a physical sensation, like a drug or a drink. It was brainless, it whipped into my blood, it made me dumb and incoherent. It removed any desire in me to write – poetry or anything else.

I was trying to speak to her. What next? I wondered. But I could tell from Amina's expression that it was no use. She could not hear me either. Perhaps that was for the best. It was sensible here to be silent, no more than shadows.

Without a word, but touching her grandmother's hand, as though giving a command, Amina led the way, granny right behind her, with her leprous hand gripping Amina's shoulder. I followed, and I was glad for all these shadows, for the crowd and the confusion and the fire and the drums. How could they notice me? But even if they could, I thought, they were so dazed and heated by the dance that I did not matter.

Amina's hut – more likely her granny's – was in the outer circle of older huts, the ones nearest to the bush that surrounded Moyo. It had its own tree – I could just make out its shape in the rising firelight, and it was larger than the other stunted trees. The smell of the old trampled corn shucks in the nearby garden was an odor that was linked in my mind with snakes and scorpions and biting spiders, which lurked in the warm, broken rubbish of the shucks.

Squinting down so that I would not stumble I banged my head against a heavy pole that served as a rafter for the thatched roof.

'What is that noise?' the old woman said, and reached for me. I guessed that was what she said: the meaning was clear enough from her gesture.

'*Fisi*,' Amina said. Hyena.

The old woman had muttered in a dialect that was probably Yao. It was a bush language associated with Muslims and Mozambique that I did not understand. But I could translate Amina's replies. Perhaps she was speaking Chinyanja for my benefit – but it was not odd for the Africans at the leprosarium to converse in several languages. The granny was still talking.

'Because I am very tired,' Amina said in Chinyanja. She lit a candle and placed it in a large tin can, which had holes punched in it.

To the old woman's croak, Amina said, 'I want to keep the hyenas away.'

Gabbling again, her granny seemed to be praying. She was at the far end of what was by Moyo standards a spacious hut, rectangular, a large single room, with two mats on the floor. She lowered herself to the distant mat and faced in our direction. She was at home in the darkness.

Except for the two mats, the exposed floor was hard, packed dirt, and the walls were mud, and dust trickled from the straws in the thatch bundles of the roof. The room stank of dirt and termites, and on the looser and untrodden part of the floor there were worm casts. The only furniture were cardboard cartons and lanterns and among this assortment a sturdy wooden crate shoved against the wall had the look of an heirloom.

I held my breath while the old woman gazed with white eyes, and then murmured.

'I am moving my mat,' Amina replied. She motioned me to her mat and I sat down next to her, carefully pulling my legs under me.

Amina's face in profile was as smooth and simple as a carving with the candlelight behind it. She had long lashes and her lovely mouth looked solemn in silhouette. She sat very straight, her neck upright and seeming so fragile that I could not help reaching and touching it. She hardly moved, not even when I touched her, and when I stroked her cheek she became motionless. That was not fear or even submission, it was pleasure. I passed my fingers across her lips and she opened her mouth and bit them with her pretty teeth. She was swift, and I could feel her hunger in the sharpness of her bite.

The old woman grunted several words, her face on us, and I watched her closely as I slipped my hand under Amina's cloth, feeling for her breasts.

The dance had grown louder. Was that what the old woman was saying? Now I could recognize some of the dancers' chanting.

'Sursum corda! Habemus ad Dominum!'

Cupping Amina's breast, loving its warmth and its contours, I moved nearer, and she sighed and moved towards me to make it easier for me. This thrilled me.

'Agnus Dei, qui tollis peccata mundi!'

I kissed her and although I could smell the dirt floor, the ants, the sweat, the mice, the dust sifting out of the thatch, there was a sweetness on her lips that was like syrup, with the tang of ripe fruit, and her skin had the heavy sensuality of freshly turned earth. She received my kiss and moved nearer still, shifting to face me, the candlelight flickering in her eyes.

Had we made any noise? The old woman uttered another remark.

'It is the zinyao,' Amina said.

The old woman grumbled as I leaned over and whispered to Amina, 'Let's go outside.'

She shook her head: no.

I clutched her as though questioning.

'The people will see us,' she whispered, as she stared at the blind old woman.

Then we lay on the mat, side by side, while I went on stroking her breasts and breathing in shallow gasps, afraid that I might be heard. The old woman's face was fixed on us. She was still muttering, but nothing she said was clearly audible. I wanted her to sleep, yet she sat upright, her eyes unblinking.

The drumming was so loud it made the thatch bundles tremble in the roof. The voices of the dancers cried out, '*Christe, eleison! Kyrie, eleison!*' and other snatches of the mass responses, as though they were incantations.

Amina's breasts were small, her body was hard and thin. It made me think of the saplings at Moyo, their long, narrow branches and small leaves. And my fingers found parts of her body that felt like the healed scars of a young tree. Amina was so small I could caress her easily with one hand. And she was so smooth.

I put my lips against her ear and said, 'When I saw you at the English class I wanted to touch you.'

My face was so near to hers I could feel the change in her expression on her face. She was smiling, I knew. But she did not reply.

'So why did you come to the class?'

'To see you,' she said.

'Did you want to touch me?'

She hesitated, and then she sniffed. It was her shy way of saying yes, a kind of modesty.

'Tell me.' I moved so that her mouth was at my ear.

'I wanted to play with you,' she said at last. The word for playing was also the word for dancing and foolery.

I stroked her arm and when my fingers touched the leprous patch, the disc of dead skin, I was not alarmed. I had been here long enough to know there was no danger to me. I slipped my hand into hers and guided it against my body, so that she would touch me. I did not have to go any further. She knew what to do, without my suggestion, and her knowledge excited me, because it showed she was a woman not a girl. Then she took possession of my whole body with the nimble fingers of her small hands. Leaning towards the little lamp she pursed her lips as though kissing the candleflame.

Just then the old woman grunted again.

'I am putting out the light,' Amina said, and her one sigh against the flame killed it and brought darkness down on us.

Seconds later, when my sight returned, there was moonlight making angular shadows in the room. There was also the glow from the *zinyao* dance shining on us. It was as though this light made us want to be smaller, and so we embraced, and touched and kissed, and moved our bodies closer. Yet even in this wonderful hug I could sense the other person in the room, the restless presence of the blind woman.

She spoke again, sounding irritable.

Amina, with a grip on my hand, said, '*Ndiri ndi mphere kwabasi.*' I have a serious itch. Kwabasi. Brother Piet had taught me that word. It was one of the sexiest things I had ever heard, and as she said it she moved my hand between her legs and helped me, working my fingers on what felt like the lovely pulp of a ripe fruit.

Amina was smiling at me as I touched her. The moonglow lighted her and her face became even more beautiful, animated with desire. Her mouth was open in silent rapture as the old woman spoke a whole rattling sentence as though uttering a proverb.

Amina put her mouth against my ear again and spoke breathlessly. 'She says, "Then scratch it." '

She slipped her leg over me and clumsily steadied herself. I propped myself up on my elbows. And she opened her cloth as I fumbled with my shorts. Then she was on top of me, straddling me.

The old woman had started moaning to the drumming and the yelling outside, while Amina shut her eyes and strained not to make a sound, as she rocked back and forth.

'*Sursum corda!*'

'*Deus meus!*'

Amina hitched herself forward and moved her hands to my face and held me as she drove her body against me, riding me. I could still see the old woman at the far end of the room, the light and shadow broken over her body like patches of liquid. It was like being in the presence of an old African idol, a great impassive lump that might spring to life at any moment and become a demon.

Yet I had no fear. I took Amina by her hips and jammed her against me and she threw her head back as though convulsed. And when she bowed down and clutched me again I thought I heard her say, 'I am not crying.' I could not hear her cry, yet her tears were running down my face, and I tasted them to make sure.

She was pressed so hard against me it was as though we were not two people anymore, but were so penetrated that we were like one wild tearful creature. She tore at her breasts and then clamped her mouth over the fingers of one hand and wept. I was intent on one drumming rhythm. If sex was knowledge, and I believed it was, I was on the verge of knowing everything.

It was heat and noise and skin and drums and fire and smoke, and the feeling of silk in every opening of her body. It was also the growl of the crowd, and it was our old blind witness. I struggled with Amina and held her tight gorging on her like a cannibal. Soon my body was sobbing, caught in a desperate panic of possession that made me reckless. And then we too were blind.

After this singular act of love we turned into two people and I knew I had to get out of her hut. It was not easy for me to leave, for as soon as I got up, the old woman mumbled, saying to Amina, 'Don't go,' or something like it, because she too stood up and began shambling to the door.

I could not go out alone or the old woman would hear. The only way I could avoid detection and not rouse her suspicions was to stay so close to Amina, so that we would sound like one person.

In all the clatter of the drumming there was another snorting noise.

'*Fisi*,' the old woman said.

'Yes. A hyena,' Amina said, as a big, bristling and humpbacked dog blundered out of the darkness next to the hut.

That was how I left, startling the slavering creature and covered by its noise. We were the noise, the hyena and me. The thing was alert but did not seem afraid. It was mangy and misshapen, and it snarled at me, not angry but annoyed, as though I was the intruder.

II

When that scavenging animal bared its teeth at me, I knew it was the end. I would have to leave Moyo, and I should pick up and go before I was sent away. Expulsion would have been so hard: facing Father DeVoss's melancholy eyes. I was ashamed on the path back. I skulked like the hyena. I went guiltily to my room, sneaking up the stairs, knowing that anyone could hear my feet.

Even so, when I said the next day, 'I have to be getting back to my school,' Father DeVoss did not protest or make an ironic remark. He nodded as he sometimes did when he was dealt a certain hand of cards.

It was settled, his silence meant that it would be soon. Perhaps he was grateful to me for sparing him the bother of banishing me from Moyo.

I had lost my right to remain there. I had at last interfered. I had used Amina and that was wrong, because it violated a strict rule. I knew the rule, but I had been curious. I had created an area of disorder. There was no way I could deny it or undo it. Father DeVoss knew everything.

And what made it hard for me was that I felt strongly that everyone else knew, too. I could not look into their faces, and when I glanced at them they seemed different – not more familiar but a great deal stranger, almost menacing. And if this was so, that everyone knew what I had done, I could never go back to Moyo. That was worse than anything.

'I am sorry to be leaving,' I said to Father DeVoss.

He did not ask why. That shamed me, too.

'Because this is the real world,' I said.

'Yes,' he said, and smiled. 'It is all here.'

He was not being ironic. It was a complete world, perhaps the only real world, and I was leaving it for the feebler and less secure world of metaphors, where leper did not mean leper.

'Maybe you can write something,' he said.

'I don't know about writing,' I said, remembering how I had shoveled my books into the ground in my attempt at a great purifying act of finality. 'It's so hard.'

'*Papier is geduldig.*' Father DeVoss had never spoken Dutch to me before. He smiled, as though he had revealed a secret. Then he explained. 'Paper is patient.'

The word paper brought to mind a piece of foolscap that my school got in stacks from the ministry, the sort I had used for writing my poems. This blank sheet had a blinding whiteness that made me helpless and stupid.

*

At the station at seven the next morning, Father DeVoss said, 'Don't forget us.'

It was perhaps just a pleasantry but I knew I never would. Then he touched my elbow and I felt the charge of his hand traveling through my arm.

The train drew into Ntakataka halt and it was all a confusion of shouting and boarding, the women with baskets, the men with chickens. This was near the beginning of its run but after just four stations it was littered with peanut shells and chewed sugar-cane stalks and orange peels. And the carriages seemed much more battered than they had six weeks ago. Decrepit and uncomfortable, they looked a hundred years old.

I sat in second class again and even before we left the station I began mentally to list what I had seen at Moyo. I wanted to write something, but I truly felt as though I would never write again, about Moyo or anything else.

Was I a writer? A writer had to get used to looking on and not interfering – being a witness. I had been passionate. Should I have kept back and been colder? I did not know whether I had made it hard on myself. I did not know that I would only see this over an enormous distance of time and space. I felt sad because I did not know how to live.

The low woods, the yellow leaves, the elephant grass, the dust, the mud huts, the unvarying bush: every landscape feature seemed to turn its back on me in my departure.

I would miss Moyo, I knew, and what made the loss of it a burden was that no one there knew what missing meant, nor wanted to be anywhere else. In that sense it was paradise.

To console myself, I looked for a young girl who might resemble Amina. I searched inside the train and looked at the people we passed in villages. No one looked like her. That thought uplifted me, but made me sad.

Moyo was unlike any of these mud hut villages by the tracks. It was static and settled, a place of monumental inertia and no drama. It was not dark, not dangerous. It went against all my notions of Africa. It was snakes and insects and curable diseases. You accepted it and left all other ambition behind.

The lepers and priests and nuns – all of them – were happier than anyone I had ever met. They had found what they were looking for.

What luck. It bothered me that I had not been able to fit in; that through my own fault I had been cast out; and that having left I would have to keep going – searching for the rest of my life for a similar place, and my mind always returning to Moyo.

I thought of what the people said at the leprosarium: There would never be a disease like this again, never a plague or a scourge, and certainly nothing like it in this part of Africa, which in a clumsy way was being purified. No plague, no scourge, and even words like these would be archaic or quaint when leprosy was gone.

Yet I was uneasy, feeling naked again, certain that I was leaving this for a greater ignorance.

THREE
Poetry Lessons

I did not understand a thing I read, nor did I begin to write any better, until I married and had children.

It all happened quickly. I fell in love in Africa with Alison Musgrave Castle, an English woman, and within three years we were a family of four. That short time crammed with events changed my life, and all of it – love, marriage, children, debt – seemed inevitable. I felt powerless against these urgencies. Yet I saw that I had to be strong. The ritual and romance of adulthood bred such intense emotions in me that one day I would see myself as a victim and another day as a hero. But really I was being a husband and father. I held my family in my hands and felt how fragile they were. Loving them made me love life and value it in a way I had never known before.

In that same three-year period we moved from Africa to Singapore. I was not ready to go home to the United States, and I wanted to see South East Asia, to be near to Vietnam, perhaps go there while the war was hot. As someone who opposed the Vietnam war, I felt obliged to be a witness. I also liked Singapore's image as a hot, sleepy backwater, full of colonial relics, crumbling houses and old habits. The time-warp of travel in hot countries, under a vast sunny sky, helped my imagination. I signed a three-year contract to teach at the University of Singapore. I had plenty of time.

My small house was now noisy with my family and several inexpensive servants. I often complained about all my responsibilities. But I was howling dishonestly, because deep down I was fulfilled.

I knew how deep my pleasure was the day I agreed to drop Ringrose's key at his house on the Jurong Road.

'I can't do it,' Ringrose said, his mouth drawn down like a dog's.

He was either suffering or else imitating it brilliantly. 'Ring Nose' we called him behind his back at the Staff Club.

He had the office next to mine. The walls were thin, I heard his telephone conversations, but everyone knew what I knew. He had just gotten divorced and the old Singapore law was humiliating. The grounds were adultery. His wife had had to name a corespondent; it was one of Ringrose's students. Ringrose countersued, named his wife's lover, Pratchett from the chemistry department, with the beard, and all the pens in his shirt pocket, and the flipflops on his feet – he had entered Ringrose's house wearing them, and the story went that he had left one behind, an incriminating rubber footprint.

After this mess was settled, Ringrose's wife had gone back to England with their two children (Colum five, Kari eight). That it was winter in England – it was never winter here – made it especially awful for the angry, isolated woman and her children. Ringrose was living in an apartment in the noisiest part of Selangor Estates, pretending that he was not carrying on with the named student, a Chinese girl, Wendy Lee, whose smooth seal-pup face still looked guiltless. Ringrose too had moved out.

'I can't stand to look at that bloody house,' he said. I had lived among English people long enough to know that he had a Birmingham accent.

Having agreed to drop the key through the letter-slot of his house, I decided to turn the errand into a family outing. Here on Bukit Timah there was nowhere for children to play. The Chinese shops were full of ambiguous wonders, like snake wine and medicinal deer antlers and jars of crumbly pickled lizards or fragile mouse fetuses. But there were drawbacks.

'Chickens!' Anton said one day, seeing half a dozen hens squawking on a counter. An hour later we passed the same shop and saw them dead, beheaded, and plucked. 'Where are the chickens, Dad?'

Jurong Road was the country, ragged uncut jungle, the defunct rubber estates, new red roads being made in the swampy ground, the old Asia of snakes and ferns and grottoes, and mossy shrines littered with blown-apart firecrackers, and small, square rubber-tappers' huts being bulldozed and buried.

Alison said, 'I wish this were our house.'

It was off the road, up an unpaved driveway, a lovely upraised house with verandahs running entirely around both the lower and upper stories, set among palms, in a garden that flourished with ferns and big-eared plants and flowering shrubs. It must have once been a rubber planter's house, an estate manager, one of those adulterous drunks that was always turning up in the expatriate stories of Somerset Maugham.

We crunched down the gravel drive, scaring the wild birds, and we all piled out of the car, as though in a park. Alison had brought a ball for the children to play with, and some sandwiches and drinks, and she joined me on the ground-floor verandah.

We looked through the windows and saw the Ringroses' chairs, their pictures, their rugs, some carved Malacca chests, their bright cushions and ashtrays and pewter mugs; a playpen, a fruitbowl with no fruit in it, vases without flowers, some scattered toys, and in a room just off the hallway a glimpse of a bedpost.

Because it was not vacant it was one of the saddest interiors I had ever seen. It was visibly haunted. The family had gone, their artefacts and their gloom remained. Everything in the house had been chosen by the Ringroses. Each silent object had once radiated hope. You could imagine the family saying, 'I love this,' and 'Let's get two of those,' and 'This is just right for the children,' and 'This is super.'

Dead echoes in the furnished house.

It reminded me of one of those tombs – Egyptian, I suppose – where pots and pans and bracelets and books, all the paraphernalia of a person's life, are buried with the corpse. The ghosts of the Ringroses still lingered. Number 538 Jurong Road was the sarcophagus of a dead marriage, and we peered inside like the living looking into the window of a burial chamber, where a family had been turned into triumphant dust and was now represented by their chairs and vases and their stuffed toys and green garden hose and their other comforts and consolations. The way the toys were propped and the cushions prettily arranged broke my heart.

'Let's get out of here,' I said. I shoved the key through the letter slot.

Alison shivered aloud and said, 'I never want that to happen to us.'

I kissed her with all the love in my heart, so that we would both feel reassured and, seeing this intimacy, the boys, watching from farther down the verandah, began to object.

'You said we could play here!' Anton said. 'That's a false promise. You broke your word!'

I took his face in my hands lovingly and said, 'I'd rather chew snot than stay around this house.'

He shrieked with pleasure and snatched at little Will. 'Daddy said . . .!'

But I was rejoicing in his excitement and thinking: We have everything!

Ringrose's house represented failed hopes, an ended life, the stage set without a play, all the actors gone, never to return. This glimpse gave me a horror of divorce: the loss, the pain, the emptiness. A family split up and scattered. You could not lose more than this.

*

So, as a married man in love with my wife and adoring my children, I was a wiser reader and a better writer, but I had very little time for either reading or writing. We simply had no money. I earned 1,400 Singapore dollars a month, which was 200 American dollars. Fifty bucks a week.

The Singapore government had found out that I was a writer, that I had written political pieces in Africa. This was a government that feared student dissent or any opposition. A flogging – twenty or thirty strokes with the *rotan*, a cane the width of a man's finger – was a frequent sentence in Singapore in the Sixties. The government approved of the Vietnam war and, as a supplier of food and technical assistance and one of the safer R-and-R locations, Singapore was making a fortune on the war. Under pressure from the ministry, the university tried to withdraw my contract. But I had already signed it. Unable to cancel my contract, the government put me on the lowest wage scale, hoping to starve us, so that we would go home. They did not seem to know that we were too poor to go home, or anywhere, and we were still innocent enough of the world not to regard our poverty as failure.

We decided to be very frugal, yet frugality did not help. At the end of every month we were deeper in debt. Alison went to work, teaching at Nanyang, the Chinese university, and when this still did not pay our bills she taught night school, English language and *Macbeth*, in the basement room of a tenement. Being poor was like a dull ache. It forced habits upon us, life lived at a slower speed. All shopping took longer because we deliberated over prices; we seldom went out – even a movie was an unthinkable expense; and for the first year with no car, having to take buses, we were always waiting by the side of the road. It did not make us quarrel, nor did it bond us; we suffered it in silence because it was exasperating to talk about never having enough.

Except for official thrashes at the embassies – especially the American Embassy – no one I knew gave parties; no one was social. Quite the opposite: people prided themselves on being loners and bad-tempered drunks. They thrived on chaos, and when they were drinking they told stories of the last time they had been drunk and what a mess they had made. If a stranger walked into the Staff Club they were generally rude to him – or her. Being awful to someone to their face without flinching while they were kept one humiliating beat behind was regarded as an art, and it was better if the victim was a woman. 'He's a rat bag,' people said admiringly of the tor-turer. Hearing that in the Staff Club, I was reminded of how much I hated the place and pitied these people, and how badly I wanted to resign and go away.

But I needed my job, and so I stayed and I listened to my col-leagues in the Staff Club whisper about each other and tell the same awful jokes and complain of the heat, or the rain, depending on the time of year. No one gave parties unless they were leaving Singapore for good. And when they left there was a sourness in the air, mingled jealousy and resentment for someone who was getting out. Afterwards we toasted 'absent friends,' talked about them constantly and it was hard to tell whether they were being ridiculed or envied. The other expatriates were older and English and had no idea how I wanted to be self-sufficient as a writer. I knew I could not afford to quit, and so I had my hands full with my teach-ing at the university English department, my writing, and my family.

A year went by, then another. Now it was 1970 and I was still on the lowest salary scale; still a lecturer in English, still teaching the course called Shakespeare's Contemporaries; still working on my novel. Africa had cured me of poetry. Fiction-writing seemed to offer a hope of financial self-sufficiency. That was what I told myself, but I knew my soul was possessed; I needed to turn what I saw into fiction, to give it light and shape. I had published two novels. Ripples still widened from where they sank; they had received respectful reviews.

And I had more to write – my head was full of plots and pronouncements, characters' names. I wrote each morning between seven and ten, lectured at eleven, had lunch, held tutorials in the afternoon, drank from five to seven and then went home to my family. It was a strange and selfish existence but it was what the other men did, the English, the Indians, the Chinese. Although we were just scraping by, we had two servants. Such was life in Singapore.

We lived, the four of us and our two amahs, Ah Chang and Ah Ho, in a hot semi-detached house of mildewed plaster so near to Bukit Timah Road that the house always smelled of exhaust fumes and all day and night we could hear the gasping and plowing of the buses. Just across Bukit Timah, in a walled compound, was Serene House, a private hotel which catered exclusively to soldiers on R-and-R from Vietnam – enlisted men. The officers stayed several blocks away at the Shelford. Serene House was a glorified brothel which was one of Singapore's secrets – open only to the military and to prostitutes. Even the police stayed away. It was run with the connivance of the United States and the Singapore governments, a supervised whorehouse. The Shelford had a better class of prostitute and a forbidding fence. I knew the Serene House gatekeeper, a Tamil Indian named Sathyamurthy, and so I often dropped in on my way home from my lecturing at the university.

The soldiers came for a week and teamed up with a girl on the first day. I saw the buses arriving every Monday, Sathya opening the gates for them and shutting them after the bus pulled away. Soldiers and hookers drifted around the neighborhood, and sat on benches near the canal, holding hands. They had their pictures taken at Luck Ong's camera shop in Bukit Timah Arcade, and after they had gone these pictures were hung in the window, Luck Ong's trophies, soldier and hooker, and they remained on display long after the hooker had moved on to other soldiers, and the pictured soldier was gone and perhaps dead. Some of the soldiers at Serene House ignored the girls, and simply drank and fought and watched cowboy movies. A few soldiers found their way across the sports field to the university buildings. One day we found a dazed soldier in our library. Ringrose wrote a poem about him. At the end of the week the bus came and took them all back to the war.

They could not draft me. I was married. I was one of those perspiring young men in shirt sleeves and sandals standing at the bus stop, among the Malays and Chinese, near Chop Keng Fatt Heng ('Provisioners') with a shopping bag of groceries in each hand. I felt burdened, I felt old, fifty or more, which seemed elderly to me then. The cars driven by Malay chauffeurs went quickly past us with their passengers dressed up for garden parties and drinks in the early evening.

Singapore was an island of party-givers, everyone drumming up business or being social. You saw their hateful faces in pictures in the *Straits Times*, hugging each other and looking damp and over-dressed and pleased. Their complete names and often their ridiculous nicknames were given in the dense captions. They were all strangers to me. They seemed not exotic but remote and foolish, inhabiting a world so different from mine that I had nothing to say to them; and they did not know me. I hated them for their parties; I also thought: Please invite me.

We were sometimes asked to parties at the American ambassador's residence. The Vietnam war caused such an invitation to be a moral dilemma, but not a serious one. We always accepted.

2

We were at an embassy party tonight.

In that Vietnam war period in Singapore when we expatriate teachers and journalists went to parties at the American Embassy, we drank too much, snatched food from trays, insulted the diplomats and businessmen, and wandered outside into the ambassador's garden and pissed on his orchids.

What we resented was the order, the peacefulness of this house, which was the United States of America. When we stepped outside afterwards, we were back in Singapore. The embassy resented us, too, but had to give the parties in order to seem unthreatening. They had no choice but to invite us, because there were so few American civilians in Singapore. Perhaps they hoped that we would put them in touch with ordinary people. Perhaps we fantasized that they would give us privileged information. What it came down to was that they were there to serve free drinks and we were invited to drink them. But we held all American diplomats in utter contempt and so, instead of rejecting the invitation, we accepted and behaved badly.

Tonight, something in the atmosphere of the ambassador's residence made me feel unwanted and anti-social. I felt like a burglar and I saw that Alison was talking with some other women, so I slipped into the library, with the idea of stealing something, not a treasure, but an object that would be of greater use to me than to the ambassador. I rationalized that a book might be just the thing.

I was leaning against a wall of shelves looking at the spines of books when a man came up behind me and said, 'The books in a person's house reveal an enormous amount of what's going on in his head.'

This was true, if obvious, and I wanted to say so, but I was flummoxed for the moment – feeling guilty, as though I had almost been caught in the act of theft. Another minute and this man might have seen me slipping a book into my pocket.

'What do these books reveal?' he said.

We were both looking at the shelves, not at each other.

I saw history, politics, biography, diplomacy, statistics, no authors or titles I recognized.

'Not much, I guess,' and as soon as I spoke I realized I was too drunk to hold a conversation.

'Nothing,' the man said. 'These books come in a job lot from the State Department. They go with the house. They're inventoried under the heading "accessories."'

I was nodding. I could not have put it better than that.

'There's no poetry,' he said. 'If there were you'd know exactly who you were dealing with.'

I liked him for saying that, but he seemed an unlikely sort to make that observation. It was the kind of thing my seedy university friends in the next room might have said, one of the extremely unpleasant intellectuals, with his mouth full of quail's eggs, his cheeks bulging. If you commented on his hogging food, he would spit egg flecks and say, 'Fuck him! We're paying for it!'

But this man was pink-faced and well-fed and wearing a dark suit and tie. You were only dressed like that in Singapore when your whole existence was air-conditioned. The wealthiest people dressed warmly and rode in air-conditioned cars. He wore a gold watch and chunky cufflinks and the sort of pebble-grained ostrich-skin shoes that were made to order in Hong Kong. And there was also a certain expensive odor about him, a lingering leathery smell of money.

He said, 'Been in Singapore long?'

'Almost two years. I teach at the university.'

'Good for you. But you seem too young to be a professor.'

'I'm not a professor. It's the British system. Only one prof – the head of the department. He has the chair of English. The rest of us are lecturers.'

'You still seem young to have a PhD.'

'I don't have one.'

It was hard for me to hold a conversation in which I had to explain things. In my drunken condition I could listen or agree, but I stumbled over my words.

'So what are your credentials?' he asked, and with this direct question he put himself in charge, which annoyed me.

'I don't have any credentials,' I said. 'And neither does he.'

I had turned back to the bookshelves and seen the spine of a slim volume: *Life Studies* by Robert Lowell.

'You're sure of that?'

'I went fishing with Cal in the Lake District just before I came here.'

The man seemed interested but somewhat disbelieving, wearing a crooked smile.

'Jonathan Raban introduced me to him. Raban's a friend of mine and of Cal's. You don't believe me.'

The man stepped back a little and said, 'It just seems so far away and incredulous.'

That was the first hint I had that he was not at home with the English language.

'Cal,' I said, 'is short for Caligula.'

'Did you catch anything on this fishing trip?'

'It was only a long weekend. It rained. Cal fell in. The rest of the time he stayed in his hotel room and read. Jonathan caught two trout and threw them back.' My back was still turned. 'And him.'

I plucked off the shelf the book *In the Clearing*, by Robert Frost. I opened it. There was a sticker on the inside cover, an American flag and an inscription. *A Gift from the United States of America.*

'Frost had no credentials. He never even graduated from college. But he taught his whole life.'

'I suppose you knew him, too.'

I nodded. 'At Amherst. One day in 1962 I followed him into Jones Library in the center of town. Up the stairs. Into the stacks. I had his new book in my hand. "Mind signing it?" ' I turned around to look into the man's big pink face. 'Frost took one look at me and said, "Do not pursue me!" Those very words.'

'That's great,' the man said, and now he did seem persuaded.

'But he signed the book. He said, "I just signed a thousand of these in New York and they're selling for fifteen dollars each." '

'You can see his objection,' the man said.

I smiled at him, but he was serious. He was still beaming at me – not smiling, yet his face was brighter than before, luminous with attention. I was not used to anyone paying this much heed to anything I said. His expression was deeper than simple curiosity. It was hunger, but more than that, the expression of someone used to getting what he wants, seeing something desirable. It was a kind of confident hunger that made me self-conscious, as though he was going to take a bite out of me.

To cover my embarrassment, I said, 'And what's your line of work?'

'Electronics,' he said.

But his face was still radiant, obviously he was still thinking of the two truthful stories I had just told him about Lowell and Frost.

'Timing devices. Circuitry. Switches. Small motors.' These words came out mechanically. He was merely reciting, as though to a fellow-passenger. But another wheel was turning in his head. 'You're a writer.'

'I've published two novels.'

'That's marvellous,' he said with feeling. 'What about poetry?'

'I used to write it but I haven't written much lately.'

I was too drunk to go into the reasons, which could have been listed under the headings Africa, Marriage, Children, Debt; and also my sense that the poems I wrote were miniatures. With fiction I had begun to write on a larger scale, and I was the happier for it.

'Is writing a good living?'

It was a terrible question but I had an answer.

I said, 'No. It's a good life.'

This impressed him, I could see. And I realized that he was not teasing me, he did not doubt me now, he was just clumsily probing.

'You must be very busy – teaching and writing.'

'Yes,' I said, but I did not feel busy at all. I was bored, I was neglected. There was so much more I could have written or done, if I were given the chance. I knew that my time would come, but for the moment I felt ignored. And as though this provoked a physical revulsion I suddenly felt nauseous and could taste vomit at the back of my throat.

'Are you ever free for lunch?'

'Sometimes,' I said. The true answer was: Every day. But the mention of food made me feel queasier.

'I want you to meet my wife.'

'Oh, yes,' I said, and started away.

'Harry Lazard,' he said, and seized my hand and shook it. 'Hey, you look a little pale.'

'I'm sick,' I said. 'Excuse me.'

And I hurried into the garden and puked behind the ambassador's ferns. Behind me, seemingly oblivious of my retching, Mr Lazard was saying, 'You're the only person here that I envy.'

Soon after I looked for Alison and we left, and Alison drove while I lay moaning.

Whenever we left the ambassador's residence the spell was broken: buses, hawkers, rickshaws, shouts, stinks, glaring lights, and air like a dog's breath that stuffed your head with humid heat. So many times I found myself back at my cramped house on Bukit Timah Road, hearing Serene House cowboy movies, the gunshots, the galloping horses, and feeling that I had landed with a bump back in my own world. It was disorienting to be at a great house overlooking the Botanical Gardens one minute and here the next. It helped me understand that we really were hard up and that in some obscure related way, the war in Vietnam would go on for ever. The Vietnam war made many Americans proud, but many of us felt like victims and were reminded of our weakness and felt like the enemy. No wonder we secretly admired the Vietcong.

I felt all that tonight too. I lay on the sofa, under the croaking fan, hating the bus fumes, thinking about his pink face, his wealth, a man not used to being the least bit impressed; incredibly, my talk of poetry – of all things – had done the trick. I had the strong sense that having met that man Lazard, something in my life was about to change.

3

Harry Lazard called me the next day and invited me for lunch. When I told him truthfully that my car was being fixed he seemed pleased. 'Don't take a taxi!' He sent his car for me, a Daimler with a Malay driver who called me *Tuan*, Master. I sat in the back, enjoying the cool, silent trip down Orchard Road, turning at Tang's, past the Strand and the Goodwood. Seen from inside an air-conditioned Daimler, Singapore seemed not just bearable but quaint and attractive. This was the city I had imagined before I had come here.

Ahmed, white gloves on the wheel, made a wide turn into the Tanglin Club. After two years in Singapore I was setting foot in the Tanglin Club for the first time; in less than a year, Harry Lazard had become a member. He had been waiting in the lobby and was telling me this as we made our way to the members' dining room.

Passing a photographic portrait of Winston Churchill, Lazard said loudly, 'His mother was an American, you know.'

At the table he explained that he enjoyed saying that about Churchill in front of the British members of the club. I noticed he had hairy ears. He refused a menu; he told the waiter that he knew what was on it; he ordered the daily special, roast beef, Yorkshire pudding, roast potatoes, and brussel sprouts. Feeling overwhelmed, I ordered the same.

Lazard began belittling the food as soon as it was served, which made it hard for me to swallow.

'You must come over to my house sometime for a meal,' he said. 'It's a funny story. My wife and I had a great meal at Chez Michel. I asked to see the chef and when he came to our table I asked him how much he was earning. He was Chinese. It wasn't much. I said I'd double his salary if he worked for me. He learned his cooking from a cordon bleu cook in Saigon. He's mine now.'

It impressed me, his stepping up and hiring someone, just like that.

'It was only a matter of money,' Lazard said. 'It usually is. Most people are underpaid in Singapore. That's the great thing about this place. They don't know how good they are. You can eat the best food in the world here.'

His Singapore was air-conditioned and pleasant. Mine was hot and crowded. His had the Tanglin Club, the golfers and polo players; mine had the University Staff Club, full of complainers. His was the Singapore of great cuisine; mine was the Singapore of fried noodles and amah's soy sauce. He was happy, I was impatient. I had no telephone, I took the bus, I swam in the Singapore River, I bought ganja from trishaw drivers. I knew my Singapore was the past and that my days were numbered.

'Do you realize how clean it is here, how orderly, and how rare a thing that is?'

I said, 'They flog people for petty offenses. They have press censorship. They're very hard on my students. Recently the government took all their scholarships away because studying English literature isn't part of nation-building. That was the expression. The government wants economists and scientists. Poetry's an aberration.'

'Why don't you quit your job?'

'I need the money,' I said and almost choked. 'If something better came along I'd jump.'

'I'm very divided on Singapore,' Lazard said, and I was glad he did not question me further about quitting. 'I'm a chemical engineer by training. My firm makes and sells chemicals, as well as electronics.'

'I'm surprised you're not four-square for the Singapore government, then.'

'I'm also on the side of the poets,' he said.

'They're burying the old Singapore. It will be gone soon. That's why I'm writing a novel about it. I want to write about the shop houses and the harbor and the hookers and Bugis Street and the trishaws, while you can still hear their jingling bells.'

'And does your main character teach at the university?'

'No. He's a ship-chandler's water clerk,' I said. 'They'll all be buried soon, too.'

'What a wonderful idea,' Lazard said.

'A novel is among other things a social history.'

'All writing is, I guess.'

'Sure. Poems, too. If you read a poem about a train in England, it will be pulled by a steam locomotive. But there are no more engines like that left. Poetry hasn't caught up.'

'A poetry reader,' Lazard said, and unzipped his briefcase with the kind of impatience that showed he had been planning this. He pulled out a thick book-shaped magazine, and showed me. *Metro Quarterly – a Journal of the Arts*. He hefted it and it opened almost by itself to the page he wanted, where a short poem was printed. I took the entire poem in at a glance: *Gorgeously, the fish fits its fins to the foam and controls the spin of its body over rock*. It was signed *Harold Lazard*.

'Tell me frankly what you think of it. Be brutal.'

'It's very good. I like its simplicity.'

He smiled. He seemed not to believe me, but I insisted.

'And obviously the editor agrees with me.'

He smiled again. He was a big man, with big hairy fingers and heavy arms. It was hard to imagine these fingers holding a pen, writing a poem, seated at a desk.

Perhaps my staring at his meaty hands made him self-conscious. He said, 'Yes, I'm a published poet.'

Over coffee he said, 'How much do you earn?'

'Fourteen hundred a month.'

'That's pretty fair,' he said.

'I can barely run a car. My wife has to work to pay off our overdraft.'

'But that's an American salary.'

'No. Those are Singapore dollars.'

Little spasms – of pain, of incredulity, almost of mockery – set his face in motion, rippled without settling, lighting separate features, and overlapping his expressions. His eyes were frozen, a calculation going on behind them. He was thinking: *Fifty bucks a week!*

'Drink up,' he said. 'I want to show you something.'

'This is where I live,' he said as Ahmed turned into a gateway in a high wall off Holland Road; but all I saw alongside the driveway were palms, and a lawn, and flowerbeds. It was not until we had traveled for some distance that I saw the house, which was enormous, with a green tile roof and white stucco that was brilliant in the sunshine. This whole estate inside was hidden by the wall, and

103

once inside the wall it was not possible to see outside – Singapore was just its steamy sky.

Big as it was, the house was a detail, and so were the lawns and flowerbeds; even the swimming pool and the arbor and trellis arches around it, even the waterfall and the stream, the marble statues, the pillars, the other buildings were mere details. Beyond the flower beds were bushes and flowering shrubs and trees, not single specimens, but a forest of them, jungle foliage of blackish green, so dense and with such a thick canopy of boughs there was darkness under it.

Near the pool, pale as marble, what I took to be another statue was a woman whom Lazard roused with a shout.

'Fayette – over here!'

The woman frowned at him, as though irritated, then saw me, and seemed to count to ten before she smiled and sat up.

'This is Paul Theroux,' he said, 'the fellow I was telling you about.'

She did not move, she watched us walk nearer, waiting with a kind of queenly restraint, while we circled the pool, making us do all the work. All the while she was dangling something from her finger, moving it like a pendulum.

'You have a lovely place here,' I said. And added, coyly trying to compliment her, 'It must be an awful lot of work.'

'It's no work at all.' The pendulum was green, a carved piece of luminous jade on a gold chain.

'I meant all the landscaping.'

'We have four gardeners.' She smiled and swung the piece of jade.

She was a bony, attractive, sharp-featured woman, quite a bit younger than Harry, probably in her forties, blonde, with pinched gristly nostrils that might have been a botched nose-job; freshly reddened lips, perfect teeth, and very pale skin, slack at her arms. Here she was outside by the pool, yet she obviously spent no time at all in the sunshine. And her pallor, which was almost that of ill health, set off her jewels – earrings, bracelets, necklace – and gave her a languorous sensuality.

She said, 'Isn't Singapore marvellous?'

Again I thought how these people, just across the island from me and behind a wall, lived in a different Singapore. I liked traveling to this country; I wanted badly to live in it. The flowers, the trees, the temperature, even the air was different here.

'Will you have something to drink?' Harry said.

'I don't want to impose,' I said.

Holding the piece of jade to the side, Fayette jammed the heel of her free hand against a push-button. In that same instant I heard a servant's squawk; then I saw him, a Chinese man in white jacket and pants, carrying a tray, emerging from the far end of the arbor.

'What do you have?'

'Anything you want,' the woman said.

'Orange juice will be fine,' I said.

'It's real fresh. Mr Loy squeezes it himself,' Harry said. After the servant had gone for the drinks, Harry Lazard said, 'There is something I'd like to ask you, Paul.'

But before he could continue, Fayette let out a sharp cry of pain that startled me, and when I turned she was on her knees by the side of the pool.

'It jumped off my finger,' she said, peering into the pool. 'I can't even see it. Oh, God!'

Harry looked suddenly stricken and helpless, and he tottered as though his indecision made him physically unsteady.

'Harry can't swim,' Fayette said with surprising satisfaction.

'I'll get it. I just need a bathing suit,' I said.

'In the changing room.'

Most of the spare bathing suits were large, making me think that everyone they knew was fat and prosperous; we were all skinny and pathetic in my end of Singapore. Even the smallest suit was large on me, but I cinched it and jumped into the pool, did a surface dive and saw the jade pendant glittering at the bottom in about ten feet of water. I missed it on my first try, but got it on my next dive. Now I saw how bright it was, emerald-green, and intricately carved.

'My hero,' Fayette said distractedly, and snatched at the jade piece without looking at me.

'That thing's worth a lot of money,' Harry said.

'What is it?'

'It's a child's burial mask, and that's the rarest jade obtainable.'

'Did you get it in Singapore?'

'Long story.'

Fayette had turned her face on him, as though dreading the story and daring him to tell it.

Harry said, 'Listen, I've got a job for you.'

After he explained, I said, 'I'll ask my wife.'

'He needs permission,' Fayette said, caressing the elegant mask of jade.

He had said, 'You're going to think I'm nuts,' and I had had to encourage him to continue, and he went on, 'I want you to give me poetry lessons,' and, 'You already passed the hardest test – my wife likes you.' I wanted to tell him that it was the craziest thing I had ever heard. But I made a serious face and reassured him that it was a perfectly normal request.

I told Alison everything. One of the clearest indicators of being hard up is that every decision is crucial; you have no cushion, and so everything you do involves risk.

'The woman sounds awful,' Alison said, 'but the man seems fine – idealistic in a strange sort of way. Poetry lessons!'

'They're what I give my students,' I said. 'At least I'd be well paid.'

'Americans are so funny. You're always trying to improve yourselves.'

'Why shouldn't this guy learn to write poetry?'

'I didn't mean him. I meant you. That salary turned your head.'

'You could give up teaching night school.'

'That's fine with me,' she said, and she laughed again, in puzzlement. 'Here is this man with pots of money, and instead of sitting around and enjoying himself he wants someone to teach him how to write poems. Doesn't he know any better?'

'But you said he was idealistic.'

'I think I meant naive. The idea that you can teach him that!'

'He seems to think I can – that's all that matters,' I said. 'It's very civilized of him!'

We looked at each other and laughed at my pompousness and hugged each other.

I kissed her and said, 'I want to tell them to shove this job.'

'It's nice, burning bridges,' Alison said. She wrinkled her nose, she made a face, she laughed again, and I loved her for her bravery.

I saw Harry Lazard again; we drew up a satisfactory agreement – I would tutor him on weekdays in return for a rent-free house and a hundred US dollars a week. It was for six months initially; but renewable. We already had our air-tickets home. When I told the head of my department I was resigning he shrugged. Half Chinese, half Indian, he was a former tax inspector named Ratnaswami, known behind his back as the Rat.

'We weren't planning to renew your contract, so it's just as well,' he said. He grinned his awful stained-tooth grin. 'We have someone else in the pipeline.'

I hated him for that but I hated myself, too: why had I stayed at this badly paying job so long? The answer was that until now I could not afford to leave.

We pensioned off the two amahs, packed our belongings – everything we owned fit into our old car – and drove across the island to Holland Road and found Lazard's wall. Alison's reaction was the same as mine had been. That this house and all its acres and its pool and its forest was so well hidden that Singapore seemed far away. Once you were behind the wall you were in a different place, that could have been a different country. It was quiet, it was hot, it was lush. For those differences alone it was worth making the move. And if I were to achieve anything as a writer I needed to have the strength to quit a job; to move on and make my own life.

We were met by Mr Loy, the Chinese servant. The Lazards were away, he said. He showed us to the guest house, where we installed ourselves, and before we had unpacked anything the children were out of the house, on the verandah and across the lawn.

I watched them kicking their old blue ball, laughing – squealing with delight – safe in this lovely place. Alison's face was light with love as she watched the children, and I knew that I had done the right thing.

4

For the first four or five days before the Lazards came back we lived the sort of life we had never known. Without servants feeding the children we cooked our own meals and we ate together on our screened-in verandah. We had the swimming pool to ourselves. We played croquet. I did no writing, but I looked over what I had written so far of my novel and it seemed fine to me, so I was confident that when I resumed it would go well. These were glorious peaceful days and I felt an almost inexpressible gratitude towards this strange couple who had taken us in. I told Alison that this was how Third Worlders must feel when Americans entered their lives. It was as though we had been rescued. Our days were sunlit, our meals were pleasant, and after we had read to the children and put them to bed we had a drink on the verandah, marveling that we were still in Singapore, and then we went to bed. We all woke together.

Alison said, 'I like this.'

We were at last a family, and family life was possible because we were together, because our needs were met, because we were living in luxury, because we were happy. And on those first days I often thought of our visit to Ringrose's house on the Jurong Road, and shut my eyes and gave thanks.

But I also knew that I had been entrapped, even if it had been in the nicest way. If Harry Lazard had a gift, it was his ability to gauge what it was that a person needed. Everyone wanted something different. Money, a meal, space; when he found this out he had them. There were many ways to a person's heart, and generosity worked best when it filled a profound need. He was not around, but because we were happy we had a sense that he was present. It wasn't poetry but perhaps, I told myself, Harry's was a poetic gift. How had he known that all this little family wanted was to pay off our overdraft at the bank and be together?

Then they returned – we knew it even without an announcement. It happened in stages, first something in the air, a tremulous attention, a sort of nervousness, as subtle as a cloud shadow crossing a meadow. The servants stopped talking loudly to each other; they worked with greater care, the gardening was more meticulous, the nagging sound of the vacuum cleaner was almost constant, flowers appeared in vases, dust covers were removed from chairs and tables, and most of all there was an air of watchfulness – not as though the Lazards might turn up at any moment, but rather as though they were already there, hovering, humming, about to explode into view.

One evening it was that, intensely, and the next morning Fayette

Lazard was in the chaise longue by the pool, in the shade of a thick awning, where I had first met her.

The children hung back, feeling that their swimming pool had been invaded by a stranger, but I gathered them up and introduced them and Alison to Fayette Lazard.

Fayette hardly moved, she tilted her sunglasses and smiled.

'We were in Bangkok.'

'Was it nice?' Alison asked.

'We're there all the time, because of Harry's business.'

Alison persevered. 'I've heard Bangkok's fabulous. I'd love to go there.'

'They have TV,' Fayette said and frowned.

Alison took this to be a joke, and out of respect laughed very hard. But Fayette's expression was not dead-pan, it was serious, and then it was grim.

'Only two channels, though. We have fourteen in San Francisco.'

We stared at her and I wished I were able to see her eyes.

'I'll bet you love watching television,' the woman said to Anton. 'What's your favorite program?'

'Television is bad for you,' Anton said in his quacking voice, with all the sententious certainty of a bright three-year-old.

Fayette turned to me, as though blaming, and she laughed insincerely.

'Television gives you square eyes,' Anton said.

Alison said, 'He's such a philistine. If Will could talk, he would assure you he quite likes the telly.'

Was Fayette wincing behind her sunglasses? We could not tell. She said, 'I hope you're comfortable.'

'The guest house is lovely,' I said.

'That's not the guest house, it's the old servants' quarters. The guest house is way over there.'

We decided not to be put off by her. We were happy enough and secure enough in each other's love that not even this woman could spoil our fun. She spent an hour outside and then disappeared. The rest of the time she kept to the big house, occasionally shimmering on to the verandah. She stayed out of the sun. She never came to the guest house – as we went on calling it. It was only at the pool that we met, and the pool was big enough so that there was room for everyone.

We had no need to leave the estate, and indeed seldom went outside the Lazards' wall. A grocer came in his van every other day; we bought what we needed and then he sought out Mr Loy. We used the pool and the croquet lawn, and we walked on the gravel path through the three-acre woods. The arrangement worked because we did not fraternize. The Lazards gave a party. We were not invited. It struck me as comic that we had met as equals at the American ambassador's house, but here we were regarded as glorified servants – at least I was. I did not mind; my family was happy.

It was more than a week after he returned from Bangkok that I gave Harry Lazard his first poetry lesson. I realized that he was very shy, that he liked the thought of my being around, and he was thrilled by the idea that I was working on my novel – he told me so, he inquired about my book's progress. But he was reluctant to expose his own talent, or lack of it. It was amazing to see this powerful millionaire made so timid by the prospect of showing me his poems.

I took the initiative. I saw him dropped off by Ahmed late one afternoon and I hurried across the lawn and up the hill to say hello. We chatted, Lazard offered me a drink; we began talking about things in general, and then about poetry. It was as though sitting in the shade on the sheltered side of the house was our way of being serious.

That first day he asked me, 'Do you have any favorite poets?'

'So many,' I said. 'One is Wallace Stevens.' And I remembered. 'He was a businessman. Insurance. Went to his office every day. His secretary typed his stuff. Have you read him?'

'Wallace Stevenson, oh, yes, he's very powerful,' Lazard said.

I was afraid to embarrass him by correcting him, and it hardly mattered, except that it gave me an inkling that these poetry lessons might be harder than I had thought.

He said, 'Do you still hear from Robert Lowell?'

'No,' I said. 'He doesn't write. Harry, I only met Lowell that one time.'

'It's not how often you meet someone, what matters is how deep an impression you make on them,' Lazard said, and this was not the poet but the businessman speaking.

'He was impressed that I caught a fish.'

'That's what I mean,' Lazard said. 'I should get him out here.'

We looked across the lawn, past the trellises, the statues, the arbors. I tried to imagine Robert Lowell sitting by the pool, a big pale man with wild hair and crooked glasses and crazy gestures, getting drunk, teasing Fayette, insulting Lazard.

'Do him good,' Lazard said.

We were seeing our own versions of the same thing.

The next day I ambushed Lazard again, and taking a cue from him I asked him who his favorite poets were.

'I'm very old fashioned in my literary tastes. I like the old masters. Shakespeare. Keats. Lord Byron. "Where have you been, Lord Randall, my son?" That sort of thing.'

'I gave tutorials on them. We had to teach all periods. What about the war poets?'

'Which war!' Lazard cried out, startling me.

'The First World War was the one that produced the most poets. I'm thinking of Edmund Blunden. Siegfried Sassoon. Wilfred Owen. Isaac Rosenberg. Have you read any of them?'

'Oh, years ago.'

The expression 'years ago' always seemed evasive and untruthful to me.

'Isaac Rosenberg sounds pretty interesting. What did he write?'

'"Break of Day in the Trenches" and some others.'

'Must have been Jewish,' Lazard said. 'Strange. A British Jew.'

'Disraeli was a Jew.'

'Everyone says that,' Lazard said.

'"Mendelssohn was a Jew and Karl Marx and Mercadante and Spinoza. And the Savior was a Jew and his father was a Jew. Your God was a Jew. Christ was a Jew like me."'

Lazard gave me a puzzled, almost wounded look. 'Are you OK?'

'I was quoting. That's in *Ulysses*. Leopold Bloom says it to some Irishmen in a pub.'

Then he was absolutely delighted, and he swished his gin and tonic and drank it and swallowed it with satisfaction and said, 'I never thought I'd be sitting on this verandah talking about Joyce's *Ulysses*. That's pretty unique!'

I just smiled. I found it impossible to reply with a straight face to such a solecism without sounding sarcastic.

We did not meet the following day, but later when he had a spare hour or two, in the late afternoon before dinner, we sat together. He was still very reluctant to show me more of his poems or even to write any, and so I suggested that we simply read and talk about poems to get into the mood.

'Good idea,' he said.

I could see that he was grateful to me for not asking him about his own poems; glad that I did not expect too much of him. He was prompt in paying me my month's salary in advance. With no rent to pay we were better off than we had ever been when I was working at the university, and at last Singapore seemed pleasant.

But inevitably, with so little to do, I felt a growing sense that I was superfluous. Whenever I saw the chef sitting behind the kitchen, reading the *Straits Times* I remembered how Lazard had gone into the kitchen of Chez Michel's on Robinson Road and offered to double the man's salary if he left. With me it was money, peace of mind, literary pretention, luxury, and a chance to live in old Singapore on the grounds of an imperial mansion, behind a high wall, with my family. It was a chance to work on my book, to be away from the bitter humor of the Staff Club. But I identified too strongly with the chef to feel much at ease.

One night on our little porch after the kids had gone to bed I said all this to Alison.

She said, 'This is the first time in ages that I've been happy. The kids love the pool.'

I suspected that Lazard knew that too.

'And I love not having to teach rotten old night school. What are you complaining about?'

'I'm not complaining. I'm just wondering.'

'Please don't drag us away from here,' she said. Settled here, protecting the children, playing with them, feeding them, she had discovered that the sacrifices of motherhood also gave her intense pleasure. And the boys blossomed in her care.

Their happiness justified everything, and was the best reason for giving this man poetry lessons.

At the next lesson, Lazard said, 'Your wife and kids seem very happy here.'

So he knew my secret. It was as though he had heard every word that Alison had said to me. But no. All he had to do was look out of the window and see them frolicking on the apron of the swimming pool. Children never sun themselves or sit by a pool; they are like cats, either active or asleep. I had never seen this little family so happy, and I wanted it to continue.

'I'd like to share one of my poems with you.'

He was apprehensive, snorting through his nose. He drew a stiff folder out of his briefcase and there, beautifully printed and mounted as though it was especially prized, was a twenty-line poem, about a traveler's inability to communicate with a non-English-speaking person. It was called 'Say Something.'

I read it, trying to think of a way of praising it.

'Be brutal,' Lazard said.

'I like its bluntness,' I said. 'It's a sort of anti-poem. Almost boorish, the way the narrator is making demands on this local guy. Willfully inelegant. Very strong.'

He was smiling admiringly at the poem.

'I hadn't thought of that,' he said. 'I think you're right.'

That cheered him up. He showed me another poem in the same folder: '*Market*' *by Harry Lazard.*

It was a clumsy poem, in short lines, listing the sights of a market that was obviously in South East Asia: the local fruit – mangoes, rambutans, durians; the cuts of meat, the stacked fish, and swatches of herbs; the bags of rice. It was a list of items.

'It's good,' I said.

'Go on, criticize it.'

'I love the line, "Dead animals for sale." '

It seemed to irritate him that I singled out this line for praise. At first he said nothing and then, 'It was an actual sign at one of the market stalls. I copied it down. That didn't take much work.'

I said, 'It's called "found art." Driftwood is sometimes found art. It takes a poetic eye to recognize that a sign like that has poetic value.'

'That's very true,' he said. 'What about its weaknesses. I'm sure it's got some. I just don't see what they are.'

'I have a little problem with "the dried red peppers strung like firecrackers waiting to go off." '

Harry pressed his lips together and compressed his face, making it fierce.

'I worked hard on that particular line.'

'The "waiting" firecrackers, is all I meant. Firecrackers don't wait. They don't do anything except explode.'

'These ones looked like they were waiting,' Lazard said. 'Didn't you ever notice that some fireworks look like that? Like they're just waiting?'

He had begun to smile in encouragement at me, nodding in a twitchy way. He wanted me to say yes. I heard a child's distant shriek and then a splash, and Alison crying out, 'Well done!'

'I guess so,' I said.

'Sure. You get the idea.'

5

It was not all misery and submission for me, giving poetry lessons. Harry Lazard did not write many poems. What he seemed to like best was sitting and talking, telling me about his life, his struggles, his success. His father, an immigrant from Odessa, had been a concert violinist, and had never made a decent living. I asked Harry whether he himself played an instrument.

He said, 'I hate music.'

I had an urge to hit him for saying this, but I did not react.

He said, 'Good for you. I told a man that once and he burst into tears.'

It would be very bad for me if I made my first million before the age of forty, he said. I told him I was not worried.

On the subjects of politics he often made a statement that defied analysis. Of Lee Kwan Yew the autocratic prime minister of Singapore, Lazard said, 'His main strength is he's a dictator, and his main weakness is he's a dictator.' This struck me as baffling, either very wise or very stupid.

One day he called out from the verandah, 'Paul, I've got someone here I want you to meet.'

Seated on one of the wicker chairs was a pale, stoop-shouldered man, seventy or so, very soft-spoken, in a rumpled shirt, obviously suffering in the heat.

'Nate, this is Paul. He's going to be a great writer some day,' Harry said. 'Nate's written some stuff, too.'

'Would I have read it?' I said.

Smiling sadly – but I took it to be the heat – Nate raised his limp fingers and waved the question away. 'I'm here collecting material on leprosy,' he said.

'There's none in Singapore.'

'I'm on my way to Johore Bahru. There are some centers there.'

'I worked in a leprosarium in Malawi about six years ago.'

I told him a little bit about the leper colony at Moyo. He became very attentive and patient, as though we had all the time in the world. He asked me specific questions about the treatment, the living conditions, and the morale. I was struck by his interest in me and my experience, and it struck me that I had rarely met someone so subdued and yet so compassionate. It was his posture and the way he moved; he took up so little space.

'Where are you from, Nate?'

He coughed and said, 'Chicago originally.'

After Ahmed took him back to his hotel, Harry said with satisfaction, watching my expression, 'That was Nathan Leopold, the child murderer. Remember Leopold and Loeb?'

He was dying of cancer, Harry said, and so they had let him out to pursue his study of leprosy.

'A guy down at the embassy put me on to him. You'll never forget this day, will you? You could write about it.'

After almost a month of this we developed a rhythm that was simple and undemanding. Except for when Harry was away, we met two or three times a week, always in the late afternoon. We chatted, we drank tea and after an hour Mr Loy brought Harry a gin and tonic and me a pint of beer. Usually we discussed poetry, but I realized that Harry had read very little and was uncomfortable being asked his opinion about one writer or another. He wanted to be my student and listen to me talk about poetry; he wanted me to listen to him discuss life, women, food, drink, the heat, power, and money. So we took turns being each other's student. He said he found this a very pleasant way of passing the time.

Weekends and most mornings I worked on my novel. When I was done for the day I swam or played with Alison and the boys. This seemed a wonderful way of living, and being productive – my novel was going well – made me feel secure. Though I was niggled by the thought that we were isolated from the life of Singapore, it was that very isolation that made this life possible.

There was not much I could do about Lazard's poetry. The man had a shaky grasp of English that was summed up in his own expression 'pretty unique.' 'I'm a published poet,' he had told me. I was amazed that this was so, and that two of his poems had appeared in a magazine. His style, if such a word could apply to flat declarative statements, was artless, almost crude, and that gave his poems a simple power that I could praise without being a hypocrite, or at least that was what I told myself.

About a week after the Nathan Leopold visit I heard Ahmed driving away and, assuming that he had just dropped Harry off at the house, I crossed the lawn and went up to the verandah. Instead of calling out, I listened. The house was very still. I could see through the window into the library and beyond it to the dining room, and the brightness on the opposite side of the house.

I stepped to the door. 'Hello?'

I had no name for him. I was uncomfortable calling him by his first name, because the very name Harry seemed so intimate; and calling him Mr Lazard would have made me feel like one of his minions, like Mr Loy or Ahmed or the Tonkinese chef, Victor.

'Paul?' I heard a voice say.

It was Fayette, but I had no name for her either, so I called out, 'It's me. For the poetry lesson.'

'Come up.'

But when I got to the top of the stairs, I saw no one, only a long corridor of doors ajar, and I called out 'Hello?' because I felt awkward using her name.

'In here.'

She was in the master bedroom, reclining by the window in her chaise longue, a magazine open on her lap. Next to her was a lamp with a pink parasol shade, and behind her was a tall antique chest, from the herbalist, with a hundred drawers, each one identified with Chinese characters. She seemed so ignorant and obvious. It was all pretense – pretending to be reading, pretending to be resting, pretending my visit was accidental.

She said, 'Sit down.'

The imperious way she said it made me resist.

'I was just looking for your husband.'

'Harry's on his way to the airport. He won't be back until Friday.'

'That's all right.'

'So it's just the two of us. What are you afraid of?'

'Who says I'm afraid?'

'Standing over there like I'm going to bite you.'

I went nearer. She pushed some magazines from the seat of the chair next to her, making it plain that I should sit there. She took my hand and held it and I could feel her greed trembling in her bony fingers. I knew it was greed from her grip; it was hunger without appetite.

If Harry had walked in at that moment he would have had a reason to shoot me, but worse than this was the thought that not far away my wife and children were playing and perhaps one of the boys was saying, 'Where's Dad?'

I primly tried to withdraw my hand. Fayette at first would not let go, and in the little struggle I lost my balance and had to steady myself on her thigh.

'What's this?'

She encircled her fingers and framed the little spot that I had touched.

'You touched me,' she said, with a kind of triumph, as though she had trapped me.

I was so alarmed I stood up and went to the window and realized that I had visibly shuddered.

She said, 'How can you write anything, if you don't know anything?'

'I do my best.'

'I'll bet you do.'

Now she was moving one propped-up knee back and forth, her pretty sarong slipping down, no panties, and I could see the dark tarantula of her private parts.

'You pretend to be so innocent,' she said.

In the gutter of the magazine was the carved jade burial mask, the child's face, that I had seen the day I had first met her. She picked it up, delicately, as though it were an hors d'oeuvre she was about to nibble – she was licking her lips as she examined it.

'That piece is worth fifty thousand dollars, US.'

'It's very nice.'

She smiled at me. That was revealing. Her rudeness had told me nothing, her nagging had simply irritated me; but it was obvious in her smile – the cant of her unsteady head, her eyes not quite a matched pair – that she had been drinking.

'It's stolen,' she said. 'From a temple.' She dangled it again. 'They're all thieves.'

Her tone that had been sweet, the coquette's cry of 'In here,' had sharpened and was now distinctly sour. I had the sense that in a matter of seconds her mood had changed and she was now very angry. In the way that lust or desire can quickly turn violent, she seemed on the verge of screaming or throwing something.

She leaned over, as though concealing herself to make a covert movement and snatched open one of the hundred drawers in the herbalist's chest, and – I saw this plainly, she was very drunk – slipped the jade mask inside and shut it.

'I have to go,' I said.

'This is your poetry lesson,' she said. 'You don't have to go anywhere.'

'You just said that Harry was away.'

'But the lesson is all paid for,' she said. 'What do you think we pay you for?'

All I could think of was that in the two years I had worked at the University of Singapore, no one had spoken to me in this way. If they had, I would have screamed back at them. How could I do that now, with my family out enjoying themselves on the lawn of the very woman who was insulting me?

'Are you trying to cheat us?'

I was so angry I did not trust myself to reply, but instead glared at her and wondered how I could leave without this woman throwing something at me.

'Harry's problem is he's always trying to better himself to make up for his lack of education. I tell him, why bother? This was a stupid idea, but he wouldn't listen. People like you are always taking advantage of him.'

I denied it, but lamely, because it troubled me that what this drunken woman said was true. Yet I still had not gotten over her dangling the piece of carved jade (that I had once brought to her from the bottom of her swimming pool) and saying, 'It's stolen.'

'I'm giving him poetry lessons. He likes them. He's learning something.'

'That's bullshit,' she said. 'He's a rotten poet and always will be.'

'He publishes them in magazines.'

'One magazine. He gave the editor a grant. If it weren't for Harry they'd go broke.'

'I think his poems are pretty good.'

'How dare you patronize my husband.'

'I'm not patronizing him – I'm patronizing you.'

'You touched me. If Harry finds out, he'll castrate you.'

I hated this woman, but what could I do? She was too drunk to listen to anything I said, and she was working herself into a fit of anger.

'Get out of here,' she said. 'What are you doing in here? This is my bedroom, sonny!'

'Is there anything wrong?' Alison said that night, seeing me shuffling in the parlor, watching her bathing the boys. The sun had set but I had not turned on any lights, and I suppose I seemed thoughtful, if not anxious, being so silent in that darkness.

I said no, trying to keep fretfulness out of my voice, yet I knew as soon as I said it that it was a mistake not to open my heart and tell her everything that had happened between Fayette and me. This was the right moment. If I did not tell her now I could never do it without seeming that I was hiding something.

She looked so peaceful. Leaning over the tub, bathing Will in the sudsy water, supporting his head, protecting his eyes from the soap, as she poured water over his hair. Anton watched, another cherub, still pink from his bath, holding his blue Ladybird book of nursery rhymes he wanted as a bedtime story.

'This little fish was actually swimming in the pool today,' Alison said, and, opening his mouth to smile, Will swallowed water and smacked his lips, still struggling to smile, he was so proud.

'Dad, will you please read to me?' Anton asked.

I kissed them all, I read to Anton, I said nothing more to Alison, and I knew it was a mistake.

'You pretend to be so innocent,' Fayette had said. But I was not pretending. I had come to Singapore for its name and its aura. I taught students because I thought they wanted to understand English literature. I moved here to Lazard's house because I thought he wanted poetry lessons, and a month ago, when he had said, 'You already passed the hardest test – my wife likes you,' I took it as praise. I had believed him when he said the magazine had accepted his poems.

I was not innocent any longer.

Lazard returned on Friday, but I did not see him until Monday. I had used the time to work on my Singapore novel. As usual he did not acknowledge the fact that my job so far had been mainly symbolic; he was in a good mood and seemed glad of my company.

After we talked for a few minutes – he was bemoaning his airport delays – he said, 'Have you been doing some writing?'

'Working on my novel.'

'That's good.'

'It's going well, thanks to –' I did not know how to finish the sentence: Thanks to your being away. Thanks to this luxurious estate. Thanks to your wife who hardly speaks to us. Thanks to my nervous anxiety in wanting to finish the book and be solvent.

'Maybe you could put in a little note or something at the beginning – how we helped you out,' Harry said.

There was not even the slightest undertone of irony in his voice, and his smug, beaky face had never looked more proprietorial. He was serious! And though I objected, and once again wanted to quit, I swallowed hard; I had a family to support. I was his prisoner. I looked at him, hardly believing his hubris, and thought: You wish.

'Or maybe dedicate it to you,' I said.

I knew he would not accuse me of mocking him. Someone incapable of expressing irony was equally incapable of hearing it.

'We wouldn't expect anything as elaborate as that.' But he seemed to be savoring the idea and liking it. 'It would be quite a tribute.' Now I could see he was eager for it, and I was pleased that my simple irony had made him greedy. He saw his name and Fayette's on the dedication page of my novel.

He said, 'Fayette told me she had a little chat with you last week.'

What did he know? What had she told him?

'Yes, I was looking for you. She said you'd already left for the airport.'

He had flipped open his wallet. He pinched out a snapshot of Fayette, and passed it to me, and he sounded like a pimp when he said, 'You see how lovely she is at forty-eight. Can you imagine what she looked like at twenty-three? She looks so sweet. People never believe me when I tell them that she wears the pants in the family.'

'It's true, she looks absolutely angelic,' I said.

'She's been pretty low these past few days. Remember that carved piece she had, that you rescued from the bottom of the pool?'

'The jade mask?' I remembered her drunkenly stuffing the exquisite carving into one of the hundred drawers in the Chinese herbalist's chest.

'That's right. Seems she lost it somewhere.'

'That's terrible. It must have been valuable.'

He was not troubled. He said, 'There's more where that came from.'

Of course: it was stolen. Someone would steal another one and Harry would buy it.

'At her last birthday I says, "Hey, this will be a first. I never slept with a 48-year-old woman before!"'

'Was she flattered?'

'She almost murdered me. She likes you, Paul.'

It was his pimp's voice, he was almost pleading, but I was sure he was only trying to be friendly.

'You won't believe this but she has barely a high school education.'

I said nothing. Some remarks were beyond the reach of irony.

'She's a little sensitive about that,' Harry said. 'I guess your wife went to college.'

'Cambridge,' I said.

'"Some of the smartest people on earth don't know the basics," I tell Fayette.'

'My wife knows the basics.'

'Fayette's in awe of you.'

'There's nothing to be in awe of.'

'Nathan Leopold said he'd heard of you.'

'Prisoners read more than the average person.'

'You're a published author,' he said.

'So are you, Harry.'

He did not smile, he looked trapped, but he did not tell me what I was sure was the truth, that his grant to the magazine was his way of getting his poems published.

He was evasive, he was untruthful; yet still I respected him, because it was in a good cause. He wanted to know what poetry was all about and, ill-equipped for the task, was willing to face the difficulty. He seemed in that sense innocent and, even as Alison had said all those weeks ago, idealistic.

We did nothing more in that lesson, but he made a point of saying that he wanted another lesson the next day. When I arrived, I was determined not to make chit-chat or to talk about Fayette. I said, 'Shall we look at Wilfred Owen?'

'I was reading it on my trip,' he said.

I had typed out the poem 'Anthem for Doomed Youth' so that we could discuss it.

'It seemed a little overdone,' Lazard said.

I wanted to scream: He was in a muddy trench! He was gassed! Shells were exploding all around him! He saw men dying!

'The thing is,' I said as though to a child, 'Owen actually saw these events first hand. It was a nightmarish war. He died. So did Rosenberg and Rupert Brooke.'

'What did Patton say? "War is hell." ' Lazard sipped his drink and swallowed and smacked his lips in a knowing way.

'General Sherman said that.'

'You sure?'

'It's in a poem by e. e. cummings called "plato told." '

Lazard accepted this and then said, 'Funny, isn't it? Poets writing about war.'

'It happens all the time,' I said. 'That's the subject of the *Aeneid*. "Of arms and the man I sing." '

But Lazard had not heard me. He was still ruminating. 'Oh, sure, they're probably good poets. But you've got to wonder what kind of soldiers they were.'

'Average soldiers, I guess.'

'What's that supposed to mean?'

'It means scared shitless.'

'Been to Vietnam?'

I said no, and I was going to add that living across the road from Serene House I had met dozens of American soldiers. I felt it was my patriotic duty to befriend them and make them feel at home in Singapore; and not one of them had spoken of the Vietnam war in any terms except horror and shame and waste.

We talked a bit more about Wilfred Owen. Harry Lazard gave the poem low marks.

That night I slept badly. I thrashed, and when I finally went to sleep I dreamed I was clinging to the side of a building, in a high wind. I woke. The wind was the overhead fan, but that was merely a detail in my dream of destitution. In the morning I sorrowed inwardly, hearing my children laugh. Only I knew that this was all coming to an end.

At our lesson the next evening I asked, 'We were talking about Vietnam yesterday. Have you been there?'

'Many times.'

This shook me.

'Most of my business is there.'

Innocent was the acceptable word; the reality was that I was stupid.

Electronics, he had told me.

'I wrote a poem on my last trip there.'

Timing devices. Circuitry. Switches. Small motors. He had also mentioned chemicals. What did that mean – napalm?

'I think it still needs some work.'

He opened the stiff office folder, and showed me the single sheet, clipped in. Its title was 'Cap St Jacques.'

He slapped his breast pocket.

'Forgot my glasses – left them upstairs.' He rose to go and then said, 'Might as well come on up. We can talk there.'

'I wouldn't want to disturb your wife.'

'She's out – at a party.'

In this seclusion and servitude in Lazard's estate I had forgotten the Singapore parties.

I followed Harry upstairs to his bedroom, and there looking like the scene of a crime was the chaise longue, the stack of magazines, the parasol lamp and the massive Chinese herbalist's chest with the hundred drawers. Lazard had once made me feel like a prisoner. I no longer felt that way, because I now knew that I could leave at any time. I had to leave. It would be hard for me to be on my own, there would be less comfort for Alison and the boys; but they would understand when I explained.

'Go on, read it.'

He passed me his poem. It was the sort of clumsy, matter of fact series of observations that he scribbled in the name of poetry. Sometimes his work was like bad prose, at other times like bad poetry. He was at his worst when he tried to sound poetic. The rest of the time the result was like notes jotted in an appointment book, or hurried diary entries.

This was about ten lines and it was dated. Its subject was the sky seen from the terrace of a fine hotel, clear air in the morning, helicopters and C-130s during the day, and at night galaxies of stars and fighter planes.

'It's a sky seen over the period of twenty-four hours,' he said.

I said nothing.

'I'm a bad sleeper,' he said.

I was holding the poem without wanting to read it again or even look at it. A hasty man would have crumpled it and thrown it into his face, but I was an enemy infiltrator, in the disguise of a simple scholar.

'That's the old name, Cap St Jacques,' he explained. 'That's where the French used to hobnob. Now we're hobnobbing, I guess you could say. They renamed it Vung Tau.'

He was still smiling at me. He began to look uncomfortable.

'Will you excuse me? I think I picked up a tummy bug in Saigon. Ho Chi Minh's revenge.'

He had not noticed that I had been silent the entire time. I watched him leave the room. And then I heard the bathroom door close and the click of the lock – that was comic: did he think I was going to intrude on him?

I went to the Chinese herbalist's chest, opened a drawer and there was Fayette's jade carving. I quickly put it into my pocket and shut the drawer.

When Harry Lazard returned, I said, 'I'm afraid I have some bad news for you.'

He looked stricken. 'You don't like my poem?'

We flew out of Singapore the next evening, stopping in Colombo, Karachi, Beirut, and Frankfurt, before arriving dazed and unsteady on our feet in London. For a week I had attacks of vertigo, an actual spiralling sense that I was dropping to the ground, and I had to look up at the sky to regain my balance.

The £13,000 I realized on the jade carving, the child's burial mask (it was Chinese, Later Liang Dynasty, say tenth century) at the auction at Christie's in South Kensington, was the purchase price of a Victorian house in Clapham. The spoils of war, I would have said, if anyone had asked. No one asked.

FOUR

Lady Max

I

You didn't become a Londoner simply by living there. After seven years I was still an alien. I wanted to write about the city from the inside, and be anonymous in the streets. I felt it was happening, I was at last becoming a Londoner, the winter I discovered Gaston's.

Only the professionals knew Gaston's. The poet Ian Musprat (*The Dogflud Chronicles*) had shown me the place. It was a small used bookshop in an alley off Chancery Lane. A square of cardboard stuck in the window was printed in Chinese characters and English, *No Rickshaw Parking* – an obscure joke. There was no other sign, but there were stacks of books.

Gaston was fussy about the books he bought and sold – they had to be new, unmarked and in demand by libraries. London book reviewers were Gaston's suppliers, and if you lingered by the plain wooden counter where the books were piled you would meet the great names, the savage reviewers, the literary hacks, the strugglers. They entered and left like punters at a pawn shop, trying to put a jaunty face on their shame. All of them were doing something they faintly despised, selling copies of the books they had reviewed, at half-price, cash.

Friday was a popular day, because it was a deadline, copy day for both the Sundays and the weeklies. After lunch I typed my review and made my way from Clapham to Fleet Street, and sold my books at Gaston's. Then I turned in my review at the *New Statesman*, nearby. I did round-ups, three or four books, sometimes as many as six, 'The Week's Fiction,' or else four travel books. The crime reviewer did many more in half the space. The *Statesman* was just on the other side of Lincoln's Inn (barristers looking silly in self-important wigs and black gowns). After I handed in my review I had money in my pocket, a check in the mail, and the weekend ahead. Saturday was for shopping, Sunday for outings with Alison and the boys – I never wrote a word those days. On Monday it was back to my novel, and I read the review copies in the evenings. On Friday I did my review, and then it was time for Gaston's again.

I liked being rid of the books, it gave me pleasure to turn a stack of bound proofs into a box of Lego, a jar of marmalade, *The Hobbit,* and four ounces of Player's Navy Cut pipe tobacco. And I needed the routine. London monotony was necessary to the writing of a long novel.

'How's your book?' Alison asked on those weekends, when she saw me looking thoughtful.

I always said my book was going fine, and it was, but I would have preferred a bit more – a bit more money; a bit more space in the *Statesman,* a lead review instead of a round-up; one book instead of four; my name on the cover of the magazine. Yet I didn't complain. I was reassured by the routine. Cozy, predictable London was at its best, its blackest, in the winter, in cold, dead and dreary January, with spring seeming a long way off. Londoners hated January and February, and often muttered as much grumblingly to strangers on buses.

For me it was writing weather, and I loved it. I was not a Londoner in the way I enjoyed those months, those fogs, those thick white skies. When it rained the city was blackened, and I liked that too. The short days and long nights kept people indoors. I worked in a small pool of lamplight in an upper room, overlooking the slate roofs and chimney pots and the leafless trees in the back gardens. Everyone else was inside, too. In the London winter I never had the feeling that I was missing anything.

I usually met Ian Musprat in Gaston's. I saw him that dark Friday in January when I came in with my stack of books. He was negotiating nervously with Gaston – dickering over a book. When they were done he stepped aside, looking fussed. As I sold my four ('God, the price of books,' Gaston said, handing me seven pounds), Musprat covertly slipped a book into his briefcase.

'Gaston made me wait, because Angus Wilson came in to sell that Christmas junk he reviewed in the *Observer.*'

'I wish I had seen him,' I said.

'He looks like the head of Girton.'

'That's a women's college, isn't it?'

'You Americans are so literal,' Musprat said, and we threaded our way through the wet footpaths of Lincoln's Inn, the short-cut to the *Statesman*.

I said, 'Did Gaston refuse to buy one of your books?'

Musprat shook his head and said, 'I bought one from him.'

'I've never seen anyone buy a book there,' I said. 'I thought they sold them by the pound to libraries.'

Musprat inhaled but said nothing, only sighed. He went very quiet. He was just my age but seemed much older. He was balding and had bad teeth, and was cranky in the way only Englishmen in their thirties could be – assertively seedy. He cultivated a look of failure, he boasted of his bad reviews. He could have passed for fifty.

I had never seen Musprat without a necktie and a jacket, and yet I rarely saw him in a place where he needed them. He wore a tie at home, in his flat in Notting Hill Gate. He told me that he put a tie on before he answered the door – a school habit, he said. So much in English life originated not at home with the family, as it did in Europe, or in the street, as it did in America, but at school – the table manners, the slang, the rules, the habits, the dress code, even the food. What was oddest of all in this school-obsessed country was that people claimed they hated school – Musprat's school poems were angry and sad. He had been thrashed by his sadistic house master, mocked for being a loner, disliked for not being a rugger hearty, and he still wrote poems about the school he had left twenty years ago. His writing was his way of getting even, and he saw his poetry as a form of revenge.

'So what book did you buy?' I asked him.

His briefcase was a battered satchel, like something else from school. He whacked it against his leg as he walked.

'Jesus, you and your bloody questions,' he said. He was genuinely irritated, but he fumbled open the flap of the satchel and took out the book, *The Dogflud Chronicles*.

'You bought your own book?'

'Rescued it,' he said. 'Some bastard sold it to Gaston. I couldn't bear seeing it on the shelf. Half-price, shop-worn, flogged to a library. It's only been out a month.'

'I think I'd do the same if I saw one of my books there.'

'No one sells your books to Gaston,' Musprat said, and he smiled. 'That's the highest compliment a reviewer can pay.'

Waiting outside the literary editor's office at the *New Statesman*, Musprat said, 'This is like a tutorial, isn't it? Clutching our ridiculous essays, waiting for our tutor to summon us.'

Musprat was smoking. He puffed out his cheeks and blew smoke.

'Hoping he'll give us an alpha,' he said crossly. 'Are you going to that Hodder's party?'

I said that I didn't know anything about it.

'It's for that boring American woman who writes picture books about Nash terraces. Every twit in London will be there.'

'So are you going?'

'It's a drink,' Musprat said, meaning yes. He looked pale and rumpled, leaning clumsily against a torpedo-sized fire extinguisher.

'Are you feeling all right?'

'Of course,' he said. He was offended by the question. 'You're always asking me that.'

There had only been one other time. I had run into him one morning in the Strand. I had said he looked ill, as though he had just thrown up. He said he had, he had been drinking the night before, but that he was sick every morning. He said, *'Don't you throw up every morning?'*

'Come in, Ian!' the literary editor shouted through the closed door.

'Just like my tutor,' Musprat muttered, and shuffled in. He was out in minutes, sighing and rifling the book locker, and then it was my turn, and the editor, Graham Heavage, immediately lapsed into his irritating habit.

'Bonjour, M'sieur Theroux, ça va? Il souffle un vent glacial aujourd'hui. Avez vous des engelures?'

That was his irritating habit. He often spoke to me in French – because of my name, because he spoke French very well, and could patronize me that way. I regarded it as an unfriendly gesture. I spoke French badly. So I always replied to him in English. This didn't bother him, but neither did it encourage him to speak to me in English. He had the sort of reddish eyes you see in most geese and in some East Europeans.

'I'm fine. No chilblains.'

Wasn't that what *engelure* meant?

Heavage was a highly intelligent but fretful man of fifty or so who had never been friendly with me. He was another tie-wearer. He was said to be an authority on Aleister Crowley – hard to reconcile this fastidious editor with the lecherous Satanist, but the English sometimes had surprising interests.

Goose-eyes twitching, he went through my copy quickly and frowned in approval, making swift printer's marks in ballpoint as he read, and then he said, 'I can't remember when anyone has used the word "crappy" in these pages before.'

'Do you want to change it to "egregious"?'

'No. Crappy will do,' he said. But he didn't smile. It was hard to tell whether he was mocking me. Still he was scrutinizing the review – not reading it, but considering it.' And you're a trifle severe with Mr Updike.'

'I hate allegories.'

'I would have said pastiche, but never mind.'

Musprat was right: it was a tutorial. No praise, only nit-picking and rather wintry irony.

Shoving the pages into a wire tray on his desk, Heavage said, 'We'll run this next week. On your way out have a trawl through the book locker. See if there's anything you want to do.'

I decided to be blunt. 'I'd like to do one big book instead of four small ones, for a change.'

'I'll keep that in mind,' Heavage said. 'As you say in America, I'll think it over mentally.'

I wanted to hit him. I was sure that he had never had any experience of physical violence, so my slapping his face would be a great shock. In this silence he had leveled his reddish eyes at me, as though he had guessed at my hostility.

'Not many big books in January,' he said, flexing his fingers. 'Very quiet at the moment, though there will be the usual logjam in the spring. Find yourself a clutch of novels, there's a good chap.'

He was saying no to my doing a lead review. So it was another week as a hack. Then he smiled and broke into French, which was my signal that the meeting was at an end.

I found Musprat on his knees, rooting around the book locker.

'Look at this,' he said. It was a picture book, *Tennyson at Freshwater: The Record of a Friendship*. 'I bags it.'

'I didn't know you were interested in Tennyson.'

'I'm not,' Musprat said. 'But look at the price. Ten quid. I'll just mention it in my round-up and Gaston will give me a fiver for it.'

*

It was a beautiful drawing room in a Nash terrace on the Outer Circle, east side, of Regent's Park, and everyone there seemed to be out of place – reviewers, writers, editors, publicists, all drinking wine and watching for the trays of hors d'oeuvres which were carried by waiters and waitresses who were better dressed than most of the guests. I had the impression of people who had just come in off the streets, drifted out of the park, where they had been lurking – they looked damp and grateful and somewhat anxious. I mentioned this to Musprat.

'They're drunk, that's all,' he said, and lunged at a woman with a tray of drinks.

While I was searching for someone I knew, a woman materialized next to me. She was almost my height, and white-faced, with an elegant neck – and a pearl and velvet collar around it – and full red lips.

'I know who you are,' she said. 'But I thought you were much older.'

People sometimes said that, because of all of my opinionated reviews – but it was only a posture I had adopted. There were comic possibilities in being full of opinions and crotchets. I wanted to be the joker who never smiled, and I was surprised when I was taken seriously.

'You're very busy, aren't you? I see your shorter pieces everywhere.'

'But mainly on the back pages.'

'I loathe self-deprecation,' she said. 'Don't be insincere. I thought your *Railway Bazaar* was brilliant. It was quite the best book I've read in ages. I gave copies of it to all my friends for Christmas.'

When someone spoke in this way I always assumed they were making it up. I simply smiled at the woman and asked no further questions. I thought it might embarrass her if I had. In any case, she was still talking.

'Your best review was from a man I saw walking along the tracks at Paddington Station. He had a copy of it in his hand. A man passing by said, "Is that book any good?" and the first man said, "Fucking marvelous, Fred."'

'I like that.'

'I thought you might,' she said. 'And what are you working on at the moment?'

'A novel.'

She smiled. I loved the fullness of her lips against her thin face.

'About a man,' I said.

Her eyes were dark and deeply set.

'He leaves home and becomes a sort of castaway.'

Still she said nothing. There was a pinkish bloom on her cheeks.

'He dies in the end.'

How was it possible for someone to hear all this and still say nothing? Her silence made me nervous.

But I loved this woman's looks, her lips, her lovely Madonna's face, her skin very close against her skull, her high forehead and her black, gleaming hair tightly drawn back. Her paleness, her pinkness had no blemish, and I found her slightly protruding teeth another aspect of her beauty. She was wearing a dark dress trimmed in velvet and lace, and although she was thin – with a slender neck and fragile-looking arms and wrists – she had a full, deep bosom that her good posture and height elevated and presented. I was accustomed to regarding lovely women as not very intelligent, but she seemed both beautiful and brainy – her silences alone seemed intelligently timed – and this combination I found madly attractive.

My tongue was gummy as I said, 'It's called *The Last Man*,' and looked down and saw that she was wearing stiletto heels – wicked shoes on thin, white feet.

'That title has an excellent pedigree. *The Last Man* – that was Mary Shelley's original title for *Frankenstein*,' she said. 'And I'm sure you know that Orwell's first title for *1984* was *The Last Man in Europe*.'

From my expression I was sure she realized that I did not know this at all.

'You could ask Sonia,' the woman said. 'Sonia Orwell. She's over there by the window – do you want to meet her?'

I said no, not at the moment, because I could not imagine that George Orwell's widow would want to meet me – I anticipated more silences.

'I really do admire your writing,' the woman said. 'In fact, I think you might have that rare combination of qualities that makes a writer of genius.'

'What qualities?' I asked, and fumbled with my arms.

'Total megalomania and a nose for what the public like to read. It's unbeatable. Dickens had it. So did Shaw. Henry James didn't have it, but Maugham did.'

'I've just been reading Hugh Walpole. He was a friend of Henry James. James was always sending him hugs. *The Man With Red Hair*.'

The woman had stiffened each time I had uttered a sentence.

'A macabre novel,' I said. 'Set in Cornwall.'

The woman said, 'You're much better than Hugh Walpole.'

It was the first time in my life anyone had ever said that I was better than a dead writer. I had never imagined that I was better than anyone who had written in the past. It had never occurred to me that I might be compared to another writer, dead or alive. The point about writing was that you were yourself – comparisons were meaningless. Nevertheless, I took this woman's assertion as praise.

She went on praising me – and I felt flustered, embarrassed and confused, like a puppy being squirted by a hose. I also found myself delighting in glancing down at her cleavage. Did women know how this warm smile-like slot excited a man's interest?

Distracted, I asked, 'And who are you?'

But she was looking across the room.

'Will you excuse me?' she said, and gave me a lovely smile, and she was away, sooner than I wished.

Had I said something wrong?

Then Musprat was at my elbow, with a cigarette and a smeared glass and flecks of vol-au-vent pastry on his tie and fingers. His eyes were bloodshot, his suit wrinkled, the knot on his tie yanked small. He was slightly hunched over and looked more fragile and elderly than ever.

'Who was that?' I asked him.

She was standing by the fireplace talking animatedly to a man in a chalk-striped suit.

'Lady Max,' Musprat said. 'She's married to a tick called Alabaster. He's something in the City. They have a house in the Boltons.'

'She seems nice.' I was thinking of her praise.

'That's the one thing she's not.'

'She's attractive,' I said.

'Sort of a bruised peach,' Musprat said.

'I like the way she's dressed.'

'She's always wearing those "fuck-me" shoes,' Musprat said.

'Don't you think she's pretty?'

'I hate that word,' he said, in a disgusted way. 'I don't want to hear it. At this point in the evening everyone looks leathery to me.'

I lingered at the party hoping to speak to the woman, Lady Max, again. She did not return to my end of the room. She was surrounded and I was too shy to approach her.

I loitered, growing sober and with this heightening sobriety felt strangely superior – not in any complicated way and not intellectually, but simply stronger and in control. The other, drunker guests brought out a kind of priggishness in me. At a certain point – when the first drunken person emerged and began to stagger and sputter – I usually stopped drinking, and began to watch, and grew sober and colder, and was all the more fascinated by what I saw.

Drunk people, loud people, obvious and angry people, people stammering and stumbling, spilling drinks and scarfing small burned sausages and cheese cubes on toothpicks. They had surrendered all power and direction, they were yelling and gasping. They strengthened me.

I did not want to be that way. I stood, growing calmer, observing them. They seemed, as Musprat often seemed to me, self-destructive and weak. I didn't see how people like that could write anything. That was my yardstick. I measured people by their ability to write. How could these people write well if they could not see straight?

Lady Max flashed past and I made after her. I wanted to hear more, but lost her in the crowd.

2

It was important in London to leave a party or start home before the public houses closed, for just after eleven o'clock the streets were thronged with drunks – all men, their faces wolfish and pale, yelling at passing cars, or else staggering and scrapping. Some of them loitered, looking ravenous, eating chips with greasy fingers out of pouches of old newspapers. All over London these men, turned out of pubs, were pissing in doorways.

That night I was delayed on the Underground and by the time I reached Victoria the eruption had occurred – drunks everywhere. The station was overbright, which made it seem dirtier than it would have in dim light, and it was old – the wind blowing up the tracks and through the barriers, rustling the newspapers and the plastic cups, and moving them through the way the tide moves flotsam. The newsstand was shut but the *Evening Standard* poster was still stuck to the wall, looking sorry in its teasing way. *TV COMEDY STAR IN SUICIDE BID – PICTURE.*

That feeling I had had at the party came back to me on the train, as I saw the drunks eating chips and dripping hamburgers, or else slumped in their seats, or swaying feebly with the swaying carriage, looking weak and tired. It was not merely that I was sober; I was also a stranger, an American, an alien, just quietly looking. I saw theirs as a peculiarly English despair – specifically London fatigue, London futility. It was their fate, not mine, and I wanted to write about it, because no one else had noticed it. I was not any of them.

Three stops, thinking these thoughts, and then I walked through the disorder of my own station, littered and dirty, its posters torn, and its black iron gleaming with the sweat of condensed fog. I liked hearing my footsteps in the stillness, and the shadows and the mist falling through the light of the street lamps, as empty double-decker buses moved importantly down the empty high road.

Alison had gone to bed. Before I joined her I crept upstairs in the dark and stood in the boys' room, listening to the rise and fall of their breathing, just the slightest whisper of it, Will's adenoidal snorting, and Anton's just audible flutter. They were both still, like buoyant things floating high and peacefully on a sea of sleep. Without waking them I kissed each boy's cheek – their faces were warm in the cold room, and their breath had made feathers of frost on the window pane.

I undressed in the dark and crept into bed with Alison. She slid against me and sighed, the bedclothes a nest of warmth. In order to ease myself into sleep I went through the chapters of my unfinished novel, murmuring the number of each chapter and the secret title I had assigned it. There were eleven so far, but I was asleep by the time I got to eight.

London nights were silent and clammy cold in the submarine darkness, and when I woke from a dream of strangulation it was as though I were suspended in this dark, vitreous silence. I had the sense of us all in the house swimming through these London nights, of night here as a sea-swell, and of us sinuously moving through it as though drifting deep in the face of a wave. I loved sleep and it was only morning that gave me a sense of disorder, something to do with the morning darkness of winter – we woke and dressed in the dark – and the clank of milk bottles, of crates shifting on the milk float, the only sound in the street, but a deranged one.

'You came home so late last night,' Alison said. 'What time was it?'

'Eleven or so,' I said, wondering why I was lying. She would not have minded my telling her it had been after midnight.

Yet she was silent. She seemed preoccupied. I sensed her disapproval.

'It wasn't much,' I said, being defensive. 'Pretty boring. I got some money at Gaston's, then Ian and I went to a book launch.' Alison said nothing. I said, 'That boring American woman who writes about Nash terraces.'

She had not heard. She said, 'The boys were up until all hours doing homework. Why do they give them so much prep? I'm going to complain.'

'Don't say anything, Mum,' Anton said.

Will said, 'You'll get us into trouble.'

'Jeremy's mum complained and Townsend announced it in class and everyone laughed at him.'

They were seated awkwardly at the table wolfing their cereal. In their school uniforms, their hair sticking up, their blazers rumpled, they looked harassed if not anguished. They ate quickly, nervously, without any pleasure, simply stoking their faces, and then they jumped up and said they had to go or they would be late.

'I'll walk you to the bus stop,' I said.

Alison said, 'I'll be gone by the time you get back, so I'll say goodbye now.'

She kissed me while the boys tightened the buckles on their satchels.

Mornings were clamorous, and I needed silence, needed the

house to myself. I wanted to see them all on their way. I could not sit down until the house was empty.

At the bus stop, Will said, 'Are you a socialist?'

'I don't vote – Americans can't vote in Britain,' I said. 'I'm just a spectator.'

'Mum's a Labour supporter,' Anton said. 'I am too.'

'That's what he told Mr Fitch,' Will said.

'That's none of your business,' Anton said.

'You can be a socialist, but if you're dogmatic,' I began.

Will asked, 'What does dogmatic mean?'

Anton was listening too, as though he had been too proud to ask.

'Something like inflexible.'

'Mr Beale is inflexible.'

Mr Beale was the hated headmaster.

All this time they were looking up the road for the bus. I hovered and yet held back, wanting to protect them and wanting to be strong. And they had the same ambivalence, liking my company and resenting the thought that they might need it. They were thin and pale, with a hint of anxiety in their soft brown eyes.

It was a cold, overcast morning of mist, with a harsh sound of traffic, and the dampness gave a greasy look to the black road and the broken pavement. Then the bus loomed and slowed, and they leaped aboard, catching hold of the rail, and when the bus resumed and went past me I saw them standing, small figures jammed in the aisle among all the heavy coats.

The house was empty when I returned. I went to my study and opened my notebook and read: *Shafts of sunlight filled with brilliant flakes falling through the green leaves to the jungle floor –* which was where I had left off yesterday to write my book review and go to Gaston's.

Shafts of sunlight filled with brilliant flakes.

I looked through the window of my study. Outside, London in midwinter was dark and the brick and stone of the old house-backs I saw looked crusted with neglect. The trees were brittle and black too, and the damp night air had left a look of slime on the slate roofs. Some windows were lighted – you could see the pale bulbs – but the overall impression was of stillness and darkness, of daylight sleepily emerging and seeping out of the low sky. In this narrow corner of the city winter seemed a kind of fatal affliction, the way a gangrenous leg turns black.

The darkness was a comfort. I was learning to live here. The stillness, and even the tomblike quality in the shapes of houses, the sense I had of being buried alive here, penetrated me; it kept me indoors and calmed me and helped me think. A blue sky would have turned my head and tempted me away, but the gray morning and the backs of these old houses and their brown bricks kept my reverie intact. I was not dealing with them or anything like them. There was no distraction here. I was writing about the jungle.

I had sketched the way ahead – I knew what was coming in the next three or four chapters. After that, I had only the vaguest sense of what I was in for. Mocking myself, I said out loud, 'Now what?'

Just as I picked up my pen, the mailman's feet sounded on the stone front steps, and I held my breath, and then letters began plopping through the letter slot. Only one required a reply, an overdue bill, and I paid it immediately, then found a stamp for it. Another, from a reader – a woman who said she liked my books – I crumpled and threw away. I lifted my pen again, but when nothing came – no word, no thought – I retrieved the woman's letter from the wastebasket and smoothed it. It was from Stony Plain, Alberta, Canada. I pulled out my big atlas and found the place – near Edmonton – and I was so touched by a message from this distance I replied to her on a postcard, thanking her for her letter.

It was then ten-thirty. I tried again, attempting to move on. *The shafts of sunlight* . . . I struggled to continue the thought, to make a paragraph, but I could not advance it.

The woman's letter from Stony Plain, Alberta, had mentioned a particular story I had written years before. I found that collection in the bookshelf and read the story. It was good. It held me. Could I still write as fluently as that? Putting the book away I glanced up and saw a guidebook to Canada. Stony Plain was not listed, but there was an entry for Edmonton. The capital. Oldest city in the province. On the Saskatchewan River. And this: *Ukrainians played a large role in the settlement of Edmonton and are still the dominant ethnic group.*

I shut the guidebook and dragged my notebook over and tried again, struggling to begin. It was now eleven-twenty. I reread everything that I had written in that chapter so far, and as I read I noticed that my fingernails needed cutting. I attended to this, paring them carefully over the wastebasket, and as I was doing so the telephone rang. It was Ian Musprat. Did I want to meet for lunch?

Snipping my nails I said, 'I'm writing.'

I believed the lie would commit me to action.

Musprat said, 'I've been thrashing around all morning. I can't do a thing. It's hopeless. How about playing snooker at the Lambourne later on?'

'I'm busy tonight.' Another lie: I must write something, I thought. 'What about tomorrow?'

'Fine. I'll see you at the Lambourne at seven. If we eat early the table will be free. I'll let you get on with your writing. I don't know how you do it.'

But after I hung up I did not write. I finished clipping my fingernails and then I filed them. It was almost noon.

At last, very carefully, I began to recopy what I had written on the previous page in the notebook, writing it on a fresh page, as though to give myself momentum. I improved it, but when I got to the end nothing more came. It was ten minutes to one. I tugged. I squinted. I saw something.

I wrote, *Just then they looked up and saw a brown face staring at them through the leaves, and after they saw the first one they saw more – three, seven, a dozen human faces, suspended like masks.*

A breakthrough at last. I had more to write, but stopped – I would save it for later. It was one o'clock: time for lunch.

Fish fingers – I loved the improbable name, like 'shoe trees' – three of them in a sandwich, a cup of coffee, two chocolate cookies, and while I ate this I listened to *The World at One*, a news program, and I read *The Times*, and I sat. The radio, the food, the newspaper – it all left me calm, and when the program ended I hurried upstairs and almost without thinking I wrote the sentence I had saved: *They looked again and the faces were gone.*

This was all I needed, because in that thought – the sight of the faces in the jungle – I saw the whole situation, my own characters, the Indians spying on them, the hint of an ambush, the jungle, the narrow paths, the hidden village. And so I spent the rest of the afternoon bringing my characters nearer and nearer – and intermittently they saw the faces – until when their path ran out they arrived at the village and were mobbed. End of chapter.

I had written 35 words in the morning and in the afternoon something like 1,500. But what gave me the greatest pleasure was a sentence containing the image, *limp green leaves like old dollar bills*.

I made notes for the next chapter, to prepare for tomorrow. *The village. Smoke. Trampled earth. Frightened children. Barking dogs. A conversation. 'We cannot help you.' 'Ice is life.' The hidden strangers*. The act of writing produced ideas and events. It was late afternoon and I was growing excited at the thought that I had moved on. I guessed that I was half done with the book. I wanted so much to be done before the summer, but ten chapters more, ten weeks, would take me into March, and if so I might be through by my birthday in April. Looking over what I had written I became hopeful. The book was strange, true, comic and unexpected – that was what mattered most. I wanted people to believe it and like it, and to find something of themselves expressed in it.

With these thoughts – my pen twitching words on to the bright paper in the pool of light on my desk, and darkness all around – night had fallen. The door to my room opened. It was Will.

'Anton's downstairs making tea,' he said.

He looked exhausted. His face was smudged, his hair spiky, his hand-me-down school blazer had shrunken on him, but instead of making him look bigger it only made him skinnier, with a thin neck and knobby shoulders.

'Hi, Dad.'

He kissed me. His hair smelled of cigarette smoke. When I mentioned this, he said, 'The bus conductor made me sit on the upper deck.'

He slumped into the armchair opposite my desk. He said, 'What page are you on?'

I looked down. 'Two hundred and eighty-seven.'

'Are you almost done?'

'Half done, I think. I don't know for sure.'

'I did an essay for Wilkins today. Two sides. *Macbeth*.'

'The hen-pecked hero.'

Will nodded. 'It's true. I should have said that.'

'You look tired, Will.'

'We had rugby. And the English essay. And in chemistry we did an experiment with sulfuric acid and Jason burned a hole in his blazer. Matron went bonkers when she saw it. In the morning there was a rehearsal for the school play. Lunch was stew. It was gristle and fat. I didn't eat it. Jam sponge for afters. Beale told me I needed a haircut. And some of the boys hid my satchel and when I found it they made fun of me. The sole of my shoe is coming off. Simon Wesley told me he hates me.'

School.

I said, 'Why don't you watch television?'

'I have tons of homework. Latin prep, chemistry and history.'

'What would you like for dinner?'

'Dunno, do I? Maybe spaghetti. The vegetarian kind.'

'I'll make the sauce,' I said. 'We'll have salad. I think there's ice cream for dessert.'

Will yawned like a cat. 'I'll have a bath first. The school showers weren't working, so we ran straight from rugby to chemistry. We were all dirty. Matron said we smelled like goats.'

That explained the mud streaks on his face and the dirt under his fingernails. My sons knew I loved them, but they had no idea how much I admired them.

Anton called out to Will to say the toast and tea were ready, and while they sat at the table, saying little, I made the spaghetti sauce – and chopped the onion and garlic and green pepper, and sautéed them with some mushrooms, then scalded and peeled the tomatoes, and tossed it all into a pot with a bunch of fresh basil and a stock cube and a pinch of crushed red pepper and a dollop of tomato paste. While the sauce reddened and simmered, the boys went up-stairs to their room to do their homework, and I went out. I bought the *Evening Standard* and took it to the Fishmonger's Arms to read it over a pint of Guinness. There was a mention of John Updike staying at the Connaught, in London to launch his new book; and I thought how Londoners knew nothing of London hotel rooms.

Later, waiting for Alison to come home, I watched a television game show with Anton, who had finished his homework, and when the host of the show quipped, 'You're like the Irishman who thought an innuendo was a suppository,' Anton laughed out loud, and I thought: I am happy. There was nothing on earth so joyous as this – the darkness, the silly game show, the thought that I had written something today, the knowledge that I was home, the anticipation that Alison would be home soon, the spaghetti sauce simmering, a pint of Guinness inside me, and most of all – the explosive sound of my child's laughter, generous and full-throated. I felt blessed.

Alison was home at seven, a bit later than usual. She too was tired, but she helped Will with his Latin while I boiled the water for the spaghetti and made salad. We ate together. The boys cleared the table. Alison did the dishes – because I had cooked – and after the boys went upstairs I read Alison the chapter I had just finished.

'It's good,' she said.

'Say something more.'

'Isn't that enough?'

'Just a little more.'

'I like the image about the leaves like dollar bills. And it's menacing at the end. I would want to read on. How's that?'

'OK.'

We watched the *Nine o'clock News*, and the beginning of a program about fruit bats, and then Alison yawned and said, 'I'm tired.'

So we went to bed. Then the house was in darkness. I was happy. What had happened to make me so contented? I could not say why I was reassured. Perhaps my novel had gone better than I expected – I had finished a chapter. But more likely it was that we were together, a complete family, a whole healthy organism, fully alive.

This ordinariness was what I liked and needed. It had been a perfect day.

3

London lies in a bowl-shaped valley sloping into the Thames – downhill from Clapham to the river and uphill again from the Embankment to the West End. London pedestrians and cyclists could feel the earth's contours beneath all these bricks. I sensed this on my last half-mile up the steepness of St James's Street on my way to the Lambourne Club, and I was imagining not that I was meeting Musprat, but that I was a member, going here each evening in the London darkness and finding it a refuge, reading *Punch* and *The Times* in an armchair in the reading room, sitting in front of the big fireplace in the lounge, standing with old men in rumpled suits.

The Lambourne Club was a bright place with tall windows and high ceilings, and it smelled of pipe tobacco and brass polish and the hot ashes in the fire baskets. It seemed to me the essence of London – a carpet-quiet place, slightly too warm, a blend of old folks' home and private school, the safest place in the world, if you were an older white male.

Joining the club was a lazy ambition, I knew that, and it didn't suit my impatient temperament – and what did I have in common with the members? But these difficulties interested and provoked me.

I mentioned to Musprat on the stairs when I saw some men in pinstripe suits that I felt out of place in the Lambourne, because I was an American.

'This club is full of Americans,' Musprat said. 'Solicitors and bankers mostly. The club wants their money. Them, for example.'

He indicated the men in the pinstripe suits. Was that the sort of person I wanted to turn into? American Anglophiles, predictable in their Burberrys and kidding themselves rigid, and going hee-haw in the club lounge with schooners of sherry?

My main objections were the strict dress code and the absence of women. How could anyone relax while wearing a suit and tie? How could any man find pleasure in a place that was so sternly masculine?

'Doesn't it bother you that there are no women here?'

We were at the bar, among the old men who looked like morticians and the toothy young men shouting at each other and the overdressed Americans.

Musprat looked around. He shrugged and made a sound in his nose. He said, 'How many women are there in your local – what's it called?'

'The Fish,' I said. 'Fishmonger's Arms. Not many.'

'Exactly,' he said. 'Irish, isn't it? All bog-trotters.'

We had gone there for a pint once when he had come over to borrow a book and he had looked around and said, 'I hate places like this.'

'I suppose the Lambourne's a bit like school in that way,' he said, and glanced around. 'Everything in London is a bit like school.'

I was heartened to hear him say it because I had already worked that out myself.

Making a face, he said, 'The food here at the Lambourne is school food. But that's not as bad as some places. Wilton's Restaurant? Posh old buffers eat there. It costs a fortune because of the food.'

'Nouvelle cuisine?'

He had a particularly aggressive laugh – the harsh triumphant laughter of a deeply insecure person. 'Nursery food,' he shrieked, showing his stained teeth.

We went into the Lambourne dining room. The idea in this club was that rather than eat alone the members ate at a common table – a long refectory table in the center of the room. In this way a shipping magnate might find himself seated next to a journalist, a diplomat next to a novelist, but the chances were that inevitably you would find yourself next to a barrister or a solicitor – so Musprat said – because there were so many of them in the Lambourne. Once it had been mainly writers, the likes of H. G. Wells and Arnold Bennett, Saki and Shaw, and its reputation had been literary and raffish. But now it was old gray men in old gray suits.

Musprat winced at the menu and held it loosely, distastefully, in his chewed fingers. The menu was a small single sheet of paper inserted in a leather holder.

'See what I mean?' he said. 'School food.'

'They didn't have smoked buckling at my school. What was it anyway?'

'Fish,' Musprat said, and smiled sourly at me in a one-upping way, and it struck me again that the English often made an effort to be such bad company – so contrary – and they often made a virtue of being peevish. Musprat certainly did. You could see them up and down the long table, frowning at their food – their school food – and cutting it and pressing lumps against the tines, loading the fork as though they were baiting a hook.

We ordered our food, and I began to hate being here.

Not only did Musprat seem older than me, he also seemed fixed and certain in his life. I had no idea what was going to happen to me. Musprat said that he knew what his whole life would be like. Already he had been married and divorced. It was an unhappy and bitter marriage but an amicable divorce and now he was quite friendly with his ex-wife, so he said. He disliked children.

Like many insecure people he was deeply and cynically opinionated, perhaps in an effort to give the impression that he was sure of himself. But his talk made me uneasy – the more certain he sounded the more I feared for him. He said he knew exactly what he wanted – the very narrow and predictable life that the English seemed to assume was the ideal. It seemed that it would be the English life without change or upheaval or, apparently, without passion. He could be tetchy and a scold – he was truthful and blunt in the way of an unhappy person who takes a little satisfaction in the hurt he inflicts on others. Because of all this, I sometimes reflected with sadness that he and I had no other friends.

He used soon-to-be obsolete and fogeyish words like 'pantechnicon' for moving van, and 'beaker' for mug. In the country, he said, he wore gaiters. *Gaiters?* He called the radio 'the wireless.' To annoy him one day I said, 'Do you call airplanes "flying machines"?' and he replied, 'No, I call them aeroplanes, which is what they are.'

We talked about his radio plays at dinner. He was writing one at the moment, about a gypsy who – piece by piece – moved an entire caravan, or mobile home, into his one-room apartment in Islington.

'I want to go on writing plays for the wireless,' Musprat said.

And as though to assure the failure of the effort at the outset, he often wrote plays in blank verse, and sometimes they rhymed.

'What about poetry?'

'Poetry-writing is shoveling shit. Radio plays reach a huge audience,' he said. 'I'm going to do that for the rest of my life. And I want to go on being in this club. I don't want to travel, I don't want to turn into a book reviewer. And I never want to go to America again. It's hideous there.'

'Sometimes I miss Boston,' I said. It was a timid confession. I missed it every day – its space and its familiar streets and smells. I missed the laughter, I missed the feel of American money which was like the feel of flesh. Reality for me was the past, and it was elsewhere. This – London – was like a role I had been assigned to play, and I was as yet still unsure of my lines.

Musprat said, 'I was in Boston for that color mag story two years ago. Boston isn't a city. Not a real city. It's about ten small towns clustered around that poxy harbour. And you find' – Musprat was cutting a very small muscle of meat, his mouth set rather severely as he sawed the gray sinew – 'that in fact Boston does not exist except as a rather spurious urban concept. I hated the food, the traffic's appalling, and you can't drive ten feet without propelling your car

145

straight into a pothole. The police carry these bloody great revolvers and they're always sort of reaching for them.'

It was as though he were describing Boston in a warning way for the benefit of someone who had never set foot in the place.

'I lived in Boston for twenty-two years,' I said, hoping to shut him up. He knew so little of the city it was futile to argue the merits of it. I had to be gentle. He was at his most vulnerable when he was generalizing like this, and his feelings were easily wounded even though he could be brutal with others.

'I preferred New York City,' he said.

'New York is never dark and never quiet,' I said. 'I can't sleep in that city.'

'London's worse in some ways,' he said. 'The air's foul from everyone breathing, shop assistants are rude, and the food's filthy.' He was still eating, chewing quickly with his stained and protruding teeth, like a rodent. 'I suppose that's why I like London.'

He was not a Londoner, though I would never have known. He had a neutral accent and a pompous and slightly cranky way of talking, always seeming to scold or correct.

'Money's not important here. Class matters. And class has nothing to do with money.'

I kept noticing that in the English – their love of being right or of setting you straight, the school-teacher sternness, because they had once been cringing students. In Musprat's case it was slightly worse, because he was from the provinces, somewhere in the Midlands, possibly Lichfield – he often made references to Dr Johnson. He needed to prove himself and yet he loathed himself for having to.

He had a keen awareness of class and with it a hatred of the class system. This caused him conflict and sometimes pain.

'People are always imitating their charlady. "The lie-dee wot does for me, comes on a weekly bie-sis, innit?"'

And when I laughed – his mimicry was a success – he was torn, having succeeded at the very thing he hated.

'Money's such a big thing in America. But no one has money here.'

He was signing the chit on the pad the waiter had brought. The waiter looked Malay but when I asked the old man next me he said they were all Filipinos.

The old man had a white mustache that was stained with nicotine, and he spoke in a roaring voice.

'Absolutely indestructible! Work for a pittance. Live on rice and fish heads. He shifted his gaze around the table, as though seeking more listeners. 'Their only fault is that they believe in an afterlife. Very superstitious. You wouldn't want to put your life in their hands, because they don't mind dying, you see. You want an atheist as your bat-man. But they get on willy-nilly. This isn't America – you don't need to take an examination to be admitted to Britain.'

The old man opposite, straining to hear, said, 'Quite. My nephew is taking his examinations. I have no idea what it's all about. When I was in school my father simply rang his old tutor and said I was ready, I went up to Trinity.'

'Maybe your nephew is in one of these comprehensive schools,' the other man said.

'Yes. I believe he is. Are they very expensive?'

As these old men continued to talk, the Filipino waiter went around the room and no one took any notice of him. It seemed to me that he could go anywhere and see anything. He was invisible.

As I watched the silent waiter, Musprat said, 'You see? That's why I like this club. Those old men.'

We were on our way to the coffee room. There were more old men among the aquatints of Indian ruins.

'She is a very handsome woman. She absolutely has her pick of men. They send her roses. Her husband knows about it, of course. Turns a blind eye. Very keen cricketer, you know.'

Another said, 'It was well known that the prince was having a little fling with her. Her husband was in the picture then. But, you know, people are always rather proud when their wives or daughters have a thing with a member of the royal family. In fact, people look up to them. It is rather an accomplishment.'

'No such luck for me,' Musprat said, and he began talking to the old man, as though he were one of them.

I had two thoughts. That this was like every overseas club I had ever been in – male, old-fangled, English, fussy and foolish – only cleaner. My second thought was more in the nature of a fear, that this life of the club and London and this talk were a sort of permanent condition – you joined and this was how your life went on, changelessly, passing on from the dining room to the bar to the library with a stop at the Gents, among these men, predictably, without surprises, until you died.

Musprat looked irritable and slightly drunk. He took a deep breath, looked briefly youthful, smiled at me, then began to cough, and coughing, became old once more.

'I really am glad you suggested this,' I said. Was I saying this because of my guilty feeling, which was the opposite of what I said? 'I remember the first time I came here, about a year ago. The winter night, when the snow –'

'Jesus, are you actually reminiscing?'

He was angry, disgusted, embarrassed. He drank some wine and made an ugly chewing face as he swallowed.

'Let's bag the snooker table before someone else does,' he said.

From the way he behaved, in this abrupt and sneering way, usually bristling, I guessed that he had been bullied at school. He was small and pale. He wore thick glasses. He chewed his fingers. He wrote poems.

In the snooker room a long bar of light hung over the table brightening the green felt and putting the rest of the room in shadow.

Musprat chalked our names on the slate that hung above the scoreboard of beads on wires that was like an abacus. He had lovely handwriting, regular and upright. School had made him, and then unmade him.

'You know who those old buffers are talking about?'

'That woman?'

'Yes. Your friend, Lady Max.'

'I don't even know her.'

And I thought: I have no friends, except you. I spent all my time writing. I had a wife and two children and they were the whole of my life, my society in London. I could not tell Musprat the truth, that he was my only friend, and this outing at the Lambourne twice a month was my only outing.

'I met her at that party,' I said. 'That's all.'

But I saw her clearly – her white forehead, her black hair drawn back, her bright eyes, her pretty mouth and thin fingers.

He had set the triangle of balls on the table. We were taking our separate shots with the cue balls to see who would break. Musprat strained and stroked and his cue ball came to rest an inch from the cushion.

So he went first, and pondered his break, and took his shot, a purist's poke. He nicked the edge of the cluster of balls, hardly disturbing the triangular arrangement.

'Your shot,' he said.

At this rate we would be playing for a week. There was a slow, tactical you-can't-see-me game of snooker that I hated, although it was said to be the real thing. And there was a speedier version, nearer the American game of pool that I was more used to, with bolder strokes, and more obvious moves, played more on the open table and less in the shadow of other balls.

I lined up the cue ball and hit the clustered balls hard, blasting them apart.

'How rash,' Musprat said. The balls were still caroming, and none were potted. 'How convenient.'

And he began potting balls. When he finally kissed one, snookering me, and I went to take my answering shot, I nudged the cue ball with the tip of the cue.

'It moved. You touched it. That's your shot.'

'It was an accident, Ian.'

'That's your shot,' he said firmly, in the stern, prissy voice he had learned at school. He chalked his cue. 'No exceptions. If we start making exceptions where will we be?'

He was ponderous as only a drunken man can be. He fought for every point and when I realized how badly he wanted to win I became bored by the whole business – the desperate fussing of his insistent competition – and wished I were home with my little family.

'Get in there,' he said – he was speaking to the brown ball. 'I've potted the pink but it's got to go back on the table.'

The idea was that as long as the player went on potting, his opponent flunkeyed for him, replacing the balls that were hit out of sequence. Flunkeying was another school role, for the younger, newer, duller boys.

We were about evenly matched, yet he won more often than I did, partly because I always let him have the disputed point and also because he was the more consistent player – not aggressive, but tenacious. No one held on like the English, and when they wanted something they knew no embarrassment. They were never more obvious or disregarding or single-minded than in this tenacity. No surrender, was Musprat's way, but winning gave him very little pleasure, it simply made him chattier.

'And it seems,' he said, continuing the line of talk that he had broken off earlier, 'that she's an admirer of yours. The Lady Max. She told Heavage. He told me.'

This was news – that she knew Heavage, who had a reputation as an obnoxious and persistent womanizer. *Poor Gillian*, people always said of his wife. He was niggardly, a trait I associated with most lechers. And I hated him for speaking French to me and treating me like a hack.

'What do you think of her?'

'I told you. A bruised peach,' Musprat said. It was his only summing-up.

'I thought she was witty.'

'That's the one thing she's not,' he said.

'So you don't like her?'

'What does "like" mean? I don't care one way or the other.' Musprat was still sinking balls. 'She always gets what she wants, though.'

'What's wrong with that?'

'She wants everything.'

He could not pot the green. He lined up his shot and sent the cue ball gently into it, and it came to rest between the pink and the blue.

'Snookered,' he muttered with satisfaction.

'Oh, I say,' an old man cried out from the shadows, and soon afterward I conceded the game.

Musprat was uncharacteristically jaunty afterward, and friendliness gave him an air of confidentiality. He wanted another drink, and then he wanted to sit by the fire, and then he wanted to talk.

He began to behave like an uncle. He said, 'How would you like me to put you up for membership? The drill is that I simply put you in the book and the other members scribble remarks next to your name.'

I did not know how to say no without offending him, so I equivocated, knowing that he would drop the idea when he was sober.

'You look like a wet weekend,' he said. 'Don't worry. I'll let you have a rematch.'

He did not know how sad I was. It was worse than he knew, and it depressed me. He had been my only friend. I had nowhere else to go.

4

'Doesn't she know you're married?' Alison asked me, the night of Lady Max's dinner party.

'I'm sure I told her,' I said, hedging. But had I? 'I only met her once.'

'I don't understand why she didn't invite me.'

The flames were gone from the grate, and there was heat from the mass of coals but little light. It was almost eight o'clock. I had sat with Alison while she had eaten – cold fowl and salad – and now she was drinking her customary cup of tea, sipping it neatly and looking comfortable in her big warm chair. She would read or watch television for an hour or so and then, growing sleepy, would crawl into bed.

Reflecting on this, I began to wish that I hadn't agreed to this late dinner with Lady Max. I was tired after a day of writing and I needed to rest, nestling against my wife in bed. These days I slept nine hours like that and in the morning, thinking of my novel, saw light breaking through the treetops of the jungle clearings.

I said, 'Would you have come with me if you'd been invited?'

'And sit in some stuffy house in the Boltons,' she said, suddenly defiant, 'listening to a lot of old bores droning on about poetry? No, thank you very much. I'd rather watch *Dallas*.'

Before I left the house I put my head into the boys' bedroom. The room was cool but the children seemed to radiate warmth – their glow was in the air – and this warmth from such a small bed I associated with their good hearts. They still smelled soapily of their baths, and I kissed their warm cheeks and whispered good night. What is it in darkness that makes us whisper?

They were in that mild twilight of fatigue that was like sinking in warm water as their breathing became shallower and they slipped softly from wakefulness into the depths of sleep.

'Why are you all dressed up, Dad?' Anton asked.

'I'm going to see a lady. Lady Max.'

'See a fine lady upon a white horse,' Will said, calling softly from his bed. 'Is she rich?'

151

'Probably. I don't know. Money's not important here. Class is the thing,' I said and was annoyed with myself when I realized I was quoting Musprat. 'You know, middle class, upper class.'

'What class are we?'

'None. We don't care about that.' I wanted to say, *I'm a spectator.* But I only half believed it. I wanted more.

The boys kissed me, and their tenderness reassured me that all was well between Alison and me.

When I left the room, I heard Anton whispering across the room to Will, 'I think we're middle class.'

Going out into the winter night took an effort of will like crossing a frontier, because I was re-entering London after a full day in the fastness of my tall house.

It was such a quiet and gentle city at night, with shadows on its face – it was a city that slept, a city with a bedtime. And in this area of south London the sky-line was old-fashioned chimney pots, slate roofs, and church spires. On these winter nights I had the illusion of being a part of it, an alien being swallowed by the city's shadows, and transformed.

I loved night-time London's sulfurous skies, and at Chelsea Reach the light shimmering in the river had the watery, dreamy quality of one of Whistler's *Nocturnes*. I was intensely conscious of where I was, and that was a reminder of another trait that Londoners possessed: we could find our way around in the dark.

All this from the upper deck of the bus, sitting at the front window, and with the sense that I was piloting a very old, low-flying plane.

Lady Max's house, a short walk from the bus stop, was one of those newly painted cream-colored Victorian façades, almost phosphorescent in the light of the street lamps, with tall bay windows and pale pillars at the top of an intimidating flight of stairs, in an empty corner of the square.

A small woman, with a pretty face and a nimble, simian way of walking, greeted me in a sing-song accent as she took my coat. Another Filipino.

Imposing from the outside, the house was moribund within, like a walk-in sarcophagus. It was the foyer's marble floor, it was the dust, it was the brittle flowers and dry plants and gloomy pictures in ornate frames; it was most of all the temperature and the smell of damp carpets – a chilly, sullen lifelessness, as though no one had eaten or slept here for a long time. Just as I thought of my own warm house on the other side of the river, I heard my name being called from a room beyond this foyer.

'Paul,' Lady Max cried out. She remained in her chair in a queenly way.

But she was so friendly and familiar I was encouraged, and she quickly introduced me to the people present who were arrayed around the room – Graham Heavage smiled and showed no sign that he had rebuffed me in my willingness to write a lead review. There was an elderly novelist named Dunton Marwood, and a couple called Lasch from South Africa, whose name I associated with anti-apartheid protests. There was a woman named Pippa who blinked repeatedly when I spoke; and the American poet, Walter Van Bellamy.

'My wife couldn't make it,' Bellamy explained to me, twirling his forefinger in a shock of his white hair.

He was famously crazy and very tall, and when he drew me over to the fire – too close to the flames, he was crowding me – he smiled his wild staring smile and said, 'You're from Boston, too.'

The fire burned but even so gave less heat than mine in Clapham. This one simply gasped in the chimney.

'I'm from Medford, actually.'

But Bellamy had a crazy man's deafness and distraction, and the glazed eyes of a man on medication.

'We Bostonians have to stick together.'

I was flattered until he squeezed my arm – too hard, it hurt, it conveyed desperation rather than friendliness. He then lost all interest in me and staggered towards the bookshelves and pinched out a volume of his own poems.

'Max was just telling us about you, so you arrived on cue, as it were.'

This was Marwood, the novelist. I knew his name from the *New Statesman* fiction cupboard; and there were always stacks of his books at Gaston's. He was married to a rich woman whom no one knew, and his reputation – though all my information was from Musprat, and it had the Musprat slant – was that he was an envious and conceited bore.

'Are you working on a novel at the moment?' I asked.

'Well done! I usually have to tell people that I'm a novelist. "You won't have heard of me," I say. "I write what is called quality fiction."'

'Marwood is the poor man's Henry James,' Heavage said. 'No popular fiction for him.'

'God forbid,' Marwood said. 'No, I've finished my novel. I'm going on a journey. Corsica – know it? Fascinating. Following Edward Lear's itinerary. No nonsense. An in-the-footsteps-of sort of thing.'

'Some journey!' Heavage said. 'Dodging holiday-makers and trippers, is more like it.'

'Graham is such a tease,' Marwood said. 'I say, your new novel sounds splendid.'

'*My new novel?*' I said. 'My new book is non-fiction. A travel book.'

'Not that. The one you're working on. Sounds smashing.'

Lady Max was smiling at me, hearing everything, seeing everything: the world was naked and had no secrets from her. But only then, seeing her regal smile, did I remember what I had told her.

'Stick to your own title,' Marwood said. 'Don't let Max put you off. She can be diabolical.'

So she had told them everything.

By then the Filipino serving woman had gone around with a tray and I had a drink in my hand.

Heavage stepped over to me. I braced myself to be addressed in French by him – how would I reply? But in an entirely friendly voice he said, 'Super review,' meaning last week's fiction round-up in which I had slashed four novels. 'Did you take anything away with you?'

'I thought we agreed to wait until some good ones came along.'

He was unruffled, he did not respond to that.

'Keen on Henry James?' he said. 'There's a new edition of his letters. Vol One just out. Supposed to be rather good, some fresh material. Might be fun, you and James, two expats.'

This was a different-sounding Graham Heavage, and he seemed to be offering me a lead piece, the sort of book that V. S. Pritchett usually reviewed. Heavage's manner threw me; tonight at Lady Max's, away from his desk, he looked seedy and powerless. This man, who was naturally and smilingly rude, who demanded sex from his assistants on the paper – who, just down from Oxford, got gladly on to all fours for him, seeing this as their way to advancement in literary London; this ugly, domineering man seemed a little silly and self-conscious trying to be friendly to me.

'Might give you a chance to talk about that very thing,' he said. 'Expatriation.'

Yes, he was offering me Henry James, a lead piece.

'I could let you have fifteen hundred words,' he said. 'The book doesn't come out for ages. You could take your time.'

I said – a little too eagerly – 'I'd love to do it. Do you know that James was apparently hit in the groin by the whiplash of a fire-hose when he was about eighteen.'

'No, but goodness knows, you might want to animadvert on the implication of this unsolicited kick in the goolies,' Heavage said, without smiling, though Marwood sniggered and Bellamy laughed out loud.

I was certain that it was because he had met me here at Lady Max's that he had offered me the lead review and that his laborious comedy was a form of friendliness. It was hard for an Englishman of his distinctly pitiless sort to attempt generosity without being patronizing, but I did not mind – at least he wasn't speaking French to me in front of all these people.

Lady Max kept her distance, though each time I looked over at her she seemed to be staring at me. Sitting and smoking, she seemed completely in charge, and she was porcelain pretty, her skin so pale in the lovely way it often was with women in this sunless country.

I was disconcerted by her not speaking to me, and by her incongruity – she was so bright, so delicate in this big shadowy house – and I was disturbed by the fact that I could not smell food cooking. I slipped into the hall to look for the toilet – the Filipino woman, correctly guessing what I was looking for, pointed to the door when she saw me hesitating. It was more black shadows, and clammy walls and cold tiles, and again I wished I had stayed home. A satirical print by Rowlandson hung above the basin.

When I returned to the drawing room, the guests were putting their coats on.

'We're going to dinner,' Lady Max said. 'It's right down the road.'

We trooped out to Brompton Road, to a French restaurant called

La Tour Eiffel, and we were shown to the sort of secluded wood-paneled private room that I associated with trysting couples or rowdy men. Over the windows hung dusty velvet curtains with fat gold tassels. After we handed over our coats, Lady Max seated us. I was confused, and I wondered if the others were too. Mrs Lasch's head was down and she was whispering urgently to her husband. The woman named Pippa was on my right, Marwood on my left.

'Where is Walter Van Bellamy?' Lady Max said.

He had gone – vanished on the way – but Lady Max laughed and said that it was just like him. 'He's crackers, you know. The real thing.'

A bored-looking French waiter in a much-too-tight shirt, with damp hair and a hot face, entered the little room and gave us menus and then recited the day's specials and the no-longer-available dishes, speaking in a parody French accent.

Pippa said, 'Do you mind? My menu is sticky. I can't stand that,' and made a face and handed it to the waiter, who looked offended.

'Shall we have some wine?' Lady Max was addressing the waiter. 'The house wine comes in a filthy carafe and tastes like nail varnish. Two bottles of Meursault, make it three, and you can bring them now.'

'Drinking Meursault always makes me think I am entering into the spirit of Camus's *L'Etranger*,' Heavage said to me.

But Lady Max was still directing the waiter. She had become a brisk and attentive hostess, from her vantage point at the head of the table. There was a tension of authority in the way she sat, in her lifted chin, in the angle of her body – she was twitching, alert, full of suggestions.

After the wine was poured, the waiter took up his pad, saying, 'And in addition, zere are fresh lobstairs zis ivneen. Zay are not on ze meenue.'

'Not real lobsters,' Lady Max said, shivering as though insulted by the word. 'They're just these pathetic little discolored crayfish from Scotland.'

The waiter simply clicked his ballpoint.

'But the potted shrimps are super.'

We all ordered potted shrimps.

'And the jugged hare,' Lady Max said, and muttered the name in French while licking her lips.

'*Civet de lièvre*,' Heavage said in his pedantic accent.

Hearing him, I thought: the English are a nation of pedants, always correcting you, and they hate themselves for being that way, because being in the right is such a dull pleasure.

Lady Max smiled at Heavage – a smile of disapproval – and said, 'They do it with chestnuts here.'

Most of us ordered that too, except Pippa, who said she was a vegetarian. Hearing her announce it, Marwood growled impatiently. Pippa conferred nervously with the waiter and finally settled on the ratatouille.

'And I will bring a selection of vegetables.'

'If you must,' Lady Max said. She lit a cigarette and dismissed him, exhaling and flinging smoke at him with her fingers, in a witchlike gesture. 'They do fuss so, and they don't mean a word of it.'

We chatted among ourselves until Pippa called out to Lady Max, 'Do you often have supper here?'

'What is supper? Is it something you eat?' Lady Max said.

Pippa made a terse explanation of the word.

'Surely this is dinner?' Lady Max said.

'Working-class people have supper,' Marwood said.

'"Working-class" is a euphemism I just adore,' Lady Max said.

The waiter began serving the potted shrimps – a small ceramic dish of pink bubbly paste, with a stack of toast.

As we spread it on the toast, Lady Max, still smoking, said, 'I do hate being served promptly. It's like rudeness, and I always think there's something wrong with the food.'

'I come to that conclusion when my menu's sticky,' Pippa said.

'Tea is a meal for them. Dinner is lunch,' Marwood said. 'I know this through my staff. They have "afters."'

'They are extraordinary,' Lady Max said. 'I always think inventing these ridiculous names for meals is a way of saving money on food.'

'And,' Heavage added in an announcing way, 'they go to the toilet.'

He was at the teasing and silly stage of drunkenness – the teasing that turned cruel and then sadistic. 'That is, working-class people.'

Lady Max smiled disgustedly. She said, 'I cannot stand that word. Does anyone actually say it?'

We laughed, everyone except Pippa, to please the hostess, as though none of us actually used the word.

'"Toilets" is an anagram of T. S. Eliot,' Mr Lasch said, but no one heard him, because Marwood was indignant again.

'And "cheers" is another one I hate,' he said.

Hearing him, or rather mishearing him, Heavage said, 'Cheers,' and emptied his glass.

Looking at me, Lady Max said, 'I love the expression "white trash." Americans are so graphic. Do you suppose we could introduce it here?'

'I'm sorry but I find this whole conversation quite objectionable,' Pippa said.

Marwood leaned in front of me and put his face against Pippa's and said, 'Miss Lower-Middle-Class-And-She-Knows-It is trying to be the sincere proletarian again.'

'Of course, with the help of your staff, you're an authority on the subtle nuances of class,' Pippa said, blinking but standing her ground.

'Yes, and rather more than I'm given credit for by second-rate book reviewers,' Marwood said, making it obvious that at some point Pippa had given one of his novels an unfavorable review.

'Someone, I think it was a shop-girl, said, "You're welcome" to me the other day,' Lady Max said, ending the stand-off between Marwood and Pippa.

'What a ridiculous American expression,' Heavage said.

'Have a nice day,' Mr Lasch said to his wife, who replied, 'Sorry, I have other plans.'

But no one took any notice of them, because Lady Max was saying, "You're welcome" is not ridiculous at all. It's an effective response. Say "thank you" in England and the other person simply mutters and chews his lips.'

'I suppose it's no worse than *prego*,' Heavage said. 'It's less objectionable than *bitte*. It's rather like *pozhal'st*.'

'You've lost us,' Mr Lasch said.

'One of those useful and happily ambiguous expressions like "I'd like to see more of you,"' Lady Max said, and she smiled at me.

Then the jugged hare was served. It came in an earthenware crock submerged with carrots and chestnuts in a brown stew. The waiter hurried back and forth, sighing, laying out the dishes of vegetables, and when he waited on me, his whole body radiated sweaty heat and I could hear him breathing impatiently.

'Bring more wine,' Lady Max said.

'Thank you,' the waiter said.

'You're welcome,' Lady Max said. 'You see?'

We were still on language. We discussed the correct pronunciation of certain English names, such as Marylebone and Theobalds and Cholmondley. This, I guessed, was all for my benefit.

Mr Lasch spelled the word Featherstonehaugh and said, 'Fanshaw.'

Marwood smiled and said, 'I've got one. It looks like "Woolfardisworthy."'

'Woolsey,' Pippa said, and turned her cold eyes on him.

'My grandfather pronounced the word "leisure" the American way,' Lady Max said, with another glance at me. 'Leezhah.'

In a solicitous, almost servile way Marwood asked, 'How is your daughter, Allegra?'

'Flourishing,' Lady Max said. 'That foolish person, Mr Pieplate – well, that's what I call him – is still chasing her. He took her to an embassy party and she deliberately wore a transparent lace – absolutely in the noddy underneath. It scandalized the Muslims there and it drove him wild. He doesn't even know she's sixteen years old. What an ass he is.'

'She might fall for him,' Marwood said.

'Lucky old Pieplate, if she did. But it won't happen. Allegra's much too heartless. They all are. That's why I don't worry about her. It's her loss. And I know how she feels. At her age I was being squired around by Boothby.'

'Wasn't he a bit fruity?' Heavage asked.

'He was but not exclusively. Anyway I fended him off.'

She said orf, as she had said lorse.

Her mention of Lord Boothby turned the conversation to the Kray brothers, a pair of London murderers he had befriended, and a lot of Sixties gossip about the Profumo affair. And again I felt this was for my benefit, as though the dinner was a little seminar on English life that Lady Max had arranged for me.

Seeing a new waiter approach, Lady Max said, 'Another waiter, another course. And this one has the implacable look of pudding on his face.'

The waiter showed no sign that he had heard this. He said, 'Shall I bring the trolley?'

'It will just be stale gateau and puddings and sticky buns on wheels.' She was not facing the waiter when she added, 'Why don't you just *flambé* some crepes for us. There's a good chap.'

For the next twenty minutes the waiter labored at his portable grille, first making the crepes – seven of them – and then folding them in a silver dish. He methodically made the sauce, scorching sugar cubes with melted butter in a frying pan and then sousing the crepes with this sauce. He poured gouts of Grand Marnier on to them after that, and set them on fire. He then rearranged them on individual plates, still spooning sauce, and served them.

This elaborate procedure killed conversation, and when we started eating the crepes, and Pippa made a remark about them – 'Delicious. This is only the second time in my life . . .' – Lady Max cut her off, as though it was bad manners to comment on the food.

'Queen Mum's out of the hospital today, bless her,' Lady Max said.

'The Royal Barge,' Heavage said, frowning drunkenly.

'I know several of her intimates,' Lady Max said. 'They call her "Cake," you know, behind her back, and I do think it suits her. Her staff are exclusively poufs. One night she got on the phone to them – they were in the kitchen. She said, "I don't know about you queens down there but this queen wants a drink!"'

It was well after midnight – you knew it from the gloomy resentment on the waiters' faces as they ostentatiously stood round after liqueurs and coffee. They had missed the last tube trains. There was only the chance of an irregular night bus from now on.

The bill, folded in half, had been resting on the saucer at Lady Max's elbow since coffee. She had taken no notice of it.

At last, exhaling smoke on it, she unfolded it by poking it open with her fingers and said, 'I'm terrible at maths. What is ninety-six divided by seven?'

Ninety-six pounds was the amount of my monthly mortgage payment and it seemed incredible to me that we had gobbled up a whole mortgage payment. And, worse, that I was being asked to pay my share. I remembered Lady Max saying, '*Bring more wine.*'

'Is service included?' Marwood asked.

'Call it fourteen each,' Heavage said.

The Lasches had gone pale, their faces displaying the agony I felt.

'And a quid each for the tip.' Heavage dropped the bill.

'Fifteen even.' Marwood began poking through bank notes in a leather pouch.

Fifteen pounds. It was what I was paid for a book review. Heavage knew that but did not seem to care. I pretended to look through my wallet, but I knew when I heard the figure that I did not have it, nor any sum near it, and neither did Pippa, and this inspired in me a sort of kinship with her. She wrote Lady Max a check, and so did Mr Lasch. I fingered a crisp five-pound note. I had some coins but needed them for the bus.

'I'll have to owe you the rest,' I said.

'I'll collect it one way or another,' Lady Max said.

The bus only went as far as the depot at the south end of Battersea Bridge, and so without enough money for another bus fare I walked the rest of the way home in a drizzling mist, kicking the paving stones.

5

The only certainty in my London life was my writing. I felt this was a way for me to make a place for myself in the city. Although the novel I was writing was a jungle book it was penetrated with London. It was my London work. And I wondered whether the opposite might be true – if I wrote a London story in New Guinea would the book seem jungly and overbright?

I needed to sit down alone and write the next day. Alison had asked without much interest how the evening had gone and I said fine.

'Rich food, small talk, gossip and indigestion. I didn't even get drunk.'

'I'm glad I stayed at home,' she said.

I somewhat envied her her indifference. It was the reason she could be so serene. But I was obnoxiously curious about everything and had to pretend not to be, because it was so unEnglish to be nosy, and to ask probing questions.

I said almost nothing else to her about the strange meal, Lady

Max's Dutch treat – the way she had invited us, ordered all the food and wine, and then charged us. I concealed my embarrassment, because I could not tell her the whole truth. How could I tell Alison these misleading details until I knew everything myself? This was a story without an ending, without even a middle. I felt sure there would be more. There would be consequences.

I sat down and continued my novel, as I did every day. I wrote a paragraph that day and a few pages the next. If I wrote nothing in the morning, I forced myself to write something after lunch. And on the days when I wrote well, I often turned aside and did a review – I had time for it because I had done my own work first. That week, after I made headway with my book, I read the first volume of *The Letters of Henry James* and made notes for what I hoped would be a lead review.

When I was stumped in my writing, I wandered around the damp yard behind my house, peering at plants. I tore old birds' nests apart to see how they had been made, I watched spiders feeding, and ants hurrying and snails dragging themselves in their own spittle across the bricks. I put these London creatures into my Central American jungle. I observed a trickle of water and, for my fiction, turned it into a river, with mud-slides and ox-bows.

Sometimes in the black late afternoon, before the pubs opened, I walked – thinking with my feet. Walking the streets, I murmured to myself, as I was doing it. There were gaps in the day that baffled and intimidated me.

Musprat called, but I put him off. I did not want to be drawn into his life – the disorderly flat, the hasty meals, his intrusive borrowing and bitching, his writer's block, and wasted evenings at the Lambourne Club.

I wrote my book. I lived in my house. I loved my family. I had no other life in London, and indeed had not realized there was another life to be had, until Lady Max called again.

'Paul, is that you, dear boy?'

It was affectation, not fooling, and her voice was unmistakable, dark brown with cigarette smoke. I was alarmed, fearing another of her meals.

But no, she was calling to collect what I owed her. She used those very words. She said I had to go with her to the William Blake exhibition at the Tate Gallery.

'I'll meet you there inside the foyer in about an hour,' she said.

That was my ten-pound repayment to her – my agreement to go. But I had done my work for the day. I did not feel I was being deceitful to Alison, though it was unfair to my sons – I knew that I would not be at the house when they returned home from school. I would miss Anton making tea and Will asking 'What page are you on, Dad?' For that I resented Lady Max's sudden presumption and her insistent *Be there*.

She was late – Londoners who regarded themselves as powerful were seldom punctual, though they always expected you to be. She arrived in a taxi and she looked rather small, mounting the wet black stairs alone. But this was a passing illusion. I had always seen her in the company of other people, and when I was next to her I felt very plain and out of step, an American again.

Lady Max had hardly greeted me. She said, 'I love being in a museum on a rainy afternoon.'

It was not rain but a low cloud, the mist and drizzle of a London winter that made the dark city even blacker.

'There's only one better place to be,' she said.

We were passing a sensual Rodin sculpture, all muscles and bumps, a couple entwined like a big bronze walnut.

'Between the sheets,' she said, 'and preferably not alone.'

She had a knack for uttering statements to which there was no reply. It was like a verbal form of snooker in which I was left holding the cue and not being able to use it.

We passed a set of big, flat Motherwells, all black shapes like moth-eaten shadows, a slashed and assertively striped Rauschenberg, a Hockney interior that sloped in three directions, a soft sculpture like a big toy, a rusty bike hung on wires, and a triptych the size of three billboards surfaced entirely with broken crockery.

The Blakes were behind this laborious frivolity, in a darkened exhibition room in low lighted showcases. Walking just behind Lady Max in the darkness I felt her warmth, and her perfume stung my eyes with sweetness. Her white face, her full lips, her large eyes were reflected in the glass, layered with scenes from *The Marriage of Heaven and Hell*.

'Ruskin called him a primitive,' Lady Max said.

'So unfair. He had great technique, subtle color, and a kind of visionary quality. Look at that composition of flesh and spirit.'

'Everyone says that about Blake.' She had not even paused or turned.

But this was a standard London put-down, the accusation that you were being hopelessly unoriginal. *Everyone says that*. It sounded cruel, but it was just another move in a chess game. In my earlier years in London I would have hated her for saying it. Now I saw it as glibly defensive – a weak kind of teasing – and she would mock me if I reacted. The London response was not to complain but to do it back and do it better.

'Everyone says that, because it's so obvious and because it's true,' I said. 'Ruskin was the weirdo, if you ask me. Not Blake. Ruskin was shocked by his wife's pubic hair. He thought she was the only woman in the world who had it, like a physical abnormality.'

'There is so much more to Ruskin than that,' Lady Max said.

'But the rest isn't as interesting,' I said.

She liked that. 'I rather like the nympholepsy. He adored little girls.'

'Kiddie porn,' I said.

'You sound so shocked. And yet Ruskin was an incredible romantic.' She was staring down at the Blakes. 'Speaking of pubic hair. Some people shave it into peculiar designs.'

'And some people twine marigolds into it,' I said, 'according to D. H. Lawrence.'

'That's such a silly book,' Lady Max said. 'It's completely unbelievable. It's all Lawrence's lurid fantasies about the English class system – virile gamekeeper, sex-mad aristocrat, emasculated lord. And apart from anything else it gives an utterly inaccurate picture of oral sex technique.'

She was bent over a lighted case of Blake etchings, her face shining at God the Father holding a set of gold compasses among jubilant angels and puffy clouds.

'She could hardly have sucked him off playing with his old job as though it was a cocktail sausage.'

She said *orf* again, slightly dignifying the shocking expression. A shadowy man nearby grunted with unease and disapproval.

Though we were still in the darkened room and I could not see Lady Max's face, I had the impression she was smiling.

'The sexual virtuosity in your novels is much more impressive than Lawrence's.'

This was an advance on *You're much better than Hugh Walpole*.

'Sexual description is the great test of literary ability, I always think.'

'It's a problem, sex on the page. You have to choose the lingo of the clinic, the gutter, or the moralist. I use all three.'

She was not listening. She said, 'The way you handle sodomy.'

My mouth had gone dry.

'You have marvelous penetration,' she said.

Snookered.

'William Blake got married in a church near here,' she said. 'Want to see it?'

She took charge and we were soon outside, in the wet air, walking along the embankment next to the whitish, depthless water, which seemed turbulent today.

'There was once a prison here,' she said, at the river's edge. 'Mill-bank. James described it in *The Princess Casamassima*.'

I had just reviewed a Henry James book and did not know that.

'Notice how the river seems to be flowing upstream?' she said.

It was true – a burst cushion, a broken branch and bits of plastic foam were floating towards Vauxhall Bridge.

'That's because it *is* floating upstream,' she said. 'It's all tidal as far as Richmond, you know. People in London are forever staring at the river, but they never see its real character, that its current changes direction four times a day.'

As she spoke she raised a gloved hand.

'I can't walk any farther in these shoes.'

These were the ones Musprat called her fuck-me shoes.

Her hailing a cab made me feel useless. And after the privacy, the intimacy of the taxi – the driver isolated, her hand resting on my thigh – there was something unexpected and punitive in the way she stepped out after the short ride and walked on, leaving me to pay the fare. In my confusion I gave the driver an absurdly large tip – he made a mocking noise at me to indicate that he was not impressed.

The church, St Mary's Battersea, was sited directly on the south bank of the river, next to a flour mill and a public house, the Old Swan – the houseboats and brick façades of Chelsea just across the water. The church was in a perfect place, surrounded by light and water, with a Thames sailing barge moored just beside it. Just upriver, above the black railway bridge, the sun was breaking from between some smoky clouds.

'Ken Tynan showed me this church,' she said. 'It's Georgian. Such a beauty.'

'Tynan the theater critic?' I asked, unlatching the large church door for her and holding it open.

'And fetishist,' she said, entering the church.

We passed though the crypt under a low wood-paneled choir loft to a side aisle glowing with patches of color from the light of the stained glass windows. I picked up a leaflet from a side table and saw that Blake had indeed been married here, that Turner had visited, and more.

'Benedict Arnold is buried here, I see.'

'Arnold, the brave hero.'

'Arnold the wicked spy.'

'Don't be so predictable.'

I approached the pretty altar and pulpit, thinking how orderly they were, and that though somewhat unadorned they were not severe, they had a purity of design, a spareness that had spirit and strength – thinking this, while Lady Max began talking again and looking away.

'The rest of the time, Tynan was gadding about in women's clothes,' she said. 'He had mirrors on the ceiling of his bedroom. He said to me once, "Have you ever tried soft flage?" I suppose he meant gentle spankings. He had well-thumbed copies of *Rubber News*. This is authentic Georgian, you know.'

She was working her way along the smooth carved pews to the altar rail.

'Is he dead, Tynan?'

'Oh, no. He's very ill, but that doesn't stop him,' Lady Max said. 'These days he dabbles in urolagnia with eleven-year-old girls. What do you call it? Golden showers – something like that? I adore these exquisite finials. What's wrong?'

I shook my head because what was there to say?

'I'm telling you things you need to know.'

'About sex?'

'About London,' she said. 'The love and knowledge of London is in all the great English novels. You're funny. You don't know how good you are, or how great you can be. Now I must go.'

We left the church and walked along Vicarage Crescent to find a taxi.

'Wilson lived there,' she said in front of a two-story house made of gray brick. 'A vastly underrated painter and great naturalist. He died at the South Pole with Scott.'

Just before she got into the taxi, she said, 'I have my accountant tomorrow, so we'll have to meet Thursday – I'll ring you.'

She did not touch me, the English seldom touched, and that left me feeling even more flustered, in the cloud of her taxi's foul exhaust.

When Thursday came, I agreed to meet her in Mortlake that afternoon. As a consequence I had a productive morning writing my novel, and, stirred by her talk, I looked forward to seeing her.

The Mortlake excursion was to another church, a Catholic one – and in the high-walled churchyard, Sir Richard Burton's tomb, a marble monument in the shape of an Arabian tent.

'This grave has never appeared in any novel of London,' she said. 'I'm giving it to you.'

I read the plaque and then began to tell Lady Max how Burton had explored unknown parts of Utah, when she interrupted.

'Because of the polygamy among Mormons there,' she said. 'Burton was scx mad but hc combined it with scholarship and a love of languages. That's why he translated the *Kama Sutra*, and he was fascinated by fetishes.'

There in the quiet churchyard of St Mary Magdalene, she spoke about some episodes she'd had with men she had known as a girl – older men in every case – and how they had involved some sort of whipping, 'and not soft flage, I can tell you.' The men had been canted over chairs while she had slashed at their buttocks, cutting them with a dog whip.

Then she giggled and pushed a branch aside and said, 'It's all school nonsense. Englishmen never get over it.'

'What about English women?'

'We're all sorts, but the most effective kind are matrons – like our prime minister. Bossy and reliable, with big hospitable bosoms.'

She put her hands on her hips and faced me, but I kept my distance.

That day we finished up at Richmond Park, looking at deer. The following day we met at the London Library, which was a private members-only club-like place – Musprat was always mentioning it. Lady Max insisted that I become a member, there and then, and I did, writing a check for the thirty-pound annual membership fee and making a mental note that I might have to transfer funds so as not to be overdrawn.

After a weekend – Saturday shopping, Sunday outing to Box Hill – I met Lady Max at Blackfriars and she took me around some rotting Dickensian warehouses at Shad Thames.

'All of these wonderful old buildings will be renovated and made into hideous little flats for awful people one day.'

That week she took me to Strawberry Hill, to Hogarth's House in Chiswick, to World's End, to the room Van Gogh had rented in Brixton; to the Sir John Soane Museum. I had crossed Lincoln's Inn Fields thirty times and had never been aware of this lovely house that had been converted into a museum of exotic treasures.

I would be looking at a gable, or some fretwork, or a picture, while she monologued in her off-hand way about something totally unconnected, usually sexual.

'I thought I had seen everything,' I would say.

'Yes, Sir John actually collected these artifacts himself.'

'I mean, about what you just said about – what's the word?'

'Oh that. *Frottage*. It's just French for rubbing. Very subtle. Not very popular. Takes ages. Who has the time, my dear?' And she turned to an inked sheet of petroglyphs. 'I much prefer that rubbing.'

At Turpentine Lane in Victoria she pointed out the fact that the houses had no front doors, and in what perhaps seemed to her a logical progression – but surely a non sequitur? – added, 'And I never wear knickers.'

She deconstructed for me – the word was just becoming fashionable among reviewers that year – the Albert Memorial and said, 'You should put this thing into a story some time,' and went on to tell me how, after the death of Albert, Queen Victoria developed a passion for her Scottish footman, John Brown.

'But why shouldn't she? Life is short, and passionate people should have what they want. It makes the world go round, and no one is hurt.'

I felt that was true, but she said it with no passion at all.

That day, walking to Kensington Gore from the Albert Memorial she said, 'I don't live far from here. You could see me home.'

She took me by a circuitous route, to show me where Stephen Crane had lived off Gloucester Road.

'His common-law wife had been a prostitute, but you know that,' she said.

I said yes, but the true answer was no.

'She owned a brothel called the Hotel de Dream in Jacksonville, Florida,' Lady Max said. 'It's perfect, isn't it? But you're much better than Crane.'

She walked briskly – in different shoes – and wore a long black coat and a velvet hat, and she kept slightly ahead of me. Then her white house loomed, looking less white than when I had first seen it, and there were patches of yellow water stains near some decayed gutters and broken-down spouts.

At the front gate she said, 'Won't you come in?'

It was a winter afternoon, blackening into early dusk.

'I should be moving along. I have to be home by six.'

She did not hear my excuses. She batted at some trailing leafless wires of clematis and said, 'This has all got to be cut back.'

I was still hanging back. She lit a cigarette.

'See me to the door,' she said. 'Don't worry. I'm not going to eat you.'

Fixed to the door was a big brass knocker, very tarnished, of a turtle with a tiny head. You banged its shell.

'I'm not worried,' I said. It was impossible not to sound worried when uttering this sentence.

'I have the feeling there is something you want – in your life, in your writing,' she said.

She released the cigarette smoke from her mouth, but with so little force that blue trails of it encircled her head.

'What is it?'

I was restless and a bit fearful standing with her in this vast creamy portico of blistered paint. She had exhausted me with her talk, though she was still bright, as though she had drawn off all my energy. I was looking into the little square at the Boltons. I seriously wondered whether there was anything I wanted. My life seemed whole and orderly; there was no emptiness anywhere in it, and so little yearning.

'I've always gotten everything I've wanted.'

'That makes two of us,' Lady Max said.

I smiled. What more was there to say?

'That is what I'm asking you,' she said. 'What is it you want now?'

'Very little,' I said, surprised that I said it.

'Then it must be something crucial,' Lady Max said.

'I wish my writing was more visible. I work hard doing reviews and they're buried in the back of the paper. My books are reviewed in these round-ups, three or four at a time. I'd like a *solus* review. I'm very happy, really. But I'm indoors all the time. That's why I like these outings of ours, I suppose. I don't have any friends.'

She said, 'That's the proof you're a real writer. How could you write so much or so well and still maintain your friendships?'

It was what I had often said to rationalize my empty afternoons. I liked Lady Max better for defending me this way.

'But you consider me your friend?'

'Sure.'

'Then you have plenty of well-wishers,' she said, 'and you will have everything you want.'

What could I say to this? I stammered and tried to begin, but she cut me off.

'It's time for you to go home,' she said, as though making the decision for me.

I kissed her cheek.

'I get a kiss,' she said, stating it to the darkness behind me.

But I couldn't tell whether this was gratitude or mockery, and I realized even then that I did not know her.

6

Sometimes it is only when you turn your back on it that the world gives you what you want.

I woke up angry and in a very short time I came to hate Lady Max's promises. I had been content until she made them. Then I disliked myself for hoping. Was it that she had made me want something that I felt was unattainable and did not really deserve? No, it was just a matter of *Don't ask*. I detested the suspense. What you want should be your secret, not spoken aloud. Revealing it had made me feel lonely.

Trying hard not to think about it, I avoided seeing Lady Max. That made life easier. She called three times, and she was sharp and insistent, and I was just dumb and unwilling. It was not only a question of my pride. I had work to do. I turned my back on Lady Max and London. This woman and the world seemed like much the same thing.

I wrote all day at my desk, until the boys returned home. I bought the *Standard* when the Fishmonger's Arms opened. I sat and drank and read, and after a pint or two I went home and made dinner for Alison and the boys. There were whole days when no one spoke to me – days of great serenity and isolation, and I wondered whether I felt this was because I had become a Londoner or that I was a true alien.

But one evening the barman in the Fish said, 'Terrible about Jerry,' assuming that I knew.

*

He had not known me, but I knew Jerry Scully. I went to Jerry's funeral out of curiosity, because I had never seen a cremation in London. And also I wanted to test my anonymity. My going to this service on a weekday morning in London was a form of open espionage.

I had not liked him much. He sat under the dartboard that no one used and often grunted at the television. He was a carpenter, a 'chippy,' he called himself, a Derry Catholic who could whip himself into a fury in seconds merely by someone's mention of British troops, or by the sight of a British soldier on the six o'clock news. Watching Jerry, or listening to his talk, I understood the ambushes, the girls who were tarred and feathered for dating British soldiers, the heartless bombings, the fathers shot in front of their children – Jerry approved, Jerry was violent. Now and then I would hear an English person say, '*What sort of monster put these bombs in places where they'll kill innocent people?*' and I smiled because I knew. It was Jerry.

I happened to be sitting near him once when Prince Charles appeared on the screen. Jerry began to spit. 'Fucking bastard,' he said, with real feeling, as though he had been wounded. I often overheard him, and most of his talk was blaming. In Jerry's eyes, Jerry was Ireland.

But, really, Jerry Scully was a Londoner. He was paid in cash for his carpentry, he also drew the dole, he lived alone, his nose dripped, he was nearsighted and wore old wire-rimmed National Health specs, and when he was not drunk he was tremulous and uncertain, his eyes goggling in thick lenses.

He shouted when he was drunk and lately he had complained of a sore throat. He was someone for whom drink was a remedy as well as a sickness. Drink made him ill, and then it made him well. He drank more and his sore throat developed a painful lump that no amount of drinking could ease. He found swallowing difficult, though he still shouted hoarsely at the television set in the Fish. The doctor gave him tablets for his throat, and when these had no effect Jerry saw another doctor who diagnosed throat cancer, and at last a specialist who told him there was nothing that could be done. He stopped going to the Fish. It seemed a very short time later that the barman said, 'Terrible about Jerry.'

According to his wishes, he was cremated at the cemetery in Earlsfield, on the number 19 bus route, and all the stalwarts from the pub showed up, looking pale and shaky in the thin February light. Some of them looked downright ruined, as though they too were suffering a fatal illness. They had that fearful and unsteady – almost senile – look of dry drunks in the daytime, before the public houses opened, and they looked lost here on Trinity Road, so far from the Fish.

There were wreaths of flowers on the steps of the red-brick crematorium – bouquets wrapped in cellophane, and flower baskets, all with messages to Jerry. One was from Mick, the landlord of the Fish. The strangest flower arrangement was a tankard of beer, two feet high, marigolds representing lager, daisies as froth. The men smiled at it, but not because it was clever. One said, 'Jerry wouldn't touch that.' Jerry drank Guinness.

Filing into the chapel, I heard a wheezing man in front of me say, 'These days I get home pissed and want kinky but me missus won't play.'

A small organ was gasping a ponderous hymn. We were handed booklets indicating the details of the crematorium service, and a short sermon was given by a man who, in this glorified furnace, was more a stoker than a priest. He spoke of the immortality of Jerry's soul and the frailty of the human flesh – the brevity of our time on earth, and our vanity in thinking that earthly successes mattered. Hearing this, I had a sense of Jerry's being precious and indestructible, and that he had carried the secret of his soul around with him all these years. We prayed for Jerry and ourselves, and afterwards Mick opened the Fish early so that we could have a drink. The drinks were free, so opening the pub at ten-thirty was legal.

Lying on the bar of the Fish that day was the early edition of the *Evening Standard*, the one that all the gamblers bought for the horse races, and in the gossip column, 'Londoner's Diary', was a photograph of my face and a short paragraph with the headline *American Author Content to Live in London*, as though it were news.

It was a comment on a quotation from my book review of the Henry James letters – though I had no idea that it had been published. I had said in an aside that I regarded London as 'the most habitable big city in the world,' and that I lived here was proof that I meant it. The diary item mentioned that I was not one of those Anglophile American professors in stiff, matching Burberrys who spent the summer swanking in Belgravia. No, I was a hard-working refugee writing my head off in Clapham. The photograph, printed small and smudgily, flattered me.

I read this three times while the others (who did not know me and would not pay any attention to this section of the *Standard*) reminisced about Jerry. I could not say why I felt there was a close connection between this gratuitous little paragraph about me, and dead Jerry Scully – perhaps it had been the preacher's speaking about the vanity of earthly success. I was aware of being absurdly pleased.

And there was more. Reading the diary item I was reminded that I had not seen the review I had written. I went next door to Patel's and bought the *New Statesman*. My name was printed large on the cover of the magazine, as large as the prime minister's (the subject of another article), and my piece was the lead for the week, the most prominent book review I had written.

I often had the feeling that only two people cared about any book review – only two people read it – the reviewer and the reviewed: the person who wrote the piece, and the person who wrote the book. It was public correspondence, a letter from one to the other that no one else read. Sometimes – certainly in London – there was a reply, when the reviewed turned reviewer, answering back. But this was Henry James: did anyone else care?

From time to time Musprat called to say he had seen a piece of mine, but he would use the occasion to tell me he had writer's block. No one else commented. But the day after the *New Statesman* appeared, Alison said, 'Several people at work today mentioned your review.'

It was a scholarly book. My review had not been brilliant. And I doubted whether they had actually read the review. But they had seen my name. The point was that I was now visible. I had been buried in the back pages before.

Heavage called me that same week and offered me a new book by Walter Van Bellamy. Had he remembered that I had met Bellamy at Lady Max's? It was *Alarm and Despondency*, Bellamy's first public mention of being treated for depression. It had to be a favorable review, but a thoughtful one, ruminative, discursive. There was nothing crooked about book reviewing, but often a good book was helped on its way, and the reviewer – in helping – rode along with it.

'I think you'll do it rather well,' Heavage said. 'I can give you fifteen hundred words.'

Space was money – the more column inches the larger the check. This was another lead review, and (because of Bellamy, not me) it was widely read and quoted. It seemed I was now publicly associated with him.

I was asked to be on the radio to discuss Bellamy's book, on the program *Kaleidoscope*, which was presented by a small yellow-eyed man in a stained cardigan who had a powerful, growly voice and who belittled Bellamy's work while seeming to praise it. He then asked me leading questions about the book and after a few minutes thanked me out loud, saying my full name, and after a burst of music – it was 'I like New York in June' – he said, 'And now another curiously different American.' He began discussing the new Woody Allen movie. For this I was paid twenty pounds.

Never mind the fee – 'money for jam,' as Musprat used to say – the fact was that I had begun to exist in London. And in my first years in London my agent had arranged for me to see a producer at *Kaleidoscope* – the idea was that I might become a regular contributor – and I had been rebuffed. It was important for me to have at last appeared on the program, because I now saw its triviality.

Was triviality the key to success? After the program, many people mentioned that they had heard me, among them was Walter Van Bellamy.

'Dear boy' – he was in a good mood – 'I heard you on the wireless.'

He invited me to tea at the Charing Cross Hotel. I wondered whether it might be another of his batty ideas, and I also suspected that he might not come. But there he was, big and wild-haired, standing in the lobby, ten minutes early.

'This was once very grand,' he said, frowning at the wan cushions of the chairs in the lobby, as the Spanish waiter set out the tea things. He was silent a moment. 'More and more I find this city insupportable.'

I was smiling. 'I've just started to like it here.'

'Tell me why.' He fixed his eyes on me like a headmaster and stared until I spoke.

'My work is going well.'

'That I understand.'

'And this city is being good to me. I am making some friends. I have a sense of belonging that I didn't have before.'

'Yes,' he said tentatively – it was not approving. I recognized the tone. He was not happy but he was giving me the benefit of the doubt. He suspected that I was kidding myself. He was exasperated and impatient, but there was too much to say for him to attempt to analyze. My mention of friends made him doubtful – perhaps a little envious and skeptical. All this he put into his yes. Then he elaborated.

'When you first come to London it seems vast – as vast as England itself. With each passing year it shrinks around you, until it is a very tight fit – your house, your room, your desk. Your art.'

He poured – milk first, then tea, then sugar. He stirred the cup, and his stirring was like a process of thought.

'I think about people who play with art. Some people in London do it. They are glamored by it. Don't play with art.'

I wondered whether he meant this personally – surely he knew better? It was obvious that I worked very hard. I guessed that he was on a medication that was making him serious and single-minded.

He said, 'Who do you see in London?'

It was a sudden question. Yes, he had been provoked by my mention of friends.

'Do you know Ian Musprat, the poet?'

'He doesn't exist,' Bellamy said. 'Not as a poet.'

'His last book won a prize.'

'There are more prizes in this country than there are writers to give them to. Name me an English writer who hasn't won a prize!'

He said this very loudly, curling his lips in triumph, and hooting afterward. Perhaps his medication was wearing off.

Finally, I said, 'And Lady Max. She's a friend.'

'Oh, God,' Bellamy said.

He gave me a twisted smile of disgust, then he sipped some tea and recovered.

'It struck me the other day that the British government ought to sell titles at the post office. They could do it the way they give out TV licenses. A little booklet with a grid of spaces. You buy stamps, a few at a time, and when you've filled it up you hand it over and get your MBE. Two booklets for an OBE. Three – a knighthood!'

This little diversion cheered him up.

'"Lady Max," someone will say, and hearing the title "Lady" you'll immediately think, "Three booklets." What is a title? What does it mean?'

I said lamely, 'I was only wondering what you thought of her.'

'One had a thing – years ago, when one first came to London and was being introduced, as it were. When one was impressionable. When one was a bit dazzled, because one knew ever so much less.' He sipped his tea again. 'But one was never glamored by her.'

I saw Bellamy to his train and walked home a little shaken by this talk. I had expected him to be crazed and colorful, but this was sobering advice – a sort of warning. It was clear that he did not approve of Lady Max. And it seemed that he was implying that my new visibility as a writer in London suggested triviality. His warning had been *Don't play with art*.

And he had put me on the defensive. People often did that when they had something to conceal. *One had a thing*. What was that supposed to mean?

But I had turned my back on the world, on Lady Max.

This was in mid-February. I was still working hard on my novel and I had now been writing it for a full year, dating my pages. I wrote two or three pages a day. It was a solemn moment when I realized that a year ago I was sitting here doing exactly the same thing, and I was still not done – not even close. Yet I was not so impatient to finish that I wanted to hurry it and fail to enjoy its surprises, its growth, its improvement – writing, polishing, rereading, and moving on.

What had changed? Lady Max had looked into my heart and stirred something and woken it with a word – made that little animal sit up and beg, then rewarded the mutt with a biscuit. Good dog. Beyond the routine of the day, which I had found satisfying, I had wanted recognition. And I had innocently imagined ways of being recognized – a lead review, my face on an advertisement, mentions in newspaper diaries.

Soon, unexpected rewards came my way – more biscuits – and, surprised and delighted, I began to wag my tail.

The *Sunday Times Magazine* ran an interview with Sir George Rackstraw, the banker. In the accompanying photograph – a portrait by Lord Snowdon – a copy of one of my novels lay next to a bunch of flowers on Sir George's coffee table, the book title and my name pleasingly visible.

My book was Sir George's secret, as though part of his intellect and imagination, and so our names were linked. And afterwards when you saw him you thought of me.

A few days later a book of mine turned up on a bookshelf in a catalogue for Habitat furniture. Another book of mine was mentioned in a celebrity column called 'On My Bedside Table.'

These appearances were better, more noticeable than good reviews and, naturally, people mentioned them to me. Several of the people were publishers, interested in my next book. Another little miracle: a letter from a movie company in Wardour Street wishing to take out a film option for *The Last Man*.

When had I revealed that now rejected title to anyone?

I called the movie producer, a man named Slack, and told him that my novel was not finished. He was not dismayed, he sounded enthusiastic – he encouraged me to finish it, and his encouragement gave me hope.

'And when you're done, give us a crack at it.'

'How did you know about my book?'

'I heard it on the street,' he said. 'There's a lot of talk about it.'

I mumbled that expression to myself. 'On the street.' My work had never been spoken about on the street before. In my mind it was a particular street, narrow and interesting, full of pedestrians. A London street.

I had another inquiry from a movie company for a novel I had published a few years before, and a letter from a firm specializing in picture books asking me to consider writing the text for a volume of London photographs.

'What we want is a sort of excursion,' the picture book publisher wrote. 'Your London.'

My London! Except for what Lady Max had shown me of those churches and monuments and back streets, my London was mainly indoors, as I worked on my book the whole day, confident in the darkness.

And all this time there were invitations. Since my lead review and first diary mention I had received more than a dozen invitations. I had received them before – to the sort of 'It's a drink' book launches that Musprat never missed. As a reviewer, I was known to the publicity departments of some publishers. But now I began to get invitations to parties at gallery openings, wine tastings for charity, drinks to publicize new lines of cosmetics, and to movie premieres. I put them on the mantelpiece, a London affectation – the thick white cards and invitations propped up over the fireplace, looking pompous.

Alison snorted at them, because she never appeared on them, not as 'Mrs,' not even as 'and Guest.'

She said, 'I wouldn't go even if I were asked.'

I too stayed away. London parties of this kind, always 'Six until Eight,' were given at the wrong time of day. My work kept me at my desk until five-thirty, and by then it was too late; I was too tired to change my clothes, to put on a tie and hurry to the West End. I had the evening meal to prepare, the boys to meet, the *Standard* to read, and rather than standing up in a noisy room drinking wine, I preferred a pint of Guinness in the funereal Fish. If I went anywhere these days it was to the Topography section of the London Library to check facts for my novel, which was set in Honduras.

At last I felt obliged to accept an invitation – it seemed rude to refuse to go to a party for the opening of a new exhibition, 'Victorian London,' at the Royal Academy. After all, I lived in a Victorian house, the authors who had defined London for me were Victorian, and the word 'Victorian' was fascinating for its ambiguity – supposedly so strict and straight-laced, but behind that pompous four-syllable façade, loaded with secrets of other lives.

There were posters announcing the exhibition on the Underground, and banners flying across Piccadilly. We had been near here, on one of our London excursions, when Lady Max had shown me Albany and its courtyard.

Thinking of her in this way, I had her fixed in my mind, and so I was startled on entering the foyer of the Royal Academy to see her. Her face was as luminous as ever, her lips as lovely, and she wore a loose, black, shimmering dress. When she spoke, she seemed impatient.

'Where have you been?' she called out, and dropped her cigarette butt and stamped on it with one of her wicked shoes.

7

If I had been walking down Piccadilly past the Royal Academy that dark winter evening and seen the glowing room and this by-invitation-only preview among the brilliant pictures I would have hated these party-goers and wanted to throw a brick through the window. What frivolousness! What privilege!

But I was inside the Royal Academy, a guest at the private affair, eating smoked salmon and having a wonderful time. It was like high mass, with all that space and light, and music too – a string quartet sonorously scraping away in a corner. We guests in the foreground were dwarfed by the looming portraits.

Victorian London was depicted not only in paintings and period costume, but in a series of elaborate interiors – a middle-class Victorian drawing room, a lighterman's cottage by the Thames, Oscar Wilde's bedroom, an ingeniously conceived view of Dickens's office at *Household Words*, each with voices and street sounds. 'Eminent Victorians' was a separate exhibit, and so was 'Clubland.' Some of it was marvelously down-to-earth – whole exhibits given over to objects and pictures describing London plumbing or London shopping – food and clothes – in the age of Victoria.

'Has this wine corked?' Lady Max was saying. 'They serve bad champagne when a decent Chablis can be had for the same money.'

I was on my second glass. People were chattering with each other, their pink, eager faces close together, and no one was looking at the exhibits. Lady Max sniffed as she turned to put her glass down.

'You would have thought they'd exhibit something a bit more up-lifting than water-closets,' she said. 'Think what an opportunity they lost – what portraits they could have hung. This is all a low-brow cheapie, on the level of a primary school pageant. Pimping for punters!'

That was not true. It was Victorian London from a new angle, and portraits of Victorians were hung everywhere. The pictures in this beautiful room made the guests seem smugger, but most of the people were improved by the setting, and looked more prosperous, hopeful and gentle. There was a sense of eagerness in the place, a vibration running through the room – the drink probably, but also the just-finished look of the exhibits, the hum of their newness – and I took pleasure just watching the play of people and lights. I was glad to be there, delighted to be anonymous. The champagne made me slightly tipsy and gave to the party the warmth and blur of a good dream.

'I can't stand another minute of this,' Lady Max said.

She hurried away and, stumbling a bit, I followed her into the foyer, where she handed me her cloakroom tag. I picked up her coat. The lining was still warm – she had not been there long. And sens-ing the scrutinizing gaze of the attendant, who had positioned him-self next to a saucer of coins, I panicked and tipped him a pound.

'Oh, good, there's a taxi,' Lady Max said in the Royal Academy courtyard.

Once again she was taking charge. She had the capacity to make me feel wonderful, but with that same power she could reduce me too, so that I felt stupid and spineless, just a snuffling creature wait-ing for a dog biscuit.

In the darkness of the taxi, as we tore through Knightsbridge, she said, 'You've been decidedly scarce.'

I agreed – yes, I had – and let myself be bullied, and even paid for the taxi and – fussed by all this abruptness – yet again overtipped the cabby. Meanwhile, Lady Max had mounted her stairs and was in the portico, holding her large black latch key out for me to take.

The turtle knocker caught my eye – it was dark and stained, with big damp fingerprints. I made a few feeble pokes with the long latch key before Lady Max snatched it away from me and expertly rammed it into the keyhole in one thrust.

To the clunking sound of the lock's works loosening, its parts engaging, she said, 'That's how it's done.'

She went inside, and I followed, as though by a prior arrangement.

She switched on lamps, lighting our way to a side room I had not seen before. It was full of books and framed photographs – clusters of faces staring and smiling from shelves, from tiny tables, from the piano lid. They peeped from the shadows, but the room was so quiet and so dark at the edges they were like creatures from another life, another world. As I raised my eyes from all these strangers, I saw that she was holding a glass of wine and offering it, much as she had offered me her latch key.

'Sniff-sniff. You have a novelist's nosiness.'

Her directness embarrassed me. I picked up a bowler hat from the piano seat and put it on – much too big. There were gold initials, *TRDA*, stamped in the hat band.

'He's out of the country,' Lady Max said. 'Please sit down. You're awfully nervy.'

Not nervy but still tipsy from the Royal Academy champagne.

She sat opposite me on the sofa, then kicked off her sharp-heeled shoes and raised her legs and sank her feet into a blue cushion. She had lovely patterned stockings, and when she had swung her legs her dress was hiked up – it was a brief glimpse but I did see her stocking tops tightened against her white thighs. I remembered, *I never wear knickers.*

'You're frightfully busy these days,' she said.

'No more than usual.'

She pretended not to hear, so as to go on talking – a London habit.

'Absolutely all over the papers,' she said in her tone of approval. 'I can't open one without seeing your name.'

'I'm doing the same amount of work. I'm getting more credit for it, though.'

'No more than you deserve,' Lady Max said, and straightened one sock with the tips of her fingers. 'You're brilliant, and it's about

time people knew it. There will be much more. This is only the beginning. Just watch.'

In the half-dark of this shadowy room, speaking from where she
sat coiled on the sofa, she sounded less like a well-wisher than one
of the witches in *Macbeth*.

'I wasn't doing badly before,' I said, and it seemed to me that I
was whining.

'Of course,' she said – she was amused at my shrilled little protest
– and she patted the sofa with one bloodless hand, and puffed her
cigarette with the other. 'Now come here and sit next to me and tell
me why you never go to parties.'

Scattering sparks as she poked out her cigarette in the ashtray, she
moved her long legs as though to make room, and feeling dog-like I
crept across the carpet and sat beside her.

'What parties?' I asked.

'The ones you're invited to.'

'But I just saw you at the Royal Academy party.'

'As though there weren't any others.'

So she knew – and she must have connived at having me invited. I
felt a bit diminished, if not put in my place, because she had been
responsible for my being on those guest lists.

'These parties take place at a very inconvenient time of day.'

'Rubbish. It is a fact of life in London that there is nothing whatever to do between five and eight most evenings.'

'I find I'm pretty busy then.'

She did not hear that. She said, 'As the French say, the hours between the dog and the wolf.'

I wanted to say: In the hours between the dog and the wolf I am
usually simmering spaghetti sauce, or gutting fish, or chopping
vegetables, or reading the *Evening Standard*, or waiting for my wife
to come home. But no – Lady Max might have understood the
cooking, yet any mention of my wife seemed out of place or unwelcome at this moment.

'I have been watching for you,' she said, and slid closer to me.
Now I could see the pattern on her stockings. Butterflies. 'This is
what I had planned. Precisely this.'

She smiled at me and smoothed her hair.

'Thank you for being so cooperative.'

What was I to say to that?

'Do you find me too blunt?' she asked.

'No.'

'I wonder if you could bear to kiss me.'

Her way of asking the question made it impossible for me to refuse. She was deft at getting me off-balance, and with just the simplest question she could control me, as though tugging at my leash. I thought: *Woof-woof.*

Of course, I heard my stupid voice saying, Don't be silly. I want to kiss you.

And I did, and the kiss was facile, tentative, clumsy, insincere, dutiful, all chilly lips, and made her frown. Her breath of burned tobacco and ashes and charred paper was moist and sooty.

'You need practice,' she said. 'Funny. One of my favorite scenes in literature is when you have that man in your novel kiss the woman and then fuck her in front of the fire.'

In a single motion, flicking her fingers, she pushed her dress off her shoulder – there was no strap beneath – and slipped her hand down and inside, and moved it over her breasts. I could see her knuckles move against the silk as she traced her nipples.

'I know I'm no great beauty,' she said. 'I have small boobs and a biggish bum.' She smiled teasingly because what she said defied me to glance at her body. 'But honestly I think I could show you a thing or two.'

She was still sipping her wine and moving her hand inside her dress, caressing herself, and still fluttering her fingers over her nipples.

'Do I surprise you?' she said. She moistened her lips. 'I think I could surprise you in lots of other ways.'

I was aware that I was leaning close to her when she removed her wandering hand, and she shrugged, straightening her dress. Then she was looking past me, as though at the window, listening hard – I could see it in the concentration of her eyes, the hint of their contraction. She was hearing something clearly that I heard only faintly.

'Wouldn't you know,' she said with utter disgust, but not to me.

The front door creaked open – I heard the chink of the turtle knocker before the door slammed – there was a stamping in the hall, a sigh, our door was flung open, and a tall young girl stood smiling in the doorway. She had tumbling blonde hair and from the rosy glow highlighting her pale skin, her bright smacked cheeks, you knew she had walked home this frosty evening. She wore a dark cape and boots, and standing there breathless and apologetic made her seem even more attractive. It was the daughter, Allegra.

'Hello, Mummy. Sorry to burst in.'

'Shut that fucking door this instant, you silly girl, and go to your room!'

The girl reacted as though she had been hit, stepping back, and the pretty redness reddened to points of color on each cheek. Then she was off – the door was shut even before Lady Max stopped shrieking.

The spell was broken and all my ardor died. It was a tone I had never heard her use before – a new voice, harsh, angry, pitiless, ignorant, more an animal's snarl than a human noise. That moment made a little welt on my memory. And I knew that after this I would never be able to look at Lady Max without also thinking of this ugly person inside her.

But she had gone quiet. She had moved her dress off her shoulder again, farther than before, and she was holding one breast like a Madonna in a Renaissance painting, proffering the nipple in her fingers for me to suck.

'Take it.'

The bluish veins in her breast made it look as cool as marble, and the smooth whiteness of the skin and a suggestion of pale hair surrounded the russet-brown of the aureole and the nipple. Against the delicious softness of her breast, the nipple looked thick, like the cut stem of a fruit.

Seeing me hesitate, she said, 'It's Allegra, isn't it?'

She held her breast, but casually, like an apple she was holding for me in case I might be hungry.

'She had arranged to meet a friend – that's what she told me. She never makes a plan and sticks to it. She's so selfish, the way she comes and goes.'

Lady Max was so certain that her daughter's appearance at the door, and her presence upstairs, were the reason for my reluctance that I did not try to dissuade her. A shudder of gratitude passed through me. I was thankful to the daughter for showing up – for provoking the mother and revealing her. And I was touched by the daughter's humiliation.

'God, I hate the young,' Lady Max said, and stroked her breast sourly, before tucking it into her dress.

She looked older and unreasonable, though I could only think of the daughter's sweet, startled face in the doorway, her uncertain posture, her sudden fear, a deer caught in the headlights.

Lady Max glanced at me. I said nothing and felt I was a coward for not defending the daughter. But there was a deeper reason: I had been so moved by the daughter's hurt I felt I might betray myself, because in a sense I fell for the daughter then, for her wounded innocence. The injustice had more than roused pity and protectiveness – it had stirred something likc love.

'I hate them for being young,' Lady Max said. 'I hate their talk.'

Now, for my own self-respect, I felt I had to speak up for the girl. I began to say how the young seemed connected to the world – they lived close to the ground, they had access everywhere, they traveled light, and they were most alive in old, safe cities like London.

But all this while Lady Max was shaking her head.

'I hate the way the young tell you things you already know, as though it's news,' she said. 'They are forever discovering the obvious – that Soho is charming, that the King's Road is stylish, that Oxford Street's a bore. And in their little papers and magazines they write about it all in sickening detail. I hate the things they buy, I hate their music.'

She lit a cigarette but without any flourish, simply snatchcd one from a silver box at her elbow and set it on fire and gasped on it.

Speaking through rags of smoke – and the smoke itself made the words visible – she said, 'And as if that's not bad enough, they tell you things you know are wrong. You want to say "Balls!" but you can't talk them out of it, so you listen, and in a month or so you have to sit through them contradicting themselves.'

She tapped the ash off the cigarette and sulked as she inhaled more smoke, blowing it as though spraying poison, blighting the air with her breath.

'That's the worst of it, listening to them change their minds – watching the young grow up.'

'It happens so fast, though,' I said, thinking of my own children.

'Not true. It takes too bloody long. I have been listening to this nonsense for years,' she said. 'And I hate the way they think out loud. I hate their ignorant opinions. I can't stand the way they change their mind.'

Saying these things with such conviction, she seemed old and cranky, and I felt at a greater distance from her – young, or at least younger than she.

'Isn't it part of growing up?'

'Why can't they do it more quietly?' she said. And with menace in her eyes she glanced up at where Allegra's room probably was. 'She was supposed to be with her friend.'

It was the most passionate she had ever been with me face to face, sitting down, and though she could be a tease or an insincere mocker I knew she meant every word of this.

And her words were tainted by her breath. The dark whiff in her breath made me squint.

She was a heavy smoker and I was sitting near. It was the odor of her lungs – not a rancid thing in her mouth, but deeper. It seemed especially odd and offensive because she was so lovely. She had stubbed out her cigarette but she smelled strongly of smoke, of black, clammy London, of sooty air and stale breath.

First her shriek, then her rant, and finally her breath again. She stank. And yet from a little distance she seemed so pale and fragile. In her rant she had lost interest in me, and she had emptied her glass. She looked peevish and distracted, though for a long while afterwards she sat there saying nothing. Then she saw me sneaking a look at my wristwatch.

'You're going to be late.'

'It's all right.'

'Your wife is going to wonder where you are.'

I hated that, I said nothing. Seeing me squirm made her smile.

'Will I keep seeing your name everywhere?'

'Who knows?'

'I think I will,' she said, and paused, and added, 'If I want to.'

*

Another London walk, homeward from Lady Max's, through winter streets. I needed that ritual to calm me. Each time I saw her I had to sort out where I was, and what did she mean, and who was I, and who was she? Part of her witchery came from her power to spread confusion, and the rest of her witchery was her beauty. But I was still confused.

I had gained a measure of visibility. She knew that and from what she said she might have even pulled a string or two on my behalf. But the writing was mine – I had done the work. Being appreciated stabilized me and made me happy at home. The routine of doing reviews made my writing easier, more confident and fluent. And she had revealed herself as rather a pest – it seemed she had been to those other parties I had stayed away from, and she apparently had lain in wait for me.

I was still walking through Chelsea, still remembering. There are certain awful sounds that enter your ears and penetrate your whole body. Her howl at her daughter was one of those. It startled me and made me fearful. Now I was bearing towards the river, walking south towards Battersea Bridge and home. The odor of burning coal fires on these narrow streets reminded me of Lady Max's breath – the sharp chimney stink of her lungs.

Though I was flattered by her interest and her praise, her sudden sexuality threw me. She had made me feel like an idiot for not responding, but – really – did she expect me to kneel and suck on her breast and then go home and kiss my wife?

By the time I reached Clapham I had worked myself into a state of grievance against her – feeling that she was presumptuous and unsubtle. I hated her greed. And she was niggardly too – I had not forgotten that dinner at La Tour Eiffel.

The phone was ringing as I climbed the stairs to my house. The ringing stopped when I opened the front door. Alison was holding the receiver towards me.

'It's for you,' she said. She covered the mouthpiece. 'A woman. Frightfully posh.'

It was Lady Max.

'I was just wondering whether you had any plans for tomorrow,' she said.

'Just work.' Writing at home gave me no convincing excuses; being a freelance writer seemed indistinguishable from someone unemployed.

'Good. Then you can take the day off and have lunch with me.'

But my walk home had filled me with resentment.

'Sorry,' I said.

She hung on, she made me struggle, but at last I got her off the line.

A week passed. More invitations. My book was going so well that

I accepted an assignment to write a piece the following week about Brighton, for a British travel magazine. Lady Max called on Monday.

'You weren't at the Heinemann party.'

'I'm pretty busy. I have to go to Brighton tomorrow.'

'I know. It's for *Travel World*, isn't it? I'll go with you.'

She was not only blunt, she was quick. I couldn't think. I said, 'I'm staying overnight.'

'Even better.'

Now she was making me work.

'It's not a good idea,' I said.

'I think it's an excellent idea. Brighton's a marvelously scruffy place, and in The Lanes there are some splendid restaurants.'

Feeling spineless and desperate, I said, 'My wife might be going with me.'

Lady Max did not hesitate. 'I thought your wife worked.'

'She does. But she's taking the day off.'

She had made me squirm again, she had frightened me, and now she was making me lie. I hated her for that most of all. We had entered a new phase of the relationship, deeper and more treacherous, and the suddenness was like some of the streets she had shown me in London, the strange alleys and cul-de-sacs off wide and well-known thoroughfares. She was insistent, I was dithering. And she had a meddling interest. How did she know, and what business was it of hers, who I was writing this Brighton piece for?

That night, after putting the boys to bed, Alison was chatty. 'Everyone's talking about you these days. They ask me, "Are you any relation to the writer?" That sort of question.' She smiled. 'I'm not sure I like it.'

I was opening my mail in front of the fire. 'What's wrong?'

'Nothing. Look at this – two publishers have written to ask about my new novel. It's not even finished and they're competing for it. And here's something from the *Observer*. They want to know if I can go to China.'

Alison was looking puzzled. 'Aren't you glad?'

'Of course.'

'Then why do you look so haunted?'

8

Again I thought: Most writers are balder and smaller than you expect. I was entering the Members' Reading Room of the London Library, passing among the men scribbling, some seated at tables, others hunched in leather chairs. There were women writing, too, but they seemed altogether more efficient, tidier, less conspicuous. It was a warm room, but with an odor of leather and old bindings, and quiet except for the rattle of pages being turned, and the hiss and ping of antique radiators.

With his back to the room, Ian Musprat was working on a poem. He was facing a window pane that was so black, so stippled with raindrops, it looked liquefied – like a tall, trembling sheet of water which diffused the yellow street lamps of St James's Square. He clutched his head with bitten fingers. Peering over his shoulder, I could see his open notebook page – crossed-out lines and doodles and, *A distant toilet flushing is like the sound of a human voice, a sigh becoming water and collapsing with a call into a pipe – always a little sad*, and the scattered words and phrases *Humptulips* and *distemper* and *How terribly reassuring*.

They were the makings of a poem – I could tell from the way the lines were set out, not reaching the right-hand margin of the page.

Seeing this small, untidy man writing made me respect him, even like him again. Writing made him seem admirable and civilized. This was what he was for, and I was impressed by his bravery. His posture gave him a look of concentration and struggle, and in his very plainness was an aura of strength. There was also something in his silence, and the way he wrote with the notebook on his lap, that gave him the appearance of a conspirator. He was so engrossed he did not notice me.

At his elbow was a plump volume, its spine printed *Mythologiques – Vol. 3 – The Origin of Table Manners*.

Only when I stood blocking his light did he look up at me, with the scowling face of a hamster waking from a nap in its nest, and he said, 'God, I'm sick of doing this.'

'How about a cup of tea?'

'There's a poxy tea shop in Duke Street.'

He tripped on the ruck of a carpet leaving the Reading Room and shouted loudly, 'Knickers!' No one stopped writing, though one man looked over the top of his newspaper.

'How long have you been a member of this library?' he asked me on the stairs, under the portrait of T. S. Eliot.

'Since Lady Max insisted I join.'

He said nothing in reply.

'What are you writing?' I asked him.

'A desperate piece of crap about hermeneutics.'

'Could you elaborate?'

'It's actually an attack on Levi-Strauss.'

'The American blue jeans?'

'The French structuralist,' he said. And he smiled. 'But that's nice. I'm using that.'

In the tea shop I said, 'I want to ask you about Lady Max.'

Musprat did not reply. He stared at the floor and then blew his nose with a stiff and wrinkled handkerchief that he held balled-up in his hand. He then frowned at the thing and said, 'I'm disgusting,' and stuffed it into his pocket.

Stirring his styrofoam cup of tea with a wooden stick, he said, 'I sort of hate her. Sometimes I'd like to punch her in the face.' He sucked the tea from the wooden stirrer and said, 'Sorry. I know you're a big fan.'

'I'm not a fan at all.'

He sipped his tea, then faced me with a little more confidence. 'You write short stories. Want an idea for one?'

He began to gnaw his wooden stirrer.

'You meet someone early in your career, when you are weak and they are strong. They are bloody rude to you. Time passes. You get a little recognition, and you meet this person again. This time they are very pleasant. They don't remember that they were rude. They actually believe they were part of your success. Yet their rudeness is all you remember – the only thing.'

He had reduced his wooden stirrer to a mass of wet splinters. He lifted the paper cup in his thin, anxious fingers.

'The first time Lady Max met me she more or less mocked me. I knew she didn't fancy me at all. Anyway, why should she? I'm a pig. After I won the Hawthornden she remembered my name and tried to be nice to me.'

'And that's why you want to punch her in the face?'

'No. I think I envy her, actually. I'd like to have her money. I'd like to have a house in the Boltons. I'd like to go around saying, "I never wear knickers." That's her war-cry, you know.'

Having finished the tea he began chewing the top edge of the styrofoam cup.

'Her mother's a marchioness. Only a marquis or a marchioness can be addressed as "the most honorable," ' he said. And he made a face at me. 'I'm surprised you don't know that. That's the sort of thing that Americans tend to know.'

'Musprat, you are such a dick.'

'I hate it when people call me by my last name. It reminds me of school.'

'What if Lady Max had fancied you?'

Now he smiled, he was strengthened, as though I had played the wrong card. He looked timidly triumphant. He said, 'I should have thought you could tell me a thing or two about that.'

That was another thing about them. The English could be so pompous and wordy when they felt they were in the right.

'I haven't touched her, Ian.'

'I don't want to know about it,' Musprat said, and made it sound like a teasing accusation. 'But it's easy to talk about her, because she makes no secret of her life.'

'Meaning?'

'She's been to bed with everyone,' he said. 'Didn't you know that?'

'I guessed,' I said. Yet I had not wanted to think about it.

'Heavage?' I said.

'She had a fairly public thing with him,' Musprat said. 'Most editors have had a leg over her. Most writers in the news. Writing's a sort of aphrodisiac to her. She's very old-fashioned in that way.'

'She mentioned Kenneth Tynan.'

'They used to show up at parties wearing each other's clothes.'

'Do you know a movie producer named Slack?'

'No, but Lady Max does.'

I named the men at the dinner party – Marwood the novelist, the South African named Lasch.

'I suppose so. She's fairly rapacious. I know you're shocked and all that, but looking in from the outside I must say I find it bores me rigid.'

In his off-hand way, blowing his nose, chewing shreds from his plastic cup, he named others, as though listing people involved in a conspiracy. They included journalists who must have put my name in 'Londoner's Diary', publishers who sent me invitations to book launches, museum directors, and the editor of the travel magazine who asked me to write the piece about Brighton. And Walter Van Bellamy. I had thought she had pulled a few strings, but it was more than that – she had manipulated all the attention that I had been receiving lately. She had tipped a wink to these old lovers, perhaps collecting on a debt from them.

'I'm not shocked,' I said. But I was.

I decided to avoid the germ-laden commuters and walked home. It was only when I took a London bus or train in the rush hour that I caught a cold. It was an easy one-hour walk through St James's Park, past the palace, and through Victoria and Chelsea; then across the river and uphill to Clapham.

Walking along I thought again about Musprat. He seemed almost virtuous in his detachment and his mockery, and his ragged clothes gave him a look of sincerity, like a mendicant monk. His detachment had given him a perspective. He looked on, he was touched by forgivable envy. His strength was that he had not been lured into Lady Max's orbit.

Putting these questions to him about Lady Max, I understood Musprat better – and that had been the case in my talk to Bellamy, too. Lady Max was the key. She had shown me London, and because it was her London, and seen through her eyes, the city was distorted for me. Yet seeing Lady Max through the eyes of others had helped me to understand London better. And of course she had helped me. The more visible I became, the clearer I could see London, because she had given me access.

The price for this was a sense of woe and a feeling of obligation. What to do about her?

*

She phoned me again several more times. She did not give her name or say hello. She plunged in – 'Well?' – and waited impatiently until I thought of something to say, and when I did my evasiveness seemed to rouse her, as though she liked the challenge of what she took to be my lack of interest. She did not know it was fear.

'I'm afraid I'm not very gregarious.'

Even then I did not say her name – still didn't know what to call her.

'We'll see about that.' And she hung up.

She regarded me as an interesting problem. But as before she worked obliquely. From other quarters came more invitations to parties, more offers of writing assignments. A television producer asked me whether I was interested in writing a play for television. Another literary editor inquired about the possibility of my review-ing for him. These were substantial offers, involving contracts and terms, with a promise of serious money.

As with Musprat, knowing these people helped me to know Lady Max better. I could place her now, I understood her society and what she needed, and that was a London knack, being able to put a person in their context. It was not a high-rise city but it was dense, and it sprawled all over the slopes of its river valley; Londoners fitted in, but each was a tight fit.

She phoned me once more, was off-hand again, and asked whether I was free for dinner that very night.

'No. I have another dinner' – and I did, with Alison, and one of her friends from work.

'Where will you be going?'

I named the restaurant.

She said, 'I'd love to join you.' She could not have been more blunt.

'And my wife?'

'I don't cope with wives ordinarily, but we do have something in common, she and I.'

I could not imagine what that might be, and said so.

'You, dear boy,' Lady Max said, but there was a contemptuous edge in her voice.

I resisted, feeling foolish, and out of cowardice canceled the dinner, fearful that Lady Max would show up and make a scene.

After that, I seemed to see her everywhere in London. It was a city of shadows, of memories and suggestions. It was a city of lowered voices. And at this dark and rainy time of year, with all its shining lights, and the mirrors of its winter streets, a city of reflections.

It was also a city of look-alikes – people dressed similarly, a familiar hat, that identical coat, the same umbrella. There were

London clothes, there was even a London walk. Londoners didn't saunter, they walked with purpose, rarely making eye-contact, their faces fixed, chin up, as though into battle, knowing it was another futile charge. Those people marching down Oxford Street were Londoners, the stragglers were foreign.

In those crowds I often saw Lady Max, her drawn-back hair, her white face, her cloaks and capes, and I believed she was watching me. Anonymity was a valuable asset here, but now I was afraid I had lost mine. Lady Max had shown me the city – its secret places; but now that I had begun to inhabit her London it seemed that I was exposed. I felt she might turn up anywhere, at any time.

It was easy enough to stay home. Life in London had given me a taste for privacy: Londoners valued their isolation – they liked to be, as Musprat said of himself, in one of his own invented words, 'un-get-at-able.' You could never get lost here the way you could in New York City, but you could hide and not be found.

I loved the seclusion of my house, and my absorption in my novel made me happy. Except for the ring of the telephone (but it was never her these days, she had stopped calling), I worked without interruption or anxiety. What other cold northern city was so protective that it allowed you to be able to write, undisturbed, of the Honduran jungle? It was the effect of all that winter darkness. Yet even at the end of February there was a suggestion of spring, the first flowers of the year – snowdrops, some early crocuses, even in the little rectangles of London back gardens the sense of rural England, the residue of the old fertile land – old roots and shrubs, old bulbs and tubers blossoming in the mud.

Then came a sound like a pistol shot, just as sudden, the same shock; the worst, most dreaded noise in London, an unexpected rapping at your door. It was she again.

9

London taxis with their engines idling make an unmistakable rattle and clack, an impatient shivering of metal that accompanies the paying of the fare. The door slams, the window is banged shut, still shaking as the cab drives off. All this I was dimly aware of as I sat

upstairs at the back of the house, writing my novel, growing doubtful of its title.

It was an afternoon of white winter light, the flowers in the back
gardens showing some small, brilliant tongues of color.

That was when the rapping came, and the door bell a moment
later, and only then did I connect this uninvited visitor to the sound
of the taxi.

'Aren't you going to ask me in?'

Nightmare was the right word: it was a mixture of the familiar
and the strange. Only in bad dreams did you meet someone you
knew in the oddest place – your mother in a locker room; or it might
be a total stranger, or someone you feared, in the seclusion of your
home.

I wanted her to go away. But she had a slender claim on me, so
how could I be rude?

Inside the house, looking at pictures, touching furniture, she said,
'This is not at all what I had expected.'

Already she was sneering, as though anticipating rejection.

'Have I ever shown you my Lears?' she said, glancing at an
Edward Lear watercolor of the Nile, and quickly sizing it up.

As she passed me on her way into the sitting room – she had not
waited to be asked – I had a sense of other men on her, and I recalled
how the bronze shell of the turtle door knocker at her house was
stained and black with fingerprints, all the men who had entered.
But this was more an odor than anything visible, and it enclosed her
body in a layer like an atmosphere she carried with her, like the
murk of dust and smoke that lay over London, so that London was
never distinct except up close. From a plane, from a distance, the
city was blurred, as she was.

'How very interesting,' she was saying.

Her manner was a little chilly. Every encounter, every conversation, I had had with Lady Max was like a job interview; but it was
she who was turned down. Today was slightly different. She was responding to me in a defensive and remote way, treating me as a male
– not a friend, or someone with a name, but a man. There had been
so many other men. And men were so predictable. This was her
weakness, her poor judgment, her bad timing, and the reason she
would fail in the end: she believed all men were the same.

This made me dislike and even fear her, because a woman with that belief would blame me for the harm another man had done her. Seeing her prowling in my house, looking two stories down at the garden below, gave me pause. Impulsive and greedy, loving to shock, capable of howling – these traits made her seem destructive.

'Don't worry. I'm not going to throw myself out the window.'

It was precisely what I feared.

'But if I did, you'd be in a jolly awkward position explaining it.'

'If you jumped out this window,' I said, and looked down at the wet paving stones, 'it seems to me that you'd be the one in the awkward position.'

'Yes. Maybe I should push you instead.'

'Why would you do a silly thing like that?'

I tried to appear calm, but what she said terrified me, and I was watching her, so that she couldn't lunge and catch me off-balance.

'Because you've been avoiding me. I don't like that.'

Was it so simple? That what made her passionate was that I was unwilling? But she was also stubborn. My refusal had made me different from the others, and it made her more insistent.

She had paused near a stack of magazines and papers on a side table. Each of them contained something I had written.

'I put those people on to you.'

'But I did the writing.'

She raised her face to me, and pursed her lips, to jeer. 'There are so many writers in London,' she said. 'Many of them are just as clever as you, but much more polite. They would have thanked me.'

She lit a cigarette, and again I had the impression, when she exhaled, of someone blowing smoke into the room.

'I don't think you quite realize what I've done for you.'

'Do I seem ungrateful?'

'Very,' she said, and looked around. 'Your little house. Your little life. Your little wife.'

She peered across the back garden to the row of houses beyond, and the sun was casting its last redness over the roofs and through the black branches and the air was thickening with twilight.

'Places like this make my heart sick,' she said.

'I can't do what you want me to do.'

'I don't know why I came here,' she said.

In that moment she looked abandoned – truly lost. Some women could seem so pathetic in their rejection, almost tragic, as though they were about to lose their lives. If they met the right man, they had a new life. Their fantasy was that a man could work miracles for them. But for most rejected men it was not tragedy, simply bad luck – the breaks, fooled again; move on, pal.

'I don't think I want you anymore,' she said, turning away, looking sad. I had never seen her in this mood and it shocked me, her mute face, her small shoulders, her slightly hunched, defeated-looking posture.

Perhaps she wanted me to say, *Tell me what to do to please you, and I'll do it*. But I could not utter those words to her. It was not a fear of sex – on the contrary, I was attracted to her. But sex for her was not the meal – it was only the first course. She would not have been satisfied until she had all of mc. She wanted more than passionate afternoons and the occasional party. I had the powerful fear that she wanted to suck my soul out of my body.

Without speaking again, she wandered out of the room and found the telephone in the hall. She picked up the receiver and dialed, and I felt sorry for her again. I said nothing, only watched her struggling, calling for help. I assumed she was calling a taxi.

'Julian!' she said.

What was this new voice? It was gleeful, it was false. There was something diabolical in the way this utterly different voice rang out of her body, as though she were a lump of ectoplasm that could be sorrowful one moment and coquettish the next. Like London itself, Dickensian in one street, dreary in another, renovated, crass, cozy, dangerous – not one city but many.

'It's me. What about our drink then?' she was saying. She stopped and listened, then said, 'Perfect.'

In this new voice she rattled on, mentioning a publisher, a magazine, an editor, a café, and she settled on a day and a time – tomorrow, in fact. The voice quacking like a duck at the other end of the line sounded surprised and grateful – a young man's eager voice, thankful for the sudden interruption on an otherwise empty afternoon. I knew that feeling.

She kept me waiting a while longer, while she chattered with this man, and then she hung up and said over her shoulder, 'Must be off. Thanks for the use of the phone.'

I touched her arm, so that she would turn and listen to me.

'A prostitute did that to me once in a hotel,' I said. 'She had finished with me. She was calling her next customer.'

'You are a shit,' Lady Max said.

I opened the front door. In our passing from one room to the other, from the back of the house to the front, night had fallen. The word 'shit' was still on her lips as she stepped on to the landing. I had always regarded her as lovely, even in her pestering and greed, but now I felt I knew her well, and she seemed ugly, bony, bloodless, witchlike.

'Don't be surprised if you find life in London rather different after this.'

It was a threat, and she left believing that I was doomed, that I would be lost and forgotten. She went into the street and disappeared, swallowed by the London darkness. I was not afraid. At once my house seemed large and safe. I did not mind being left behind if it meant that I would never have to see this woman again.

The children came home from school a few minutes later. It was Friday, two free days ahead of them, and they purified the house with their laughter. From that day the weather in London improved.

*

Spring came. Alison knew nothing except that for a period I was very happy and productive. My book was still unfinished. But a book was not a job or a project – it was part of my life, and I liked my life.

Still, when I wrote a review or took a trip, I remembered Lady Max's threat, which – more and more – sounded like a witch's curse. Defying it strengthened me – and I was even bolder when I realized that she could not destroy me. It meant that my writing mattered, and that she had not created me, nor was she involved in my achievement. Public relations were her game, and so it was with witches.

Once, I saw her at a publisher's party. She seemed ugly, almost monstrous to me, with her huge, white forehead and popping eyes and her greedy mouth and red claws. I intended to say hello, but I had ceased to exist for her. There was a London way of dealing with people you had written off. She froze me and then cut me – did not see me, although she certainly noticed me. She radiated a poisonous awareness of me as she made a beeline for a young writer at the far side of the room, the same Julian she had called from my house that last day.

I went home happy and did not see her again. Lady Max had taken Julian as her lover. He was her project now. He was a northerner, new to London, and he lived in Hampstead and wrote of misery in provincial coal towns. Was Lady Max the reason he was all over the papers, being helpfully mentioned and reviewed and offered work and short-listed for the spring book prizes? Time would tell. In the meantime, Julian became known – as perhaps I had been – as one of Lady Max's young men.

'I think Julian is a fearful little tick,' Musprat said.

We had resumed our snooker games, but not at the Lambourne. Musprat was avoiding the Lambourne because he owed so much money, both in club dues and bar bills. We played these days at the Regency Snooker Hall in Clapham Junction, two pounds an hour, tea and pork pies extra, and a Cockney lad with earrings and tattoos at the cash register saying, 'Is that the lot then, guv?'

'But she's worse,' Musprat said. 'You know that.'

I said I didn't. I wanted to encourage him, to hear his version.

'I think about her every time I do my taxes,' he said. 'She doesn't pay, she's not English.'

'Of course she is. Her mother's a marchioness.'

'But Lady Max is American. She took out citizenship – for tax reasons. Carries a US passport. How else do you suppose she manages to go on living in London?'

I should have known. Yet I was grateful to Lady Max. She had shown me that I would never be a Londoner. That was a valuable lesson. And because I had not been her lover I could see her clearly, and London too. So I knew the complex fate of being an alien here, and I felt confident of a time when I would write about her and her city, and my life there.

FIVE

The Writer and His Reader

I

Anthony Burgess enjoyed the story I told him of how the distinguished critic and poet, William Empson, author of *Seven Types of Ambiguity*, interrupted himself while discussing an obscure metaphysical poet with a friend of mine and got on to his knees and said unambiguously, 'I want to put your pretty little thing in my mouth.'

My friend, who was a great reader and who loved Empson's work, said no thanks in a stammering voice and helped the professor to his feet.

The poetry discussion continued for another hour, at which point Empson's charlady served them tea and cookies.

Empson said to her, 'He won't let me kiss his pretty little thing.'

The charlady laughed indulgently and poured the tea. She said, 'These Yanks!'

Prof. Empson, seventy-something, lumpish and elderly, with gray flesh and wild hair and bristly cheeks, wearing a shapeless woolen sweater, stared at my friend, his discolored teeth showing through thin lips, smiling and 'looking thirsty.'

That was when my friend made for the door. He was shocked and, because it showed, Empson just laughed at him. Burgess laughed at him too when I told him the story in London, and I did not understand why until years later I read Burgess's autobiography and discovered that at various times during his first marriage he and his then wife had experimented with a *ménage à trois*. 'I've tried just about everything Burgess wrote.'

I told Sam Lettfish that story, too. It fell flat. 'Empson isn't collected,' he explained. So the story bored him. But, 'I'm one of

Burgess's greatest readers,' he said. 'I'm a book-lover. Does that sound corny?'

No. Just American.

He said he had brought three boxes of Burgess's books for the author's signature.

'I keep doing these wacky things!'

This was at an event in London, a staged interview with me, where Burgess was the special guest and I prodded him with questions. Afterwards, members of the audience came forward with copies of books for Burgess to sign and the one with the most books was this man Lettfish, who was told to stand at the back of the line, because he had too many books, three large boxes of them. Lettfish also had a man to carry his boxes. Lettfish was not happy about being made to wait.

That was when he made the remark about being one of Burgess's greatest readers, and he added, 'I'm kind of a little Burgess myself.'

We were standing near the line of people waiting for signatures. Burgess and I were being given lunch by the South Bank people, and I wanted Burgess to meet my son, who had just begun to study Russian.

'He is the most articulate of modern novelists. I've been collecting him for years. There's tons of material.' Lettfish was agitated. 'I've got the largest Burgess archive in private hands. I'm as bad as he is!'

Modern Firsts, it was one of the passions of the early Eighties, along with junk bonds and antique maps and Japanese netsukes, good clean collectibles. The books had to have dust-jackets, 'original wrappers,' no foxing or stains, nothing ex-library.

'You must have some Burgesses,' Lettfish said, looking me over as though he had just realized that I might have some value. 'I'm always searching for association copies.'

That was another prized category in the Modern Firsts, an item such as Stephen Spender's own copy of Eliot's *Four Quartets*, 'with some marginal comments in pencil and ballpoint in Spender's hand.'

'Funny you should mention Empson. I've got William Empson's review copy of Burgess's *Nothing Like the Sun*. Bound galleys. Mint.'

'I just read paperbacks, and throw them away,' I said, to tease him.

'Letters, notebooks, manuscripts,' he was saying. 'The corrected typescript of *The Doctor is Sick*. I paid seven thousand for it. Listen, if you've got any Burgess material you want to sell, get in touch.'

He passed me his business card and signaled for his book-box carrier to join him in line. And when it was his turn, he stacked up his Firsts and Burgess put his elegant and easily readable signature on the half-title page of each one, while Lettfish pressed him with questions.

' "You're nuts," people say to me. I don't care. I'm as bad as you are!'

Burgess was hunched over the books, perspiring, working his pen; he heard nothing. I examined Lettfish's card. He was an attorney, with an office, Littler and Lettfish, in New York City and another in Lincoln's Inn Fields.

The signing over, Burgess got up and stretched and clawed at his hair, and turned his back on Lettfish and the rest of his readers.

'I'm rather peckish,' he said to them as they closed in on him. 'You will excuse me, won't you?'

'You know, that last man, with all the books, is a real collector of yours,' I told Burgess at lunch. 'He owns the largest Burgess archive in private hands.'

'What man?'

'Lettfish. He believes you to be the most articulate of modern novelists.'

'Ballocks.'

After that, I began hearing from Sam Lettfish, polite but persistent notes and phone calls. He invited me for lunch, and he asked me again whether I had anything to sell – letters or postcards from Burgess. Lettfish sought me out because I was friendly with Burgess, and Burgess was rarely in London. I resisted his invitations at first, but then in a moment of weakness I asked Lettfish's help. He gave me legal counsel and quickly solved for me what could have become a terrible tax problem. Lettfish refused payment. I was so grateful I made him a gift of a Burgess postcard to me, written half in Malay, in Jawi script.

This exchange of favors between Lettfish and me put us in touch and kept me respectful.

'That was one great momento,' Lettfish said – it was his usual pronunciation of the word. 'Hey, you're worse than I am.'

My instinct was to be courteous and not alienate bankers or tycoons like Lettfish, because they were well-connected, and who did I know? The fact that they did not mention their power only made me feel weaker. I saw Lettfish occasionally, but I felt he had no interest in me. 'Do you mind not smoking?' he said to me one day after lunch as we sat drinking coffee. He was the host, so I put my pipe away. Then we resumed our conversation. Our talk was nearly always about Burgess. Talking about him excited Lettfish, but it made me miss him.

I valued my friendship with Burgess because I felt that I somewhat resembled him. We had both been raised Catholic, in the age of the Latin mass, and as the liturgy had become folksy and English-speaking, playing show tunes after the Consecration instead of the Agnus Dei, all that hugging and hand-holding, he had lapsed and so had I. But the Church had done its work, my conscience was like a black maggot in my mind, and we went on, still regarding our souls as stained indelibly with sin.

The young sinner from the provinces, escaping from a large, messy family, is a familiar literary figure in a great tradition, as both a writer and a central character. That was Burgess in Manchester, and me in Medford. But instead of finding our fortunes in the metropolis (London in his case, New York in mine), we had expatriated ourselves and headed for distant parts of the globe – Europe and then the equatorial world. His first good work was done in the tropics, and that work had inspired me to do mine, in a similar sort of place. I remember the rainy Saturday afternoon in 1964 on which I bought the Penguin edition of *Time for a Tiger*: in Nyasaland, at the Limbe Trading Company, three shillings and sixpence.

Reading it, I felt vindicated in my decision to have gone as far away as possible, and I was heartened that he had found a subject in his remote place. His book convinced me that I could do the same, write about the post-colonial world of a small newly independent country. At that time few writers had done it, just Burgess and Naipaul. I needed the encouragement of their example: I was alone; I knew that from 1963 until 1965, when I left, I was the only person in the central African country of Nyasaland writing a novel, and then I was the only person in Uganda doing it.

Burgess was prolific, impatient, funny, modest, self-mocking, with a gift for mimicry. He wrote everything, he wrote with both hands. I was not the linguist he was, and I knew nothing of music; yet his example gave me heart. He was a traveler, a teacher, a natural expatriate; he was a perceptive and witty critic, he had no literary circle. He was old enough to be my father. That was crucial. I admired him for the way he had made himself a grand absentee.

I read everything of his that I could find, about a dozen novels. I kept traveling, and I went on writing. After I married Alison and we moved to South East Asia, I finally met Burgess with some of my colleagues from the English department in 1969, in a Chinese restaurant in Singapore. He was passing through on his way to Australia. His jet-lag gave him the sleepless, puffy face of someone on medication, and he was slightly drunk and dyspeptic, but indignant on our behalf because the Singapore government was leaning on us, saying that the study of English was useless.

'English literature is probably the greatest the world has ever known,' Burgess said that night drinking gin in a towkay's shop, rocking on a wooden stool under a croaky ceiling fan, among the strung-up air-dried ducks and the trays of chicken feet. 'And since literature is all about morality, it is the most civilized discipline imaginable. That's why the politicians are against you.'

'I don't care,' I said. 'I want to become a novelist.'

'I know your work,' he said. 'You are already a novelist.'

'I mean, make a living at it.'

'Just keep away from Hollywood. "Never any luck with movies," Scott Fitzgerald said. "Stick to your last, boy." Look at me. My relationship with Hollywood is a case of unrequited love,' he said. 'And I only made about fifteen thousand Straits dollars on *A Clockwork Orange*.'

'I want to leave here,' I said to him in a confidential way.

'Stay in Singapore as long as you are able to write. Try to avoid getting sand-fly fever. That turned my first wife into a dipso and eventually killed her. You'll know when it's time to leave.'

Soon after, I resigned my university job to give Harry Lazard poetry lessons, a leap in the dark that brought me to London like a refugee, where I carried a green Resident Alien card for a year and then was granted permission to live there with my wife, Alison, and our two sons.

Five years passed. There was the night of the staged interview with Burgess, and my first meeting with Sam Lettfish. Afterwards, at one of our lunches I mentioned Singapore. Lettfish said, 'I like the Singapore parts of Burgess's *Malayan Trilogy*,' and then, 'I had a friend in Singapore, Harry Lazard.'

'I knew him,' I said.

'I represented him in a very big case involving apparently forged end-user certificates in the sale of military hardware.'

'I gave him poetry lessons,' I said.

'Fayette, did you meet her?'

'Sure,' I said, and I wondered what more I dared to say.

'She had a steamy affair with President Sukarno of Indonesia in the Sixties,' Lettfish said.

I tried to imagine the big blonde woman, a Jew from South Carolina, taking on the dictator known to his people as the Great Bung.

'She's as bad as I am,' Lettfish said. 'Worse.' And he added, 'Something like that can make a woman's husband very insecure.'

'He introduced me to Nathan Leopold, the murderer,' I said.

'Harry's as crazy as me.'

'I wonder where Harry Lazard is now?'

'Israel, I imagine,' Lettfish said. 'He was pretty broken up after Fayette left him. Did you say "poetry lessons"?'

'Yes,' I said, and I explained.

'He's worse than I am!'

But I was thinking how I did not know Lettfish, nor had I really known Harry Lazard nor his ex-wife. Lettfish knew me superficially, I hardly knew Burgess, Lettfish did not know Burgess at all. Yet we were paddling on in this shallow pool of names and acquaintances and trivia and pretending it was reality.

Burgess was still in England then. I thought that he was living in Fulham or Putney, somewhere in the riverine suburbs of west London. We were fellow reviewers in London literary journalism, appearing in the weeklies and Sundays and selling our review copies at Gaston's. But after Lettfish inquired (he badly wanted to meet Burgess privately), I discovered that Burgess lived in Brighton 'in the gull-clawed air.'

'It must be Hove,' Lettfish said. 'Enderby lived in Hove' – naming a character from one of Burgess's novels. 'Remember when Vesta Bainbridge visited him?'

It seemed to me that Lettfish was once again confusing art with life, but it turned out that he was right. I asked Burgess the next time I saw him at Gaston's and he confirmed that he was indeed living in Hove on the south coast, but that he was planning to leave pretty soon.

'I hate the light here,' Burgess said. 'I need more sunlight. I can't work in this inspissated darkness.'

He also hated paying English taxes. 'I've been a fool long enough.' He contemplated living in Ireland, but he was too Irish himself to be happy there. He left England for Malta, found it repressive and priest-ridden, moved to Monaco, then Italy, and traveled a great deal, teaching and lecturing in the US with the reels of *A Clockwork Orange* in his luggage, which he showed to impress or amuse his audiences.

After Burgess left England Lettfish sought me out more often, precisely because Burgess was not around. I sometimes had a drink with Burgess when he passed through London, I occasionally bumped into him in New York, and we presented a joint lecture in Strasbourg. By then our age difference did not matter. I had never been his protégé, only his acquaintance. He was a man with no intimates.

One of the characteristics of English writers was that they all spent time on Grub Street and many went on living there. They were generally hard-working and unsnobbish and entirely democratic and uncompetitive. A writer's life was harder but simpler there since writing was classless and essentially unprofitable. We read each other, we wrote about each other; even the grandest hacked at reviews. Everything was fine until an English writer struck it rich with a bestseller in America, or a movie; and then his money set him apart, and he was sneered at and envied and sniped at, and he became 'the shit in the shuttered chateau,' loathed for having a good income and a life of ease.

Burgess was kind to me but he could be irascible, and the way he puffed his foul-smelling Schimmelpennick or held it in his trembly fingers like a smoldering pencil, made my eyes water. He loathed the English middle class and grew very cross at what he took to be manifestations of philistinism. Even in casual conversation he used his writing words – 'vatic,' 'idiolect,' 'thaumaturge,' 'claudicate.' He insisted on staying in the best hotels, always Claridge's in

London; and he pleaded poverty, perhaps because he was self-conscious about his hard work, and his prolific output. Though he tried to be frugal, he was a lavish tipper, as people from humble origins often are, out of fear and sympathy, understanding the people who serve them, knowing how weak and envious they can be, the big tip a clumsy attempt to placate them.

'Does he drink?' Lettfish asked me. Lettfish was a cautious drinker – overalert, nursing his half-pint of beer, always mistakenly calling it 'bitters.'

'A certain amount.'

'I'll bet he's as bad as I am,' Lettfish said. 'I'm always swigging something.'

Burgess drank a great deal, but he was not a drunk. He was far too dedicated to his writing to coarsen or belittle it with booze. It was only after his day's work was done that he guzzled gin, swilled wine, hoisted glasses of beer. 'Are you leaving that?' he once said to me in a London restaurant as I put down a glass of wine I could not finish. And then he drained it in a single gulp. He was a marvel to me, with an active mind. Alcohol gave him back his Irishness and made him forgivable. The few times I had seen him drunk he had a look of vulnerability and pathos that you see on the faces of some people who equate drunkenness with shame, a look of suffering and guilty surprise.

I never knew any writer who worked harder or was more generous. Of course he had his pick of the best of the week's books, while upstarts like Ian Musprat and I rummaged among his leavings. But it was only Burgess who was intellectually equipped and had the style and the confidence to review the new edition of the *Encyclopaedia Britannica*, or the *Oxford English Dictionary* or, as the sequence was published, the eleven volumes of Pepys's *Diary*. He still made time for his friends, for students, for aspiring writers. He wrote an introduction to the French translation of a novel of mine, *Les Conspirateurs*, and, as a joke, signed himself 'Antoine Bourgeois.'

He kept at it, writing, and composing music. 'As for writing assignments, I accept all reasonable offers,' he said, adding, 'and many unreasonable ones.' He was perhaps too restless and prodigious and impatient to be a great writer, but then greatness did not matter to him; he wished only to write well and be original. He was never cruel. There was wisdom in his generosity. I saw that as his greatest gift. That he could stand apart and see the value in someone else's effort.

'I tried to write a travel book once,' he said. 'We took a trip in our Bedford Dormobile to southern Italy – Calabria, actually. It was great fun, the food was wonderful, and every day I sat down and wrote about it, with the idea of doing a travel book. After about two weeks I saw that everything I had written was rubbish.'

'I'll be looking for your travel book about Italy.'

'Couldn't do it,' he said. 'But I'll tell you something. I read your book, *Railway Bazaar,* once a year.'

That was a Burgess compliment, and typically grand, but I knew he liked the book and now I had an inkling of why he liked me. I had written something that he had not managed himself. He had become my reader, too. But it was also the reason I admired him, and many other writers, because I saw myself as incapable of writing what they had. Not knowing exactly how a writer wrote a book, yet being fully aware of a brilliant writer's ability to enter the reader's soul: that was the key. How did they do it?

A reader might admire a writer, but only another writer saw the magic. I sometimes felt I was his only reader. That was why I was puzzled and amused by Lettfish, who because he collected his books felt he owned a piece of him. It offended me that Lettfish did not see the misery in a bright page of print. The presumption in his expression 'I collect him' gave me the creeps.

I was in awe of all fine writers' achievements and was still trying to understand the mystery of their lives. I knew what few readers knew, that you had to be that particular writer in order to write that particular book. My admiration for their work grew out of my puzzlement: I could not imagine how they had done it. Such writers inspired me by first proving I was stupid, and then making me feel wise. A person reading a wonderful book is overwhelmed by feelings of inspiration and ignorance, bafflement and belief, and becomes a sort of dogged, dazzled apostle, limping after the priestly figure of the writer.

I knew how ordinary writers had produced their books. It was no secret. There was a fine carpentry, obvious to another writer, that was woodwork but not art; you knew all this joinery and how it was hinged. Non-writers often recommended books to me; I would mention New York City and they'd say, 'You should read . . .' and they named a current book, and there was no way that I could explain to a non-writer that such books might be energetic and newsworthy but that they were uninspired and over-praised. I looked at them and knew just how they were made. I did not mock, but I felt I could do the same – indeed, I had done it.

But so many other writers were brilliant that it made me love the act of writing and hope to be inspired and not intimidated. I never compared our work; I often compared our lives. I did not know a single writer who was any good who had had it easy.

Burgess had been hard up like me. The struggle had made him cranky and generous and it had energized his books and made them live. His books might look artless but they had vitality. He loved language too much for his books not to seem somewhat mannered, yet I saw that this extravagant wordplay was a handicap; not eloquence, but clumsiness, more like an endearing speech defect, a lovable lisp.

I loved his work because it was not brilliant, and yet it disturbed me and seemed to defy gravity and, hovering, giving the illusion of concreteness, it contained enormous ambiguity, a floating pillow stuffed with impartial paradoxes – Burgess especially mingled good and evil. He was one of the handful of writers whose work I admired because although I could not duplicate it I saw how it was attainable. He had talent but not genius; that was another reason I read him closely, because I could understand and learn. These writers inspired me not to be like them but to be myself; they filled me with a desire to write my own fiction.

Burgess at least stayed abroad, for tax reasons, though he made Joycean noises about art and exile. Lettfish pursued me more than ever and became strident in his invitations, about half of which I accepted – for lunch, for drinks. It bothered me that I did not reciprocate. It did not bother him – rather, he seemed to enjoy the idea of my indebtedness. I wondered why I put up with him and I decided that his collecting fascinated me, the appetite it showed, the eye for detail, the patience, the need to acquire, most of all the wealth it illustrated.

It was another of Lettfish's expressions of power that he included in his collection insignificant and high-priced articles of Burgess's life because they were so scarce. Lettfish owned one of Burgess's old passports, a pewter mug from Kota Bharu presented by the Sultan to Burgess, a leather satchel once owned by Burgess, a paper napkin Burgess had doodled on – not words or sketches but notes and lines of music, a Russian–English dictionary with Burgess's bookplate, an airline ticket (London–New York) in Burgess's name.

Lettfish did not boast about these items. 'I'm always buying these crazy things!' If he had been a collector and no more than that I would not have agreed to see him. But he was a reader. He had read everything that Burgess had written. Knowing the work was as important to him as owning it. He could quote whole paragraphs verbatim, he could repeat dialogue, he knew the characters, what they ate, how they dressed, their reactions. We were in a restaurant, where the service was slow. 'I know what Victor Crabbe would say at a moment like this.' In a pub, Lettfish turned and said of the barman, 'He looks like Paul Hussey,' naming another Burgess character. It pleased me when Lettfish said that Burgess's work gave him a sensitivity to language and a feel for geography – the Russia of *Honey for the Bears*, the England of *Enderby*, the Malaya of *The Long Day Wanes*.

'Does the Africa of *Devil of a State* ring true?' Lettfish asked me. 'You've lived there.'

'It's all made up. Burgess set the novel in Africa so that he wouldn't be sued for libel. It's really about Brunei.'

'Mind not doing that?'

I was puffing my pipe. I palmed it, inwardly raging, insulted at having to carry out his order.

'What was I talking about?' Lettfish said.

'I haven't the slightest idea.' I stared at him.

Lettfish sniffed and said, 'So that country Dunia doesn't exist?'

'*Dunia* means "the world" in Malay and, I think, in Arabic.'

Such trivia made me seem knowledgeable, and so he ended up valuing me.

I'm kind of a little Burgess myself, Lettfish had said, when we first met. What did he mean by that? I supposed that he identified with the Burgess anti-hero, how he was always victimized by women, and drank too much, and complained of ill-health, and was overcharged, and snubbed. Burgess's men were in constant physical discomfort, they were romantics, they tended to be well-read, they always wore badly fitting dentures. They felt out of place in big cities, especially American cities; they were frightened by crime, by young thugs, they traveled a great deal, yet they hated it. They were morally strong, often indignant, but they were physical cowards. They were accident-prone, ending up disabled and broke rather than dramatically dead. They were self-mocking. Even the dimmest of them were able to speak several languages.

They were in short all of them Anthony Burgess.

Burgess's books were Lettfish's education. They simplified his adjustment to living in England, and because Burgess was expert at describing the discomforts of London, and his uneasy sense of Englishness – a provincial, a Catholic, who had earned his literary stripes in the colonies – Lettfish was vindicated in his own London uneasiness.

At one of our lunches, Lettfish – who was always the host – asked me how I liked living in London. I told him the truth: I was happy here. Afterwards I pondered the happiness, the way that sometimes on a tube train I looked at the face of a lovely woman, pondering the obvious, scrutinizing her nose, her eyes, her hair, her skin, her lips, her legs: what element, or combination of them, accounted for this beauty?

My London happiness was my big brick house, the quiet street, the way my desk faced Victorian windows, the giant sycamore outside, the backwater of South London. It was my family most of all. I hardly thought about living in London. I lived in a house. I was a member of a family. I worked indoors. The city was out the window, beyond the sycamore and the garden wall: the glimpses of wet roof slates, the black streets, red buses – and everything in the foreground was private, personal, safe, lighted with love and warmth, fragrant with flowers and food. That was my London – my house.

Burgess's books helped Lettfish like England better. They gave him a certain style – that is, he saw that his own style was quite good enough. Burgess's characters were human beings, like the writer himself. And beneath the surface of Burgess's writing, where mockery became fondness, was an affection for Americans and a resentment of England. Burgess was one of those class-hating and reluctant Englishmen who was happier among Americans, because they were generous and didn't judge, and yet perversely he kept a sneering stiff upper lip only when he was talking to Americans.

Lettfish's vocabulary was crammed with Burgess words. Who else said 'proleptic' or 'pelagic' or 'claudicate'? Lettfish also used the words 'halitotic' and 'lexeme' correctly. He sometimes overdid it with something like 'brachycephalic.' I had the sense that Lettfish was a better man for knowing Burgess's work; and reading the books that Burgess reviewed he was better read; better able to cope in London; funnier; more conversational. Burgess, a relentless pedagogue (so many of his fictional characters were English teachers), was Lettfish's teacher.

He implored me to arrange a dinner for him and Burgess. He had been asking me to do this for some time, but – as I told him – I hardly saw Burgess in London. Once he had left England I saw him only a few times. He came unannounced and was hard to pin down and furtive in a way I associated with most writers, and he always left in a hurry. I did not really want to have dinner with him. We could never be close friends. I wanted simply to know him and to go on being his reader.

It was about this time that I stopped reading my day's work to Alison in the evenings. With both children at school during the week, our lives changed, we worked later than usual – dinnertime could be flexible: there were only the two of us. The evening had once been long and eventful, beginning with the children's dinner, ending after our meal, as I sat reading the two pages or so I had written that day. Now it was different, emptier, Alison's day was longer, we sometimes ate separately, and now and then I went to bed alone, or she did. Though she always read the finished typescript, I had stopped reading to her. I sensed that something important was ending between us but I could not say what it was.

Lonelier, more susceptible to offers of hospitality, I saw more of Lettfish, and he reminded me each time that he was eager to have dinner with Burgess. I was willing to arrange it – I owed it to Lettfish, I felt. But it was not possible because Burgess was unavailable; that is to say, in Italy, or else in Los Angeles.

And I reminded Lettfish – who paid no attention – that Burgess was not a close friend but rather an acquaintance, whom I had known ten years, having met him in 1969 in Singapore. It was now 1981. I had no friends in England, I had numerous acquaintances. I had no friends anywhere. Burgess said the same thing. Friendship in any intimate sense, implying sacrifice and love and an unquestioning willingness to confide, is almost impossible for a writer. My writer acquaintances – Ian Musprat, for example – did not have any friends, either.

Still, Sam Lettfish, the collector, the lawyer, the version of Burgess, wanted to meet his favorite writer. I said I would try to fix it. Then one afternoon I was asked to appear with Burgess on a TV program to discuss Graham Greene's work – the occasion was a new novel. Burgess flew in from Monaco. The taping was done at the BBC in White City in the afternoon, and while we sat in the fake library set of the studio waiting to begin I said to him, 'Are you and Liana free for dinner tonight?'

He said he was free, but that Liana was back in Monaco, laid up with a broken ankle – she had slipped on a hotel step in Monte Carlo. A horrible business, he said. He had sought compensation, the poor woman had not been able to work; but not only had he not received any money, Liana and he had been persecuted by the hotel's lawyer.

'Come to my house. You can forget all about it.'

'That is very kind of you.'

And after the taping I called Lettfish.

'I apologize for the short notice, but can you come to dinner tonight?'

'Sorry,' he said. 'I have a very important meeting with a client who has just flown in from Geneva on a tax matter.'

'What a shame. Burgess is coming. I knew it was crazy, inviting you at such a late hour.'

Was that a challenge? My earpiece on the receiver seemed to crackle and glow, as though charged with a jolt of electricity.

'I'll be there,' Lettfish said.

2

As a host, bringing together Burgess and Lettfish, the writer and his reader, I felt an apprehension that a marriage broker must know intensely when making an introduction, because even when prospective marriage partners might seem equal, one does most of the speaking, the other the listening. It was the physical business of it that puzzled me most, because I always imagined the writer and reader as separate people, not two big men in the same room. Perhaps that was why I had done nothing in the preceding years, and had been not lazy but afraid.

I called Alison from the studio where we were taping the Greene program. This was just minutes after Lettfish told me that he was coming. Alison made a sound that indicated exasperation, unwillingness, resentment, a sudden gust of impatience that the telephone wires made even harsher. It was just a sigh, a syllable, intelligible only to a spouse and only after years of marriage; a long-married couple has a perfect ear for such uncooperative murmurs.

'What's wrong?' I said, because I knew this sound was a serious objection.

'Does it have to be tonight?'

'Yes.' There was so much to explain. All the months and years that had passed since I had first met Lettfish had led to this moment. 'Shall I tell you why?'

'Don't bother. If you want to have these people over, fine. But I can't help you. We've had one crisis after another all day here. I was hoping I could go home and put my feet up. Have an early night.'

'I wasn't asking for your help.'

She made another noise, just air, that was like the beginning of a howl.

'Please,' I said, and I meant: Give me a break, yell at me tomorrow, swallow your anger, play along and don't embarrass me.

'It's a week night.'

'I have to do this.'

She said, 'All right,' and though there was a reluctance tucked into its intonation, saying yes under protest, she was relenting. She knew desperation when she heard it.

After I thanked her she said, 'Why are you doing this to me?' And before I could reply to that, she said, 'It's your dinner,' and hung up.

Those responses were part of that dispute. They were lines. In marriage many conversations are the same conversation; we had been having this one more often lately, especially after I had stopped reading my daily pages to her. That part of the evening had been important, when, as a writer, reading to her, I made her my reader.

Your dinner: that was fine with me. I had started the event in motion and I had to see it through. And now I knew that at a certain point tonight, probably just after dinner, when I was taking orders for coffee, Alison would say, 'Now I am going to be very rude and uncivilized. I have to get up early tomorrow. I'm not even going to ask you to forgive me. Good night.'

Early on, I had the sense the dinner was going to be a failure. The conversation with Alison confirmed this fear.

We rarely entertained. I have already mentioned that I had no friends in London. My London door was always locked. No one ever dropped in. No strangers entered the house. I had not had any friends since I had gotten married. In my peculiar temperament that the passing years intensified, I regarded other people as intrusions and placed a special value on being alone.

I was reflecting on this as I made the dinner. Because Burgess had mentioned curry with approval in his Malayan novels, I decided to cook a prawn curry, with channa dhal. I bought two pounds of prawns at the fishmonger's in Clapham Junction on my way home from the Greene program and walked back through the rain.

The Malayan touch was coconut milk. I found a large can of it at a Jamaican grocery on Northcote Road. Back home, I put on the rice, peeled the prawns, chopped the garlic and onions and green pepper, sautéed them, then made a flour and curry powder paste, added water and vegetable stock and thickened it. This gave me a half-gallon of curry sauce. Half of it I would use for the prawns, adding coconut milk to it; the rest for the dhal, to which I added red pepper and two chopped tomatoes and some crushed cardamoms, along with three cans of chickpeas.

While the sauce simmered I chopped a cucumber for the yogurt raita and made a plate of sambals, garnishes that Burgess would recognize from his days in Kota Bharu. It was almost seven. If we ate at eight-thirty or thereabouts, then there would be enough time for the dhal to simmer and reduce. It was simple cooking but its strong flavor made it seem ambitious. The thing was to avoid overcooking the prawns. I intended to put them into the sauce just before the meal so that they wouldn't curl and toughen and become flavorless.

Alison came into the kitchen just as I finished the last chopping.

She poured herself a glass of wine and said, 'What are you going to give them to drink?'

'There's wine and beer.'

'What if they want whiskey?'

'They can have wine instead.'

'Oh, God.'

'All right, will you go out and buy some whiskey?'

'This isn't my dinner party!' Alison said, and the note of hysteria in her voice made me fearful.

I said, 'You're right. I should have some whiskey. I'll go get some from the off-license.'

'I'm so tired.'

She spoke in a persecuted way. That was a definite signal that she would go to bed early, leaving me to handle the guests.

Rain in London had a sooty quality that soaked the city in its own smoky odor. I walked quickly through the drizzle. The corner shop, the Paki store as it was known – though the owners were Indians, Hindus, from Gujarat – was open all hours, and sold groceries and tobacco and newspapers and overpriced liquor, as well as renting TV sets. They were young, with a fat, squally infant and a slavering guard dog: England's new nation of shopkeepers. I bought a bottle of Scotch and, passing the Fishmonger's Arms, I glanced in and wished that I could be sitting there irresponsibly reading the evening paper over a pint of draft Guinness.

At the house I saw Lettfish at the front door, his hands in motion.

'There's no answer,' he said to me.

'My wife probably didn't hear the bell' – *It's your dinner!* – 'but at least you found the place.'

Lettfish said, 'I've never been to this part of London before,' and it seemed to carry with it a hint of rebuke.

Leading him in, I remembered that tomorrow was rubbish pickup day. I put out the barrels.

'What's the word they use for those things?'

'Dustbins.'

'I love it.'

'Dustmen are coming tomorrow,' I said, 'with their dustcart.'

I had rain on my face, curry stains on my shirt, my hair was wet, and I was breathless, gasping as I let him into the house.

Lettfish looked around, made a beeline for my bookshelves and gave them his lightning scrutiny, and then he snatched at volumes, opening them to the copyright page, smoothing the dust wrappers, assessing their value.

'Whiskey?' I asked. The fresh bottle was under my arm.

'How about a gin and tonic?'

216

'I don't have any.'

'Wine, then. A red – cabernet.'

'You got it.'

I poured him a Beaujolais and smiled, defying him to object.

He was restless, asking where Burgess was; and Alison was up-stairs, so I could not get on with setting the table or any other pre-parations. He required me to be with him.

The etiquette for a guest lay in reading what the host had to do and then either helping or else getting out of the way. All guests were supposed to know that. But Lettfish was so used to being a host that he was a bad guest, knew nothing about the respons-ibilities, how demanding it was to strike the right balance between being helpful and being intrusive. Being a guest involved a large measure of generosity and tact, cooperation and intuition. He was inept, and I began to see that his always assuming the role of host had made him selfish.

When Alison appeared, I said, 'This is Sam Lettfish,' and I ex-cused myself and went back into the kitchen. I tossed the prawns into the skillet of bubbling curry sauce that was creamy with coco-nut milk, and stirred them until they turned pink. They had such delicate flesh and were so easily toughened, spoiled by overcooking, I took them off the stove and ladled them into a double boiler.

'Bonnet, wing, wing mirror, boot, petrol tank,' Lettfish was saying as I returned. One of his favorite topics: English nomen-clature. I guessed it was my mention of 'dustbins' that had set him off. He found the words uproariously funny. Alison's eyes were glazed. In a moment she would say that she was hungry.

'Sam's a book collector,' I said, as a way of getting him to change the subject.

'Paul's worse than I am,' Lettfish said. 'Pretty exciting, Anthony Burgess coming over, eh?'

'I must confess that I am not a fan,' Alison said.

'All those big words,' Lettfish said.

'I know the meaning of the words, I don't regard them as very big,' Alison said. 'No, it's those Burgess women. They are so frightful.'

'I guess I'm a sucker for crazy broads.'

'If they were truly crazy I would pity them, as one does. But they are simply objectionable.'

'It takes all kinds.'

'It doesn't take castrators.'

'Maybe I'm just stupid for liking his books,' Lettfish said.

'You don't understand,' Alison said, and smiled, as though to placate a simpleton. 'Like him by all means, but please don't try to make me like him.'

'I can relate to his output.'

'Whatever that means,' Alison said.

'"Relate" means understand.'

'"Output" was the word I was questioning.'

'Hey, you remind me of my wife.'

Alison smiled again, not mirth, but rather a look of pure disgust.

'You're as bad as she is!'

Staring at him, her smile fixed, not trusting herself to reply to this, Alison said, 'Paul tells me you're a lawyer.'

She was wondering how anyone this silly and casual could hold down a serious job. I knew that Lettfish's nervousness was making him chatter in an infantile way.

'What you'd call a solicitor, though I don't do much soliciting' – he paused for a reaction: there was none – 'mostly tax matters, corporate mergers, estate planning, licensing agreements. We don't live in separate countries anymore. We're part of a global tax and banking structure.'

He went on in this vein while we listened – Alison thinking of her hunger, I worrying that Burgess might not make it and, if he did, that the prawns would be tough from sitting in the heated sauce. Lettfish seemed very serious when talking about his legal work, but his seriousness did not make him sound intelligent or articulate, only monotonously dull.

'I'm hungry,' Alison said.

Lettfish did not hear her. He was still talking. 'I've been facilitating joint ventures in carbon. The British carbon industry is booming. That's not a widely known fact.'

'I think I can understand why,' Alison said, smiling again.

There was a thump and clatter in the street and it sounded like one of my barrels going over and losing its lid. This sudden sound was followed by a distinct but distant curse.

'What's that?' Lettfish asked me, looking worried.

'Burgess, I think.'

He had not yet begun to ring the bell when I opened the door. He was wiping his tweed jacket with his pocket handkerchief. His hair was wild, his face wet with rain, his tie yanked down, and there was a new tear, with a smeary stain, in the knee of his trousers.

'Pranged my leg,' Burgess said. That was another characteristic of Burgess heroes, and Burgess: they were accident-prone. 'Some bloody fool left his dustbins in the footpath. When I lived in England, the dustmen carried them from your garden and put them back.'

'That doesn't happen in Mrs Thatcher's England, ' I said. 'Come in, have a whiskey.'

'Splendid.' He entered, still scrubbing at his soiled jacket. 'What a lovely house. Those Victorian windows are so graceful. A touch of Malacca' – he was passing the carved settee. 'I should love to see these aquatints in daylight. Paul, it's a real home! My place is such a hovel – but we're working on it. Yes?'

He had come face to face with Sam Lettfish.

'And you are?'

Before I could speak, Lettfish said, 'One of your fans.'

'No, no, no. Terrible word – fans, fanatics. It's madness.'

'One of your readers.'

'Better,' Burgess said, chewing his teeth.

He was still wet from the rain, bruised from his fall, distracted and seemingly blinded by coming indoors into the light on this winter night. He was stumbling and stammering, and it occurred to me that he might be a bit tipsy. He was still in motion, moving from room to room.

'Hello.' He saw Alison leaving the kitchen.

'Your meal smells delicious. I love curry. There's none to be had in Monte Carlo.'

'Paul's done the cooking,' she said.

Lettfish hovered, waiting for a chance to speak again.

'This is Sam Lettfish. You met long ago at the Festival Hall,' I said, handing Burgess a whiskey.

'Lettfish,' Burgess said, and squinted in concentration, as though he had just been asked a tricky question. He chewed on the syllables of an unspoken word. 'Lettfish, are you a Lett?'

'He's as crazy as I am,' said Lettfish.

'So Lettfish does not speak Lettish,' Burgess said. 'Are you leftish, Lettfish, or flatish.'

'Crazier.'

'A lott is a fish,' Burgess said. 'Lettfish might be a corruption of lottfish.'

'I'm a Jew,' Lettfish said.

'To a non-Jew that explains everything,' Burgess said. 'To a Jew, it says nothing.'

I went into the kitchen to check on the meal. Alison stood at the counter, refilling her wine glass.

'I'm awfully hungry,' she said. 'Do you mind if I eat right now?'

'Please wait for us. It will look ridiculous if you eat by yourself.'

'Paul, how many of Burgess's books do I own?' Lettfish called out.

'Please join us,' I whispered to Alison, but putting my arm around her she recoiled, not wanting to be touched. I left her sulking in the kitchen. To Burgess, I said, 'Sam's a collector. He's got quite a library.'

'For a lawyer, I guess,' Lettfish said. 'I get a little tired of dealing with industrial litigation relating to faulty fall-away sections.'

Burgess became alert.

Lettfish said, 'I prefer something flavescent.'

'How much is that in real money?' Burgess said in a snarly American accent.

'Your tie is flavescent.'

Burgess sipped his whiskey and licked his thin lips. He looked very frail and had that same doped-up look I had seen all those years ago in Singapore, when I understood that a writer is always two people.

Lettfish said, 'Acrotism.'

'Don't mention religion,' Burgess said, the same snarl.

'My pulse is acrotistic,' Lettfish said. 'You are claudicant.'

'Once you've started using words like that, because you like the sound of them, you're lost. The world has no use for you. No one wants to read them.' He looked at Alison, who had wandered out of the kitchen, looking haunted and hungry. He said, 'Transponder.'

'The rice is overcooked,' Alison said.

Lettfish said, 'Before there was good quality control, the transponder market gave us a lot of billable hours.'

'Finite amplitude waves,' Burgess said.

Lettfish brightened, hearing the words, and said, 'I had a case of copyright infringement involving electronic monitoring, using those. We had trouble getting the case to court because the infringer lived in Monte Carlo. He didn't count on us having a partner in the principality. Kleinvogel. The infringer settled.'

Burgess had his glass to his lips, but he did not sip. He said, 'Fall-away sections.'

'Your military type uses different specs and usually a titanium bolt in the linkage,' Lettfish said.

'Observe how this description derives from the solid field of technology,' Burgess said.

Alison had brought the serving dishes of curry and all the rest of the meal, to the table. She said, 'Shall we sit down?'

'There is something essentially philistine about technology. And the law is just book-hating.'

'I love your books,' Lettfish said.

'Ballocks,' Burgess said, taking a seat at the table. And he leaned over to Alison and said, 'I think it's all going awfully well.'

He was drunk. I could see that from the way he had heaved himself into his chair, from his breathlessness, from the way he sat. And Lettfish watched him eagerly, with a mixture of respectful caution and genuine bafflement – innocence and disbelief.

I was grateful when, unbidden, Alison began passing the rice, and then the dishes of dhal and prawn curry.

'I'm sorry your wife's not here,' Alison said.

'Liana broke her ankle. Tripped on a child's toy left on the marble stairs of one of our leading hotels. Took a header. We tried to sue. We were threatened with destruction by the hotel.'

Lettfish said, 'I might be able to help.'

'Haven't you done quite enough?' Burgess said, with a screech in his voice that made Lettfish wince.

Then Burgess became preoccupied – finished his whiskey, spooned chopped banana, murmured the word 'sambals,' and he did not look up as his hand moved crabwise towards his wine glass and his fingers snared its stem and hoisted it. He drank, he did not notice that his last outburst had silenced the table. He ate, working his mouth as though the food were too hot; but it was his bridgework in motion, his useless teeth were part of his unmanageable mouthful.

'You're the writer chap,' he said, mimicking a pompous fruity voice. 'Isn't it interesting, the number of writers who went to medical school – Joyce, Maugham, Chekhov, William Carlos Williams, Voltaire – the list is endless. And yet can you name a single writer who went to law school?'

'Robert Louis Stevenson,' I said, hoping it would calm him.

'To please his father. He despised the law. But there's no one else.'

I said, 'Anthony Trollope must have known the law. There's a very good legal judgment, the definition of "heirloom" in *The Eustace Diamonds*.'

Lettfish, grateful for my intervention, eagerly looked at Burgess for a response.

'Trollope was a civil servant, a postal official. It was his business to know the law, since he drew up postal treaties. I was thinking of a writer who actually practiced law in the way that Chekhov practiced medicine. You can't name one.'

He faced Lettfish, he chewed his teeth, he sipped his wine. All this mouth motion seemed like aggression, and even his food-flecked lips were threatening.

Alison said, 'I fancy he's pulling your leg, Mr Lettfish.'

Lettfish stared bug-eyed at his plate and in his silence he seemed to glow with rage and disappointment.

'Does anyone mind if I smoke?' Burgess said.

He was lighting up as he asked the question, and he blew a cloud of smoke over the remains of the dinner. Sam Lettfish shut his mouth and kept his head down, like a man in a storm.

'I'll make coffee,' I said.

Burgess said, 'Do you have tea? I'd love a mug of strong tea. Two tea bags. Two sugars. Just a drop of milk. Lovely.'

'Nothing for me,' Lettfish said.

'You're the writer chap,' Burgess said again, and grinned horribly at Lettfish.

Alison pushed her chair back and said, 'I hate to be a spoiler. Please don't get up. I must go to bed or I'll never make it to work tomorrow. Good night.'

She was smiling but it was not a smile. I thought of her saying, *Why are you doing this to me?*

Burgess and Lettfish said good night. I went into the kitchen and put the water on for tea.

I heard Burgess saying, 'So Kleinvogel is your partner in the principality . . .'

They spoke back and forth, in short slap-like replies, while the kettle boiled and I made Burgess his cup of tea.

When I returned to the table, Lettfish was saying, 'I imagined you'd be above all that.'

'Of course I am,' Burgess said. 'My ivory tower is the perfect height, and I sit there paring my nails, oblivious of the lawsuits brought against me.'

'If Kleinvogel knew of your standing in the world of literature he wouldn't have proceeded against you.'

'That's ballocks. "So you're the writer chap." His exact words.' Spit flew from Burgess's lips as he spoke.

'Kleinvogel's a great litigator.'

'Kleinvogel is cauchemaresque.'

I handed Burgess the cup of tea.

'Everything's going awfully well,' he said, and smiled, and he blew on the cup and then set his lips on the rim and began sucking at the tea, and eyeing Lettfish. Then he uncorked the whiskey bottle and poured some whiskey in, filling the cup.

'What book of mine do you especially admire?'

'*Nothing Like the Sun*,' Lettfish said in a small voice.

'It's a parlor trick. My least achieved novel. It's a thin idea, tricked out with Elizabethan verbiage that I pinched from old glossaries. Wrong again, Max.'

'And the first *Enderby*.'

'Meretricious,' Burgess said.

'*Devil of a State*.'

'A victim of threatened litigation,' Burgess said. 'The libel lawyers made me rewrite it.'

Lettfish said, 'Paul told me – '

'You see?' Burgess winked at me, then turned to Lettfish. 'So you're here selling – what? – military hardware and children's toys, pretty much the same thing. And what I want to know is, do you miss American food? Sara Lee cheesecake – that sort of thing?'

Lettfish shook his head from side to side, as though he had just received some very bad news and was like a man grieving.

'I used to eat it myself,' Burgess said. 'I won't hear a word against it, Max.'

'My name is Sam. Kleinvogel is Max.'

'Tell me,' Burgess said, 'why is your neck turning purple?'

Lettfish's face was twisted, he looked miserable, stung by the conversation and sickened by Burgess's cigar smoke. He was trying to be brave, yet the ordeal showed on his face – not only pain but a deeper and more lasting look, a sad scowl of disenchantment.

Compressing his lips, Burgess hummed a few notes, making his jowls flap, and then sipped his alcoholic tea and spiked the cup with more whiskey.

'You can't read, Max,' he said, and stuck out his jaw. Now I could not look at his mouth without imagining his set of false teeth.

He ground out his cigar butt and lit another one and blew smoke assertively, squinting behind it, as though planning an attack.

Lettfish lifted his head and, scarcely controlling his anger, said, 'You've got to be kidding.'

Burgess smacked his lips and took out his fountain pen and drew on a napkin, a stave of parallel lines, then rapidly like hanging fruit on these lines he inscribed a series of notes.

'Go on, what does it say?'

Lettfish folded his arms. 'That's music.'

'A four-year-old could have told me that. Go on – hum it.'

'I will do nothing of the kind.'

'Anger makes some people crude, and it turns others pompous,' Burgess said. 'So you can't read the simple phrase.'

'What is this, some kind of test?'

'Exactly,' Burgess said. 'Gesualdo. Know him?'

'I haven't read him,' Lettfish said. 'Sorry. I can't read everything.'

'He's a musician, Max. Sixteenth century. But very modern in his tonalities. That' – he pointed to the notes – 'is the opening of his madrigal "Moro, lasso." '

Lettfish looked again as though he were grieving.

'Max, a knowledge of serious music is essential to an understanding of my work.' Burgess began to hum, and though he seemed drunk and rumpled, his humming was precise and tuneful and was like a reminder that he was sane.

Over this humming, Lettfish said, 'I own every book you've ever written.'

'Too bad you can't read, Max.'

Lettfish smiled hopelessly and got up to leave.

'I wasn't asking you to like me,' he said.

'Cauchemaresque,' Burgess murmured, as I saw Lettfish to the door.

Lettfish's last words to me were: 'I always felt there was something missing in his books. Now I know what it is. He's a very sad man.' But it was Lettfish who seemed heartbroken.

Burgess was smiling when I returned to the room.

'I think it all went awfully well,' he said, and went on humming the complicated music.

It was the last time I saw him. Lettfish too stopped calling me. And Alison said, 'Don't ever do that to me again.'

SIX

Man Alone

Rupert Moody told me the story of Arturo Tripodi and so I knew there must be something missing in it.

We were in London. He had come over to my house on his bicycle. He said, 'My wife's down in the country. I'd be there myself but I'm fronting a TV program for Julian. Stop looking at me as though I'm a media slut!'

It was late summer, a season I was so unused to in London (I normally spent the summer on Cape Cod) that it seemed like a different city, and another of its lives was revealed. When London dried out in the summer heat and became parched, its surfaces cracked – the brick walls, the stucco façades, the pavements. It was a shabbier city, with a look of exhaustion, the split masonry, the trees heavy with dusty leaves, the grass a blackish green, clumpy and uneven, thick hedges and untrimmed rose bushes leggy and out of hand, needing to be dead-headed. The magnificent flowers of spring and early summer had vanished and gone to seed. There were no blossoms in August, and the days were either clammy and humid or else sunk in harsh headachy heat, with dense gassy air. In summer the city was overwhelmed by its weather, and with its windows open, noisier. The English seemed self-conscious in the street, looking vulnerable and underdressed, their flesh exposed, either very pale or burned pink.

'My wife and I were supposed to be in Tibet, but this TV program came up,' Rupert said. 'We'll head for India in October. It's a better month anyway and there's that fantastic puja there at that time, the Kumbha-mela, which is absolutely not to be missed. What are you doing?'

Irritable in the city heat, I was writing a novella. I told him. I had sent my wife and children to Cape Cod; I was in London alone.

'And what does your little family think of that?'

'I'm not very popular these days.'

'I was in Amsterdam last month. People were raving about you. You're big in Holland, you know.'

'Someone interviewed Alison recently. She was quoted as saying "Even genius has to do the dishes." '

'Oh, yes, the death of the artist is the pram in the hall.'

'I don't have that problem. It's just that writing seems to be a very anti-social activity. Wouldn't you hate to be married to a writer?'

'My wife writes all the time. She's always scribbling her head off.'

But I was thinking about my house, my marriage, and wondering whether I had overstayed my welcome.

'What is this novella you mentioned?'

'I started it in May. The trouble is, it's not portable. I can't leave until I finish it. I like it too much to leave it behind. So I'm here alone until it's done.'

It was, I said, about a young American woman, Lauren Slaughter, leading a double life, as a political science researcher by day and a social escort, a glorified call girl, by night. It seemed to me to be the best way of revealing the layers of life in London. This American had penetrated to all levels of English society, from her Brixton bed-sitter and her research institute in St James's, to her luxury flat in Mayfair, where her address, Half Moon Street, would give the story its title.

The grand people who ignored her as a lowly and underpaid re-searcher later hired her through an agency, and as an escort she dined with wealthy oil sheiks. Such a woman was at home every-where and nowhere, for without a husband she had no status. But she was one of the few people who knew her way through the London labyrinth. Being American helped; being intelligent and pretty were also crucial. She did not mind being a prostitute – in fact, she rather enjoyed it, the glamour of it, the way it balanced her other life. She had no money. She had no conscience.

Rupert said, 'My wife met someone exactly like that at a dinner party in Belgravia. "Are you with Whitey Grutchfield?" "Oh, is that his name?" the tart said. Sir Stafford Grutchfield.'

Moody plied me for more details of Lauren Slaughter. He con-sidered himself an outsider, and was always mocking the English, liked the lowlife aspects of my story, the obscurity and audacity of the woman, the vicious sex, the money changing hands, the way in which a grand figure – a total mystery in the House of Lords, an enigma to his family and friends – was naked before the eyes of an American popsie, who knew all his secrets. These things fascinated me, too. I asked him about Sir Stafford Grutchfield's tart.

' "I just met this bloke tonight – the agency sent me." My wife had to bite her tongue so she wouldn't laugh and cause an uproar. The Duke of Westminster was there!'

So, as a sort of gift in return for my telling him this story, Moody told me the story of Arturo Tripodi. And he suggested that I might make it a companion piece, as another example of someone who lived in London in complete obscurity and had a secret.

Tripodi lived across Wandsworth Bridge in Fulham, on Musgrave Crescent, facing Eel Brook Common, in a tiny terrace house. Rupert seemed to be suggesting that I make Lauren Slaughter and Arturo Tripodi neighbors in Half Moon Street, off Piccadilly, one person going down in the world, the other moving up. The street would be their only link – that, and their other lives. They might bump into each other on the stairs one day, no more; yet there would be resonances.

I had read Arturo Tripodi, I had heard that he lived in London, but I associated him with Cairo or Rome. It thrilled me that a great writer, someone I associated with Egypt and Italy, had turned up in a small street across the bridge from my own house. He was an Italian, from a merchant family that had lived in Egypt since the early nineteenth century. He was fluent in Arabic, he also wrote in French. He had a very strong accent. You had the impression, when he spoke, that his English was faulty. And yet he was one of the great prose stylists in English.

'My wife saw him in Paris on that program "Apostrophe." His French is perfect, as you would expect, with a slight Arabic accent. That was how I got so friendly with him. You have to meet him.'

'I guess I will, one of these days.'

'No, that's why I'm in London. I'm doing a program about him. The talk is that he's on the next Honours' List for a knighthood. And I have the key to his house!'

'How did you manage that?'

'I needed it for the program. Tripodi's too deaf to hear my knock, and his housekeeper's too lazy to go on answering the door.'

It was typical of Rupert to invite himself and me to tea at Arturo

Tripodi's house. He said the old man would be glad to see us. And that I had to meet him in person before I saw the TV program. Afterwards, when I had my story, most of it, the essentials, or so I thought, Rupert told me the rest and I realized that I could not write it down, nor could I assign Arturo Tripodi to a flat in Half Moon Street. I knew his secret, but it had to remain a secret. If I suppressed the secret, and the truth about Tripodi ever came out, I would look credulous and naive. Rupert knew that. And so I simply remembered it, to write about some other day.

Now Arturo Tripodi is dead; so is Rupert Moody. I can tell the story.

The afternoon tea in Fulham at Tripodi's was not eventful. The old man was stout, he was deaf, his sight was poor. He wore a heavy pair of eyeglasses, a hearing aid bulging in one of the earpieces. He wore thick-soled shoes, though he clearly did no walking, and they looked wrong for his small house. He wore baggy pants, a rumpled jacket, a tie. I doubted that he had dressed up for me. It was a European habit, a tweed jacket and tie on a hot summer afternoon, and this effort making him seem more disreputable than if he had worn rags.

I asked him a question, something about living in London, hoping for a usable reply.

'Rupert knows all the English intellectuals,' he said. He had not heard my question. Perhaps he was offering me a compliment.

But 'intellectuals' was a word that no one in England used. In English it had an old-fashioned and faintly ridiculous sound. It was a European word, an intellectual was a European, someone who spoke with a strong accent and who dressed like this man, in cheap itchy tweeds, and sat in his jacket and tie in an overstuffed chair, wearing heavy shoes, among bookshelves. Who smoked a pipe and ate heavy meals, served by a devoted old woman with a mustache.

'There are no English intellectuals,' Rupert said.

The old man did not hear that either.

In spite of the heat, we drank hot tea, and Tripodi remained in his tweed jacket. There were herbs in the window boxes and pictures on the walls of classical scenes – Piranesi prints, Greek ruins, and in several vases there were dead flowers. I could not tell whether they had simply expired and blackened or else been deliberately dried. Whatever, they gave a funereal effect to the room.

Arturo Tripodi was not an exile but a distinguished foreigner, as famous for his social commentaries and his historical insights as his gloomy exoticism. In America he would have been required to integrate and become a loyal American. In England such a man was expected to be aloof, and would become famous for his foreignness, for not quite fitting in, as Joseph Conrad had been in his day. Tripodi was well-known as part of an unEnglish élite which included George Steiner and Sir Isaiah Berlin and Elias Canetti, all British passport-holders and the sort of citizen aliens I myself might become if I persevered.

Arturo Tripodi was also famous for being penniless. A wise old man with no income, he lived by winning prizes. There were endless literary prizes in England. That was the gift the English gave him – not for work he had published but for work in progress, for his very existence. He knew the judges intimately, yet it was not dishonest. He deserved the prize money; it was enough to get by on, not enough to make him prosperous. It was niggardly, narrow English patronage, the award with a sonorous name. When I saw on his book jackets *Winner of the Bowood-Hancock Prize*, I was reminded of the royal warrant (*By Appointment to H R H The Prince of Wales*) on jars of mustard.

Tripodi had published a memoir which he called a novel, a number of essays and commentaries, an analysis of Moorish thought in Spain, a recent piece on the death of Nabokov, a long piece on the artist Balthus, a book about Italo Svevo's novel *Senility* that was longer than the novel itself. It was felt that he would some day win the Nobel prize; it was almost certain that soon he would be offered a knighthood – more patronage – and that he would accept. Already he was treated as though he had been ennobled.

The mustached old woman I expected to find was not there. He made the pot of tea himself, with great care, as though carrying out a tricky chemistry experiment. He served us some stale biscuits. He was alone. In spite of his heavy accent he was known more for his talk than his writing, and better known for his silences than his talk.

Rupert had warned me what to expect before we arrived: 'My wife asked, "So what is the significance of your analysis of solitude?" and he said nothing. He just smiled. Not a word. Fantastic!'

Tripodi was remarked upon for needing no one, for being solitary, for studying it – his history of loneliness. He had been working for many years (Rupert's wife said thirty years) on this book about solitude, *Man Alone*.

He said very little that afternoon. I could not always fill in the gaps of his famous silences. He was very deaf, he was almost inert, he sat and drank tea, slurping it.

Whether it was the thick jacket, or the gray cast to his skin that made it opaque, or a shifting light in his eyes, I had the impression that there was someone within him, inside this suit, this body. He was not attentive, but he seemed preoccupied with that person inside him. Was that what Rupert meant?

'Wait and see,' Rupert said.

When it was over, I was glad to leave and I knew exactly why as I drew a deep breath of fresh air in the street outside. It was the suffocation of Arturo Tripodi's place, the small room with all the dusty books. And it was the bloodless man himself. I understood for the first time how philistines viewed bookish people – as heartless and unphysical and time-wasting talkers. The talk itself in that accent was almost incomprehensible, and so I could scarcely make out what Arturo Tripodi was saying. Now I could identify with the simple soul who was antagonized by a pedant. True, the word 'intellectual' was seldom used in England, but 'pseudo-intellectual' was uttered all the time. Yet I felt that this man who was made entirely of thought, without a heart, was eternal and indestructible.

'I'll tell you all about it,' Rupert said.

'When?' But I didn't mean when. I was thinking: Will you tell me everything?

'You're just like my wife!'

Rupert was still dubbing his program about Tripodi. But he had wanted me to meet the man first, to assess my reaction. I told him what I felt.

Of course Arturo Tripodi was brilliant, I said. But he was all thought. He did not act: a head without a body. I was inspired by his work, but face to face, in his airless room, I was appalled by the rigid way he sat, by his jacket and tie. His accent was so strong it seemed deliberate and assertive. 'No heart' seems like a figure of speech until you meet a man with such a pale face and a huge gray forehead. And he was deaf. He made me feel ignorant and restless and alive.

My reaction delighted Rupert, and very soon after that he invited me to watch the unedited tape of his program about Arturo Tripodi.

'There's a clue in it, and it probably won't survive the final edit,' Rupert said. 'My wife insists that I leave it in.'

I met him at the BBC building in Shepherd's Bush. We watched the tape in a studio that had the look of a laboratory and the smell of a stuffy old parlor. There were cigarette butts in the used styrofoam cups on the cloth-covered table, and a glass carafe half-filled with cloudy water. How I hated these studios. I knew I could never work in television or radio, because all broadcasting was done in rooms without windows.

'Rolling,' Rupert said. He was eager, bright-eyed as always. I recognized the small house. 'Establishing shot, for my introduction, or maybe get him talking over the titles.'

It was the house in Fulham, the park, Eel Brook Common, Musgrave Crescent, the King's Road in the distance, the camera shortening its gaze and becoming intimate, withdrawing into the room and tracking across bookshelves to the chair where Arturo Tripodi sat.

'Julian called that his "Fellini sequence." '

'*There is no such thing as a novel anymore,*' Tripodi said. '*It is an obsolete form. Like the sonnet. Like the verse play. How can anyone believe in it?*'

'*What will take its place?*'

Rupert's voice; but he remained off camera.

'Isn't he supposed to be deaf?' I asked.

'The questions were written on big pieces of cardboard. We had a girl holding them behind my head.'

'*What has already taken its place? The work that is nearer to autobiography or memoir. That is why Svevo is so important. His work is more modern than Joyce's. Joyce knew that, which was his motivation for bringing his work to the notice of European intellectuals.*'

'*But surely the so-called memoir is as much of a conceit as the novel?*'

You could see Tripodi peering forward, his hands to his temples, steadying and directing his glasses, as he read this question.

'*It is nearer to reality,*' the old man finally said. '*It has more shocks and they are real shocks. Real flesh, real blood.*'

'*What other examples are there of this new form?*'

'*There is of course my work. But I would prefer to mention the paintings of Francis Bacon. Of course they are not pieces of writing but they are the best example of the kind of fictions I am describing. How different they are from the formal portrait. People are so solitary when seen from an oblique angle, so defenseless when seen from behind. It is the posture of retreat. The pain, the screams, the flesh, the nausea, the eroticism. The candor.*'

'*But*' – Rupert had adopted a teasing tone – '*my wife is always saying that Bacon's paintings have been superseded by abstract expressionism.*'

'*Your wife is mistaken. All abstract art is little more than decoration. Any painting that is not figurative has no reality. It is merely design. Mondrian is simply superior linoleum. Albers is wallpaper.*'

'*You sound so certain.*'

Tripodi hesitated. He leaned forward again and said, '*Excuse me, how much longer will this take?*'

'*Just a few more questions.*'

But this reply was not written down. Tripodi did not hear it. He looked around again.

'*Time will tell. Jackson Pollock might be interesting as an example of someone who is in extreme mental crisis, but his paintings have no artistic value.*'

'*I thought we were talking about the novel,*' Rupert said.

And so the program continued, the old sage unmoving in his chair, his hands grasping his knees. He was alone, he was hardly physical, all mind, like a decrepit pope in an old portrait.

Tripodi lifted one hand and waved it in impatience. This was a sign of life. There was a sudden cut, the film cartridge had to be changed, a black and white clapperboard swung shut with a crack, *Tripodi BBC Arena 16/8/82*, and restarted.

'*Flaubert never married. He worked. He wrote.*'

'*I'm married and I like to think that I –*'

But Tripodi did not hear him. It was a comment, not a question written on a card. Tripodi was still talking.

'Madame Bovary *is as modern a novel as it is possible to be. But the house of fiction has many rooms. The novel as we know it is no more than an entertainment – an amusement.*'

Tripodi went on, speaking in abstractions, and I found myself missing connections, as the talking head explained the future of fiction. I realized as I had at his house in Fulham that I was not made for such arguments. I needed something more concrete, or else I was turned into a grunting philistine. Tripodi in this program was an intellectual in full cry.

Rupert said, 'I'm losing you, Paul.'

'No. It's interesting.'

'Your eyes are glazing over, as my wife would say.'

'OK. I really don't know what he's talking about.'

'Because you take a traditional approach. "He said, she said. The clouds, the grass, the trees."'

'I don't write stuff like that.'

'I'm teasing you. But don't you realize that this man is describing exactly the sort of book I am trying to write?'

'Is that why you want me to see this?'

'No.' Rupert was smiling. 'Didn't you notice anything strange in it?'

I started to answer. Rupert began rewinding, making Tripodi clownish, doing everything rapidly, backwards, twitching. And then Rupert hit the Play button and the tape began again from *You sound so certain.*

I saw the old man hesitate and then turn. Rupert froze the tape.

'What do you see?'

'Nothing.'

'Look again.'

A blur, a figure in the distance glimpsed through the window moving towards the back door, just the back of a small head and narrow shoulders. It could have been a cluster of leaves blown by the wind, a gulp of light, the snap of a clean rag.

In the foreground Arturo Tripodi had turned and I could see the back of his neck – stringy, weak, pathetic, too small for the collar and tie which, on this poor flesh, was bunched like the drawstring on a loose bag. People are so solitary when seen from an oblique angle, so defenseless when seen from behind.

'What is it?'

'You mean, "Who is it?"' Rupert said. 'Remember that blur.'

'Your wife?'

Rupert laughed so hard at this I knew my fumbling question had to have a private meaning that excited him, even though his shrieking laughter was like mockery to me.

At last he wiped his eyes and gasped and said, 'The charlady's daughter, Clara.'

So there was a mustached old woman who looked after him. I said, 'You want to tell me something.'

Rupert's eyes glistened with excitement. His expression was lit with the knowledge that he was about to tell me something I could not even guess at. That was one of his most affecting traits, the way his face shone as he screeched. Being wise is someone's knowing something you don't. He was usually absent, but when he showed his face he was enthusiastic, which was more than I could say for Arturo Tripodi.

With his hand on the tape machine Rupert kept the moment frozen – the blur at the window, the turned head of Tripodi, the feeble neck, the posture of retreat.

'When we were done,' Rupert said, 'and had put the furniture back, we thanked him and left.'

Again I saw the hot little room of dusty books in my mind, and the overdressed old man in his heavily upholstered chair.

'I was halfway home when I remembered the key that I had been given to let myself and the crew in with. I still had it. I couldn't call him – he was too deaf to hear my explanation. That was why I had the key in the first place, because he couldn't hear the door bell. The arrangement was that I would put it into an envelope and push it through the letter slot.'

He smiled, he pressed his fingertips together as though he held a key.

'I was going to send my wife, but she was down in the country and wasn't due in London until that evening. So I went back, and – I didn't have an envelope – I let myself in through the front door. Arturo Tripodi was not in the parlor.'

I saw Rupert in the parlor, holding his breath, peering, listening, his face shining with pleasure.

'I could have put the key down. But I had plenty of time. I didn't have to meet my wife until seven. Something made me hesitate. It was his voice. I thought I heard the word "trance." That seemed to me perfect.'

He looked for my reaction, and he seemed to be enjoying the suspense, the way I hung on, waiting for his next word.

'He was seated in the library, his back to me. Just a few feet from where we had recorded the program. It's a small house, with more rooms than you might imagine, but this was the next room, just a few feet from where he had discussed the new novel so seriously, his concept of fiction. Candor. Solitude. Man alone.'

Rupert was gleeful, his fine skinny fingers trembling.

'He sat in his big hairy jacket, but he was not alone. He was watching a small girl, the one there' – the blur on the tape – 'and she was naked. She was so pale, so fragile, no more than eight or nine, no breasts, wearing only a pair of white socks. Her eyes were large and fearful. You can imagine. And Arturo Tripodi was whispering, "Dance, dance."'

That was the story that Rupert told me.

A few years later Arturo Tripodi died of heart failure. Rupert Moody died of AIDS.

SEVEN

The Shortest Day of the Year

I

A writer often chooses to leave a chapter out of a book. I have always been fascinated by the undressed father and daughter in that ramping perversity Edith Wharton deleted from her novel *Beatrice Palmato* (see the appendix of Professor Lewis's biography of EW); there is the dreamy river chapter that Mark Twain left out of *Huckleberry Finn*, and the sexual ambiguity J. R. Ackerley excluded from *Hindoo Holiday*. There must be thousands more. I suspect this writing to be revealing stuff, but it may be suppressed on other grounds – that it offends polite taste, or strains credulity, or seems inappropriate. Or is it simply a bad fit? Whatever, it is a question of timing: writers are careful not to throw anything of value away. The fact is, no matter how bizarre or scandalous, the sunken chapter always surfaces.

I traveled the coast of Britain in the spring and summer of 1982. Afterwards, writing *The Kingdom by the Sea*, I sometimes returned to a seaside place to verify a fact or confirm an impression. Anton and I spent some summer days in Orwell's Southwold, Will biked with me, checking place names on the Isle of Wight. Soon, autumn had emptied the summer resorts, and the gusting winds made them barer still. They were blackened by the sweeping rain of late November. The seas were higher, the cold strands were narrower, the surf noisier. But these were seasonal variations, differences in smells and skies; they did not alter the judgment in the manuscript I carried with me from one place to the next.

Four days before Christmas I was in Yorkshire looking at a section of coast I had missed north of Whitby. In the spring, for the purposes of my book I had taken the branch line from Middlesbrough. This time I was walking. I thought I had set off in good time, but as twilight gathered the shadows I realized it was the shortest day of the year.

Dusk slowed me down, and at Runswick Bay and Kettleness I found it hard to see my feet. It was that uncertain time of day, just after a winter sunset, when the way is made visible by the pale sky showing in puddles on the muddy path.

And then everything was black. I stumbled on through the wykes and dumps until I saw a wavering light. This is how I came to Blackby Hole.

The village was not yet visible. But I knew there were cottages hidden in the nearby darkness, because there was in the air the cozy burned-toast smell of smoke from coal fires, in those days the sharpest odor on frosty nights in English villages. There was only darkness and this coal smoke for a few hundred yards, and then clammy air rolled over me. The next time I saw the light it was smudged and refracted by the drifting fog.

This was the North. I had expected Christmas snow; but the sea fog was much stranger and just as cold and penetrated deeper. It was as if I lay with my face against a marble slab, and the ghostly progress of surf, flopping and gasping on the foreshore under the cliffs, suggested terrible things. I imagined stepping off one of those cliffs, or else the crumbly cliff's edge collapsing under me and the loose chunks of headland bearing me down and flinging me into the black water of the North Sea. The fog had settled and thickened, shrouding the coast, and muffling all sounds except that of the suffering sea.

I regretted this trip already. England is one of those safe, overdeveloped countries where a traveler like me has to go to a great deal of trouble to place himself in danger. After days of struggling against the tameness and safety of the coastal footpath called the Cleveland Way I had at this dark hour now succeeded in placing myself at risk. And Christmas was another peculiar problem – the holiday was like an ebbing tide that left all strangers stranded. I might not be able to leave until I was released by the next tide, the normal working days that were more than a week away, or perhaps well into January.

Alison had said, 'If you're not back well before Christmas . . .'

And had not finished the sentence, so as to send me off imagining what the dire implications of the rest of it might have been. She felt, with some justification, that I had let her down many times in the past.

The swimming light showed me a stile. I plunged over it and into a narrow lane. I heard the creak of a sign before I saw the pub itself – the Crossed Keys. And cottages appeared as faint shadows of dripping walls and shuttered windows. I was muddy and cold, so I considered warming myself in the pub. There was a cardboard sign saying *Vacancies* in the window; yet I procrastinated. If I could find a bus or a lift out of the village, I would leave this very night. I was sure that if I stayed I would discover nothing beyond what I could now see in Blackby Hole. It was a tiny place. *Move on*, I thought. And then I saw the crackling fire in the Crossed Keys.

I did not notice at first that there were people in the pub. I saw tangled strings of Christmas lights and hanging ribbons. And there were bunches of holly among the horse brasses on the beams, one round holly wreath on the wall, and a twist of tuberous mistletoe drooping over the door. Because these plants were real, and dying, they seemed less festive to me. Then I saw people: two men in chairs and a woman on the far side of the horseshoe shape of the bar. They had not moved when I entered. I had taken them for pieces of furniture – it was that kind of country pub. But why should they care about me? They must have seen plenty of travelers like me, muddy and sodden from the long-distance path that cut through the village. I was haggard from almost two weeks of this fact-checking, and wearing ridiculous hiking boots, and masked with a beard I had grown because I was sick of seeing my face in hotel mirrors.

And who is a more unpromising companion than an unshaven middle-aged man bent under a battered knapsack? He is encircled by a damp odor of frugality and monomania. He will accept a drink from you but he is unlikely to buy you one in return. Go about your business, don't make eye contact; he will leave soon. He will never come back. Anyway, he might well be a lunatic or a child mo- lester. Hiking in the dark alone so near Christmas? If he had a home he would be there. All this and much more. No one acknowledged me, or spoke.

So I was the first to speak, but I had to wait some while for an op- portunity. The bell over the door tinkled as a little old woman in a loudly crackling plastic mackintosh entered with a small wet dog.

'A tin of shandy and a packet of cheese and onion flavored crisps, there's a good lad,' she said.

It was worth a day's hard slog through drizzle to be rewarded by an English sentence like that. I copied it into my notebook, while she was served.

At the sound of the bell a man had appeared from a back room of the pub. He grunted and filled the woman's order, and I noticed that he handled her money clumsily, using all his fingers. He had the dirty fingers and enormous thumbs you associate with a strangler.

The woman fed the potato chips to the dog, talking the whole while – reminding the animal to watch its manners. And then she was gone. That was my opportunity.

'I don't think I've ever seen a dog do that.'

When I spoke, the two men in the chairs stood up and left the pub, plucking at their knitted jumpers and yanking their caps down.

'I wonder whether it's hard for him to swallow them,' I said.

'I reckon it's right easy like.'

That was the man behind the bar, probably the landlord of the pub, a balding round-eyed fellow in a knitted jumper that was much too big for him. He looked at me briefly and said, 'I'm stopping inside for my tea,' and he left.

'They don't like to talk about Mrs Pickering,' the next voice said. It was a woman on the other side of the bar. 'You've driven them away.'

'I have that effect on some people,' I said, and when she obliged me by laughing I added, 'Why don't you join me? It's much warmer here by the fire.'

To my surprise she took the other chair by the hearth and said, 'I never know whether it's all right to sit here. There are a couple of old boys who always use these chairs. The fog probably kept them at home.'

She had beautiful teeth, and bright eyes, and soft hair cut short, and a pale indoor complexion. Lost in studying her, I gabbled without thinking, wanting only to keep her there by the fire. I had not spoken to anyone all day. Such long silences always made me feel invisible, so talking to that woman I became real again – and more, I became hopeful.

'And what is the mystery about Mrs Pickering?'

'No mystery. It is well-known.' The woman stared solemnly at me and I was sorry I had been so chirpy. 'She murdered her fiancé.'

I tried to remember Mrs Pickering's face. I strained, and recollected a sad shawled figure in small boots. I recalled the crackling raincoat, the fingerless woolen gloves, and I had her whole sentence (*A tin of shandy and a packet of ...*) written into my notebook. But I could not see her face. My distinct memory was of a wet terrier smacking his jaws and half choking in her effort to eat the potato chips.

'Not everyone is what they seem.'

'She seemed very sweet,' I said.

'I was thinking of her fiancé. He was a busy-body and a terrible bully. Like a lot of men with sexual problems he was very aggressive and violent. The local people knew what he was like, and what she had to put up with. It was only strangers who were fooled by him. She killed him one night with a billhook. He deserved it. She was given a suspended sentence – an incredibly enlightened decision on the part of the judge. But no one likes to talk about her. They think everything you say about her is gossip. And it is, really. Where have you come from?'

Her explanation was also a warning. I accepted it and answered her question, saying I had come from Whitby.

She had been so straight with me and so friendly I wanted to avoid my usual fictions about being in publishing and telling her whatever name came into my head. I wanted to tell her that I had written the first draft of a book about traveling around the coast of Britain and I was here looking at places I had missed the first time around.

'By the way, my name is Edward Medford.'

The false name slipped out, in spite of my desire to tell her the truth. I almost laughed at the absurdity of it. Then I saw that it was my name, that whatever I said, because I had said it, had to be true; and that it was also the case with writing – that the act of writing made the word true.

'Can I get you a drink?'

'I'd love another drink. This is whiskey and lemon,' she said. 'I didn't have any in the house – I'm battling a cold.' When I returned with the drink she was stoking the fire, tonging lumps of splintery coal from a scuttle. She thanked me for the drink and said, 'I'm Lucy Haven.' From the way she smiled I knew she wanted to say something more.

'Yes?' I said, to encourage her.

'Today's my birthday,' she said, 'Saint Lucy's Day. Thus my name.'

'Happy birthday.'

'I'm no saint, though,' she said, and laughed softly.

She might have been forty, she could have been a bit more, and she was restrained in the most dignified way. She seemed wary when she smiled – she breathed in nicely when she did so. She struck me as independent and fearless, and solitary, if not lonely. I liked her sensible clothes and heavy boots, her knitted scarf and thick coat. She seemed self-reliant and frank. She was not afraid of me. I found her extremely attractive.

We talked about the fog, the crumbling cliffs, the Crossed Keys, and the distance to Saltburn, where there was a railway station. Then I said, 'What's there to do around here?'

'I listen to the wireless or play my gramophone most evenings, and I have my knitting.'

Those old-fashioned words were among the loneliest I had heard on the coast of Britain.

'And I do a great deal of reading.'

I was too depressed to think of a proper response. I stroked my beard and saw that my silence was making her self-conscious.

'I suppose it's a very quiet life. But it suits me.' She leaned forward and said, 'What's that insignia on your tie?'

'Royal Geographical Society,' I said. 'I wear it when I'm hiking. Helps my morale.'

I lifted the little gold emblem with my thumb, offering it, so that she could see it better.

'Ties are very phallic,' she said.

I let the thing drop. *Ties?*

'It's obvious, isn't it?' she went on, perhaps because I had not said anything. 'I read somewhere that neckties didn't become popular until the sixteenth century. And that was when the padded codpiece went out of style.'

It did not seem possible that anyone could say this without smiling, and yet her face remained expressionless, while I straightened up so that my tie wouldn't dangle. I smoothed it against my shirt.

'I suppose beards are, too,' I said. 'Phallic symbols.'

'Yours is.'

It was the first one I had ever grown. I thought it made me look beaver-like and fat-faced; but when I heard her make that extraordinary remark, I felt I had succeeded at something I had not been aware of having attempted. I had always resisted growing a beard, because I felt that a beard brought on a personality change – it happened to many men. She clearly approved.

'Some penises are phallic symbols,' I said.

'You're an American, aren't you?'

'Yes. I came here to get lost.'

'You came to the right village.'

We had another drink, and another, and went on talking in this friendly way – she was full of unexpected remarks. The wind in the chimney disturbed the fire. It had become a bleak, murky night; no one else entered the pub.

'What time does this place close?'

'Half-ten,' she said. 'But if we left before then he'd probably shut up shop. It's a filthy night.'

'But if we left, where would we go?'

She gave me a lovely unexpected smile – and it was more than a facial expression: it was a beautiful thought in her eyes and her mouth.

'My cottage isn't far,' she said. 'We could have a drink there. You haven't let me buy my round!'

'It's your birthday, Lucy.'

All the while I had been wondering how this might end. I still did not know, but at least I had a chance. And it was not as a traveler wanting to be welcomed and warmed and told a good yarn; but for something more. I liked her, and I was grateful to her for taking charge of me.

The landlord was not at the bar to see us leave. I was glad of that. I felt somewhat furtive and sheepish, as if I were sneaking away with Lucy Haven. I was also ashamed of this furtiveness.

'That's a parasite,' she said as we passed under the mistletoe.

She led me out to the narrow road, where the fog was swirling and drizzling in the dimmed Christmas lights of the pub windows; and then she turned into one of those country lanes that is like a deep trench. Although it was dark, Lucy did not hesitate, and I followed the sound of her footsteps grinding the damp pebbles in the lane. We had left the hamlet of hidden cottages and were headed for the cliffs. I could hear the waves dumping and sliding in the deep hollows below.

'I always imagine there are people down there,' she said of the sorrowing sound of the waves.

'Very cold people,' I said.

'Very dead people,' she answered, and then, 'It's not much farther.'

At once her footsteps went silent as she started down a muddy path.

I was baffled by her remark, trying to fathom her changes of mood, when she called out, 'There it is.'

Lights burned in three or four pretty windows, and although they were blurred by sea mist they helped me pick out the contour of this cottage, the low slanting roof and the bulging walls. I could hear the sea clearly now: it was just beneath us, thrashing softly, sounds of anguish and collapse.

It seemed a remote and solitary place, and I reflected that I would have been frightened to be alone there. But all its desolate characteristics made it an excitement and a pleasure to be there with Lucy Haven. I was about to enter this stranger's life. It is a traveler's thrill: to delve and then move on – like passing through a pool of light.

'I always leave the lights on,' Lucy said, as she opened the front door. 'I hate to come back to a dark house.'

On the way from the Crossed Keys I had entertained the fantasy that Lucy Haven might be a witch or a murderess. It had been a spooky encounter, the business with Mrs Pickering and the chance meeting with Lucy. *She killed her husband* and *Not everyone is what they seem*, and the sudden invitation to her cottage on the cliffs; and her remark, *Very dead people*.

Inside that sense of mystery vanished. It was a tidy place, penetrated with the odors of good bread and healthy cats and green plants. Its warmth heightened these odors and made them fragrant, and the warmth itself was a reassurance. If it had been cold in the cottage I am sure I would have been apprehensive. It was rather shadowy – only the lamps near the windows were burning – but I could see the pots of ivy and the fruit basket on the scrubbed pine table, the cat asleep on the sofa near the fireplace, and I could hear a clock's hurrying tick. Along one wall were bookshelves, and there were some pictures on another wall. But these were obscured by shadows. I did not want to see them, I did not want more light than this; I liked the fire and the dim lamps and the plump sofa and the thick rug.

'I've been making a jumper,' Lucy said. I suppose she thought I had been wondering about all that knitting paraphernalia that lay on the ladderback chair. 'I had hoped to finish by Christmas, but there's not much chance of that – Christmas is Saturday.'

'Is it for someone special – the jumper?'

'Yes,' she said, and looked very serious and intense. 'Someone in Africa. I'm a sort of godmother to a little girl in Lesotho. Actually she's quite a big girl now. I send a lot of knitted things to her. It can get very cold in Africa.'

She handed me a glass of white wine and we toasted each other.

'Happy birthday,' I said.

She frowned and said, 'Happy Christmas.'

I sat on the sofa, making room for her to sit next to me, but she chose to sit on the rug, before the fire. A cat went to her and she gathered it into her lap and stroked it.

'She calls me "Mummy,"' Lucy said, and smiled, but not at me. 'She's a fifth former now.'

We went on talking – about the work of the missions in Africa, about the Yorkshire weather, about the pleasures of radio programs and the tastes of herbal tea; but all I thought was how badly I wanted to make love to her. I could begin by getting down beside her on the rug in front of the fire. I did not want to make it obvious. As we talked, and as she refilled my glass, I grew steadily more dreamy with desire. Time passed; I was attentive, awaiting my chance.

She said, 'I think this silly cat has been in a fight. He's got a torn ear.'

'Let's see,' I said, and scrambled next to her.

The torn ear occupied us for a while, and the fire warmed my face, and I was sleepy with wine. At last, sensing that I was falling, I put my arm around her, then squeezed her shoulder and leaned to kiss her.

She arched her back and stiffened as though I had driven a spike into her.

'What are you doing?' Her voice was cold with contempt.

I did not know what to say.

'Do you think I'm just going to tumble into bed with you?'

She said it with such a sneer that I was on my feet before she had finished speaking. She had made me ashamed of myself. I backed away, stumbling slightly – it was like being thrown out of bed. I said, no, of course not, it was the furthest thing from my mind; and, my, look at the time!

'I have to go,' I said. 'Where's my pack?'

She switched on another light, and I was going to the door, eager to run. The overbright light made the cottage seem less friendly and rather poky and cluttered. Now I could see the books on the shelves. I was slinging on my knapsack and studying the shelves and, with nothing to lose – I had already touched bottom – I spoke the malicious thought that was in my mind.

'Have you read him?' I said. I was at the door, waiting for her parting words.

'Paul Theroux?' she said, and brightened: the good thought showed in her face. 'Oh, yes, I love him. He's smashing.'

2

I hesitated at the door of the cottage, then smiled at Lucy Haven and took hold of my beard. She did not have the slightest idea of who I was. She had rebuffed the man she knew as 'Edward Medford.' But, 'Paul Theroux? Oh, yes, he's smashing.' I wanted to laugh. I certainly wanted to stay longer. And I wanted to tell her my name.

Lucy said, 'You don't have to rush off like this.'

The words were hospitable, but they were face-savers; her ones insisted that I must leave soon.

She said, 'I think I've offended you.'

'Not at all!' I said – much too heartily, because I meant it. I had thought of teasing her a little and then saying, Guess who I really am!

'I mean I offended your masculine pride,' she said.

With a difficulty I hoped was not visible to her I suppressed my reply to this.

'I think you misunderstood me,' she said.

A lovely unattached woman's invitation to a half-drunk stranger to walk to her isolated cottage on the longest night of the year, her birthday, to split a bottle of wine – this was a misunderstanding? It seemed a reckless if wholly unambiguous offer of casual sex to me.

Or had I misread her signals and jumped to conclusions? That was probably what she meant by 'masculine pride.' All the while she thought she was being kind to a lonely traveler. And yet in England, and in some other places, 'Do you want to come to my place for a drink?' had nothing to do with thirst but a great deal to do with hunger. Didn't she know that?

'But stay a little while longer,' she said. 'We might as well have the other half.'

In fact, I had leaped up so quickly I had left my glass with wine still in it. As she handed it to me I dropped my knapsack to let her know that I planned to linger.

'I think you had the wrong idea about me,' she said. 'It's strange when one lives alone. One is unaware of giving off a lot of contradictory signals. They think I'm a bit mad in the village. I know they talk about me behind my back. "What does she do up there all alone?"'

'What *do* you do?'

'I have my wireless and my gramophone,' she said. That sad old refrain. 'And my books,' she went on, and gestured at the shelves where perhaps a thousand paperbacks were tightly fitted.

Following the bookshelves brought her back to the fireplace. I stayed where I was, near the books I had written.

She put a few small pieces of coal on to the fire, and pushed them with the tongs. It was a statement – that she wanted the fire to burn quickly and die, and – specifically – for me to take the hint and go. She did not want to throw me out, but she was trying to make me understand that her friendliness was formal – the same sort of philanthropy that motivated her to send wooly jumpers to Africa. She was not generous; she had been kindly in a tentative way. All the presumption had been mine.

I thought: She deserves to know that I have lied about my identity.

I would have told her who I was, except that I had the strong feeling that she did not think Edward Medford was a very nice person. It was more than that business about my masculine pride – an expression I hated; it was that she did not like me much, didn't like my appearance. I had simply landed up here, an ignorant American. I wasn't jolly, as hikers were supposed to be. I was a bit of an oaf.

All this prevented me from blurting out my name. And at last, thinking about it, I was glad I had given her a false name – especially a ridiculous one like Edward Medford. I wanted her to mock my name privately to herself and be mistaken. *Americans have such extraordinary names . . .* Wrong!

I said, 'You know, back there at the pub, you really didn't have to ask me to your cottage for a drink.'

'You looked a bit lost,' she said. 'And it's almost Christmas.'

'So I'm your Christmas act of charity,' I said.

'And it's my birthday. Perhaps it was a little present to myself, too.'

'Make up your mind,' I said.

'You sound cross.'

It was unreasonable of me perhaps, but I felt she was being patronizing. I was still stung by the rebuff, by her exaggerated words – all the futile theater in, *Do you think I'm just going to tumble into bed with you?* But more than that, she made me feel I was just another muddy hiker who had stumbled into Blackby Hole.

'I'm not cross. I appreciate your taking me in,' and when I saw the effect this had on her, I added, 'But don't worry, I won't stay long.' She did not react. I said, 'Frankly, I thought you wanted a little company.'

'You thought I was lonely,' she said, and she laughed gently. 'That's actually quite funny.'

'Don't you ever get lonely?'

'I don't have time! I'm desperately busy.' And her one-word shout was like an explanation: 'Christmas!'

'Have you ever been married?'

'No,' she said, interrupting me.

'Do you – ?'

'Questions,' she said, and then looked away. 'I had a fiancé once. He died, regrettably.'

'The world is full of good men,' I said by way of consolation.

She was insulted by this, and stiffened as she had when I had touched her. 'I didn't think of him as a man.'

I said nothing – allowed a moment of silence out of respect for this man's memory.

'A few years ago I was seeing someone.'

She hesitated. I thought: Seeing means everything.

'But he went away.'

The words were sad, but she was fairly bright – there was no remorse or self-pity in her tone, only a wistful echo. That was what I had found so attractive in her – her spirit, her sense of freedom; and I had thought she had chosen me. I knew better now. She only wanted chat. So I chatted.

'You must read a great deal.'

'You find that strange,' she said.

That irritated me. I did not find it strange at all. I was glad! But it was her way of being smug.

'It's not only you – a lot of people find it strange. They wonder what I see in an author or a book. But I can't describe the experience. It is magnificent – entirely imaginative and creative.' She smiled at me from a tremendous height of accomplishment and intelligence. 'Look at it this way. It is my version of hiking. New paths, new scenes, new people. What rambling is to you, reading is to me. It's my fresh air.'

In the raw, simple tones of an untutored hiker I asked her, 'Would you recommend any of these books to me?'

'All of them,' she said. 'I only keep the books I intend to reread. The rest I give away.'

'So you wouldn't say that some of these' – and I waved my hand at them – 'are better than others?'

Something sadistic in me demanded that she say my name before we could go further.

She said, 'I love reading about distant places.'

'What – this stuff?' I said, and let my fingers hesitate on *The Mosquito Coast*, *The Great Railway Bazaar*, and the rest of them standing under the author's name, between Thackeray and Thomas.

'Anything that feeds my fantasies,' she said.

'I'd love to know your fantasies.'

'It's to do with travel mostly. I dream of sunny countries and blue skies. Steinbeck – the wonderful towns he writes about. Monterey, Fresno, Pacific Grove – such lovely names. Fruit trees. Just the words "orange groves" make me sigh. I think of the sun on the rows of pretty trees, and heating the roads and the rooftops. I see the bright houses and the little patches of shade under the green trees and the vines. I dream of Mexico too. Very hot and dry – the desert is sort of odorless, you know. Nothing decays, everything withers beautifully, like pressed flowers. I dream of small towns in endless summer . . .'

She was describing the opposite of Blackby Hole, where the rising wind of December pushed at the window panes and howled under the eaves, and the sea that reminded her of murmuring ghosts spilled its cold surf down below on the hard shelf of beach.

Lucy Haven was still talking – now about small hot towns in Middle America: fresh air, good food, friendly folk and sunshine. She also saw herself in the African sun, and in a bungalow in Malaysia, and taking a stroll in China. They were simple visions, and strange because they were not at all extravagant. They were not expensive or luxurious – no five-star hotels or gourmet dinners or native bearers.

'We're on a picnic,' she was saying, 'sitting on very green grass on a riverbank in the sun. We have food – I've made sandwiches, and everyone is drowsing, and someone says, "Let's do this again tomorrow!"'

And then I saw it, too. We were together, Lucy Haven and I, in California or Mexico, packing a picnic basket and setting off under a blue sky. I had an intense sight of it, which was the more passionate for its simplicity. It was possible and more than that – it was easy. She did not know how attainable it was. I could tell her. I had so often bought tickets and visited such places; but I had been alone and restless, and I had left thinking: Some day I will come back with someone and be happy.

Lucy had risen from the sofa. I smiled at her and prepared myself to say everything that was on my mind and I was eager to know what form her astonishment would take.

But before I could speak, she smiled – a smile that took effort – and she said through her teeth, 'Hiking boots!'

We both looked at my feet.

She said, 'Those little treads pick up mud and carry it indoors and drop it. Look.'

I was standing on a green square of carpet. There were small pellets of mud, like chocolate bon-bons, all around my boots.

'I'm really sorry,' I said, and raised one boot, balancing myself unsteadily on the other. 'What a mess I've made.'

'Please don't move. You're making it worse.'

'Shall I take these muddy things off?'

'I don't know,' she said. She was exasperated and upset, and there was a squint of pain in her eyes as she looked down. 'I wove that carpet myself – on a hand loom. I did a weaving course in York. It took me ever such a long time. You can't see the pattern very clearly, but I've based it on a Kashmiri design. It's vines and lotuses.'

'Muddy lotuses.'

'I'm afraid so, yes.'

Her voice was flat and disappointed. She wanted me to go through that door and keep going – hike out of her life. She had not asked where I was planning to stay. I had no place to stay! I suspected that she wanted me to know that I was no longer welcome. I had drunk all her wine and asked too many questions and tracked mud on to her handmade carpets.

People who live successfully in solitude live with elaborate rituals and strict rules. I had broken a number of her rules. She wanted me out. More than that, she now wished she had never seen me.

And that made me stubborn and rebellious. I smiled at her. I knelt and untied one filthy boot and then the other, and stepped out of them; and walked across the room stroking my beard – making her wait; and then back to the bookshelves and said, 'But what do you really think of him?'

'Dylan Thomas?'

'No.' I could not utter my own name to her. I feared it might give me a sudden brainstorm and that everything would come out. I tried to be casual; I wagged my fingers. 'Him.'

'Paul Theroux?' she said.

I clutched my beard merely to make my head move in a noncommittal way.

'I've read practically everything he's written that's in paperback. The novels, the short stories, the travel books. *The Great Railway Bazaar* was the one that started me off. That's travel, but it's not an ordinary travel book. It's mostly him, so you feel at the end of it that you know him pretty well. He's wonderful on people. The men he writes about are very vivid – funny, too – but most of his women are absolutely awful. Your stockings must be wet through. You're leaving damp footprints on my floor.'

It was a stone floor, my feet were so cold my toes were turned up like Turkish slippers. She had not asked whether I was comfortable, nor invited me to sit down. She was too absorbed talking about this smashing writer, who was so wonderful on people.

'They'll be here tomorrow,' she said, looking down at my foot-prints on the flagstone floor – not disappointment this time but dis-gust. 'I hate feet.' She was grimacing at mine. 'The Thais are right. There's something really sickening about them. If you point your foot at a Thai, he will be so insulted he might try to kill you.'

'No kidding. I didn't know that,' I said and made a mental note to write it down as soon as I could.

'It was in one of Theroux's books.'

'Are you sure?' And I thought: Surely not.

'I cannot abide that question and I never answer it,' she said, and frowned at my feet.

She had been talking about feet in general, but her manner indi-cated that she was talking specifically about my feet.

It was a winter night near Christmas; the fog and sea mist lay thick against the coast; I was a perfect stranger. If Lucy had warmed to me, welcomed me, or showed any concern, I would have been very direct. I would have divulged my name, and then I would have left. If she had been hostile I would have done the same, but for an-other reason. Yet she was indifferent to me. And because I was certain that I wasn't going to tell her my name – it would have been embarrassing otherwise – I asked about this writer she loved reading. What was he like?

By way of answer she said, 'There was once a very mysterious writer called B. Traven.'

She put it in the most condescending way. She was giving me in-formation again: I was the simple-minded hiker and she the omni-vorous reader.

'No one knew who Traven really was,' she said. 'You've probably seen the film *The Treasure of the Sierra Madre*. He wrote that book and a number of other books. No one could put his hand on his heart and say that he had ever met Traven. Traven had gone to great lengths to protect his identity.'

'That's very interesting. I think I saw that movie on TV.'

'I knew who Traven was,' she said, ignoring what I had said. 'I had read his books. And from internal evidence I knew what Traven looked like, where he came from, what he ate, how he dressed, his opinions, all his habits.' She looked closely at me. 'I knew the color of his eyes. Writing reveals everything.'

She smiled in satisfaction, and then blinked at me, perhaps wondering whether I could understand the complex implications of this unique insight.

'And I was right,' she said. 'A few years ago, a book came out about Traven. It was all there – everything I had deduced. His eyes were Prussian blue.'

'And so you've figured out this other fellow.'

'Paul Theroux, yes. Every bit of it.'

'He's very hunky, very sexy, very – '

'You're mocking me,' she said angrily.

Of course, I was – out of nervousness, out of panic. But I was mocking myself much more. I wanted badly to interrupt her.

'I think of him as tall and rather shy. Very gentle and' – she smiled and looked away – 'very funny. Not a joke-teller, but sort of end-lessly amusing in a droll sort of way. And a little frustrated. Why would anyone spend all that time traveling if he was contented?'

'As a hiker I can tell you that travelers tend to be optimists.'

'You can be frustrated and still be optimistic,' she said.

True; she had me there.

'And I know there's something wrong in his marriage,' she said.

My indignation took hold of me. I said sharply, 'You know that?'

'Yes. Writing gives everything away,' she said. 'He might be un-aware of it, though.' She was not looking at me, but rather was studying the American writer's many books, the row of them on the third shelf. 'I'd so like to meet him.'

I had hold of my beard again, this time to keep my hand from trembling. I said, 'Sure, but what then?'

With defiance she said, 'I think we'd have a smashing time. I think I could make him very happy.'

Then she glanced again at my feet – my wet socks – and looked at me with pure hatred. Her eyes were large and deep brown and be-cause they were turned against me they were cold and bright with ferocity. They said: Get out of my house.

I wanted to go. I walked to the door. Lucy stepped out of my way, as though giving a leper a wide berth. She moved slowly; she was thoughtful. She began speaking, not to me but to the room, as though continuing a thought that had begun in her head.

'But of course I'll never meet him. I'll never go to California, or see Africa. I won't go to medical school. I'll never learn to play tennis or ride a horse. Bridge will go on being a mystery to me. The

Queen won't come to my wedding, and even if I do marry he'll be more a companion than a lover, and I'll never have children. I won't get an award at the Woman of the Year lunch. I'll never have a computer or a motorbike or a Rolls Royce. I doubt that I'll ever learn to speak another language. I won't discover or explore anything. Nothing will be named after me.'

Now she looked at me. I had put my shoes on. I could not have told her my name now for anything. Her words came from something much deeper than a mood; they were based on utter conviction, the most severe variety of the pessimistic English belief *Nothing great or good will ever happen to me*, and in her the fatalism amounted almost to paralysis.

She sounded sad. It seemed to me now that it would only make her sadder if I told her who I really was. Perhaps I could have, earlier this evening; but it was too late now. I was sorry, because she obviously did not like me very much, and I still found her attractive.

'On the other hand, nothing awful will come my way,' she said. 'I've survived a few calamities and came away relatively unscathed. There won't be any disasters. I don't know why I'm telling you this, but I know I'll live. Like this. I'm quite happy, actually.'

'You've been very kind to me.'

'No, I haven't,' she said, and laughed carelessly, with a little crazy shriek in her laugh. 'I've tormented and disappointed you.' And she handed me my knapsack. 'But you know nothing at all about me.'

There was an unpleasant thought showing in her face and her eyes were demented for a second as she turned away from me.

I wanted to tell her my name then, but after all that time and all this talk would she have believed me? Whether she did or not I could not win and what I told her would seem like mockery.

'You had better go.' She spoke it like a warning.

Into the darkness: the sea fog blinded and soaked me. I crept slowly down the soft, sinking path, and loud waves broke near me under the cliff. I was not able to draw an easy breath until I was back in the dim lamplight and the homely stink of the coal smoke in the road at Blackby Hole.

The Crossed Keys was shut, but I raised the landlord by rapping. Aye, he said, he had a room – five pounds, in advance; and he promised me a good breakfast, which would be served by his missus in the lounge bar in the morning. Nay, it wasn't far to Saltburn, and dead easy, he said, to find a rail connection to London.

'I'm sorry to get here so late,' I said.

'We're used to being knocked up at all hours, being on the coastal path,' he said, leading me up the narrow stairs. 'All sorts of hikers come through.' By then we were under the light in the upstairs hallway. He looked at my face with sudden scrutiny, as though he saw something wrong.

'I know you,' he said, in a puzzled voice.

Was he too a reader?

'I was here earlier, having a drink.'

'Aye,' he said. But he did not smile, nor say anything familiar. 'When that woman was in the bar. Gives me the creeps, she does. That queer one.'

'Everything you say about her is gossip,' Lucy Haven had said of Mrs Pickering. But the landlord was still frowning at me.

'That killed her lover,' he said.

'Yes,' I said, and felt that I was in the know. 'Poor old Mrs Pickering, with the dog.'

'Mrs Pickering never hurt a soul! Nay, I mean that witch of a woman, Lucy Haven. Ah, you're a stranger – what do you know? Lucy Haven killed her fiancé. This was years ago. She was declared mental, and she got off. She claimed the bloke was a beast and she used a billhook on him while the balance of her mind was disturbed.'

He shoved the door open, clicked on the light and showed me into my tiny room.

'Round the twist – aye, pull the other one, my lord!'

I tried to interrupt him, as he talked and punched the mattress and pointed to the towel and soap. But I had no question to ask. I merely wanted him to stop talking, because I was afraid to hear any more.

'Lucy Haven!' he said, and drew the curtains. 'Aye, but there was another lover. No one knew the bloke. He disappeared. Could have drowned him. No one missed him.' The landlord nodded slowly, and let this sink in. 'She's never hurt me – she don't like me – but she's death on men she loves.'

And then in his friendly Northern way, out of the side of his mouth, he urged me to sleep well.

EIGHT

A Part in a Movie

I needed interruptions in London because I worked alone, haunting the house all day, growing ghostlier as I wrote, and a phone call was the proof I needed that I existed. I was especially glad when the phone rang that October afternoon; I had just finished another page of my China book and I felt it was going a bit too well. A book stuck badly was a misery, but if writing came easy I suspected it of being over simple and second-rate. (This opening, for example – the previous three sentences – has taken me two days to work out, about ten false starts.)

There was no voice on the line, just a ping, a pause, the gasp of exhalation you get when you open a coffee can, and the sense of a hollow tube rather than a wire to my ear. I became alert, knowing it was a transatlantic call.

'Hi, Paul. Guess who?'

I hated that. Boldly identifying my voice, this woman demanded I do the same, as though testing my friendship. I guessed right – Ariel Draper.

'Where are you? Don't make me guess.'

'Los Angeles.'

There was warmth in the city name and sunlight too. Mid-afternoon here was dawn there, but it was more than just a matter of light. A call from the United States was to me like a beckoning signal from a distant glowing planet.

'I'm doing another picture with Peter. We were talking about you yesterday.'

'How is he?'

'Great. He said to say hi. But the producer's English. "Ask an American what time it is and he'll tell you how to make a clock." He said that to me yesterday. I know you're working on a book, because you always are. What's this one about?'

'China.'

'I love it.'

'Except it's not done.'

'How's it going?'

'Slowly.' Never tell the truth about what you are writing and it remains yours. 'It's a travel book, so at least I know how it ends.'

'I've got a terrific story for you.'

People always offer stories to a writer, as though handing yarn to a knitter. The stories I got were sometimes better, but more often worse, than the people believed. There was always an important question that the storyteller could not answer. At their best they were colorful and neat, like urban legends, rather than the ragged maddening episodes that possessed my imagination, that I recognized as life.

One, told to me by a Dutchman over dinner, took place in Eindhoven, this man's home town. Each Saturday night after the war an old couple, whose son had been captured by the Germans, waited at the Eindhoven railway station for him to return. It was always on Saturdays that the trains brought the prisoners of war home from the German camps. In the first year after the war many of these Dutch soldiers got off the train to meet their joyous relatives, and then there were fewer, and at last in the 1950s, none.

But still the old couple went to the station every Saturday, and they waited for the train from Germany, and when the passengers had all filed past them and the station was empty, the old couple went home. They persisted in this same way for years, because they had no news, and they wanted to be at the station for their son, if he was still alive. It was a ritual – and what began as a rehearsal for a homecoming turned into a vigil.

'I used to see them watching the passengers' faces, looking for their son,' the Dutchman told me. 'Even when they were ill, they waited at the station.'

He went silent, remembering the old couple at the empty station on a Saturday night, and how they had always gone home alone.

'It might sound terrible to say,' he concluded, 'but I was relieved when they died. It was agony to see them at the station, week after week.'

That was one I liked – *I was relieved when they died* – because they had been waiting and rehearsing, preparing for an event that never happened. Yes, it was a good story, but how could I make more of it, or connect it to anything that I might write?

Ariel's stories were always good, but unusable.

'I just finished casting a film about necrophilia,' she had told me once. 'I know it sounds gross, but it's being done in the best possible taste. Stop laughing. Anyway, I found this wonderful young actress, who is just so good at playing dead in the sex scenes. The other day during one of these scenes a fly landed on her eye and she didn't blink. That is acting.'

Ariel's phone calls from California delighted me, as though I was getting news from the real world.

'Tell me.'

'Better still, I'll send it to you,' she said. 'It's not really a story. It's a script.'

'You want some script advice?'

'No. I want you to read it and see if you're interested in acting in Peter's new movie.'

'Are you joking, Ariel?'

'Absolutely not. It's not a big part, but you'd be perfect.'

'I've never acted in a movie.'

'No problem.'

'Ariel, don't send me the script. I could never be in a movie.'

'Why not?'

'I'm not an actor. I don't know the first thing about it.'

'That's what directors are for.'

'I don't want to learn. I'm a writer.'

'The guy's a writer,' she said. 'That's the whole point.'

'I can't do it.'

I looked at my watch.

'I have to get back to work.'

There was a bit more, just pleasantries, and then I hung up.

My China notebook lay open beside my pad, a page about early summer in Guangdong province: the heat, the rain, the bamboo thickets, the screech of cicadas. It was in my head: I could feel it and see it, but I could not get it on to the page.

I wrote no more that day. I tried, I doodled, I manipulated a sentence; but nothing would come. The unexpected struggle, without a result, left me tired and irritable.

The next day I made a start, a few words, but could not move further. I abandoned it and went for a walk. My normal time-killing hike took me down the hill to the river, across the bridge and either east to the Tate Gallery, to look at pictures, or straight ahead, up Beaufort Street, to the ABC Cinema on Fulham Road. I walked towards the river in a cold drizzle, but at the bridge it turned to heavier rain and began smashing at the trees and tearing the withered leaves from the boughs. I boarded a 49 bus and stayed on as far as the ABC.

An afternoon movie was harmless enough, but it remained for me a guilty pleasure. Once I had seen Ringo Starr there alone – sunglasses, beard, collar up – buying a ticket. I stood behind him, knowing we were doing the same thing. What was he hiding from?

The movie today was *On Suspicion*, an English low-budget film about the visit of a team of US cops to Scotland Yard. The cast was impressive, I recognized many of them as actors from the Royal Shakespeare Company, but try as they might, English actors could not do American accents. They sounded so hollow and posturing, and attempting American snarls they came off sounding like Irish rustics. It destroyed all credibility. You simply did not believe a thing a person said, if you kept noticing his accent. The paradox was that it had to be transparent – not there, in order to be something.

After the movie, I went to the Pan Bookshop nearby, bought a copy of the novel *On Suspicion*, and read it on the bus and saw how believable the plot was. I took a professional interest in the way the book had been adapted.

Back home at my desk, among my China papers and yesterday's false starts, I thought of one of the actors who had played an informer. He had one line. It was, '*They're all the same. Rats.*' He was American. Throughout the action you remembered that word, 'Rats.' The set of his jaw, the push of his vindictive lips. He was not incidental; it was an important element. It was inspired casting. I liked him, and I found myself thinking: I could do that.

But it was wrong to think about it. I was a writer. An actor – a performer – was the opposite of a writer. Any writer who tried this was doomed. Sam Shepard was a less interesting writer after you saw his face all over the screen. How could you take the writer Harold Pinter seriously after you saw Harold Pinter the actor hamming it up? Jerzy Kosinski had appeared in *Reds*. Kosinski had committed suicide.

I could not work the following day. Though Alison called from work about a BBC party we had been invited to, I said nothing to her about this offer of a part in a movie. It was another of my secrets, but not a very big one, because my mind was made up. I looked at my China notebooks, grew tired in anticipation and told myself I was uninspired. I needed an idea – a thought, a phrase, a word, anything. I decided to take the day off and go to Cambridge, to see Chinese paintings depicting foreigners in the Fitzwilliam Museum, for my China book. What did we look like to the Chinese? Even if I did not find the big-nosed, red-haired, foreign devils, it was worth the trip from Liverpool Street. Solitary train journeys, even short ones, calmed me and gave me ideas.

And I looked up Anton. We met at a pub near his college, Clare. When he asked me how my China book was coming along, I found myself telling him about the movie offer rather than about the book. Was I thinking that someone his age – twenty – seemed to be closer to a knowledge and experience of the public taste, particularly where movies were concerned?

Anton said, 'That is so cool. I wish someone would ask me to be in a movie.'

'Would you say yes?'

'Not half!'

Then he got embarrassed in advance for me – for himself.

'But you're not going to do it, are you?'

I stuck out my jaw and pouted. 'Go ahead, make my day.'

He frowned, he shook his head and glanced around to see whether anyone had heard me, then leaned over to me and said, 'You're not acting. You're indicating.'

It was the unexpected word, 'indicating,' that made me pause.

'Pretending. Going through the motions,' he said, and tapped his chest. 'It's not in here.'

'Don't worry, I hate acting,' I said. 'I hate watching people do it. I don't want to observe it. It's embarrassing.'

'There's such a thing as great acting, though.'

'I hate great acting more than any other kind of acting. "My kingdom for a horse." I'd rather watch amateurs or improvisers – those Mike Leigh people.'

I thought of the loud shouting stamping people on the London stage. I had gotten little pleasure from all the hours I had spent at the theater. I simply did not believe actors any more than I believed in puppets. But there were movies that had gripped me by the throat and left me gasping with admiration.

We always talked like father and son, but today I was the son, and his face was pale and paternal and studying mine as he hid his uncertainty, his apprehension that I was in danger of making a fool of myself. It had been a mistake to raise the subject; I had not told him enough.

Pondering this on the train back from Cambridge, finding the rain-flattened fields restful, I was grateful for Anton's giving me the word 'indicating.' There was a kind of writing that was indicating, too – just tentatively sketching. Ever since Ariel had called to offer me this acting part, I had stopped writing and begun indicating.

What I resented about many actors was that they were being paid and praised for doing something I knew I could do better. You could see them acting. There was such a thing as an actor's face, an actor's hair style, an actor's laugh. Actors did not even walk like real people; they were slow and self-conscious. It was so much better when a person was doing the human thing, reacting, as in the old Sixties movies that had influenced me, particularly Fellini's, where he had obviously used amateurs. Such people had real faces and real voices. I thought: The very idea of hating actors is probably a good start. In this role I would not act at all. I would deal with it as I dealt with my writing, existing in every word I wrote, in every character.

I woke the next day to good writing weather – cool, a stillness in the air, in the muted light a sense of harmless gloom, a low London sky full of gray tumbled stuffings. I sat, but I could not write; and there was nothing to distract me in the mail. Perhaps the script had been held up by British customs, as sometimes happened with business documents in this suspicious bureaucracy.

The guy's a writer. That's the whole point. Ariel had insisted on that. Only a writer knew about writing, which was why I had never felt at a disadvantage in being interviewed on television – had never been nervous. There was nothing that anyone could ask me about my work that I could not answer, no question about my life that I had not already mulled over. My books were the visible part of my mind. And I could not separate my writing from who I was. It was not work I performed, it was a process of my life

The clouds became obscured in a shower of rain spattering like crystal beads against the back garden and sluicing the slate roofs of the smaller house next door. I watched the gutters fill and run over, drenching the bricks; and the leaves being torn from the trees and falling in heaps, thickened like wet rags, and a cat compressing itself under a bush. The windows were pelted with heavy raindrops and water ran down the glass panes. Dramatic weather thrilled me and made me restless. I was now too excited to write.

I watched it and thought how writing was all I had ever done. It had protected me, kept me from having to get a job, insulated me, insured me against ever having to work in an office, liberated me from the servitude of a salary, emancipated me and made me sane. I had no boss. I did not need permission to write. But all actors had to wait for their cue. I had no employees. I was free. What actor could say that?

Only a writer knew these things, and only a writer could act the part of a writer. I was being asked to consider the part of the American writer in this British movie. That suited me. Because that was who I was, an American writer in London. Living in London was more a science than an art, it was an acquired taste, and you got better at it. I had developed those skills – not Anglophilia but tolerance and lowered expectations. I was a spectator, a witness. The more I thought of it the more I thought that Ariel had made an inspired choice in asking me to accept the role.

Another few days passed. I still could not work on my China book. I did research instead. I wandered the stacks of the London Library, searching the indexes of travel books for the names of the obscure towns where I had stayed in China, looking for inspiration. I made notes and tried to be busy.

Another wonderful story, told to me by a woman in New York City, was about a woman friend of hers who had met a man on a plane. The man was dark – perhaps Middle Eastern; they swapped telephone numbers, and within a day the man called to invite her to dinner. The woman said she was busy – she was going away for a week. When she returned, she found that a large potted plant had been delivered to her. A few days later there was a basket of gourmet food, and not long afterwards a messenger arrived with a bracelet. All the presents were from the man she had met on the plane.

The presents seemed so odd, so premature, that she called the man to tell him to stop. He had changed his telephone number. She could not find him. And he did not stop. He sent her a new refrigerator, and it was filled with bottles of expensive Chablis. He sent her a king-sized bed. Then a CD player and many discs. And there was more. It got so that the woman was hesitant to go home in the evening, so fearful was she of what she might find waiting for her. Now there was a present every day. They arrived in such profusion that it became a physical impossibility for the woman to send them back. Yet she did not have room for them in her small apartment.

A dog was delivered. And then a motorcycle. By now the woman had called the police, but they did not take the complaint seriously – giving someone presents was not a crime, and it was hardly a nuisance. Yet for the woman it was worse than theft, she was half out of her mind with worry, the intrusion of all these unwanted presents was like the worst hostility – valuable jewels, a Finnish sauna in a crate, a new car. She could not sleep. She lay awake, expecting the door bell to ring with another delivery, and there was something, nearly every day. She lost her appetite and became depressed. And where was the man? He was hiding, and relentlessly sending her presents. Now she hated him, and the onslaught of presents proved to her that he wanted to drive her crazy.

She saw a psychiatrist, who after a few sessions simply advised her to move. And so she did, changed her job, relocated, and hid, her whole life changed by this chance encounter, almost destroyed by the gifts.

But, 'I never did find out what happened to her,' the woman told me when I quizzed her. This was the very thing you wanted to know. Unanswered questions always made me think that I was dealing with an invention – probe further and there was emptiness. Perhaps the woman did not exist; perhaps it had never happened. And it was not only that the man had been persistent; would the woman really have been so demoralized by the presents?

The word 'story' always made me smile. What's his story? Just a story. A likely story. Story suggested an insubstantial invention, a wobbly vehicle for an unconvincing proposition. Ask too many questions and it collapsed.

I was waiting for the script – so I could not work. Then, at last, when the script came I could not work, because I was reading the script. It was called *Mystery Man*, a title I hated and wanted to change. It was a love story. The lovers were English, the male lead had a friend, called the Writer in the script – no name – who loaned his apartment to the male lead so that he could have an assignation with the woman. Therefore, I was the key man. I got the plot rolling. In the novel I was the narrator, an American writer. The novel was a reminiscence of my English friends.

Most of my lines were in the opening scene:

> Writer: *You lucky dog. I'll bet she's beautiful.*
> Jack: *She's only twenty.*

I could almost believe that this older Englishman might find happiness with a dreamy twenty-year-old, even if the happiness was not long-lasting; but what about Allison (as she was named in the script)? The story needed cynicism, selfishness, manipulation.

> Jack: *Don't you want to see her?*
> Writer: *Curiously, no.*

Wrong, I scribbled. Americans did not say, 'Curiously, no.' This was English writing, the slightly pompous, sniffy, weighty way of an urbane Englishman. If you knew them you knew that it was an insufferable affectation; if you did not, it was just baffling or else mildly threatening.

I did not have much dialogue, the script was childishly spelled ('sizzors' for scissors, 'miniscule'). I was described walking around my flat in Chelsea (more believable in Battersea or Islington, I thought), showing my friend my gadgets – coffeemaker, Jacuzzi, cable TV, video camera, all the items that figured later in the plot. I did not describe them. I showed him how they worked. That was simple enough acting.

But would an American writer own such things in London? I made a list in the margins of the script of all the things I actually did own: a rowing machine, a working samovar, a wind-up gramophone with an old 78 of Heifetz playing Handel's *Largo*.

After I had finished reading it, I flipped through and saw that I had scribbled so many notes on the pages it looked like one of my own rough drafts. I wanted to discuss the changes. And then I remembered that it was a script that had been sent for me to consider playing the role of the Writer. Peter was not looking for a script doctor to fix the lines, just an actor to say them, an actor to walk around, to be directed. Idly, wanting to respond, I dialed Ariel's number, but put the phone down before there was a ring. Surely they would call me. They did not want any actor; they wanted a writer.

The following day I reread the script and, instead of working on my China book, I learned the Writer's lines. They were few but significant. I had made some changes in my own lines, improved them – Americanized them. It was not presumptuous. They would be grateful for the changes. I looked over my China notes, but with one ear cocked for the phone – Ariel's call. There was no call.

At the BBC party, several people asked me what I was doing. I had not been working. I had been away from my book for a week. I noticed that these party-goers, all BBC producers and editors, self-consciously spoke in exaggerated American accents whenever they used certain words or phrases. They mockingly said 'You're welcome,' and 'It figures,' and 'You gotta be kidding,' and it struck me that the English were at their most comfortable hiding behind accents. His mustache wet with wine, one small balding Jewish man named Meyer began to monopolize Alison's attention with his many accents, a different one for each sentence, like a man speaking in tongues, a kind of glossolalia certain English people were prone to when they were nervous. Not acting, but indicating.

I turned away from them and lit a woman's cigarette.

'That was nicely done.'

I was so surprised by the compliment I could not think of a reply, and then she too asked me what I had been writing. It was my usual superstitious reflex that made me deny that I was writing anything. But I realized that it was the truth. I had not been able to get back into my China book. All I did was stare at my notebooks. I wanted to confide in her and say I've just been offered a part in a movie. What would she say to that?

On the way home from the party I said to Alison, 'Remember Ariel Draper, that casting director?'

'That calls up at the oddest hours? Yes, I remember her.'

'She offered me a part in a movie.'

'You're joking.'

'No.'

Then she went silent.

'So what do you think?'

She said, 'I'm trying to think of something clever, like, "Is it another instalment of *Planet of the Apes*?" '

'I know. It's ridiculous. I just thought you'd be interested.'

'What did you tell her?'

'That I had a book to write.'

Yet I saw this movie more clearly than my book. The car arriving at my house each morning to take me to the studio outside London, probably Pinewood, the one at Iver, in Buckinghamshire. Lunches at the studio restaurant. Chit-chat with the actors. I knew from experience that there would be a great deal of rehearsal and repetition and that I would have a lot of time to kill. I could work on my book then. And I was the only American on the set. I would be a little exotic for that reason, and because I was not an actor. I caught myself feeling a little superior to all the rest of them, and corrected myself. I imagined the others' insecurities, their slighting remarks, the misunderstandings. The flirtations. And the meals with the director and producer – a time perhaps for pitching projects of my own. Using the notes I had made on this script, helping to write another draft, I might become involved in rewriting the script.

Sometimes these reveries maddened and embarrassed me, sometimes they were a consolation.

In my reveries I did not win an Oscar, I was not nominated; but my performance was remarked upon, and I was asked to play in other movies. Because acting was out of date and formal and self-conscious, the thing was to have real people in these parts. I was noticed because I was not an actor. I was real. I was the writer Paul Theroux.

And yet, even as this thought occurred to me, I knew I had done no writing lately. I disliked my indicating; my rationalizing, my ridiculous patience, my new alertness to the ring of the telephone.

Waiting – I thought of myself as hanging – not able to work, I was asked to write a story about Sicily for a travel magazine.

'I can't,' I said, because I was waiting for the call. I was sure the telephones were terrible in Sicily, and I did not want to be there when the call came. I said I was busy. This happened several times – travel offers. Each time I thought: I'll do it after the movie.

Alison said, 'Are you all right?'

My gloom was not from writing. It was from not writing – not writer's block but a sort of block from not being able to live and believe in myself. The thought of a part in a movie had rid my mind of all other thoughts.

'I'm fine,' I said, and kept my secret to myself until I found it so hard to bear that I called the studio.

'*Mystery Man*.'

I asked to speak to Peter.

'Who shall I say is calling?'

I lost my nerve and hung up.

Not being able to work I walked the streets. I went to more movies and, examining actors' performances, became convinced that I had a career. It made me secretive and self-regarding. I looked at myself in plate-glass windows, in mirrors. I dressed carelessly, as though I did not want anyone to recognize me. When people glanced at me, I turned away.

I had always suspected that I did not belong in London, but contemplating this part in the movie I was convinced of it. I was encouraged by the discovery. These feelings made me think I could give the movie credibility. I felt restless here. The writer in *Mystery Man* was like me, a witness, someone watching the rain come down, waiting to go home.

These empty days and my non-working gave me the feeling I associated with actors. It was easier, I felt sustained, as a non-working actor rather than a non-working writer. Waiting, not working, made me feel I had turned into an actor. No one could challenge me, and yet I knew there had been a change in my mood. I was tormented by the calls for work, more frequent now, as though I sat there, waiting to be summoned.

Alison said, 'I'd love to read some of your China book.'

'Most of it's provisional – I'm still scribbling.'

There was no more of my China book.

Resolute, grimmer than I wanted to be, hating the submissive way I sat there dialing the number, I called Ariel in Los Angeles.

The message on her answering machine was obviously designed to discourage actors looking for work. '*I'm away from my desk this week – traveling*,' she said. No indication where she was or when she would be back. '*If you want to leave a message you can call . . .*' and she gave the number of her secretary. *Get in line,* was the implication. *Don't bother me – there are a million people like you.* There was no way of leaving a message on this line.

'Rats.'

Eventually, to take my mind off my part in the movie, I started working on my travel book again. I could not leave it unfinished; I would have to complete this book about China in order to be available for the movie. That was the story I told myself to give myself the heart to go on. I labored at my desk, I listened to Chinese music, the Red Guards singing *Dong Fang Hong*, 'The East is Red,' and I looked at maps and my notes, and slowly, my chair creaking as I shifted in it, hesitating, I resumed my travel narrative.

And then, somehow, I knew the part was not going to happen. I was sure of it. How was it possible? I had heard nothing. Shooting was about to begin. The Writer was a key part. I had been a fool for ever thinking it would have been possible.

And I felt more than ever like an alien – someone who will never belong, like the man in the movie. An American in England knew so much about broken promises.

So, one day, I woke up and did not want to get out of bed and begin waiting. I lay there, deciding what to do, and in seconds I sat up and rejected the movie. I began to rebuff their attention, turning them down, not angrily but in a tetchy, preoccupied way, interrupting their appeals. It seemed like another reason to leave England. I wanted to take a long trip. I wanted to be unobtainable.

Please, Paul.

Sorry. I'm much too busy. It's not my line of work.

And I realized that I had already had this conversation, on the first day.

'Are you joking, Ariel?'

'*Absolutely not. It's not a big part, but you'd be perfect.*'

'*I've never acted in a movie.*'

'*No problem.*'

268

'*Ariel, don't send me the script. I could never be in a movie.*'
'*Why not?*'
'*I'm not an actor. I don't know the first thing about it.*'
'*That's what directors are for.*'
'*I don't want to learn. I'm a writer.*'
'*The guy's a writer. That's the whole point.*'
'*I can't do it. I have to get back to work.*'

I hated Ariel. She was not a tease. She was the devil, offering me the earth and then skipping off.

Even so, hardened as I thought I had become, I was excited when she finally called me, a month or so later. I listened, breathing in a shallow, nervous way. She was gabbing. Was this a lead-up to the explanation of my part in the movie? No. She began talking about coming to London.

'Auditions?'

'No, just a vacation.'

I risked the question. 'Whatever happened to that part you offered me?'

'The writer? Oh, Peter got someone really good. He was considering you, though, for a while. Do you think you would have done it?'

For a moment then, all life left my body and I was rigid, wooden, holding the phone in my hollow hand, and then as though I had sneezed out my soul and been blessed, my spirit re-entered me and I felt ashamed and tricked.

'No,' I said.

'I've got a story for you.'

'Yes?'

'The other night, Dickie Bellford's underwear party,' Ariel said. 'It was the usual thing, people had to come in their underwear or they weren't admitted. We all knew what was going on, so we were prepared. But some people tried to crash it, and that's where it got interesting. First, were these hot shots from out of town. They stopped laughing as soon as they reached the door. Two huge black bouncers with wire coat-hangers grabbed them. "Take your clothes off or get out." They got out. Then a really rich Italian executive came with his date – the girl was already in her underwear. The Italian didn't think the rule applied to men. The two black guys came up to him with the wire hangers. "Take your clothes off." You should have seen him in his boxer shorts, and his hairy chest and skinny legs, looking like some guy that was totally lost. What do you think?'

'It's good.'

'You think it's stupid.'

It was unusual and diverting, but did it bear any relation to anything I wrote? It seemed to me unusable, like the other stories – of the Dutch couple, and the gift-victim. Perhaps the reason I was so ready to listen to them was because they convinced me of the reality of my writing. I was always greedy for more, as though they had an accidental significance, and I would see their meaning afterwards, like parables I had to live through to understand.

NINE

Traveler's Tale

The way that people, interviewers especially, sit down is usually a good indicator of how long they are planning to stay. Miss Erril Jinkins – the name was apparently correct – lowered herself slowly into the leather armchair in the sitting room of my suite at the Regent of Sydney, going silent as she sank. She was tall and symmetrical and she shifted her weight and crossed her legs as though locking her body on to the cushion and sealing herself there. The chair itself responded to her – flexed and hesitated and seemed to steady itself with an abrupt chair-like grunt of acceptance.

Miss Jinkins had seemed primly and rather prettily dressed, but when she sat down her prim clothes sort of winked and surprised me with teasing illusion. Her dark blouse was translucent and created a shadow play of the curves beneath it; and her skirt was split to her hip, showing me the entire shapely length of her slender leg.

There was something about her name, about so many of these Australian names, that made me think of a criminal or a convict. She was an elegant woman, but 'Erril Jinkins' had an old crude misspelled strength and suggested to me a hint of wickedness.

'I've interrupted you,' she said. 'Writing home?'

Her alertness alarmed me. So she had seen the letter I had begun, that lay on the desk across the room, with the stamped envelope.

'Yes, I've been away too long.'

'Didn't I read somewhere that you're divorced?'

'You may have read it, but it's not true. I am happily married,' I said. As soon as the words were out of my mouth I regretted them for their self-congratulation. Superstitiously I thought: Who heard that?

Erril Jinkins took out her tape recorder, she held it like a small sandwich, she set it on the table between us, she smiled, she peered forward without seeing much, she batted her eyelashes. I was appalled by her slowness and her patience.

Her smile made me uneasy, too. She seemed to be warning me of an awkward question.

'Mind if I use your facilities?'

I hated that – hated her asking, hated the phrase – and why hadn't she asked me before she so ceremoniously sat down in the chair.

'Just through there,' I said, as she slowly rose to her feet. The curtains of her skirt closed on her thigh as she stood and started away. What is it about the click of a woman's heels on a polished floor that is so arousing?

I went to the far window, where a telescope on a tripod was trained on the opera house. I shortened the focus, from the opera house, to the harbor, to the bustle at Circular Quay, and watched the people buying tickets, boarding ferries, relaxing. A man sat on a bench in the sunshine, a sandwich in one hand, a paperback in the other. He munched and he read. I was thinking, *I want to be that contented solitary man*, and I wondered what I was in for with this woman.

*

Now and then an interviewer, while asking something predictable and dull, lets drop a fact that stops me cold.

The journalist in San Diego whose husband got her a big blond surfer for the night as a present for her fortieth birthday. The tiny and rather plain spinster who profiled me in Denver and who said she had taken every drug I could name. 'And I still drop acid now and then.' The thirtyish woman reporter in Houston who told me how, early in her marriage, their coke parties frequently turned into orgies, and how she had often ended up with two men in her bed, one of them her husband. 'But nowadays life is pretty quiet. I mean, we have kids and a mortgage.' The broadcaster who was leaving his wife and three children to live in Tucson with another man. The Chicagoan who divorced her lawyer husband after he decided to become a plumber. The radio journalist in Baltimore who had abandoned her husband and three children to follow a fat Indian herbalist-guru to Canada. The smirking girl in Kansas City who told me how her brother, nicknamed 'Butter,' had made love to a mother and daughter at the same time, and when I frowned, wondering how, she added, 'Tag team.'

'But this interview is supposed to be about you,' they say, and they laugh and change the subject. I comply, because the sooner I answer their questions the sooner it is over and I am free to sit on a bench in the sunshine and eat a sandwich and read a book.

'I'm sure you've been asked all these questions before,' the interviewer says at some point, and I always protest: No, no – I find yours interesting! It hardly matters. I am on autopilot, answering the same questions I have been asked for the past almost twenty years. Why did I go to Africa? What is so special about trains? Do I use a word processor? Which is my favorite of my own books? Who are my favorite writers? If I could go anywhere in the world which country would I choose? Have I ever, in traveling, been in fear of losing my life? Was the hero of this book or that based on anyone in particular? What do I think of the nasty piece about my book in last Sunday's book review?

One interviewer is eighteen and a bit giggly, just out of school and still lives with her folks, and really wants to tell me about her baby sister. Another is elderly and nervous, quite unlike the young interviewer who just left the room wearing an Elvis badge. Many are unremarkable-looking women who startle me by mentioning drugs or multiple divorces or the sudden throwaway, 'Well, I happen to know that because I was sexually abused myself as a child.'

These interviewers squint at me and then rush away and describe me in their newspapers as *relaxed . . . ivy-league . . . horn-rims . . . candid . . . evasive . . . polite but distant . . . friendly but formal . . . younger than I expected . . . taller than I expected . . . shorter than I expected . . . middle-aged . . . very fit . . . somewhat pale . . . ill at ease . . . bumbling . . . transatlantic.*

I am not dismayed. I learned long ago that a newspaper page is not a mirror and seldom a window.

But I often think: I should do a profile of them. I would be better at it and they too would feel self-conscious when I mentioned how they clawed their hair and dropped their notes and spilled their drink, and got my titles wrong: *Riding the Red Rooster, Riding the Iron Monster, The Great Train Bazaar, My Secret Life.* That simple little fellow in Christchurch, New Zealand, who praised me for writing *Walden*. There is always a tape recorder that won't record, and always the same comment: 'I was always afraid that this would happen.' There is often an interviewer who arrives late and apologetic because she has a serious problem at home (sick child, ailing parent, damaged pet). Their bitten fingernails, their touching admiration, their ill-concealed malice or envy, their sadness, their mention of deadlines. All that and 'How long does it take to write a book?' and 'Do you respect your characters?' and 'Which is harder to write – fiction or non-fiction?'

But what remains with me is the sorry way they walk, and their plastic briefcases and their fatigue, and their shoes – especially their shoes, so trampled and misshapen they have come to resemble a battered pair of human feet – and I decide to do nothing, not to write about them, because every one of them is overworked and underpaid.

*

Only then did I hear a toilet flushing, like the sound of a failed explosion, and a door slammed, and I looked up and saw Erril Jinkins. She had been gone all that time. She made her way back to the sitting room, and she thanked me and motioned with her hands – I guessed they were somehow still damp – and she got back into the chair in the same serious way.

'Nice place,' she said.

It was the Presidential Suite, and I almost told her so, but I was getting it at a greatly reduced rate so that hacks could come in and scribble, as she was doing now, *Sumptuous suite ... deep armchairs ... patterned wallpaper ... signed prints by well-known Aboriginal artists ... flowers ... oriental carpets ... view of harbor ... brass telescope ...*

'I didn't choose it,' I said, despising myself for bothering to explain. 'It was assigned to me.'

'I've been here before,' Jinkins said.

I looked sharply at her. Surely a lie?

'John le Carré,' she said.

She squinted and smiled and glanced around the room.

'What is it about hotel rooms? They make me feel sexy.'

She was still looking hungrily around the room.

'He had me in stitches,' she said. 'He insisted I call him David.'

I tried to imagine his insisting, and when she glanced up at me I think she realized that I didn't believe her.

'That's his real name, of course,' she said.

How easy it was to be with an author who was wary of throwing his weight around out of a fear of being called arrogant or pompous. The idea was to put your best foot forward, to treat all questions as though they were well-intentioned and all interviewers as intelligent and serious. Play the game and they will be gone soon, was my usual tactic.

'It's impossible to open a paper without seeing your face,' Jinkins said. 'All those articles about you! All those book reviews!'

I found myself being apologetic once again, but she interrupted me before I could get very far.

'How long were you in China?' she asked.

'About a year, on and off. But the funny thing is –'

'I was there for two years,' she said, cutting me off. 'First in Shandong, in Dongfang – the oil fields – and then in Hami. You didn't mention Hami.'

'I passed through it on the train to Turpan,' I said.

'You should have stopped. It's on the Silk Route, very Muslim, the food's beaut. I got to know the people there pretty well. They can be super friendly. They've got all sorts of grievances with the Han Chinese, of course.'

'I mentioned that,' I said quickly, but before I could say where, she was off.

'Such as marriage laws, family size, freedom of religion, permission to travel to Mecca to make the Haj – all sorts of stuff. But I found that if you learned the language you could get to know them really well.'

'So you learned Mandarin?'

'I meant Uighur,' she said confidently, pronouncing it Weegah. 'Yeah, I learned Mandarin, but most of the Uighurs are suspicious of you if you speak it to them.'

'Uighur is supposed to be very difficult.'

She shrugged and dismissed this. She said, 'The script's a bugger, though.'

'You can write it, too?' I was astonished that she had learned this maddening script of curlicues and doodles.

She nodded and I wondered whether she was lying. She said, 'That train connects to Korla – in the desert.'

'Korla is closed to foreigners,' I said.

She smiled again and now I knew that this smile was a show of defiance and contempt. She said, 'I spent a month there. I lived in a village with a Uighur family. We lived on mutton and goat's milk and that fabulous bread they call *nang*. They treated me like one of the family – showed me a forbidden oasis, taught me how to ride a camel, took me hunting. Wolves,' she said, before I could ask. 'We killed three huge ones. They made a pelt into a waistcoat for me. When I left, I gave them my Sony Walkman and a compass, so they'd always know which way to face when they prayed. In return they gave me a samovar. Antique. Russian. Worth loads, I reckon.'

Her interruption exasperated me, yet I envied her – not only the trip to Korla, but living with the family, speaking the language, even the samovar. I had seen these bright brass urns in some Uighur houses in Xinjiang but no one had presented me with one. I suppose it would have helped if I had been a beautiful sturdy Australian woman, with all the time in the world. Most of all I envied her those weeks or months she had spent without the necessity of having to meet a deadline. I loved the casualness of it, the wallowing in all that exoticism, her independence and anonymity. It was obviously real travel: hardship and pleasure in the great naked, undeveloped landscape of Xinjiang.

There was something so artificial about a travel book: taking notes, and then lugging your notes back and making them into a book, as though in justification of all that self-indulgence. Yet what was more self-indulgent than writing such a book? As a writer who traveled, I felt somehow that I was forever having to account for my movements, and in so doing having to make them seem as though they mattered.

'So you've done a lot of traveling?' I asked.

'Travel is in your head – people are in your head.' She smiled and went on, 'The best fun I've ever had was driving slowly through the African bush, wearing my Walkman and listening to the soundtrack of *Diva* while looking at elephants, fifteen or twenty at a time, foraging and walking – opera and elephants and dust.'

I could see it just as she described it and I set the scene in the dusty bush of Malawi where I had seen elephants.

'In China,' she went on, 'it was "Daisy, Daisy, give me your answer, do," while looking at three thousand people cycling through

Tiananmen Square – that was amazing. It was – doesn't James Joyce call it an epiphany? It is impossible to put the feeling into words.'

She was right – a travel book was such a feeble duplication of the real thing, and some of the greatest travelers never wrote a word; their names are not known. They are the people, like Erril Jinkins, that one spots in the bazaars of distant places. You look again, in order to catch their eye, and they are gone. Their stories are never told.

'I've traveled in Europe and Asia. I was on the hippie trail in the early Seventies.' Here she looked closely at me and smiled, searching my face for a reaction. 'But mostly it's been South America. Down the rivers.'

'I've always wanted to do that,' I said.

'It takes ages but it's worth it,' she said. 'It's impossible unless the Indians help you. I flew to Colombia – Bogota. Then Chaviva. Have you been there?'

'I've heard of it,' I said, and wondered whether I really had.

'Then down the Rio Meta, to Puerto Carreño, in a canoe. That's on the Venezuelan border. Then down the Orinoco, about four hundred miles or so. Very nice.'

Erril Jinkins no longer seemed like an anonymous woman in glamorous clothes, but rather a genuine person, with a name and a past. Her strength and courage were far more attractive to me than her beauty, but they made that beauty itself something powerful.

She said, 'I discovered then that there are places in the world where no one has ever been. Not just mountains that no one has yet climbed, but valleys never seen, rivers no person has ever paddled in. Real wilderness, virgin territory. What Sir Richard Burton called "Nature in the nude." That ought to be the whole purpose of travel, don't you think? To find those places and then to keep them a secret.'

She recrossed her legs and smiled again. What lovely teeth she had.

She said, 'Let's talk about your book.'

While she had been talking about the wilderness, I had revised my opinion of her. Of course there were always these interviewers who needed to tell their stories – they sought out a writer not to listen but to talk. They were competitive, they were aggressive, they could be very boring. She was none of these. Perhaps she had set out to impress me; if so, she had succeeded. I had to admit that even if half of what she was saying were true she was special. I didn't mind her monopolizing the allotted hour – which was, by the way, nearly over.

She asked, 'Do you ever invent in your travel writing – I mean, make things up?'

'No. I put it down the way I –'

And just like that in the middle of my sentence she interrupted again, as though I had not been speaking at all.

'Ever try to, lie, make your trips sound better or worse than they are, in order to amuse your readers?'

'I was about to say –'

But I got no further.

'Because there's this theory going around that travel writing is a kind of fiction, that invention and imagination are part of the process of the writing. Maybe it happened, maybe it didn't, what does it matter, you know?'

'That's not my theory,' I said, wondering whether she was going to interrupt. 'I try to describe things as they are, as they happened. I pride myself in telling the truth, because the truth is always more interesting than anything you can invent.'

She reached over and snatched up her tape recorder and switched it off. 'That's a good ending. Thanks for the interview.'

I almost said, What interview? I certainly had not told her much. She had not seemed to notice that. She took her time putting her notes away and zippering her tape recorder into her handbag. By now her hour was gone – she had run over, not that it mattered.

The moment was crucial – the last interview of the day, the last interview of the week, in a hotel room in a strange city, the whole weekend ahead, yawning emptily at me. I wondered whether I should offer her a drink. We would talk about the city, the brevity of my visit, the real anxieties of a book-promotion tour. Such candor could be risky.

I hesitated because I felt sure she would accept. A drink meant two drinks, and dinner was a strong possibility, and so was the rest of the evening. The offer of a drink to a stranger in a city like this was a serious gamble. Yet she was someone I wanted to know better.

'Will you join me for a drink?'

She reacted brightly, as though it was just what she had been expecting me to say, but instead of saying yes, she clasped the arm of her chair and stood up. The split skirt is made for movement, not for repose. There were several distinct phases of her standing up, like an elaborate dance step that grows bolder. But this was a step backward.

'Thank you,' she said, meaning, No, thank you. 'I don't want to keep you. You've given me so much of your time. And I am sure you have other plans.'

'I don't have any other plans,' I said, and instantly regretted saying it.

'But I do,' she said.

Then she was on her way out, her resonant heels mocking me on the polished floor.

＊

I had my drink alone, and I rather resented the way she had used my time and tested my patience. I hated her mention of my letter home. I did not want to think that she had also teased me.

She was a traveler, there was no doubt of that. Her aloofness, the evidence of her strength, was both the most attractive and the most irritating thing about her. She clearly felt that the way she traveled was superior to my plodding progress and the incessant *Look at me* of my travel writer's note-taking. She was the traveler. I was the hack.

It gave me an idea for a short story, one that I had never read but now badly wanted to read, which was my certain proof that writing it would be a good idea.

A travel writer is on a promotional tour in a distant city. Not Australia, say New Zealand – make something of the starkness of the wind-scoured streets of Wellington. This friendly fellow is interviewed by a woman journalist. Describe the chilly hotel room, the pearly light in the seashell sky, the passersby, all those hats, all those fuzzy sweaters. Instead of allowing the writer to answer the questions, the woman simply rambles on, interrupting the writer's replies. She tells him about her travels, and he knows her adventures are more colorful than his. He becomes fascinated and interviews her. She is the subject of the story.

The short story would be the portrait of a traveler, but the irony was that the traveler was an obscure and unremarkable-looking woman in this bleak city, off the map. It would be a way of illustrating something that I felt strongly – that the great trips, the painful ordeals, the dangers and mishaps and close-calls, are faced by people who never write a word. The real travelers are people the world does not know.

Call it 'Traveler's Tale.' It was a good story, to be told in the first person. I would make her unattractive and earthbound for effect. *She was one of those heavy people whose clothes, much too tight, make them seem not just uncomfortable but swollen – and perhaps still swelling, perhaps explosive, the clothes dangerously full and strained, as though threatening to burst.* I would call her Joylene, I could make her a tease, a liar, a bore, or a slut. At first she would seem rather stout and lonely, a bit pathetic and self-absorbed, radiating gray monotony like a damp odor. But by the end of the story you would see – I would make you see – that she was brave and imaginative, that she had endured the hardships of travel and discovery.

And of the narrator – this man who had stories to tell of his travels, of his minor fame and his numerous books and friendships – you would hear nothing at all; nor would the interviewer learn anything of him. Joylene would go heavily away with her own voice on the tape.

Back at the telescope – but by now night had fallen and my eyes were glazed – I realized that I would rather have had that quiet drink with Erril Jinkins, the pretty girl with the funny name. I wanted to ask her more about the world's wilderness, of the places where no one had ever been. Now there was a list of places worth noting. It was one of my own favorite subjects, almost an obsession with me: undiscovered lands.

I had my short story. That was some consolation, one of the rewards of solitude. It had not been an entirely wasted book tour.

*

But the tour was not over. The phone was ringing – very early the next morning. And when a phone rings and a voice I barely recognize says accusingly, 'I'm right downstairs in the lobby,' I become anxious. It can be a worrying announcement.

There is first of all the suddenness, and the proximity of the person; and the fact that they are in the lobby means that your escape route is cut off. What else can you do except listen for more?

'Shall I come up?'

I did not know how to reply. Worst of all I could not immediately identify the voice. But then I knew. Even though I had not expected her to call, I had been thinking of her. It seemed willful and perverse, as though she had appeared because I had been thinking of her, as though I had conjured her up like an imp.

A minute or so later she was leaning on my door-chime – Erril Jinkins. But no longer was she the glamorous interviewer in the split skirt and filmy blouse and clicking high heels, moving past me in a gust of perfume, all her clothes lisping and teasing me. No, she was dressed in an Indian shirt and blue jeans, and in sandals she was smaller and simpler. She walked without a sound, she had no odor, she sat lightly in the same chair. It was a Seventies look: she was the hippie traveler, ready for anything. In these street clothes she seemed impartial and self-possessed. This was how she had dressed in South America and China.

I said, 'What a surprise. I thought I had seen the last of you.'

'I reckon you were wrong.'

This was the proof that she was a traveler – she was curious, not to say nosy; she was game, even a bit arrogant. She had certainly startled me. And wasn't it a risk, dropping in on me like this?

'It's a lovely day,' I said. 'Do you want to do anything? Or go anywhere?'

She said no. Without makeup she had a slightly different face, more subtly expressive but just as bright, with sleepier eyes and pale lips and a girlishness that I had not seen yesterday.

'So you really don't know who I am?'

This threw me.

I said, 'Have I met you before?'

Instead of saying yes or no, she made a sound in her throat and said, 'Don't you recognize my harsh, antipodean groans?'

I laughed out loud at the absurdity of it. What was she talking about?

She removed a thick paperback book with a torn and illegible cover from a cloth shoulder bag.

'I bought this bag in Afghanistan in 1973,' she said. 'The town of Herat, to be exact.'

'I've been there,' I said.

'Indeed you have,' she said. 'May I sit down? I want to read you something.'

There was something in her tone that made me suspicious, and so I gestured to a chair rather than uttering a pleasantry such as *Be my guest*. I was not sure I wanted her as a guest.

She sat, and flattened the book on her knees, and leaned and read.

'"He put me in second class with three Australians. It was a situation I grew to recognize over the next three months. At my lowest point, when things were at their most desperate and uncomfortable, I always found myself in the company of Australians, who were like a reminder that I had touched bottom. This trio on the Lake Van ferry considered me an intruder. They looked up, surprised in their meal: they were sharing a loaf of bread, hunched over it like monkeys, two boys and a pop-eyed girl. They grumbled when I asked them to remove their knapsacks from my berth."'

Here she looked up at me, to smile, but it was a smile of defiance.

'And it goes on,' she said.

'Don't bother – I remember it.'

But she ignored me. '"I did not sleep well, and once I was awakened by the harsh, antipodean groans of the girl, who, not two feet from me, lay beneath one of her snorting companions."'

She put the book down.

'That was me, more or less. You say you don't remember me, and yet you wrote that in your *Railway Bazaar*.'

I said, 'A long time ago. Was it really you?'

'And my boyfriend. And Kevin, Andy's mate. Andy and I got married. We traveled a little and then we moved to Darwin. Andy was a geologist for a mining company. We got a divorce a few years later. Then I did the rest of my traveling. But that trip through Turkey and Iran was one of the best in my life. I was happy. I didn't realize you were spying on us.'

Oh, God. I said, 'Why didn't you mention this yesterday?'

'I just wanted to talk to you. And I had an article to write. I know you wasted your time. Now I'll tell you why.' Her eyes were harder, colder, her scrubbed face was fiercer than I had yet seen it. She went on, 'You think people are insects to catch and exhibit. Their clothes. Their eating habits, their groans. And if they're not ugly you'll make them ugly, or if they're not pretty enough you'll beautify them to please yourself. And the most bloody arrogant thing about you is that you think that once you've written about them they're yours – they belong to you, because you've stuck them on the page.'

'I think the opposite,' I said. 'Once it's written it's not mine anymore, it doesn't –'

But she was already talking, interrupting, a flat-footed Australian, eager to have the last word and shove off.

'We have our own lives! We can make our own choices,' she said, sounding rehearsed. 'I don't belong to you. I'm not the person you made me.'

I started to speak, but she hadn't finished.

'I'm real,' she said. 'Are you?'

'We'll see,' I said, as she left, banging the door so hard the telescope rattled on its tripod.

That was like a suggestion. I took up my position, searched for her on Circular Quay. I did not see her, and so I went to my desk and began writing.

TEN

Forerunners

The pushy man at the Edinburgh Festival kept saying to me, 'You mean you haven't read Andreas Vorlaufer?' and I thought: No, but has Andreas Vorlaufer read me?

I had already made myself unpopular at the festival by refusing to sign 'An Open Letter to the government of Kenya.' The Kenyans had put a poet into prison. A fiercely freckled Welsh woman in a long hooded shawl that gave her the look of a gloomy druidess introduced herself as Bronwyn Thomas and thrust a clipboard and pen at me.

'Agostinho Neto was an Angolan poet,' I said. 'The Portuguese government put him into prison. He was one of the first prisoners of conscience that Amnesty International adopted, and their pressure got him out of prison. Some years later, after Agostinho Neto became prime minister of Angola, he began throwing his political enemies into jail, and Amnesty had to plead with him to let them out.' I smiled at her, because she looked murderous. 'That's one reason I'm not signing.'

'You're being totally illogical,' Bronwyn Thomas said.

'No. It's proof that poets can become tyrants, too,' I said. 'You know, Chairman Mao managed to be a dedicated poet and an imaginative tyrant.'

'You're saying, "Do nothing."'

'"Tear him for his bad verses." Ring a bell? *Coriolanus*,' I said. 'Why does it always have to be poets?'

'I thought you cared about human rights.'

'I do. I was just filling you in on some background.'

'Then why won't you sign this letter?' Miss Thomas demanded.

'I never sign anything I have not written myself,' I said, and walked away, as she muttered after me.

People usually say the wrong thing to writers. I know it is hard to

284

say the right thing, but why should I want to sign someone's ill-written protest, or chat about someone else's bestseller, or the newest travel writer? Believing that I will be grateful for the suggestion, they say, 'You've got to read this,' and I always think, No, I don't, though I might smile and make a careful note of the title. I want what I think most writers want: unqualified praise. Criticism is never helpful and always boring. If you cannot encourage me, please leave me alone.

If I have to listen to anyone, I want it to be the person who remembers something I once wrote that contained an insight or a joke that is still funny. How wonderful it is to be told that a thing I wrote has not been forgotten and that the memory of it continues to give pleasure. It touched you, it has never been reprinted, and yet you quoted it accurately to me and it still sounds fresh. It reminds me powerfully of an earlier time when I was young and anxious, under-paid, working much too hard – burning brightly.

No one says those things at British literary festivals, which is another reason why I hate them. I had only been to one before Edinburgh, and that was Cheltenham – a tea party as big as a town, books as theater, writers as performers. Dogs walking on their hind legs were what I thought of. It was bad for everyone. The people watching should have been home reading, the writers should either have been writing or else doing something equally dignified – anything except blabbing and making faces.

Writers when they are away from their desks look so pale, so poor, so hunted. We really shouldn't go out at all, and certainly not to literary festivals, where we are such dismal advertisements for our work. Those novelists with sex on the brain show up and – she's fat, he's pimply and past it, she's posing, he's faded. This is embarrassing. For every second-rater with lovely hair and good clothes there are fifty disappointments, and nearly always it's 'I thought he was taller,' 'He shaved off his beard,' or 'He's the one with the yellow tie.' We are urged to drink at these get-togethers and that makes everything worse. We are not at our best when people are staring at us. Just the other day a fairly well-known woman novelist said she had been lying about her age. 'I have been forty-seven for the past ten years' – nicely put, but what's the point? Surely the work has nothing to do with the flesh. All that matters is that the gyroscope within us still spins and stays upright.

Why should I care who Andreas Vorlaufer was? I did not even want to be here. But I had agreed to come to Edinburgh because I liked the city's black heights and narrow streets, its wind and rain, and I had been promised a good hotel, at which I planned to finish a piece I had been writing about Robert Louis Stevenson. My publisher had made it easy for me, and vanity did the rest. I sat on a panel with two novelists and poets, all of them envious and unfriendly and one frankly angry with me.

'I hear you refused to sign the open letter because you think Jerry Njoki is a bad poet.'

I just laughed and thought how rumors are a form of wish-fulfillment. As you know, I said nothing of the kind.

The panel discussion went on until late, but I pitched in. I did my stuff, hating my over-simplifications, and I left the stage thinking: Never again.

So when this free-loading travel writer started praising Andreas Vorlaufer I could not honestly object. I deserved to be tortured like this. I would never make this mistake again.

'He writes about trains. He's been to Africa and Asia. He's supposed to be really good.'

'What do you mean "supposed to be"?' I said. 'You haven't read him?'

'He hasn't been translated into English, but he's really popular in East Germany. He's from Leipzig. Someone told me about him.'

It had all been passed along, secondhand! Time to leave, I thought. But on the day I planned to flee I shared breakfast with a stranger who introduced himself as Andreas Vorlaufer.

He was in his seventies. He had thin, mousey gray hair and a sharp nose and the sort of East European suit that looks like an English boy's school uniform, the jacket too tight, the trousers not quite long enough, the socks wrong – purple in his case.

'You write about trains,' I said, to be polite.

'I used to, long ago,' he said.

He had the overtidy way of eating that deprived people learn in frugal, failing countries, something to do with starvation and manners, a slow ritual to make the meal last and to avoid waste. He spread jam on his toast as though cleaning the knife blade. He opened a small envelope of sugar and emptied it into his coffee without spilling a single grain; and after he stirred it, he tapped his spoon against the lip of the cup, saving the droplets of coffee.

'Do you read German?'

'No. Someone told me about you. And I have written a few things about train travel.' A few things!

He went on eating his toast, sipping his coffee in his methodical, rationing way, showing no interest in me. If I had praised him, I am sure he would have listened.

'Your English is very good.'

'I have traveled extensively.'

I wanted to tell him: People who speak English well know better than to use the pompous word 'extensively.'

'Though it has been exceedingly difficult at times to purchase tickets.'

'Exceedingly' was another one, and so was 'purchase.'

But I said, 'I lived in Africa for quite a few years.'

'So much of the world is English-speaking. Africa. India. Singapore. And America, of course.'

Was he putting me on? I said, 'You've lived in all those places, really?'

'Yes,' he said quietly. 'And I have written about them.'

I did not say that so had I – I hated the sort of conversation between strangers that turned into a tennis match. He seemed just as happy to leave the subject, and he only became animated when I asked, 'What do you think of the festival?'

'It is like all literary festivals. It is a tea party, everyone is very polite. No one says anything about the horror and boredom of writing. We are performers, like dogs walking on their hind legs.'

I stared at him. Hadn't I felt precisely that way, in just those words?

'These novelists with sex on the brain,' Andreas Vorlaufer said. 'She is fat. He is pimply. Everyone is disappointed. People say, "I thought he was taller," "He has shaved off his beard?" or "He is so old." It is most humiliating, don't you agree?'

I think I nodded. I registered the phrase 'most humiliating' – native English-speakers didn't say that either. I looked closely at him.

'Physically we writers are of no importance. It is the thing within us that matters. Spirit or thought. It is a kind of gyroscope. This festival is a huge English tea party. The Kenyan poet that everyone is so concerned about – why is it always poets?'

'So you didn't sign the open letter?'

Vorlaufer said, 'I have an inflexible rule of never signing anything that I have not written myself. But no matter. I came for other reasons.'

'So did I.' I got up from the table, feeling that I was being mocked and diminished by this stranger.

He stood and bowed slightly and I thought how there is something almost oriental in some Eastern Europeans, and something deeply melancholy – their sad eyes, their sallowness, their cynicism, their school clothes.

I checked out of the hotel and set off to do what I had come to do – visit Robert Louis Stevenson's childhood home at Swanston, on the outskirts of Edinburgh, under the Pentland Hills. I hired a car and drove out of town, following signs, and had no trouble finding the turn-off to Swanston. Suddenly I was in the Scottish countryside, of steep grassy hills, and heather and gorse and blowing broom. The small village was at the end of a steep, narrow road, six or eight cottages and one detached house, the whitewashed manor where Stevenson had spent most of his summers as a boy.

It was a majestic house of stucco and mellow granite, surrounded by a low wall and old, twisted trees. On this windy late summer day the trees were struggling, their leaves turning over and looking silver in the cloud-muted daylight. The grass streaming under the wind had long, beautiful tassels. The sheep on the hillside were motionless and when the sun broke through the rising meadows were mottled with scraps of cloud shadow. Swanston, shaped like a bowl, holding only this manor house and a few cottages, was as peaceful as a valley can be, and even the clusters of ravens in the oaks looked as unthreatening and emblematic as heraldic symbols.

The gate to the house was ajar, as though in welcome. I did not need to push it open any farther to slide through. I rapped on the heavy front door and thought how this venerable door could have been the same one that Stevenson had swung open. Waiting for an answer I heard laughter inside – children – and a woman's voice. I had to rap again before anyone heard, and when I saw the children and the television set I understood the delay.

'Yes?' The voice was gruff, the woman indistinct – she had not opened the door very wide. And yet I could see beyond her to where the children were watching television. I saw the toys, the calendar, the picture of the Queen. It was an unremarkable interior but its plainness was not the worst of it. The wood-paneled walls were scratched and marked with clumsy drawings, the floor had been splashed with paint, a hunk of plaster was missing from the ceiling, and what I could see looked cluttered if not vandalized. I thought of Robert Louis Stevenson and did not want to see more.

I said, 'Isn't this Stevenson's home?'

'There's no one by that name here,' the woman said, in a voice filled with suspicion – and now she was easing the door shut.

'I'm looking for Swanston House.'

'This is Swanston House.'

'But who owns it?'

She was still talking as she shut the door, and so I was not sure whether I heard 'the Council' or 'the Corporation,' but in any case I got the message: she was a tenant, living here at a reduced rent, with her big messy family, and she was sending me away.

I turned to walk down the path and saw a familiar figure glance up at the house and walk on. It was the old man I had seen that morning at breakfast.

'Herr Vorlaufer.'

He was puzzled. 'You know me?'

'We met at the hotel this morning.'

He smiled. Did he remember? He hardly seemed to care. He did not ask me my name.

I was still shutting the gate. I said, 'Robert Louis Stevenson used to live in this house.'

'Yes. I know. That is why I came here.'

You could not tell that man anything.

He was still walking slowly, saying, 'There is a lovely path to the top of that hill.'

He seemed to be pointing to a row of gnarled trees. No hill was visible here – just a damaged wall and two sheep which were un-shorn and looked overdressed, not to say top-heavy.

To call his bluff I followed him. I had nothing else to do. I had found my story: being turned away from Stevenson's house by a suspicious Scottish mother protecting her children and her TV set was better than being allowed in for a tour of the damaged premises.

Vorlaufer led the way and forty feet on he stepped away from the road on to a narrow path, and there was the hill, as he had said.

'Do you mind if I come with you?'

'Not at all,' he said, though it sounded to me like utter indifference.

'You said you lived in Africa and wrote books about it?'

He smiled indulgently. 'You would not have read any of them. They have not been translated into English, though there are many. One of my first was about a girls' school in Kenya.'

'There aren't many girls' schools in Kenya,' I said. And I was going to say that I knew why: because I had done the same thing, written the same book.

'This one was in Embu,' he said.

'It's still there.'

He was not listening. He was picking his way slowly along the path, talking softly in the patient, wondering way that old people talk about their early lives. There was a note of detachment in his tone, too, as though he were talking about someone else.

'I wrote two other novels, and then I went to Singapore,' he said. 'If you stay too long in Africa, something happens – you turn into a white person. It is much better that Africans should run their own affairs. I saw that I didn't belong. Anyway, I was curious about Singapore.'

'So was I when I went there,' I said. 'I wanted to write about it.' Did he hear that? 'I did, actually. A novel.'

'I found Singapore a disappointing place,' Vorlaufer said.

'Did you write anything there?'

'I had a family to support,' he said. 'I was young. In those days I could write a novel in six months or less. That one was about the old Singapore – brothels, bars, and hot steamy streets. The hero was a sort of misfit. If I call him a procurer I would be misrepresenting him.'

'I understand perfectly,' I said. 'My book was very similar to yours.' If not exactly the same, I wanted to add.

He was walking in front of me on the path, which was too narrow for us to walk side by side. It was not more than a rut through the grass and I had the feeling that it was one the sheep had made with their mincing little hooves. I could not see Andreas Vorlaufer's face and did not know whether he heard me.

'It seems a trivial book to me now. The central character was fifty years old. I was hardly thirty when I wrote it.'

So was I, I thought. I said, 'I thought you wrote travel books.'

He heard that; we were talking about him now.

'Many travel books,' he said. 'I used to live for travel. I went everywhere by train.'

'You don't say?' I hurried after him. 'It's a shame the books aren't translated.'

'Who in the English-speaking world cares about East German literature? Even Thomas Mann is not read today! And my books' – he flung out his hand to dismiss the idea – 'they were probably put off by my titles. None of them sounds right in English.'

'Give me an example?'

'A literal translation of my best-known book would be *The Great Railway Bazaar*.'

I stared at the back of his head, wondering whether he was smiling as he walked on. Did he know who I was?

I said, 'There is an American who wrote a book with that title.'

'Yes. So I was told,' Vorlaufer said. 'But I used it first. My book was published in Leipzig in 1946.'

'What did you do then?'

'The book was a modest success. I continued to write novels. I went to South America. I resided in Britain, and did some traveling there.'

'Resided' was another one of those perfect, pedantic words that gave a foreign student away.

'And you continued to write?'

'Indeed' – yet another – 'a novel about a family in Honduras. It's setting was the Mosquito Coast – a good title, I think. A novel set in the future. Travel books. China.'

'More train trips?'

'After the China book I stopped writing about trains.'

The path had widened slightly. I walked a bit faster to be abreast of him, so that I could see his face – and I expected a devilish grin. But he was frowning, feeling the strain of this steep path, and he was breathless from all the talk. If what he said was mockery he was making a good pretense of looking deadpan.

I said, 'What exactly did you write after you finished your book about China?'

I had just finished my book about China.

'My children were at university –'

'Two boys,' I said.

'Yes. And so I traveled around the world with my wife.'

'I was thinking of doing that.'

He did not care what I was thinking. He said, 'My situation changed. I went back to the Pacific and wrote about myself. There is no word for *Bildungsroman* in English. Then I wrote about the South Pacific.'

'I have never been to the Pacific,' I said.

'I wrote less,' he said. 'I became involved in films.'

'Oh, God.'

'I lived in America. I was happy there. I had lived in London for many years. Did I mention that?'

'Yes, you said for about twenty years.'

I wondered how he would handle my niggling deception. He appeared not to notice. He said, 'Eighteen years.'

'I have lived in London for seventeen years myself,' I said, and immediately sensed a shadow pass over me.

'Yes, I wrote less,' he said reflectively. 'But I began writing about myself.'

'And none of it has been translated.'

'Not into English. *Meine Geheimen Leben* was eventually filmed.'

He must have seen me squint at him, the title meant nothing to me, not even the English version I could manage.

He said, 'You don't speak German?' and shrugged.

'Have you been happy?' I asked suddenly.

'That is a desperate question,' he said. 'There are other ways of asking it, but it takes a lifetime to answer.'

Only his words were philosophical. His way of saying them was impatient, and I knew he was bored – he wanted to get away from me and my questions.

But I persisted. I said, 'Can't you tell me anything specific that has happened to you over the past few years?'

I was hoping for some good news, or any encouragement; and I watched his face closely for some sign of it. Finally, he shook his head as though refusing to speak.

I said, 'Back there you used the expression "My situation changed." What did you mean by that?'

'My wife and I separated,' he said and made the utterance tragic and bleak by giving it no emotion.

And I felt a terrible pain, as though a dull knife had been drawn through my heart.

'Why?' I asked and hardly managed to speak the word.

'Oh.' Then he thought a moment, looking into the distance, all the bald hills. 'Our children were not living at home any more. My wife and myself were each busy with our own lives. I think, for a crucial period, we forgot how necessary we were to each other's happiness. I know that, because when we separated, something in me was wrecked, and then it was clear that we could never go back.'

'What made you separate in the first place?'

'A writer is alone too much,' he said. 'That solitude can make a person think that he is missing something. That he is not living. It is simple greed, like Dante's Ulysses – you know the lines? "Nothing – not fondness for my son, not piety for my father, nor love for my wife – could dampen my ardor for experiencing the wider world and human vice and courage." Something like that.'

'So you got exactly what you wanted.'

He smiled at this. 'What we want is distant and dim. That is why we desire it. Distance is the great maker of fantasies.'

'If it were close and you could see it, you wouldn't want it?'

'The things that people crave the most are never near to them,' he said. 'That is why they are craved. The Hindus are right. The world is *maya*, an illusion.'

'I would be very happy if you told me you haven't suffered,' I said.

'Everyone suffers,' he said. 'I have, too. But on the whole I can say I have been very lucky.'

'That's good to hear.'

He lost his smile. There was nothing for a moment – just a blankness in his eyes, and then his whole face seemed to tighten with reluctance.

'I must tell you one thing. When I was your age I was on very good terms with the world. Perhaps too long. It ended suddenly, and I became lost, more unhappy than I have ever been in my life. I consoled myself by saying it was for the best, and perhaps it was necessary.'

This made me feel very sorry, and I knew the feeling would stay with me and become sorrow, like an illness I would have to learn to live with.

'Worse than that, after some years – and I am not speaking of any war – I had personal reasons to be convinced of the existence of evil.'

That shocked me, just the word 'evil' was enough. But as he said it he turned and hurried up the path, as though to emphasize that he did not wish to answer any more questions. I followed at a distance, and within a few minutes we were at the top of the hill. Just past the gorse bushes that densely covered its summit there was a strong wind blowing from the west. I was almost knocked down by it, and then I looked back at Swanston in the valley below. Andreas Vorlaufer had been right: it was a lovely walk.

'You know this place,' I said. 'You've been here before.'

'Once. I was thinking of writing a piece about Stevenson,' he said. He pointed to the small village in the valley. 'I went to that manor house.'

I stared at the house, the front door I had knocked upon an hour before.

'I never finished the piece,' he said. 'I was forty-nine. I met a man.' He was still peering down, into the valley, and his smile was grim. 'It's a strange story. You would never believe it.'

ELEVEN

Champagne

Sometimes you hear a strange name, one you have never heard before and, soon after, you keep hearing it; and everywhere you turn you see it. It was that way with Andreas Vorlaufer. As soon as I got back to London I saw a piece about him in the *Times Literary Supplement*. He was alluded to in another book review, he was mentioned in the preface of a collection of Dürrenmatt's short novels that I happened to pick up, and there was a quotation from him on a calendar that was sent to me, something about travel being 'the saddest of life's pleasures.' Like the details of his life and work that Vorlaufer had told me, that too sounded familiar.

A few months later, feeling a loneliness that kept me from writing, I took to walking in the afternoons, waiting for the pubs to open. Passing a secondhand shop on Lavender Hill I saw in the box of battered books out front a volume of short stories about London, all written by foreigners. One of them, translated from German, was entitled 'Champagne.' The author was Andreas Vorlaufer.

'How much is this one?'

'One book for fifty pee, three for a pound,' the junk dealer said.

It seemed less like a business transaction than a ritual, buying a book from a man with dirty hands. And reading the story seemed like part of the same dark ritual.

This is what I read.

'Champagne,' by Andreas Vorlaufer

I had already opened the bottle of champagne, but out of courtesy had not formally drunk any. I had sneaked half a glass, because I was still a little nervous. I was about to sneak another when I heard her.

There are announcing sounds of approach that only spouses or the dearest companions make, like friendly signals that mean, It's only me. The sounds are slight yet so distinct that they create the sense of a loved one's arrival like instant premonition. I heard no more than the vibration of a latch key, and then the lisp of a raincoat passing a door jamb, and the footsteps – those particular shoes; and not a sigh, but just an audible breath like a low, murmured word of yearning. All of these; and so I called, 'I'm in here!'

'So it's going to be a celebration, then?' she said, as she entered the warm room.

Her eyes were glazed from the freezing air and the darkness, her pale face seeming apprehensive, as though seeing something pleasant that might turn out to be an apparition and trick her; all that – uncertainty, anxiety, happiness, fear – flickered in her expression, until I kissed her lips that were still cool from the night air. I clasped her hand and was surprised and even shocked by how cold her fingers were.

'My tiny hand is frozen.' And she laughed. 'I feel like the little match girl.'

'I think you're confusing your heroines. Here, this will bring color to your cheeks.'

'Lovely,' she said, seeing that I had filled the glasses. 'I won't say no. Is it champers? Crikey!'

Every word of hers was her own and I saw that there was no one like her in the world, and that we had a special language of precious clichés, like trusty artifacts and baggage, a whole culture of two people, with its own rituals and humor and habits, that had taken a whole long marriage to make. Happy people were able to talk this way, in their own private expressions and words, which had a meaning for them alone, and were untranslatable.

I handed her the more graceful glass of the two, and said, 'To us.'

Only then did she hesitate, her lips regretful, her eyes losing their light, a sadness in her jaw.

'Please,' I said and managed to tap her glass with my own.

'Is this a mistake?' she said. Her spirit was receding swiftly, the champagne flute was limp in her fingers, about to spill.

'No, of course not,' I said. 'This was the whole idea. Please drink up.'

'Oh, all right,' she said and sipped and smiled and got brave in that same instant.

She went to the window, which the night had made into a mirror, and she said, 'I look like a little old lady,' and she began to look uncertain and a bit tearful again.

'You look fantastic,' I said. 'Sit down – let's punish this bottle.'

She was dressed in her tweed skirt and thick sweater, her boots wet from her walk from the station; and her fatigue made her seem lovelier, a look of bored and weary dignity that gave her loftiness and grace.

'Did you make a booking?' she asked.

'Yes. At the Orangery.'

'So it's going to be a slap-up, then?' she said, approvingly, in the language we shared.

'With all the trimmings.'

'Do you mind if I smoke a cigarette?' Jutta asked, as she did before she lit up in the house or the car ever since I had given up smoking eight years before. I was struck this time by her politeness in always asking.

'No, go ahead,' I said. I refilled our glasses and we drank again.

'We mustn't get tipsy or we won't appreciate our food,' she said, in her mocking nanny tone, and she sipped her champagne and smoked and regained her look of serenity.

'I've had such a busy day,' I said. 'Last minute things.'

Jutta's expression said nothing and seemed composed, but I knew what a tumult it masked.

'I managed most of them, but when I tried to call Wolfie on that Trinity phone number there was no answer.' I drank some more champagne while at the same time feeling deceitful that I had sneaked half a glass and feeling that this cheating had nullified our toast. 'In Germany some students have phones in their rooms.'

'Life is ever so much better in Germany,' Jutta said. 'And there's our poor little Wolfie stuck in Cambridge.'

People like us, intimate and loving, were seldom literal, and spoke in code, and so the simplest, lamest ironies were fond and funny.

She drew her glass away when I swung up the bottle to fill it again.

'Don't. If we haven't drunk it all, we'll have some for later.'

I did not protest that it would be flat by then. I was reassured by the hope in her using the word 'later.'

'And I know when I've had enough,' she said, and laughed, as she always did when she was consciously quoting one of her mother's nagging mottoes. 'Let's be off.'

She then got a slender knife from the drawer and stuck it into the bottle of champagne, its blade just penetrating the wine.

'That'll keep it fizzy.'

I helped her on with her raincoat that was still damp from her walk from the station, and I got a pang when I saw the worn patch at the edge of the collar – the seriousness of work clothes, her stoicism, it was all so solemn; and nothing made me sadder than her frugality, because it seemed so brave and futile.

So I hugged her, to console myself, and she accepted the embrace at first, then resisted – stiffened, almost fending me off.

'That's enough of that.'

She led the way through the foyer, and passing the chair next to the telephone on its small table, the stack of envelopes, she said, 'What's that?'

'Christmas cards.'

'Of course,' she said, her voice going small.

I went to kiss her cheek in the doorway, and she drew away, lifted her cheek to deflect the kiss, making my kiss seem like something insincere, almost a betrayal. I thought she was going to cry again, but instead she snorted and clapped her gloved hands.

'I hate January,' she said.

There was no snow, only the cold rain that had fallen on the city, giving it the pasty gleam of boot polish, and a clear sky, tattered clouds rushing under the stars and above it all a blackness. The wind harried the branches of the leafless plane trees at the edge of the common, and for once I regretted the cold and the blackness and the damp streets and the foretaste of frost in the air.

'What is it?' Jutta asked. She always knew when I had something on my mind.

'I was thinking: bad weather in a place always makes me remember.'

'Yes. Whenever I think of Singapore I remember the flooded culvert on Bukit Timah Road,' she said. 'Or the way that sun faded everything we owned.'

'We were so poor,' I said.

'What did it matter?'

'I hated it. Taking the bus. Being frugal. Feeling like a victim.'

'God, you sound so pathetic!'

She punched my shoulder, and I laughed and we held hands and walked across the Common, stepping around the puddles, passing under the tall iron lamp posts, and the skeletal hawthorns, and a wooden-slatted bench that had been wrecked by vandals. The restaurant, the Orangery, was on the south side of the Common and on this Saturday night in January it was less than half full. Steam had condensed on the plate-glass windows and it was drafty, a chill in the air, the way all large rooms seemed to me in the winter in London.

'Would it be all right if we sat over there near the radiator?'

'Absolutely.'

'Nice to see you again, sir,' the waiter said to me, showing us to the table I had indicated.

He left us with a menu and the wine list and after he had gone, I said, 'When I worked at a restaurant that was something we were taught not to say. "Don't recognize the man. Don't say his name if he's with a woman. Maybe he told her his name was Smith, and you just called him Jones. Maybe he's with his wife tonight and told her he'd never been here before."'

'That's paranoia.'

'It's politeness. And it's saved some marriages.'

Jutta looked rueful, she went quiet. Then she said sharply, 'Have you ever been here with anyone else?'

'No.'

'You can tell me the truth, Andreas. What difference can it make now?'

'That's the truth,' I said.

It was, and it bothered me that it did not matter anymore to her. A stranger would have guessed that she was looking at the wine list. I knew that she was not reading anything, not looking at it, just brooding in a sudden mood of gloom.

'I hate it when you say my name like that. It sounds so hostile.'

'More paranoia,' she said.

The waiter had appeared behind me, making me glad that I

had not said anything awkward. I was thinking: I don't want to remember everything, especially of this, and I realized – while I was regretting that we were here at this meal, she was regretting it too, and that was what she was thinking when she seemed to be staring at the wine list.

'Something to drink?' the waiter asked.

'A bottle of champagne,' I said. 'The Veuve Cliquot will be fine. Number twenty-two.'

Jutta said, 'Are you sure you want a whole bottle? They have halves of the Laurent-Perrier.'

'I'm sure,' I said, not to her but to the waiter, who hurried away mumbling with insincere servility that came out sounding pompous.

'You'll have to drink the lion's share.'

'As the only lion here, that is the most obvious thing for me to do.'

The waiter brought the bucket first and then the bottle, and he made a production of wrapping it in a napkin and easing out the cork with his thumbs. All of it was meaningless ritual after that – the pouring of a mouthful, the tasting, my saying, 'Fine.'

'Celebrating?' he said, as he filled the glasses.

'Yes,' I said.

'No,' Jutta said.

Smiling in confusion, he went away without taking our orders, and a moment later reappeared, apologizing, recited the night's specials.

'How do you know that sticking a knife into a bottle of champagne keeps it fizzy?'

'Stabbing anything keeps it fizzy,' she said. 'You of all people should know that.'

I said, 'How about splitting the bouillabaisse?'

On the menu it said: *For two persons.*

'I'd rather not,' Jutta said, and it sounded as if she was reproaching me by asserting her independence.

'Leek soup and quail for me,' I said.

'I'll have the kipper pâté and the eggplant.'

'When it comes you can say, "I'm the stuffed eggplant." '

She smiled a little but became serious again and said, 'So what are we celebrating?'

She seemed angry and I began to regret that I had urged her to drink champagne at home, fearful that she might cry, or even shout. I shook my head so as not to excite her. Anything I said in reply might be regarded as a provocation.

'Those weren't Christmas cards,' she said. 'I know what they were. Change of address cards. I'm right, aren't I?'

'Please,' I said, to calm her, and then: 'Let's talk about something else.'

'There is nothing else. I hated those cards.'

'There's nothing odd about moving, darling.'

'Don't call me darling.'

'OK. If you promise not to call me Andreas.'

I looked around the restaurant to see whether anyone was listening and in a way to gauge what would happen – who would witness it – if, as I feared, Jutta might stand up and howl at me. Lowering my gaze and sinking in my chair, making myself seem small and harmless, even insignificant, perhaps pitiable, I held my breath. And then I drank some more champagne, keeping silent.

She said, 'Don't worry, I'm not going to freak out.'

She knew exactly what I had been thinking. The waiter approached with our first course. I let him set out the plates, holding my breath, and then I said in the lightest way I could muster, 'So how was work today?'

'There are moments when I feel that nothing is real but evil, nothing true but pain.' Then she smiled in a haunted and horrible way.

'Oh, God,' I said. 'That's the saddest thing I've ever heard. Jutta, are you that unhappy?'

'No. I was quoting,' she said. 'That's Monkton Milnes – Lord Houghton. He was Sir Richard Burton's patron and poor old fellow, he got pretty depressed at times. I was editing a program about him today.'

The moment passed, though the quotation stayed in my mind as indescribably bleak. Jutta was still talking in an animated way. 'Burton was a bit like you, actually. Banging around the world. Always writing, interested in everything, a dab hand at languages and arcane lore. *A History of Farting*, if you please. *The Arabian Nights*. A selfish beast, too.'

'Still, he discovered the source of the Nile.'

'No, he didn't. John Hanning Speke did. You didn't know that?'

'I forgot. That's right. There was a kerfuffle and Speke committed suicide.'

'It might have been an accident,' Jutta said. 'You'd better listen to the program.'

'I definitely will. Burton hated inconveniences but he enjoyed hardships. I can relate to that, as the jargon has it.'

'"He was my god," Isabel said. Maybe I should have been more like her,' Jutta said. She smiled at me. 'Knock, knock.'

'Who's there?'

'Isabel.'

'Isabel who?'

'Isabel necessary on a bicycle.'

When I laughed she seemed to grow sad, and then began working her knife through her pâté with more force than was necessary. 'No,' she went on, 'I am not a doormat,' and slashed again at the pâté. 'Did you do anything about putting the car in my name?'

'I sent the papers by registered mail.'

'What about the house insurance?'

'Navin said he'd send the forms. He said it's no-fault insurance.'

'That's what we should have had from the beginning,' she said, and then, 'But it's no one's fault.'

I said, 'It doesn't seem possible that Navin was at our wedding.'

'And still alive. The Africans must be dead – that funny little clerk, and your house girl, Veronica. She stole flowers and put them all over the house.'

'Not for the wedding. She did that when you first visited my house. She was trying to placate you.'

'It's the old servant fear in Africa. As soon as the bwana gets married the mem sacks all his servants.'

'But you did fire her.'

'She was very dirty. There were cockroaches in the kitchen. And that reminds me. In the typescript you had me saying "bloody." I want you to change it.'

'It's fiction.'

'I never say "bloody!"' Her sharp voice rang in the restaurant. No one looked up, but her raised voice caused a silence and a sense of people listening hard.

'Of course I'll change it,' I said quickly. 'Do you remember that Englishman who came and said, "Why, this Kraut's married an English rose."'

Jutta smiled, remembering, and then said, 'Let's not talk about the past. It just makes me sad.'

'How do you think Wolfie will do in his finals?'

'You'll miss them. You're really letting him down that way.'

'I can't take his finals for him.'

'You know what I mean.'

I realized that I had been protesting dishonestly. I was being evasive. We both knew that.

'I'm sorry.'

She frowned. '*Sarig*,' she said. 'Old English. It means sad.'

'Sorry is the name of this country. Sorry is what you say to the person who just stepped on your foot. I've never heard the word spoken so often. I'll bet there's a village in England called Sorry. I'll bet there's a local product – jam or a local wine. Sorry Jam, Sorry Champagne.'

'Are you drunk?' Jutta asked. 'When I was at Cambridge, Wittgenstein gave us a whole lecture on *sarig* and its variants.'

And through a haze of wine I saw her in the lecture hall in rainy Cambridge in the famous snowy winter of 1947, watching Wittgenstein through her steel-rimmed specs and writing in her notebook, so serious in her black gown, hard up for money, scrimping to get by, anxious and lonely, because her whole life lay ahead of her – all this. It was a pathos I found unbearable.

'Why are you crying?' she said, shocked at my tears.

'I was thinking of you at Cambridge. Those stories of how you had to be so frugal. Your cold room. The disgusting food.'

'It wasn't so bad,' she said, and the idea that she was being brave made it all worse for me.

'The past is so sad,' I said. 'All that innocence.'

'Please, Andy, you're blubbing. People will see you.'

The worried way she said that reassured me of her sympathy and kept me sobbing softly, snuffling, the tears flowing fast. She took her napkin and dabbed at my face.

'I get so unhappy when I look back and think of how hopeful we were. Nothing is sadder than that. Just two little people. We had so little – we were starting with almost nothing. Once I found a pair of your shoes. You must have had them a long time ago. They were cheap ones and all worn out. I held them in my hands and cried the way I am doing now. The sight of them tore at my heart. Why does the past seem so bleak?'

She held my hand, more like a mother than a lover, taking charge of the hand, but softly, and I was comforted.

'You're being a little melodramatic, Andy.'

'Marrying you was the best thing that ever happened to me,' I said, and licked at my tears.

'That's sweet of you to say. But please let's not talk about the past.'

'I don't remember bad things in our marriage, only good things.'

'It doesn't matter,' she said.

Her eggplant arrived, and my quail, and when the waiter had made his little bow and withdrawn, Jutta poked at her plate.

'I can't eat a thing. What a wicked waste.'

'Have some bread. Otherwise you'll get drunk.'

'I think I'm drunk already.'

She twisted the bread with her fingers, ripping the crust, pulling it apart. Seeing that I was watching her, she became self-conscious and offered me some, and I took it like communion. She did not eat any. She sipped her wine and she relaxed, easing herself back, one shoulder higher than the other; and she smiled.

Instead of eating we drank more of the champagne, drank faster than the waiter could keep our glasses filled, and so I kept snatching the bottle from the bucket.

'We should have come here more often.'

'There are so many things we should have done more often,' I said. 'And some not at all.'

'I don't want to think about that.'

'More wine?'

'Shan't. Won't. I know when I've had enough.' As she spoke she was rooting in her handbag, shuffling the contents.

'I'm paying,' I said. 'That was the agreement.'

'No,' she said, still searching in the bag. She began to cry, a sudden gust, her face crumpling, her look of panic replaced by one of utter misery. Her tears flowed, as she dug among a hair brush and a compact and a clutter of tickets and pens. They were the tears I had feared all evening, and they were piteous, and she said in a voice aching with grief, 'Oh, God, I've lost my credit card!'

'Let me look,' I said, and took the bag, and clawed through

it, so sad to see all these worn objects, the scratched compact, the broken purse, the hairs snagged on the bristles of the brush, the smears of ink on the ballpoint pens, the tickets that were used, punched, clipped and out of date, all those trains to work, all that effort. And she sat helpless, weeping, while I searched, and she still looked sad, even after I found the card.

We quarreled a little over the bill again, and I reminded her of what we had agreed, and I gave the waiter my card. When he returned, he said, 'I wanted to ask you the last time you were here whether you're the writer?'

'I'm the writer.'

'I envy you. That's the life I'd like. I love traveling myself. I've been all over Europe, but I suppose that's not really traveling by your standards. Any more trips planned?'

'I don't know.'

Jutta said to the waiter, 'He means yes.'

Outside the restaurant, I said, 'I wonder if that waiter saw me crying.'

'I'm sure he did.' She walked a few steps then turned to me and said in a breathless, gossipy voice, 'Andreas Vorlaufer, the famous writer, was at table eight last night, blubbing.'

That made me laugh, and that laughter saved everything. Her mockery was like proof that there was nothing she could say that would offend me. We understood each other perfectly, without having to be gentle. There was something unshakable, indestructible that bound us together.

'And so was his wife,' I said. 'He must have made her cry.'

Jutta's laugh delighted me, and we crossed the Common under the lamps, saying nothing more, just holding each other to keep from slipping, because we were both drunk, and the temperature had dropped. There was ice on the footpath, the shallow puddles had frozen. Side by side, steadying each other, propping each other up, we made our slow way home through the night, which was hard and dark and clear, ice crystals on the footpath and frost in the grass, and even the stars and the cold cloud-smudged moon seemed like aspects of this black, frozen city.

Entering the house, stamping to warm our feet, I had a proud almost exalted sense of fulfillment, for the house was large and solid, ten rooms piled on four floors, crammed with furniture and paintings; and the sharp odors of floor wax and brass polish and the lingering aromas of burned candles and leather bindings and exotic carpets seemed to give it greater substance, the suggestion of trophies, the accumulation of almost twenty years of love and work, this whole heap from the revenue of my writing, all of it risen from a thin trickle of ink. Yet there was a shadow over it, that was partly the hour of the night, and my mood: I felt an anticipation of emptiness, as though I had just entered my own tomb.

We stood wordlessly, still gasping from our walk through the thin wintry air, looking at each other in a silent pleading way, as though fearful of speaking.

Finally she said, 'There's half a bottle of champagne left.'

There was the bottle, with the knife jammed into it.

'It will go flat if you don't drink it.'

'Leave it,' I said. 'I have to get up early. Six probably.'

'Crikey, that's the absolute crack.'

How I loved the way she spoke to me in her own untranslatable language.

She used the downstairs bathroom, I used the upstairs, and for the next ten minutes or so water rushed up and down the house, fountains and cataracts sounding in the walls.

The bedroom was in darkness when I entered, but I knew from the vaguest flutter of breath that she was in bed. I slipped beneath the duvet, and moved into her orbit of warmth.

And there we lay, all night, holding each other in the close and steadying way that we had crossed the Common, balancing on the ice. But we under the covers, generating heat.

Often, sleeping, the image came to me that I was buoyant in an enormous ocean, submerging myself in sleep. Sleep was not the act of swimming, not action at all, but rather a sense of submersion in the deep currents of that ocean's darkness, among flitting slivers of lighted fish, the odd phosphorescence I always saw glimmering when I was in a dark bedroom. And holding my wife was the best version of that, sinking with her, clasping her from behind, and then shifting and feeling her roll against my back and ride me down to the profoundest, the darkest depths, where there were no dreams, where there was nothing but sleep.

The alarm's ringing was harsh and sudden and too loud, like the signal of the direst emergency.

She woke a moment after me, as I was kissing her.

'Andy!' she said.

But I had slid out of bed and was snatching at my clothes.

'I'll miss my plane.'

'No, please, no! Come back! Please, don't go. What will I do without you – no!'

And worse than the words was the sound that followed, not a scream but a sob, the most grievous I had ever heard, as though she were strangling on blood, the nearest thing I had ever heard to someone dying. It was her own sound.

Sometimes in a big parking lot you hear a car door slam, and you note it, the strength of it, the grunt, like the chop of a cleaver; then there is a pause, someone sucking air, and an un-earthly howl. I had shut the door, and I knew I would go on hearing that cry of pain wherever I went, for the rest of my life.

*

It was the saddest story I had ever read.

TWELVE

The Half-Life

I

After a marital separation, because of the awful things you say or hear, you start using public phone booths more – anyway, I did, for their privacy and anonymity, to avoid embarrassment. And they all looked alike, indistinguishable, allowing me to forget the bitter conversations and the hopeless silences. But in a short time an odd and unexpected thing happened, and it frightened me, and a sadness entered my soul and sank it. That capsize made me see that I had never been to a place like this. The traveler was now a castaway. I did not know how I had gotten here; I did not know how to leave this lonely country where phones had faces.

The phones were memorable, each in a different way. Every one of them, even the most humdrum and seemingly featureless one took on a particular appearance, its own look. In nightmares inanimate objects often have personalities – the wicked chair, the menacing tree. This was the phone with a memory. My misery made them unique, gave them a history. One represented tears, another stood for a particular crisis, and others still for pain or certain ugly words or a vow. Their low hoods and half-walls gave them the look of hi-tech confessional booths, all pretty much alike, yet I think of these plain objects and it amazes me to reflect on how powerful the associations are. A bank of phones now looks to me like a wailing wall.

There is a phone at the Delta Shuttle at LaGuardia that is hideous for me to look upon – I pass it with my eyes averted; another on the corner of 57th and Madison makes me sad; one in a bank of four in the service area between a McDonald's and a Total gas station, northbound on Route I-95 in Connecticut, after Exit 12, Rowayton, where I begged and pleaded; another at Hyannis Airport; one at the rest area on Route 3 at Exit 5, near the wooden totem pole of the elongated Indian, where I heard myself being called a shit, over and over.

Just as bad, I heard a woman screaming a few phones away – she was in her early twenties, in jogging clothes, howling, 'You fucking bastard!' She could only have been using those words in speaking to her ex-husband. I thought of her too when I saw the phones. Who would have believed that a nickel-plated box and a plastic receiver and stumpy apparatus could stand for so much passion and pain?

I had moved back to the United States and no one was waiting for me. I went home to an empty house. I was slow in everything I did because I was grieving and needed the delay. Failure is the taste of your own blood in your mouth. I left London so abruptly no one knew where I had gone and so I received no mail. I wrote myself a postcard:

> Dear Paul,
>   How are you? I haven't seen you lately. I hope to
> see you soon. Take care,
>   Paul.

Soon after writing it, I found it between the pages of a book. I smiled at it, and then I panicked and tore it up, fearful that someone might see it and think I had lost my mind. Whenever I got into the house, I only turned on a few of the lights, preferring not to see the rest, so that I would not have to see how empty my life had become. Half the house was in darkness.

The refrigerator was half full, one towel on the rail instead of two, one chair at the table, one glass instead of a pair, one car in the driveway, and I have mentioned elsewhere how I had begun to sleep on the left-hand side of the bed, with the other big empty half unoccupied. I was too old to begin to sleep in the middle of the bed.

I was sad at the deepest part of my being, a sorrow like a sickness, and I was not strong enough to write or travel. Instead I became very interested in counting. It was not a passion but a science, a way of turning my life into numbers.

It started with a watch that had so many dials the makers called it a chronometer. It gave me the date, the day, the month, the year, the hour, the minute, the second. I bought a scale and weighed myself, but dissatisfied that it was just a wavering needle I bought another more precise one, which showed my weight in a digital window, with pounds and ounces. I weighed myself morning and evening, and I learned that I weighed less in the morning, gained three or four pounds during the day, and lost it overnight. I began counting the days since the separation, the number of beers I drank, the miles I drove, and added them all up, I did not know why, though I found the numbers consoling.

I bought a Schwinn AirDyne stationary bike with a pulsometer and hooked myself to it, reading numbers while I pedaled, the watts, the minutes and seconds, the RPMs, blood pressure, calories. I bought a Concept II Ergometer rowing machine and stroked 2,500 meters a day, and then 5,000 and more, monitoring the strokes per 500 meters, the calories, the watts, the distance, eventually rowing 2,500 meters in 9 minutes and 54 seconds. I counted the days, the weeks, the hours. I counted my money, my years, my days on earth.

I who had spent my life making notes and writing stories stopped writing anything except numbers. Computing my life mathematically, I imagined that my autobiography might look like one of those slender books, all logarithms and mathematical tables. What kept me at it was that the numbers were constantly changing, and I saw myself in a cockpit scrutinizing fifty gauges which told me everything. I needed the numbers, I needed their fluctuations. I counted everything, and it mattered more to me as a series of numbers. I was sick of words.

At night before I slept I itemized the food I had eaten, not the substance or quality but the calories. I added up the pictures in my house, what I had paid for them, computed their appreciation, made a total of this. If I saw a stack of books or magazines, I did not read them, I counted them. I ran through the ages of every family member, of the countries I had visited. If I saw birds on the feeder, I counted them. I took pleasure in looking at the thermometer in the window, for the opportunity of seeing the liquid rise and fall throughout the day. It was a Cape Cod winter, with great variations. At night, waking to grope towards the bathroom, I detoured past the thermometer. I relished the variation of a few degrees. It gave me an enormous thrill of hope, a rush in my blood, I had no idea why.

I counted the days since I had last been together with my wife.

The days since we had last been happy, our years together, the months of our courtship, the significant dates, the ages of our children at specific times. Old friends whom I had not seen for fifteen or twenty years – I computed their present ages, surprising myself by figuring that they were in their sixties and seventies, and V. S. Pritchett was ninety, as old as the century, and, thinking of him, I reflected that I had lived half my life.

I counted the years I had left and became very sad and it was all worse for having nothing to do. I saw no one. I hardly left the house. I knew that any rational person would determine that I had gone insane, and so I avoided the company of other people, and was glad I could not write because if I did it would only prove that I was crazy. *Dear Paul, How are you? I haven't seen you lately . . .*

Now and then people wrote to me and told me about their lives. They tried to explain how empty their lives were, their jobs, they described their spouses and co-workers. They believed that I would understand because I was a writer who had written joyously of the earth and its wonders. I was busy, they thought, my life was full. I did not dare to write back or I would frighten them by saying that there was only half of me here. They were wrong about themselves, they were wrong about me. And what was the good of writing if all it ended in was a lonely man lying on the left side of the bed making sense of the cracks in the ceiling that resembled numerals?

There seemed an enormous difference between the author of my books and the person I had become, and no one would know because the sad inarticulate man I had become could not write a line.

I wanted to go away. I was too fearful to set off. I was not strong enough to travel. I clung to what was familiar, but still felt like a stranger, and that was odd because I was home, the place I knew best, and I felt I did not belong.

That was when I began using the public phones, believing superstitiously that a different phone was a new chance. Soon I realized that each phone left me with a painful memory. And then I used the public phones in order to hide the memories. When would I ever again see that roadside telephone in Connecticut? But the day I did I almost wept and my throat ached with sadness. And so the world that had seemed so benign to me, so safe and neutral and indifferent, began to take on aspects of unfriendliness, even menace. Those wicked telephones and all the angry spouses using them, the pretty jogger transformed into a howling witch. I developed unhappy memories of the most ordinary places and I began to understand the truth of places being haunted.

I had nothing to do – no job, no friends – and too much time. I had come to the end. All that effort, all that hope and ambition, and now I was alone, with nothing. I had started life believing I was special. Didn't I have a gift? Now I was like everyone else, and I saw that nearly everyone was sad. I had never understood this before. I was alone, with half of what I had had, and half was a diminishing amount and seemed as though it would soon be nothing.

I did not envy anyone, except the person I had once been, whom I had destroyed, and the worst day of marriage was bliss compared to this. A particular day came to mind when, after buying our house in London and getting deeply into debt, Alison and I had left the children with a babysitter and spent a whole day cleaning, she on one floor, I on the other; and with nowhere to cook – the kitchen was unusable – we had gone to a café and sat there, tired, silent, eating dry sandwiches, hollow-eyed, almost too tired to hold a conversation. In retrospect that seemed romantic – such effort and such rewards had followed that struggle.

That was one of the happiest days of my life. But this was simply dreary and on most days it was a misery of changelessness, relieved only by my continual counting – minutes, ounces, meters, dollars, years.

I was a measurable being. Writing blurred or contradicted this exactness. I did not write anything, I did not go to movies, I was indifferent to the news, except when it was about natural disasters or man-made catastrophes or crime, and then I watched, stonily, with grim satisfaction. It gave me no pleasure, but I was now and then a witness to a sort of suffering, or agony, which proved that I was not alone.

Thinking that reading might ease my pain, I tried to recapture the pleasure of books I had loved. I began to reread *David Copperfield*. I came across this: '*And since I've took to general reading, you've took to general writing, eh, sir?*' *said Mr Omer, surveying me admiringly. 'What a lovely work that was of yours! What expressions in it! I read it every word – every word. And as for feeling sleepy! Not at all!*'

I stopped reading novels altogether, or anything except newspapers or trashy magazines. I became submerged in what I thought of as the public consciousness. I had once thought of myself as unusual, but now I saw how similar I was to so many people. I followed Hollywood divorces, studying the details of movie stars and musicians and public figures who were going through the process of separation, and how each move they made was noted and described. I found a deeper meaning and a kind of eloquence where before I had only seen a cliché: *Says he is trying to get his life back on track ... Every moment has been a living hell ... Has found it impossible to focus on his work ... Claims something just snapped ... Feels as though everything he had worked for had been destroyed ... Misses his kids ...*

Nothing I read or heard in this period was truer to me than the sentiments in country music, a kind of clumsy poetry about being wronged and abandoned and let down. I listened to those songs, appalled by the exactitude in their lyrics, and sometimes tearful with recognition. And these simple, almost artless songs proved to me that I had up to then deceived myself and wasted my writing talent. And then I had to stop, because I could not listen without wanting to cry.

My story was in the newspaper almost every day – in *Father Appears on TV to Demand Access to Children*, in *Phone Booth Torched by Estranged Husband*, in *Ex-Wife's Boyfriend Disfigured in Scalding Attack*, in *Mystery Deepens Over Author's Disappearance*, in *No Apparent Cause in Fatal Crash*.

I concentrated on my numbers. Science was the thing, there was always something of that on television. I liked a program I saw on the Discovery Channel, about carbon dating, the way it used the expression 'half-life.' Half the film was a serious cartoon, the other half a clowning scientist. In the notebook I normally used for story ideas, that was now blank and unused, I scribbled this:

In physics a fixed time required for half the radioactive nuclei in a substance to decay.

Half-lives of radioactive substances can range from fractions of a second to billions of years, and they are always the same for a given nucleus, regardless of temperature or other conditions.

If an object contains a pound of radioactive substance with a half-life of fifty years, at the end of that time there will be half a pound of the radioactive substance left undecayed in the object.

After another fifty years, a quarter pound will be left undecayed, and so on.

Scientists can estimate the age of an object, such as a rock, by measuring the amounts of decayed and undecayed nuclei in the object. Comparing that to the half-life of the nuclei tells when they started to decay, and therefore how old the object is.

That explained it, I knew: a complex countdown, the algebra of death. I was forty-nine.

I was not suicidal. Suicide took willpower and determination. People who failed kept trying. I was merely miserable. But misery meant fluctuation in weight, exercise tolerance, pulse rate, and this kept me counting.

I started buying things, only realizing after I got home that I owned them already. I pondered over a short-wave radio and finally bought it; but I had one, a similar model. I had forgotten. A pair of blue jeans: I was thinking, I need them, but I didn't. I had another new pair I had not even worn. A cashmere sweater that was $400 – now I had two of them; a bicycle, a rifle, a popcorn popper, a video recorder; more. It was as though I was furnishing and fitting out another life, not realizing that mine was already furnished, with those same items. I shopped, with the knowledge that I was trying to fill the void of my sadness with material objects, anything to divert me or make me happy. Strangely, without any conscious intention, I only bought things I already owned. I felt humiliated by the expense and the duplication, and instead of filling the void they confused me with chaos and clutter.

For uncritical and anonymous company I drove to Boston – sixty-four miles – and found a doctor with an office on Charles Street, near the corner of Revere Street, who would see me twice a week, a woman, and fortunately she was good-looking. It heartened me to think that I had noticed and that I had been attracted to her pretty face and fine hair. I needed to be in the presence of someone pleasant, who did not know me.

It would have been so humiliating for anyone to know who I was – the man who wrote about marriages and love and freedom and strange places. I remembered how in a dismal place I would think: At least I have this to write about. That gave me hope. The hope had lain in my ability to turn around and write about my inconvenience.

I had thought of it as suffering, but now I knew it was not that at all. This was suffering and it paralyzed me. The sickness of separation, the half-life I lived, was one such experience I would never return to in writing. I would go on living in it and no one would ever know. Hopelessness is the knowledge that nothing will change and that there is no future, only an eternal and desperate present.

Yet I had begun to like being unknown, because I was so ashamed. I had to be unknown driving to Boston, eating alone. It would have been horrible to be recognized. 'Are you the writer?' a woman asked me in a gas station, when I showed her my credit card. I said no, because my eyes were glassy with grief. And what I said was true – I was not the writer any more.

A man behind me was holding a chrome gas cap.

'What do you get for these?'

'Those run twenty bucks.'

I had forgotten how Americans spoke to each other; it seemed as though I was losing the language. I would have to learn it again, sentences such as, *Come on in and let me fix you breakfast.*

But no one was fixing me breakfast. It was pitiful being anonymous and alone, but wouldn't it have been much worse being known and observed? I still had my secret, even living this half-life.

Dr Mylchreest was from Argentina though the name was not Argentine, was it? I knew nothing else about her. I had asked, but they don't tell you.

2

'So where are you now, Mr Medved?' Dr Mylchreest asked me.

It was the question she always resumed with each time we met. As for the name, I invented it for myself, and it was different from any other I had used in the past, so that with this new name I might enter another life. I believed that I must not be known; that the psychiatrist would only understand me if she didn't associate me with writing.

I was a physicist, I told her – particle physics. Boston was full of scientists. My field was studying the half-lives of radioactive nuclei.

Those were the only lies I told Dr Mylchreest. She was intense, with beautifully lighted eyes that gave her a penetrating gaze, and bonily attractive, with rubbery lips that were most expressive in reflection. She wore long skirts, modest-seeming, but I could see that her stockings, judging from her ankles, were black with intricate lacy patterns.

Though her mistakes in English masked her shrewdness, her tact and her eyes and her silent patience made me garrulous. Her questions were all the more confusing for her heavy accent and I was always taken aback when, translating what she had said – the way you do with someone whose English is faulty (with that accent how could they be bright?) – I realized that her question was illuminating.

I used to try to imagine which country that surname belonged to. Manxland? Denmark? Holland? And what was her connection with Argentina?

'I once met Borges in Buenos Aires,' I said.

'Yes?'

Then I remembered I was supposed to be a physicist.

'At a conference on molecular particles, Borges read us a poem. Did you ever meet him when you were there?'

She smiled, and made me ignorant; she knew that my ignorance would keep me curious and respectful.

'Go on, Mr Medved.'

'Please call me Pavel.'

I wanted her to inquire about my name ('Slavic?'), because although it seemed like an exotic corruption of my old alias 'Medford,' it was Russian for 'bear,' but better than bear. It was one of those glorious praise names that tribal people give to dangerous creatures, meaning to propitiate them. Medved meant 'honey wizard.'

She did not ask me that. She did not ask me anything. I was in a conversational void and, a listener by nature – an interrogator only when I wanted to get someone talking – I felt awkward and unreasonably pressured in her office. Stubborn, hating the silence, I wanted her to talk.

And I was unused to talking about myself. My method was fiction, expressing myself through my characters and finding satisfaction in remaking my world, giving it wit and life, claiming it for myself. I had trained myself to write about my life in a way that had always worked for me. There was a writer, a glimmering fabulist within me; that was who I was. This essence was enclosed by a physical being – a weak, hairy 49-year-old servant, who was responsible for bearing this small wavering flame, serving it, sometimes well, sometimes badly – falling down, sleeping late, quarreling; sometimes weepy, hating noise and disruption; distracted, yawning, restless, bored, silly. That was the half people saw, not me. I was the ageless spirit within who expressed himself in fiction.

Now this clumsy servant was the only presence left. He was no writer – there was no writing. The light was out, or dimmed. Only the physical presence and the dead eyes remained. I was used to excusing his sloppiness or lateness with the other self – outshining it, as it were. Inside was light, outside shadow; but the light was substance, the shadow was illusion. I did not expect Dr Mylchreest to understand this paradox, and I had already told her I was a physicist, so there was no need.

I was Paul Theroux the writer, but as there was no writing I was left with this other self. It did not matter what the servant's name was. I habitually gave strangers false names for myself, trying them out; and false occupations – geographer, teacher, publisher, printer, cartographer, fisherman. It was important to me not to tell the truth, because I needed to hold on to my secrets. Secrets were the only true power I had. The servant was there to listen, to sit and be dictated to – not to write about himself. He was uninteresting, the valet of my imagination.

It was how I had spent thirty years, but now the other half was gone, as I say, and Dr Mylchreest was listening. I had too much to say – and who was talking? – so I did not know how to begin.

'So, where are you now?'

Her method was free-floating Freudianism. I was the one who was supposed to carry the conversational ball.

'I'm fine,' I said. 'I had a pretty good week, though I didn't work much.' She was waiting, and I was wondering who was saying this – my servant or my other self. 'I didn't work at all.'

She knew this was disappointing to me. I had told her how much my work mattered. I was writing a report on my research into carbon disintegration.

'That was painful,' I said. 'And somehow, without my work to occupy me, my physics problems, I dream more about my wife. Awful dreams.'

Her silence insinuated itself like doubt, demanding that I offer a proof of what I had just said.

'I'm in a house with a lot of people. I know my wife is there, somewhere downstairs. I'm having a drink, enjoying myself, then I realize that I have to find her. There is pandemonium. I finally find her and she screams at me and leaves.'

'Does this tell you anything about your feelings?'

'Oh, that I'm feeling guilty,' I said. 'But I knew that before.'

Dr Mylchreest laughed. I needed that, a hearty shout of denial. I needed someone to point out that I was mistaken. But Dr Mylchreest would not make it easy for me by telling me why.

'Dreams are not as bad as reality,' I said. 'I mean, sometimes I see her. That's much worse.'

'Shall we go into that?'

'When I drive up the expressway I usually take the Chinatown exit. Near Tufts Dental School, on Kneeland Street, there's a homeless woman, late forties or so, who's always walking up and down, very agitated. She's in rags, yet she has an intelligent face and looks well-bred – but lost. She was once beautiful and happy, maybe a little nervous. I think she was married to someone who left her. She went mad, vanished, no one knows she's a street person.'

'What do you think her husband was like?'

'It was me.'

'And she's unhappy?'

'She's schizo.'

'Why do you use that word?'

'Doesn't it mean split personality?'

'It doesn't mean anything.'

'Look, this woman has been driven crazy,' I said defiantly. The word 'crazy' jangled there in the air between us like an obscenity. 'She is lost and sad. She was abandoned by someone like me.'

'So it is not that she resembles Alison, but that her husband resembles you?'

'Something like that.'

Dr Mylchreest nodded, waiting, wanting more from me.

'Alison was not my wife – she was my life!'

Then I began to cry.

Dr Mylchreest allowed me to compose myself. I wanted her to take my hand, or hug me, or hold my head. But she remained silent until I had stopped sniffing. 'You have your own life,' she said. 'And she has one. She isn't a street person. She is in London, working. You told me yourself.'

'No, I've ruined her – destroyed her.'

'Do you mean you destroyed yourself?'

'Yes. In the process of destroying her.'

'Tell me how many conversations you've had with her lately.'

'None lately.'

'What do you know about her?'

'Nothing.'

'You said at the beginning of the session that you were feeling fine. Yes?'

'Yes.'

'How do you really feel?'

'Miserable.'

'Go on.'

'What do you mean "Go on"? The word "miserable" has a specific meaning in English. It is rock bottom – sick, sad and hopeless. How can you analyze it? I feel like shit.' I had begun shouting. 'Can you imagine analyzing shit?'

I lowered my voice and I was aware that I was paying this woman to listen to me. It made me self-conscious, and unwilling. I understood the impotence that some men experience with a prostitute when they are up in her room and, after she has counted the money, she opens her legs.

Dr Mylchreest said nothing – was still listening to anything I might want to say, or even shout.

'Sorry,' I said.

She dismissed this. She was supposed to listen to tantrums. My outburst was the reason she cost me $180 an hour.

'No. Go on.'

'What I mean is,' I said in a subdued tone, 'misery is an absence of feeling. So I have very little to describe. If I were happy or fulfilled, I think I could have a long conversation. I could describe something. But my misery is a mud puddle – shallow, dark, nothing there, no subtlety.'

'Try to look beyond it. Try to imagine what would make you happy. Ideally, what would your life be like?'

'That's easy. I want to be working in an upstairs room, waiting for my kids to come home from school. Then I want to watch TV with them and hear them laugh. And cook dinner for my wife, who will be home around six-thirty. Later, after the children are in bed, I want to have a drink with her and talk about the day.'

One of Dr Mylchreest's strengths was that she was imperturbable, and listening to me just now she showed no emotion, her face was blank, yet her eyes were pierced by a shifting light that was both bafflement and curiosity. Surely, she was intrigued by what I had said – its suddenness, its unexpectedness, its love.

'That is the past, isn't it?' she said quietly.

'Of course it is. You ask me what I want. I want it to be 1978.'

'But you left it, not so?'

'I can't remember what led up to it. There was just a day when we agreed to split up. The day came, and I had to go.'

'You told me it was a mutual decision.'

'Did I say that?'

She stared at me, as though disappointed that I had forgotten this simple thing.

'It was an awful parting. I woke up knowing I had to leave that day. It was like having to face a firing squad at dawn. There were tears, but no recrimination. Just sadness.'

'Like being shot by a firing squad, you say. Do you feel you died?'

'Half of me died.'

I was silent for a long time, lost in the emptiness of my mind – nothing there, no words, no emotions, just a strange, pathless landscape that I the traveler had never seen before, and where I was now lost.

'The word "exile" is used a lot,' I said. 'I think it is a very outdated word. You know it?'

Because English was not her first language I instinctively verified important words, which irritated her, I think, because she knew them all. It was her accent. Whenever she used a word it was changed; her pronunciation seemed to give it a different meaning.

'Conrad – you know him? Joseph Conrad the writer?'

Her shrug, different from the blank smile she had given me when I had mentioned Borges, conveyed an insulted reply, yet also a measure of respect for the range of my references. I was not only a physicist, I also read the classics.

'Conrad was always described as an exile. So was Nabokov, and

Solzhenitsyn, and all those people who come here and make a bundle of money publishing their prison diaries.'

Again I sensed that Dr Mylchreest was uncomfortable, wanting me to get to the point.

'Now I understand exile. It means losing everything – wife, children, house, country. It means banishment – in a sense the opposite of confinement, but just as awful, having to contemplate every day all that you've lost.'

'Like Joseph Conrad, you say?'

'No, no. There are no exiles anymore in the old sense. Political exiles, dissidents – that's all old hat. Except for a handful of people – and most of them are Tibetans – any of them can go back. But for people like me, exile is a reality. I have lost everything. Now I am in another country. I don't know how I got here. I've never been here before. I don't know how to get away.'

'Haven't you been in strange countries before?'

If only she knew!

'Yes.'

'You said you had lived in London for a period of time.'

'Eighteen years.'

'That's a long time,' she said, and this banal response was intended to encourage me to see myself as adaptable.

'I had planned to stay for ten. After that I just procrastinated. Then I left.'

'There must have been many obstacles that you overcame.'

'Yes, but in England that doesn't prove anything. You're the Yank. After fifty years you're still the Yank. If you forget, they remind you. And your kids are the Yank's kids.'

'You are speaking as though you were an exile then.'

'No. Even then I knew I wasn't. In 1971, just after I got there, I was in a country pub in Dorset. I had rented a cottage just down the road. The local farmhands were always complaining about strangers moving in and putting the prices up, and what buggers they were. I listened to this for a few weeks. Then one night I said, "Look, I don't know what you think of me, but let me tell you that I have no intention of staying here. As soon as I make some money, I am leaving this village, and I am never coming back." After that, those people were very pleasant to me.'

'Don't you feel as though you have come home?'

'The irony is that I came home only to find myself in exile. I don't know where I am. I didn't realize that in losing my wife I lost everything. I didn't live in a country. I lived in a house – a home.'

'Why do you think –' She was about to say: Why do you think you can't make a new home? But I did not want to hear her say it.

'I'm lost here and I can never go back!'

That session, like many of them, ended in tears, and it was terrible because Dr Mylchreest was so punctual; and so there was no consolation, but only the reminder that after sixty minutes her intense alertness dimmed and the temperature in the room seemed to go down a few degrees; it was time for me to go.

I was reluctant to leave – I wanted to continue, to talk about something else, or to listen to her. I was attracted to Dr Mylchreest. I knew nothing about her, and she had kept me in the dark so that I wouldn't fantasize; but my knowing nothing kept her mysterious and made me inquisitive. I could see that she was intelligent. She had large feet and she was big-boned and somewhat humorless, but she was strong and practical, and her loose clothes and full skirts and heavy sweaters did not hide her figure, but rather emphasized it.

She had a splendid angular body, and I wanted to hold her, and for her to hold me. It was hard to be in this room with her week after week and not touch her. I wished at the end of each session that I could go home with her. I wanted for us to forget everything else and watch TV in our pajamas and eat popcorn; or else rent a video and lie in bed, propped by pillows, drinking wine and watching it.

It was not love. She was the only person I saw or spoke to. I knew I could get along with her and I liked her physically. I could not prowl around, or look for women as I once had, because of AIDS. I was cautious, even somewhat fearful when I thought of approaching a strange woman.

We got through a month of this, twice a week, and I began to see psychoanalysis as a permanent part of my life: the 64-mile drive to Charles Street on those winter afternoons, puzzling over what I would say – the sort of idea that I might have explored in a short story before; now it was fodder for therapy, blunderingly blurted out in a simple form. Afterwards two Coronas and a plate of quesadillas at Amigos, and then the drive back, my mind blank, my body exhausted, depleted from the talk and the long ride.

Exile seemed to me the most accurate way of describing my state of being. I had used the word many times in writing, but only now did I see its meaning. It was a secular form of damnation; a half-life, halving again every second in an almost perpetual diminishment. Exile was not a metaphor. I was an exile and I believed I would stay that way. It was no good to see myself as cast out, as though I had fallen from grace. I had not known any Eden. The closest I had come was at Moyo, in 1964. That leper colony had been my paradise.

But this was a different exile. As a traveler, I always had vivid dreams in strange countries – something about those clammy rooms, those lumpy beds, that sour air, the nameless nighttime noise. In those places someone would call out, in Gujerati, in Hakka, Quechua, or Ilocano; and I had no idea of what was being said. But this atmosphere penetrated my sleep and gave me dreams.

So I dreamed here, vividly, in this place that was no longer my home. They were incomplete dreams of exile and crime. I had become a broken writer babbling in his sleep, and the dreams were like the faded remnants and rags of my work.

'It's the same one,' I told Dr Mylchreest.

An old dream that I had been dreaming since arriving back in the United States – my public phone booth period; I thought of it as 'the suitcase dream,' but now I saw the point of it. I was involved in a murder. I did not do the chopping but I had wordlessly agreed when the other people – three men – asked me if I would help. It was my car, I knew the owner of the suitcase, I even had a sense that I knew the victim. No one had a name in this dream. The unsuspecting victim was snatched and killed, then chopped in half and crammed into a suitcase.

The crime itself was a small part of the dream. The rest was our driving, the men and me, with the leaky suitcase on the back seat: up the turnpike; at the pickup window of a drive-in restaurant; in a rest area; in heavy traffic; a long red light, a child with a diseased face staring out the rear window of the car in front, a big slavering dog barking at the suitcase. We were stopped by a policeman. 'What's in the bag?' He did not notice the smear of blood on the handle. But each time the question was asked, I was farther and farther from the car. I was like a ghostly spectator. I always got away.

When I woke up in fear and dread, I was gasping, drenched in sweat, my hair soaked. I was furtive in the dream; awake, I was sick with guilt, and it stayed with me, a sense of woe like nausea.

Then I needed Dr Mylchreest, to tell her the dream. What would I have done without her? I used to think that with Alison; even in the worst moments I had not been able to imagine life without her. When my life had been whole, I would have used such a dream in my writing. Now I had no writing and no wife; I had Dr Mylchreest. Flaubert's lover, Suzanne Lagier, told him, 'You are the garbage pail of my heart, I confide everything to you.'

'Try to identify the men, Mr Medved.'

'I might have been in high school with them.'

All my dreams seemed to be high-school dreams.

'That's helpful.'

'I hated high school. I had some friends, but I was fearful.'

'Go on.'

'Of ignorance. Stupid people always seemed capable of terrible cruelty. And intelligent people were mocked. It was as though a bright person was a homosexual. Homosexuals were mocked in the same way.'

'You've made an interesting comparison.'

'Oh, God,' I said.

Her lovely face said nothing, but behind it the flash in her eyes revealed a tumult of speculation.

'You think because I am making that comparison that I am unconsciously saying that I might be gay. Don't you see that I am stating it like that so that you will understand?'

'There are so many ways to describe something, and yet you choose those words.'

'There are many ways,' I said, trying not to shout, 'but this is the clearest comparison. My imagination was my secret. At my school, if a secret got out, if any detail were known – a liking for something odd, a funny middle name, anything – you were subjected to unmerciful mockery. No one was gay – no one admitted it. But there must have been many. So they had to listen to mockery about faggots, homos, queers. If you were smart you were "Einstein."'

'What about the victim?' Dr Mylchreest asked. 'In your dream. Do you want to talk about it?'

'I have a feeling it's a woman. I sense that I know her.'

'But you say that you are the driver of the car. You were not the one who killed her. Correct?'

'It's as though I did it.'

'Yes?'

'The point is that when I wake up I feel guilty not because of what I've done, but because of what I know.'

'The guilty feeling doesn't go away?'

'No. I sense the crime has not yet taken place. I feel it is going to happen, and only I know where and when. If I puzzle out the dream, I could save someone's life.'

'Yes?'

But Dr Mylchreest did not seem to be seeking more information about the murder victim in my dream.

I said, 'If this is precognition it could be very serious.'

She did not respond to this. She had become motionless and deaf. I felt awkward, like someone still talking on a telephone line that had been cut off, and I realized that my hour was up.

'I'd like to stay a bit longer.'

'That is impossible.'

'Is there someone waiting?'

'It's five past five, Mr Medved.'

'I'd appreciate it if you called me Pavel.'

'As you wish. Pavel.'

'I'd like to see you three times a week instead of two,' I said, and the words sounded to me like those of a man wooing a virgin in an old-fashioned courtship.

'It might be difficult, but I'll look at my appointments.'

The lamps outside were large and blurred by whirling snowflakes which wrapped them in great yellow gusts that slanted towards the wet street.

'It's snowing.'

'Yes.'

She wanted me out of there, and her urgency made me linger. I fastened my attention on her body – her lips, her legs, her hands, her eyes. I did not want to leave. I clung to her.

'Your time is up,' she said, and she had never looked prettier to me, though I could only think that she was waiting there for the next man like a hooker in a room turning tricks.

3

Driving back to the Cape, I was weary, sorrowing in a new way. In those few minutes of her urging me to leave, Dr Mylchreest had uncovered a tangled feeling within me. She had not simplified it, only unintentionally exposed it, and left me with the open wound. It was new and raw, still bleeding. I could not hug the pain away. The pain was love.

I saw clearly that I could survive the loss of my other life and everything that I had known, if I had her, Dr Mylchreest. I desired her with a love that overwhelmed me because I was wounded and she was a whole woman, practical, attentive, intelligent, and lovely. I had the sense that I could awaken a sexual impulse in her and that in time, when I told her who I really was, she would understand the necessity for my deception. Then we would live together: I saw the house, the bed, the books, the wine, the table set for two. I would resume writing. She would commute to Boston and keep office hours. We would be complete. And it was possible. The decision was hers: she was at the age when the door was about to shut for good – we might have some children.

This was at first a fugitive thought. But it grew, and before our next session it dominated everything I did, everything I thought. It was as though I had discovered that I had a serious illness and at the same time realized that only one person on earth could cure me.

It was love, I knew, because it was pure pain, like the worst hunger combined with the worst loneliness, a wasting disease that gave the sufferer an intimation of death. Its pathology was partly a form of madness. I had to have her any way I could, and I saw that it was worse, more desperate than being without my wife. It was my next step. I had no idea it would happen so quickly, and it frightened me and made me sick when I considered the agony of being in the same room with Dr Mylchreest. I wanted to hold her, hug her, kiss her, bury my face against her. I wanted to devour her, actually to eat her, and for her to demand it, to lie naked and murmur, 'Take me.'

I had last felt this way in high school, desperate and frustrated and helpless. I knew it would frighten her if I told her how I felt, and so I concealed my feelings towards her but in the sessions after this I talked about sex – dreams, impulses, episodes from the past, many of them invented. A common theme was that I was highly charged sexually and that my marriage had been awkward as a result – my wife unwilling.

'I needed it, not just for reassurance, but because I think of sex and work being the two most powerful human drives.'

This was a blatant appeal to Dr Mylchreest's Freudianism.

She said, 'And what response did you get?'

'Most of the time, not a lot,' I said. 'I am an incredibly passionate person.'

She smiled and said something like 'Anyhow.'

It was her intrusive accent. She was trying to say '*Annie Hall*.' She asked me if I had seen the movie. I said yes. She reminded me of the scene where Woody Allen tells his psychiatrist that Annie is frigid: 'She only wants to make love three or four times a week.' At this moment Annie is telling her psychiatrist that Woody is rapacious: 'He wants to make love three or four times a week.'

I resented her using this insubstantial and jokey movie to respond to the serious point I had made. How would she like it if I compared her to one of the New York psychiatrists in a Woody Allen movie? But I resisted. I could be hurt, but I was too deeply in love with her to be discouraged.

'And polymorphous perversity,' I said. 'I often feel a strong urge to experiment.'

'Yes?'

I was watching her closely, those eyes with their own life.

'I cannot be indiscriminate, though. Very few people in my life have moved me. I have very rarely been in love.'

'When you have been in love what has attracted you?'

'Strength, beauty, intelligence, honesty, character. It is partly physical, but it is more a kind of knowledge – looking deeply into a person's soul. There is no other word for it.'

'And this feeling, does it make you happy?'

'It makes me sick.'

'Go on.'

'I'm sick now.'

'Yes?'

'Doctor, I love you. I can't bear to be without you.'

She was not fazed. She said, 'This is natural, a consequence of the therapy relationship.'

'I mean it.'

'Of course. You are transferring. We can work through this transference-love.' She smiled and glanced at her watch. 'Next time.'

In my love I could not separate myself from Dr Mylchreest – there was no boundary between us, we were the same person. My time was up. I felt ashamed, humiliated, but what did it matter? I was convinced of my love, but though I dragged myself away I knew I was incomplete in leaving her. I was eager to return, and yet dreading it for the way I suffered when I was with her, sitting near her when I wanted to be on her, tearing at her clothes, pounding deeper into her.

It took my mind off my separation, yet it was another problem and an unexpected one. I had been numb before, not knowing what had happened to me. Now I knew the solution: to love Dr Mylchreest and be her lover. She was my salvation. I had left Alison. It was illogical to go back. I needed to continue, to move on and find my missing half. Dr Mylchreest was my other half, my other life. With her I was complete.

At the next session I said, 'I have the strongest urge to make love to you. I can't bear the thought of living without you.'

'Let's talk about that.'

'But I want to hear what you have to say.'

She smiled in a superficial way and said, 'I am your therapist. Any relationship other than a professional one is out of the question.'

'Are you saying that you are not attracted to me at all?'

'That's interesting. Do you often wonder whether women you don't know are attracted to you?'

'No. Only the few I've loved.'

'What qualities do you imagine they see in you?'

'Please stop asking me therapist questions. Doesn't it mean anything when I say that I love you?'

She frowned and when she did I saw how easily she assumed the expression as though this disapproval came naturally to her and was part of her face. She said, 'You must consider what you are saying and where you are. You are my patient. I have been careful. You know nothing about me.'

'I know more than you think.'

Though I was bluffing, I could tell from the way she tried not to show it that she was worried.

'You need to work through these feelings, Mr Medved. If you do, and understand them, you will know more about yourself.'

'I know everything about myself. I want to know more about you.'

That pleased her, as though after all I was admitting my ignorance.

'You are the only friend I have,' I said, and it sounded pathetic to me. 'I'd like to take you to the Boston Symphony next week, and then to dinner.'

'You must stop fantasizing about this.'

'You encouraged me to fantasize.'

'To understand your fantasies, not to give them reality,' she said tersely, as though snapping a handbag shut.

'What is the point of fantasizing if you don't experience it?'

She said nothing. That meant she wanted me to reflect on what I had just said, the absurd echo of it. But I did not find it absurd.

She was smiling her insincere smile again.

'Next time,' she said.

'I had the suitcase dream again,' I said. 'It was more specific. The woman is someone I know fairly well – not Alison. Instead of protecting her, I allow the others to kill her. She is dismembered and crammed in the suitcase. Although there are a number of close calls, even with police, we are not caught. The suitcase is found in a locker in South Station. I could show you the locker.'

'Did you witness the woman being dismembered?'

'No. I turned my back on it. But I heard it, like a butcher hacking ribs with a cleaver, the knock of a knife on bone.'

'And how did you feel when you heard it?'

I stood up and said, 'Jesus, Dr Mylchreest, I am an intelligent man. I've read Freud – not just the obvious stuff but "The Future of an Illusion" and "Civilization and its Discontents." I can prove by algebra that Shakespeare was the ghost of Hamlet's father – look, you don't even get it! I know particle physics. I have been to India and China and Patagonia. I am moved by metaphysical poetry. I collect Japanese prints. I own Hokusai's *Red Fuji*. I speak Italian and Swahili.'

I stopped – not because I was short of examples but I was out of breath.

Dr Mylchreest said, 'What do you conclude from this?'

'That I am a Martian. I am lonely here – not in this city but on earth.'

'Obviously. Perhaps this is why you chose therapy.'

'No, I don't need therapy. I need you – your love.'

Her face was expressionless, as always, but her eyes were vulnerable – it was her youth. An older woman would have been hardened to this, but I could see that she was struggling to contain her emotion, to disguise it and take command of this session. But it was hopeless for me. The only way I would succeed would be by embracing her, fumbling with her clothes while she feebly protested and allowed me to run my hands over her. I saw this all being enacted on the carpet of her office while she howled into my mouth.

'Please sit down, Mr Medved.'

I hated that – her flat tone, her irrelevant demand, a slight curdled tone of pity in her voice. I did not want her to pity me, much less analyze me. I wanted her to fear me.

'The woman in the suitcase,' I said. 'It was you.'

She tried not to wince. She said, 'Go on.'

'There is nothing more to say except be very careful, Dr Mylchreest.'

'Yes?'

'I am not here because I am lonely. I came because I was desperate, and I stayed because I fell in love with you. I will fall out of love – no one is more repulsive than a pretty woman who proves to be a deceiver.'

'You did say that you were lonely.'

'Of course I'm lonely!' I shouted. I had nothing to lose, I would never be back. 'But it's not that I am alone now. I have realized lately that I have always been alone and that I was kidding myself, whistling in the dark, when I thought otherwise. Loneliness is the human condition. Loneliness is why everyone does everything they do.'

'You came to me because you had a problem with it.'

'I don't have a problem with being lonely!' I was howling again. 'I want to know why I am alone. I am almost fifty years old and I have no one – not one person. Tell me why I'm alone. See, you have no idea!'

'We have been talking about the past –'

'I was always the way I am now,' I said, defying her again.

She nodded, allowing the silence to penetrate the whole room, and then said, 'I sense that this might be our last session.'

'Yes. You are beginning to look pathetic to me. Like a murder victim.'

I admired her for ignoring my saying this.

She said, 'Freud always believed that literature was a way of approaching the unconscious. He said as much to Arthur Schnitzler. You know him, his play *La Ronde*?'

'You are confused. Schnitzler's play is called *Reigen*. Max Ophul's film of it is called *La Ronde*.'

She merely shrugged. 'And Harry Stack Sullivan,' she went on, 'a brilliant psychoanalyst and also someone who wrote well about Herman Melville. And of course, there is Simon Lesser's book, *Fiction and the Unconscious*.'

'I knew Lesser at Amherst.'

'His grasp of Freud was not great but his understanding of literature was extremely subtle.'

'I thought it was the other way around. He made such heavy weather of Dostoyevsky and yet he couldn't read Russian. It's obvious that Prince Myshkin in *The Idiot* has a problem, but is it – as Lesser says – homosexuality? He said that was everyone's problem. Flaubert. Hawthorne. Poe.'

'And you think he was wrong?'

'Wouldn't it be truer to say that Lesser might have been explaining his own sexuality? That was such a dark secret in the 1960s.'

'It's still something that people hide. I'm interested that you raise the question. Would you like to pursue this – homosexuality?'

'You think you are being subtle. You are making the clumsiest and most naive connection.'

'Mr Medved, you should not dismiss the reading of novels for psychological insight.'

'I can't read anything when I am depressed. It's too demanding.'

'What about novels directly relating to your state of mind?'

'Even worse.'

331

She smiled and this smile was the most final expression of a farewell.

'There is really nothing more I can do for you,' she said. 'Nothing more I can say. Now it is up to you.'

So it really was over. She seemed to understand that a part of me was refusing to be involved and instead lurking in each session. This was no spectator, idly standing aside; it was the writer in me, not a casual onlooker but a passionate witness. Therapy could not work while this part of my mind scrutinized the process with such icy detachment, but that was the great thing about being a writer in therapy – of course you failed, because you needed your secrets, but you always had the last word.

Feeling sentimental I took pity on her. I said, 'The woman in the suitcase. I was lying. It was not you.'

'Should I thank you?'

'No. That's just the way it was. The victim was a jogger in her twenties, blonde, a divorcee from somewhere on the South Shore.'

She said nothing, she was no longer interested in the details of my dreams. 'You have to help yourself.'

'By reading?'

'Or writing.'

'That's ridiculous.'

'Just read for pleasure.'

'I always find it harrowing, I'm sorry to say.'

'That might not be a bad thing. When I can't do any more for them, I always send my patients away with a book list.'

It annoyed me that she had the list so near to hand. It was as though, long before I had told her, she knew that this was going to be my last session. She gave me a four-page list and I could see something foreign in her typing – the machine, the spacing, the punctuation; the list had its own order, its own clumsiness, like a bad translation.

I saw my name at once, near the bottom of the third page, four of my novels.

'Paul Theroux.'

'You should read him.'

I looked her straight in the eye: Did she know who she was talking to?

'And what will I see?'

'You will see whatever you want to see,' she said. 'But you might look closely at the way he deals with marriage, the complexities of freedom and dependence.'

'You think he's put my marriage in his books?'

'Oh, no. They are all totally different. I want you to see how different it can be for each person. But his characters have hope, they are resourceful, imaginative. He might have answers for you.'

'There are no answers. You've just proved it to me.'

'I am speaking of suggestions. His writing will show you possibilities. Half an answer,' she said. 'You supply the other half.' Perhaps she knew who I was – perhaps she was telling me to look at my own writing and see the work that I had already done; that I had to understand that the only way out of my dilemma was to write, as I had before, and then I would recover my missing half.

A month later, the suitcase was found in a locker at South Station. It had begun to smell, because it contained the dismembered body of a 22-year-old woman, recently divorced, from Plymouth, who had been abducted while out jogging.

THIRTEEN

Medford – Next 3 Exits

I

Three days after I stopped seeing my psychiatrist I got into my car and drove to Boston, as though it was a habit I could not break. It wasn't the session with Dr Mylchreest, but the drive I needed. I had come to depend on the twice-a-week routine, and I wanted to be out of the house – playing the radio, being busy, counting the miles, eating afterwards. The transition from afternoon to evening, light to dark, especially that ambiguous hour in winter when it is neither and both, was the hardest part of the day. And today it was snowing again – light dusty flakes as insubstantial as ashes and as aimless, not white but bluish-gray and sifting from the low seamless sky of the dark city and melting on the pavement and making the small stones beside the road damp and black like dog noses. But the distant hills that were visible from the psychiatrist's window had been white.

I was thinking, as I passed Mylchreest's Storrow Drive exit, that the sessions themselves which I expected to resemble a spell in a confessional, were more like visiting my tutor, presenting homework – my dreams, my fears – having it graded, and repeating this same business three days later. It was a monotony of effort made into an elaborate ritual, another secret. And what for? It did not help me to live any better. It was like school, the most hateful aspect of school, that it was not life but a dated rehearsal for living. I stopped seeing the shrink because I was holding back, the way I stopped writing a daily diary long ago when I realized there were things I did that I did not write down. If you did not tell the whole truth there was no point at all in anything you did.

There was something still wrong with me, but the thing that was wrong had made me a writer, and maybe I would write again. Never

334

mind that I did no writing now; at least I was fully awake, and my alertness and my fragile state made me remember everything. The drive, though, the sense of having something to do on a particular day, at a specific time — that helped me plan my week. It gave me a sense of anticipation; then the day itself, which was dominated by the session and excited my mind; and on the day after I felt slightly behind and busy and that gave me a sense that I was working.

Most of all on this drive I was experiencing American roads again — the size of them, the speed, the way the highway signs are full of choices and reminders. I listened to the call-in shows on the radio as only solitary people do, and I understood the confusion and anger. I listened to the lyrics in country music, the way they described my own feelings. And the expressway through Boston, Route 93, was not a corridor leading through a ribbon of land — no great American road is. It is a highway in every sense, signposted for places, some of which were very distant, because that was another feature of the great highway, and showing *Kennedy Library* and then *Chinatown* and *To Providence and New York*, and past *For New Hampshire and Maine* a green sign just as large reading *Medford — Next 3 Exits*.

At each session I had talked about Medford more, something to do with the signs on the highway, the sight of snow, and at the end of the twenty-odd sessions, when I gave up on it all, Medford was on my mind. I puzzled over the thought that I had not gone there from somewhere else; I had been born there, and I had left. So I associated the word Medford with departure.

I went there this winter afternoon like a dog, agitated by being near something he doesn't understand, just to sniff at it. Medford Square was the intersection of five wide streets, Main, Forest, Salem, High, and Riverside Avenue. The city square was shabbier but the river beside it had kept it the same shape. Medford was distinguished by the Mystic River. It was pretty but sluggish as it had always been — dark, silent, still. The river had made the place rich. Ships built on it sailed to Boston and the world. We all talked about Medford ships and Medford rum. The last Medford ship was built in 1873 and there had been no rum for years — you had to go to Somerville to buy liquor.

The main library — the old Magoun mansion — was gone; a supermarket-style library was in its place. And now the interstate,

335

Route 93, roared past Medford and above it, a thoroughfare as lofty and large as a Roman viaduct. It had slashed the town in two and obliterated my childhood home: 76 Webster Street and my dog house were now gone, replaced by the ramp at Exit 33; and Water Street was gone too, where we used to go coasting, our word for sledding. It was late and dark. I was surprised by the snow, its whiteness here.

The next time, three days later, I went to Medford, I took my cross-country skis.

You revisit your past and it looks very small, people say – your house, your school, your old street, that fence, that park. But no, Medford looked larger, broader, more shadowy – was it the snow? Certainly the snow simplified it. The trees I remembered as small were enormous and the steep lawns were piled with snowdrifts. The river was half-frozen, long green ribbons of weed pressed against the underside of the ice and all streaming in the same direction.

Its businesses were faltering, Medford looked unlucky. The deli now a convenience store, Star Market an auto-parts franchise, the diner a fast-food joint, the movie house derelict. Discounters flourished where once had been locally owned stores staffed by the owner and his children. The old men's clothing store, the only place you could buy expensive shoes or a cashmere coat or be measured for a suit, was now a franchise hiring out cheap tuxedos. Returning, I was reminded of what the place had been and who I had been. At last, separated, broke and unemployed, I belonged in Medford. My sense of strangeness matched the strangeness of the place. It would have been worse for me to have to return penniless to a sneering, prosperous city. I felt the way that this place looked. The town was older, run-down, seedier, a bit lost. Like me.

But nothing had changed in the woods to the north. The charge of snow, this volume filling the bridle paths of the Fells, was exactly as I had remembered. I parked on South Border Road and skied through the softness of it in the early darkness, and all that was different was, at the margin of the woods, the sound of traffic on the interstate like an endless train of freight cars. I skied in a large loop, taking in all the places I knew from South Border Road, past the bouldery hillside we called Panther's Cave, to the Wright Tower and the Sheepfold and small, dangerous Doleful Pond, where we skated in the winter but avoided in the summer because of its reputation for quicksand.

Forty years ago I had skied here as a boy, my dog Samson plunging ahead, up to his chin in snow, and snowflakes all over his tongue; with wooden skis and leather bindings and bamboo poles, but in this same darkness and freezing air that was faintly dusty with frost and the pinched odor of dead leaves and the dried needles of pitch pines, a sharpness on the wind of frost crystals, the cold that drops on you when darkness falls in winter. Apart from that distant traffic and Samson's gasps, there was a silence in the woods, the same woods with the same snow, the woods I had always known. This was the first sense that I had had of a return home, because I had spent so much time here plinking beer bottles with my rifle and building fires and climbing the rocks and doing exactly what I was doing now, tramping on cold, squeaking snow, suddenly overtaken by darkness on a winter afternoon, feeling my way along and then blinded by headlights as I reached the road.

With my skis on the roof rack I drove back into Medford Square and, thirsting for a beer, down Mystic Avenue. Once there had been a big wooden roller-skating rink here, the Bal-A-Rue, that was also a hangout for sailors from Boston on shore leave, and now it was a body shop surrounded by junked cars, and beyond it, just over the Somerville line, a bar, the Mystic Lounge.

It was dark inside, the booths lit by dim red bulbs, and it stank of cigarette smoke and stale beer. I bought myself a glass of draft and on my way to a booth I passed by the jukebox. I fed some quarters into the slot and punched in three old songs. And then I sat and sipped my beer and listened to Ray Charles's 'Born to Lose,' and Chuck Berry's 'No Particular Place to Go,' and the last one, Jim Morrison's haunting lilt, 'People are Strange': and I smiled, tasting my misery with a little jolt of alcohol, and took a self-pitying satisfaction in our mutual ruin, Medford and me.

A teasing voice from the booth behind me said, 'Hey, you got a problem, guy?'

I turned to see a plump girl and her tattooed friend — tattoos on her neck and arms — smiling knowingly at me from the next booth, as though I had described my mood by my choice of songs.

'No problem,' I said, and I laughed because I was so pleased that someone had noticed me. For two months I had been a wraith, invisible, silent, nameless, walking through walls.

'You actually been skiing?' the tattooed friend asked, seeing my ski jacket and the goggles and gloves I was holding.

I got up and joined them, saying, 'Oh, yes,' grateful to them for speaking to me, but I hesitated when I saw that there were two young men with them. They were pale, sour-faced, sulking on the seat opposite, their hair in their eyes, and one of them was very drunk, with cracked lips and his dirty white fingers gripping a glass, an inch of liquor in it. He jiggled the glass as he raised it to his mouth and he shook the scum of spittle on its surface. None of them sat straight – they curled, with their feet up, like dogs in a small room.

'I've been cross-country skiing up the Fells.'

'Where's that?'

'The Fellsway,' I said and began to elaborate, but the girl had no idea of the place I was describing and the others looked bored, and so I stopped.

'Get me another drink,' the drunken man said.

'I'll get it,' I said and called the waitress over and ordered five beers, and was at once self-conscious, slightly embarrassed that I was buying a round in the English way, so that the others would be part of it, and would buy their rounds in turn, obligated in a little ritual of mock comradeship.

But one of the young men said in a slurred voice, 'It must be cool to have a job,' and I saw that I had been impulsive and obvious, and that they had no money and that no one would buy me a drink.

'My name is Paul,' I said, raising the bottle; and clinking their bottles with mine, they told me their names. The young woman who had spoken to me was Vickie – her friends called her Weechie. The other woman was Bun-Bun: a small tattoo on the side of her neck, another – a bluebird – on the back of her hand. The young drunk was Mundo. His sulky friend stared at me, and Weechie said, 'That's Blaine. He's toasted. He's smoking a bone.'

With a smile of hatred, Blaine palmed the roach and snorted.

'I know where he means,' Mundo said. 'The Fellsway is where I like totaled a car and they had to like cut me out of it with a blow torch that took like a week.'

'He gets drunk and goes up 93 and closes his eyes and counts. Just to see what will happen.'

'What happens is he crashes into the guard rail,' Bun-Bun said.

'I like got up to forty-eight once,' Mundo said. Mundo had an asymmetrical head, one eye higher than the other, cheekbones out of alignment, and his speaking of car crashes called attention to his lopsided face. 'Then I got wrecked.'

'What is it about counting?' I said, remembering how I had spent the past two months counting everything in my life – minutes, pounds, meals, telephone poles.

'Counting is just nuts,' Bun-Bun said. 'If you're obsessing you count. There was this bitch in the consignment shop where I work and she counted everything about a hundred times and then touched all the doorknobs before she left. She finally went nuts.'

Her deliberate way of speaking, as though she had a morsel in her mouth, made me very attentive, wondering why she didn't swallow. I waited for her to smile and then I saw a glint, a flash of bright silver on her tongue.

'What are you eating?'

'Show him, Bun-Bun,' Weechie said.

'It's a stud,' Bun-Bun said and stuck out her tongue and showed me the silver ball fastened near the tip of her tongue. When she clicked it against her teeth, I saw there was another on the bottom. 'A barbell, like.'

'Didn't it hurt?'

Bun-Bun frowned at this obvious question and said, 'I liked it.'

'Body-piercing,' Weechie said.

'What's it for?'

'He wants to know what it's for!'

'Where'd you get your tattoos?' I asked Weechie.

'Tattoo party.'

'How does that work?'

'Everyone goes, and you pay about fifty bucks and you drink and hang out, and the man just does one after the other. It's cool. There's one tomorrow night on Riverside Avenue. We're probably going.'

'I used to deliver newspapers on Riverside Avenue. It was on my paper route,' I said. They stared at me. I said to Weechie, 'So what do you do?'

'I work at a pet shop in Wellington Mall.'

'Near the drive-in movie?'

'That closed about a thousand years ago,' Weechie said.

'How about you?' I said to Blaine.

In an angry defiant way, staring hard at me, his eyes blazing in his flat white face, he said, 'Does this dude ask a million questions or what?'

'He's wired,' Weechie said.

It was my old instinctive interrogation, and curiosity, all the piercing qualities of loneliness that filled my head with details and made me restless until I found some kind of order for them. This intensity preceded my writing, and although I was awkward being noticed in my questions I felt there was hope for my writing something; perhaps my being with these people, and risking the questions, meant that I was emerging from my depression.

'I used to live in Medford,' I said, to give them some information. 'I was born here.'

'About six hundred years ago,' Blaine said.

'Don't pay any attention to him, mister,' Bun-Bun said, and I was sorry she said it that way, because hadn't I just told her my name?

'I went to Medford High.'

'My old man went there,' Weechie said. 'Eddie Faganti? Maybe you know him?'

'What year did he graduate?'

'Somewhere in the Sixties,' Weechie said.

I nodded and said the name rang a bell, because I was afraid I would lose her if I told her that her father was younger than I was. And to change the subject I turned my attention to the plastic bag on the table next to Weechie and asked her whether she had been shopping.

'What's with the questions, man!' Blaine said, sounding fierce. 'Does this guy suck or what?'

'Behave yourself,' Bun-Bun said, with a motherly sort of strength and authority that impressed me. And it worked – Blaine sulked but he shut up, looking chastened. 'Hey, excuse me,' Bun-Bun said, 'I've got to take a wicked leak.'

'It's just videos,' Weechie said, as I moved to Bun-Bun's seat in the booth. She showed me the two video cassettes in the bag, *Die Hard* and *Half Moon Street*.

I felt a rush, my blood whipping through my body, and I said in a stammering way, 'I wrote that one. It's Sigourney Weaver and Michael Caine. See, my name's probably on it.'

But there was nothing on the plastic cassette except a smudged and torn label and a hand-scrawled number.

'There's this cool scene where she's on an exercise bike, all sweaty,' Weechie said. 'Bun and I love her. She was great in *Alien*. She like blows this drooling space lizard away. *Working Girl*. That was pretty good too.'

Mundo said, 'It like sucked.'

I said as clearly as I could, 'I wrote the story that they made this from,' and showed them the cassette of *Half Moon Street*.

But though they heard me, they said nothing. It was as though I had spoken to them in another language, something so ridiculous and opaque they could only hear it as a noise but not translate it. Weechie had turned away laughing, and even Blaine was smiling, because Mundo had farted loudly and was saying, 'I like stepped on a duck.'

I sat there in the booth, clinging to the edge of the seat, where Bun-Bun had been squatting, feeling like a hitch-hiker in an already full car of people who knew each other; knowing that there was not quite enough room for me, yet not wanting to get out and be left on an empty road so late with the prospect of no other ride. I needed the ride.

'Did you see *Caddyshack*?' Weechie asked me.

'No,' I said. 'I was probably traveling when it came out. Maybe it didn't show in England. I used to live there. I'm a writer. I write books. I write movies, too.'

'That's like stupid, isn't it? I mean, no one writes movies. It's all like photography and acting. Explosions and car chases. What's the writing?'

'Scripts,' I said.

Mundo was breathing deeply, gargling beer at the same time, drunk and deaf. Bun-Bun had still not returned from the toilet, and the other two looked so dull I had the feeling again that I was speaking to people who did not know English. But it was I who was the alien.

'Screenplays . . .' I said, aware that in divulging this I was telling them the truth about myself, and that in wanting them to hear me and to understand I had to be very particular, perhaps tell them much more than I had told anyone else. Already, after just a few minutes, I had told them more than I had told Dr Mylchreest. But they were still dull, and more people had come into the bar, music blared from the jukebox, the television over the bar was showing a hockey game and, attempting to be heard above the din, I sounded as though I was pleading.

'. . . for movies.'

'You make movies?' Weechie said.

'Yes,' I said, to keep it simple.

'Hey, maybe I've seen some of them.'

'That one,' I said, tapping *Half Moon Street*. 'But the first one I did was with Peter Bogdanovich. *Saint Jack*. Ben Gazzara was in it. They actually made it in Singapore, where the book is set, in 1978.'

'I was six years old,' Weechie said.

'I lived in Singapore,' I said. 'Three years. Teaching, doing some journalism. Even smoked a bone occasionally.'

Blaine looked at me as though he had suddenly heard something intelligible and said, 'You got any dope on you, man?'

'*Half Moon Street* was made in London. The book's got some life in it, but the movie's flat and it's not too accurate. Listen, I should know. I lived there eighteen years. I left there when I left my wife. I left my writing too. What was it? Something about leaving the house, leaving my routines – leaving people who cared. Who wants to sit there and bleed every day if no one cares about what you write?'

Weechie squinted at this, then said, 'What we mainly do is we mainly rent videos, and I get a special deal on them for working in the mall, which I do at the pet shop, like I was telling you.'

'*The Mosquito Coast* – ever see it? It's supposed to be Honduras but they made it in Belize. I traveled there – all over Latin America, actually. It was the trip I wrote about in *The Old Patagonian Express*. Then I got the idea for the novel. A guy, an inventor, who wants to take his family and get away from it all. But he finds out that you take your problems with you – all your flaws are portable. Ironic, isn't it? Like I have to discover that again, first hand.'

Blaine was gnawing his finger, Mundo pursing his lips over the top of the beer bottle. And Weechie said, 'I wonder what's taking Bunny so long?'

'Harrison Ford was in it.'

'I don't get him at all,' Weechie said.

'And River Phoenix.'

They stared at me and at that moment, having said so much, feeling self-conscious, I stood up and said that I had to go to the toilet, although I didn't – I simply needed to turn away from them for a little while. I passed Bun-Bun on the way, and said hello, and in the men's room I looked in the mirror and wondered whether I was drunk. I had told them more than I had told my therapist. They knew everything, even my name. They did not care, they had hardly heard me, they did not know; I was an alien, a different life-form, and gabbling, imploring them to understand, I did not even speak their language well. I wanted to be with them, to know them better, because I felt that they were the simplest people on earth, and that I could resume with them, like the Martians in those sci-fi movies who insinuate themselves in the life of the earth by taking the form of workmen. But I had failed, even telling these people everything, ingratiating myself; and so I decided to drive back to the Cape.

Passing the booth, I lifted my hand to say goodbye and I was surprised by Bun-Bun's smile of welcome and approval and the friendly way she patted the seat for me to sit down.

'Hey, so you know River Phoenix?'

On our way up Mystic Avenue shortly after that, Blaine was talkative. 'I scored some speed in the shitter using my stamps,' he said, and when I asked if they were food stamps he said, 'You know any other kind?' At the take-out pizza place Mundo was drunkenly seated with his head down, while Blaine gabbled, 'River Phoenix is one of the greats,' and, as though offering proof of it, he added, 'You can see that he does drugs. If only he didn't have that dorky name.'

'Like maybe he was born there,' Weechie said and Bun-Bun agreed.

They stood at the counter helping me choose the pizza but continually glancing back at the two young men, one mute and drunk, the other stoned and garrulous; and I was reminded of mothers I had seen in stores, with their children, nervously tending them, looking weary and overworked, afraid that they will break something or annoy other customers.

And then we left and turned towards the Medford end of the avenue, Weechie and I in front with one pizza in a box, Bun-Bun behind with the other pizza, and Blaine working his arms and bouncing, and Mundo stumbling at the rear. I was glad to be with them. I did not want to go home alone. I needed their company, and their sense of anarchy and general acceptance – they were outlaws and misfits, I needed that. I also needed them as a ragged little family that was disorderly enough to make room for me.

'I've never seen *Die Hard*,' I said.

'I've seen it about ten times,' Weechie said. 'Have you seen the other one, *Half Moon Street*?'

Already she had forgotten what I had told her. And the others clearly did not care that I had written it. But what did it matter? It only meant that I could not impress them by boasting of my feeble celebrity. But also, perversely, it had the effect of making me feel strong, like an exercise in humility; and telling my secrets to people who did not understand was a way of my keeping my secrets while at the same time proving my strength.

We crossed Mystic Avenue and walked under the glarey street lamps, through the low walls of blackened crusty snow that had been plowed from the road and dumped here. A slanting chain-link fence ran along the perimeter of some brick apartment houses.

'Where are we?'

'You come from Medford and you don't know the projects?'

There was a hole in the fence, triangular, bristling with metal strands, an icy path under it. We cut through and followed the casts of dark footsteps through the snow to a broken door, and a vandalized hallway; up some stairs to an apartment barricaded with three padlocks fastened against hasps that had the look of tarnished belt buckles. Just before we passed under the portico I had looked up and seen a woman staring out an upper window at me, and I felt a thrill.

'It's my mother's place,' Weechie said. 'But she's in Cambridge, currently living with her boyfriend.'

The word 'currently' stopped me.

'He's a cop,' Bun-Bun said. 'But he's OK.'

A baby screamed behind one door, a man howled behind another, a woman talked monotonously behind a third; they might have been television programs, but it was impossible to know for sure, and anyway it did not matter. This was where everything came together, overlapping, indistinguishable – life and TV, petty criminals and the police, custody battles and child abuse, welfare, food stamps, theft and generosity, the smell of smoke and oil, frying pans, spaghetti sauce, burned meat, onions, in the sour, boiled air of the tenement hallway.

There was something raw about the projects, especially this particular one. It was a place with no innocence, and because of that it excited and disgusted me, the way brothels had done in other countries, and this was just like a brothel. It was so easy to enter and leave, and it had some of the same odors, seedy and sexual, the sound of violence in the shouts and the sight of danger on the scrawled door jambs and walls. Voices mounting in an argument on another floor, the nakedness of it, the aggression, the unembarrassed squawks. A young, pretty woman squeezing past us on her way down the broken stairs. That was it: that she was so pretty and sweet-smelling, and the place so wrecked, and in a horrible slumming hunch I could imagine her boredom and her toughness.

I had been roused by merely kicking past the gutter and entering the building. There was no pretense here, and if there was a risk it was one that might be rewarded. You could go down Forest Street or Lawrence Road and never get nearer any house than the front gate, the houses were dark, silent, enigmatic. But here there was light and noise and smells. This brick tenement full of people was unlovely in a way that was viciously attractive to me.

Weechie undid the padlocks and pushed the door open. The apartment seemed neat compared to the vandalized hallway, and its warmth – the radiators pinging – made it seem homey. A big worn sofa and some armchairs faced the television set and this room, with posters on the walls, opened on to a dining area, a kitchen, a chipped table. It was bare and so it seemed tidy even though it was not clean. A small dog skittered out of a back room and yapped at me and then began humping my leg, while I tried to pluck him away.

'Bingo, get away,' Bun-Bun said, almost gently, but the dog hung on, his hairy hindquarters warming my leg. 'Bingo doesn't get the big picture.'

'I got him at the shop, where I also got them posters,' Weechie said.

Now I looked at them: bright blown-up photographs of puppies, of kittens, one of parrots.

'My mother wants them sconces for her place.'

Sconces? Such an elegant and precise word, and I was not even sure what it meant until I saw the light fixtures on the wall, and realized that Weechie, this simple woman in this poor room in the projects, had taught me the meaning of an old English word I should have known.

Bun-Bun put out some paper plates and napkins, while Weechie opened the boxes of pizza. Mundo stumbled to one of the chairs, like a dog to a box and curled up and hugged himself; Bingo climbed on to him and went to sleep himself. Blaine tore off two pizza slices and ate them, walking up and down, murmuring as he chewed.

I sat at the kitchen table with Weechie and Bun-Bun trying to decide which of them was the more physically attractive – Weechie with her sallowness and the tattoos on her thin arms, or Bun-Bun's hearty plumpness and the stud through her tongue. I felt I would go for Weechie – her look of ill health, which might have been merely the bad light in the apartment, made her appear submissive and undemanding.

I said to Weechie, 'So where do you sleep?'

'We're in there,' Bun-Bun said, with more authority than seemed necessary, and as though dismissing any further questions.

'I'm on the couch,' Blaine said, snatching more pizzas.

'Don't drip!' Bun-Bun said, as Blaine bobbled a slice and got sauce on the carpet. It seemed pathetic and foolishly brave, her howling at this nasty young man over a spill of goop on the frayed and faded carpet.

'My mother was like, "Where have you been?"'

They all had that way of suddenly starting stories without any prologue, in the middle, plunging in, with no other reference, losing you immediately until you listened hard.

'All that shit about how late it was,' Weechie went on. 'But she was really asking me about boys. Was I fooling around with them, and stuff. She didn't say sex, but that's what she wanted to know. She didn't realize that I was doing like two or three pipes of crack. I comes back wasted and she's like, "So who's this boy you're dating?" And I'm like, "Dating? You mean getting me stoned?" She'd make me play cards with her, whist and shit like that, to figure out if I was drunk, which I wasn't, but she was only worried about one thing, like, was anyone doing me.'

Bun-Bun let out an unholy laugh that called attention to itself, not as mirth but a reminder.

'I had a heavy crack habit.'

Blaine said, 'I don't want to hear about it.'

'I just stopped going home. And after my mother moved in with Lenny I came back, which was kind of ironic, him being a cop.'

I felt comfortable, seated at this kitchen table with these people who had accepted me without any questions. I said, 'It amazes me to think that I grew up in this city, and then I left – and I don't know a soul. So a few hours ago I was skiing through the Fells, and here I am eating pizza, feeling strangely as though I'm home.'

Blaine grunted. Bun-Bun blew her nose on a paper napkin.

Weechie said, 'So what about the videos? I got to return them both tomorrow whether we watch them or not.'

I sat in one of the armchairs, my legs stretched out, feeling a chill and a weariness – the fatigue of skiing, and beer and the pizza and the small warm room, Mundo moaning in the other chair and Blaine looking agitated and Bun-Bun and Weechie on the sofa, side by side, like parents among their big clumsy kids.

My eyes were heavy, and I was too tired to shut my hanging-open mouth. I knew it was open because somehow the violence of the video, its vibrations and its explosions, even its voices registered on my tongue. The ceiling light warmed the skin on my face.

'He's asleep,' I heard someone say and after a moment I realized they meant me. The unconcerned way they said it reassured me that they would do me no harm.

2

Waking after a night's sleep was always a shock for me – not just being jarred from the other life of my dreams, but also having to get up and face the day. How odd that this had been going on for fifty years and I still had not got used to it. Today it was worse than usual and somehow I knew that this morning was one of the lowest points of my life.

It was dark, the darkness stinking of stale food and dust, when I woke, and where was I? The old mildewed carpet seemed to purr with tobacco smoke and sent an itch into the air. Even in the dark you knew this place was dirty. I lay very still, with an animal's anxious and unblinking alertness, until the cold gray light gave the window a definite shape. I had no idea where I was, and then saw a torn comic book on a battered coffee table and became frightened again. Outside, what I could see of the world was being wrapped and inconvenienced by the thick white bandage of a blizzard.

Sometimes a snowfall can make you feel you are being buried alive. But this snow, this silence, this twilight atmosphere of the storm helped me by softening the shock of waking, which was intense here. I lay folded awkwardly in an armchair, in a room I did not recognize, under pictures of tetchy cats and sorrowful dogs, one person collapsed on the sofa and another in the chair opposite me, his arm over his head. The muffled sound of traffic moving through the snow in the street told me there was something happening outside in spite of the storm, wheels sending an up and down hum through the room, making a loose window pane tremble in its crumbly putty.

So I was alone, having woken among strangers in a poky apartment in the projects, unknown among these ignorant people. The snow improved it a little by putting it all in black and white, giving it drama. The cloudy light soothed me. It was a poor place, where no one knew me or cared whether I lived or died. I had never entered here before. I thought: I am back home. I remembered a line from *Black Spring*, in which Henry Miller had urged me to leave Medford, saying, *O glab and glairy, O glabrous world now chewed to a frazzle, under what dead moon do you lie cold and gleaming?*

I cringed at the thought of what I had said last night, but I played it all back and I saw their faces and I realized that they had not even heard me. Even deaf people would have had a reaction to what I said, would have looked at me closely and read my lips and tried to understand. But these people were utterly indifferent, selfish, obtuse. I was grateful to them for not caring, for having no memory for anything that I had told them.

It was seven-fifteen. I had been in the apartment for nine hours and twenty minutes. I had eaten two and a half slices of pizza and drunk three beers. I had spent twenty-two dollars on them. There were eighteen ornamental brass tacks on the long side of the old coffee table in front of the sofa, where the comic book *Awful Dwarfs* lay; ten on the end, probably fifty-six brass tacks altogether.

I heard water running and then someone muttering, oddly similar sounds drizzling in the next room, and then, 'I'm going to be late for work.'

It was Weechie, yawning, rummaging in the kitchen, opening and closing the refrigerator door, gathering the video cassettes into a plastic bag.

'See you later,' Bun-Bun said. 'I just have to find my keys.'

At the door between them there was a kiss, a beautiful murmur, a moment of the most casual intimacy, a sweetness that made me envious.

'Love ya,' one of them said, and I lay there in the shadows with my back to them, regretting my lost love.

As soon as Bun-Bun had gone too, I got up and put on my shoes and stretched and wondered what to do. The two men – the children in this odd little family – were still asleep.

I looked in the refrigerator, not for something to eat but just to see what was there. A box of crackers, another of cocoa puffs breakfast cereal, a jar of peanut butter, a bottle of pickles, another of ketchup, some jam, an uncovered bowl of leftover beans, and what looked like a large bar of soap with teeth marks on it and a bite out of one end. There were dishes in the sink. I used the bathroom, which smelled of herbal shampoo and a perfumed powder which stung my eyes. The bathroom was the only place in the apartment where I saw any books. They were paperbacks: *The Raven Master*, thick with dampness, and *Rubyfruit Jungle*, with a nail file serving as a book mark.

Uncomfortable in the apartment, feeling like an intruder, I left by the front door, my eyes numbed by the strange light of the snow storm. The snow was not deep but it covered everything, and the cold day, the knowledge that the snow would not melt, seemed to give it a solemnity. Below me, on Mystic Avenue, I saw Weechie standing at a bus stop. I walked over to her.

'Can I give you a ride?'

She hesitated, actually drew back, then recognized me. 'Didn't even know you had a car.'

Just then a car went by, a Mercedes speeding, throwing up salt-melted slush, and a woman at the wheel on the phone, talking fast, going to work. I felt envious and insignificant, until I thought: But who would I call?

'All I have to do is find it.'

I had left it parked in front of the Mystic Lounge. We walked towards it and saw that already the plows had pushed a high embankment of street-soiled snow against it. But it was a four-wheel-drive Pathfinder and I had no trouble bursting through the snow and on to the road.

'You work at Wellington Mall, right?'

'You got a good memory.'

I said, 'You mentioned something about a tattoo party.'

'A like great memory,' she said, nodding.

'I've never been to one. Will you take me?'

'Anyone can go, it's no problem, but OK. I'm meeting Bun-Bun after work,' she said, and then with a shudder of anticipation: 'I get so hyper just before these tattoo parties.'

The strangeness of this sentence and the excited way she said it were all the encouragement I needed to spend the day in Medford and meet her and Bun-Bun. She sat in the front seat and, as we crossed the river and traveled up the parkway, under the interstate at Exit 31 to the mall, she smiled to herself the whole way, holding her hands to her heart, as though cherishing a secret.

'You're a writer,' she said after a while, as though to show me that she had remembered something of me, too.

'Yeah, but today no writing – I'm going skiing.'

'You can drop me here,' she said, being considerate as we neared the mall, because a snowplow at the mall entrance had snarled traffic. And outside the car, she said, 'So where's your skis?'

'On the roof rack.'

She laughed, because having left them on the roof rack I could not expect ever to see the skis again, and this was usual to her.

She said, 'They ripped you off,' and did not even pause to commiserate. The fault was mine.

'*Bastards,*' I muttered, and drove farther up the parkway to a diner, where I had breakfast and read the *Globe*. Then I parked my car in Wellington and took the T into Boston, and browsed in bookstores, and crossed the Common and walked up Boylston to the library, killed another hour, had lunch, and continued on the T to the Museum of Fine Arts, where I spent the rest of the day in a desperate stupor of contentment looking at pictures and being grateful for the snow that had kept everyone at home. When I left the museum, the snow had stopped falling and the night was cold and clear.

Later, it seemed very odd to be ducking through the rip in the chain-link fence and making my way through the fresh snow to the apartment in the projects off Mystic Avenue. But already it was like a routine, I knew the way, I had learned how to go home.

Blaine in a baseball hat and winter coat was sitting cross-legged on the sofa smoking a joint, watching television. He was barefoot, his ankles very white. He was staring hard at the TV screen, where a man in the crude disguise of a wig and sunglasses was talking fast, and a description flashed under his face, *Is Unfaithful to his Wife But Does Not Want a Divorce.*

'It's the sex, sure, but it's also the thrill of it. And I need it. Hey, I love my wife . . .'

A woman in the audience was shouting, *'If you love your wife so much why are you catting around?'*

'Ever hear anything about morals?' another woman said with indignation into a microphone that was being held by the host, a black man with a shaven head and a bow tie.

'Look, lady – no, I listened to you and now it's my turn. We tried counseling, we tried therapy, we tried videos. We tried sex toys. You heard what I said. It didn't work, nothing –'

'You are going to break up your marriage.'

'It's holding my marriage together.'

His confident logic made me sad.

'Now let's hear from . . .'

'Where's Mundo?' I asked Blaine.

'In the bar. He like lives there.'

'You think he has a drinking problem?'

'No. Do you? People who get judgmental – they got a problem. You hear what I'm saying?'

'Yeah, sure.'

'They got the fucking problem.' And he gripped the remote and throttled it and the TV gasped and there was Nelson Mandela.

'I got such a problem with blacks,' Blaine said.

'He's South African. He was in prison for twenty-seven years. I remember his trial. I was in Malawi. Central Africa. He –'

'Africa's so screwed up,' Blaine said, and pressed his thumb into

351

the remote again, and got a hockey game – men sprinting at each other like gladiators, swinging sticks. 'Mundo had a breakdown, man.'

The word was wonderful because it never had to be explained. A breakdown was sudden, inconvenient, understandable, worthy of pity. No blame was attached, nothing was expected from you. A breakdown made you an invalid and won you sympathy. My struggling against it, my pride, putting on a brave face, all that had accomplished was to isolate me and leave me friendless. Or perhaps – it was just possible – I had spent a deranged twenty-four hours. My sitting in this dingy room in the Medford public housing projects on a cold evening with a druggie my son's age watching a rerun of *The Montel Williams Show* and waiting to be taken by strangers to a tattoo party – perhaps this was a breakdown?

'I was messed up too,' Blaine said. 'I had job burn-out.'

He zapped the hockey game and was now watching an old John Wayne movie, *The Wake of the Red Witch*.

'I saw that movie at the Medford Theater in Medford Square in about 1954.'

It was a crucial scene, John Wayne helpless in an old-fashioned diving suit, looking for the pearls, has his air-tube severed and begins to drown, his helmet filling slowly with water.

'Does this thing suck or what? An astronaut trying to swim!' Blaine switched back to Montel Williams and the adulterers.

'*I always use false names. That way I keep everything separate. My wife never . . .*'

There were unselfconscious scuffing footsteps in the hall. Bingo began to bark furiously.

'I could make a movie,' Blaine said. 'I've got some incredible ideas.'

Bun-Bun came in, pink and gasping from the cold and the climb up the stairs. She yanked her wool hat off her wild hair and laughed, glad to see me. She knelt and scratched Bingo and said, 'We had your book! Did I tell you I work at this consignment shop in Somerville? Your book was there in the box. The other woman read it. Cheryl – she's the one who told me.'

'Now you can read it,' I said.

'No. We sold it. What I'm saying is, I told Cheryl your name and she knew you. She read your book in high school, and she said we actually had the book in the shop. '

'They didn't like me at Medford High and now they're reading my book.'

'She went to Somerville High,' Bun-Bun said. 'But I can relate to what you're saying. People hassle you but they won't let go.' She looked at Blaine. 'This guy's a famous writer.'

'Ever watch this shit on acid?' Blaine said. It was auto racing. 'It is so cool.'

'But did Cheryl like the book?'

'Yeah. She even told me a little about it.'

'The plot?'

'No, the guy. He's kind of bummed out, but he's real focused.'

'Right.'

'So he decides to like get away from it all. He needs to be like validated.'

'With his family,' I said.

'Cheryl didn't mention any family. But society the way he sees it is in denial.'

'Right. America seems corrupt. So he goes to Central America.'

'Is that where this pond is?' she asked.

'He's in the jungle.'

'In a little cabin, right? He real, like, centered?'

I fell silent. I said, 'That's *Walden* by Henry David Thoreau.'

'Isn't that your name?'

'Pretty close,' I said.

Blaine said, 'I'm going to call my movie *Deal With It, America*.'

I said to Bun-Bun, 'How about that tattoo party?'

'I'm supposed to meet Weechie at Dunkin Donuts in a half an hour.'

As we were leaving the apartment, Bun-Bun looked across the room to where Blaine lay crumpled on the sofa, his baseball hat on backwards, working the remote switch between his toes, while he sucked on a joint and tapped the ashes into the small opening in the top of a can of Sprite. In a sudden reflex he swigged from the can, got ashes in his mouth, and gagged, and spat, and swore.

'He's real high maintenance,' Bun-Bun said softly as she shut the door on him.

*

353

The donut shop on Mystic Avenue was bright and warm and smelled of freshly made donuts.

'You want some?' I asked.

'I never eat donuts,' she said. 'I never eat anything. Know how I got heavy? Apples. They're all sugar.'

We went outside and watched for Weechie, but all I saw was a man in a new car in the parking lot making a telephone call from a cellular phone and gesturing in an insistent way with a cigarette. He was the sort of nasty little thug that I had seen long ago in Medford, and he looked the same, the greasy slicked-back hair, the pudgy face, the dark thievish eyes. I had feared their stupidity more than their violence, and I had fled from it as soon as I was able, making my exit from Medford at seventeen and never returning until now.

'Them phones are so cool,' Bun-Bun said.

The man got out of the car, cursing, still yakking on the phone. He had short legs and shiny shoes, and he slipped on the ice as he passed me, and almost lost his balance.

'The fuck you lookin' at?' he said to me, regaining his balance and turning his stumble into a little strut. He pushed the door open, lifting his elbows.

I had grown up there, I had heard that question a thousand times, and after fifty years I still had no answer to it except what I said to Bun-Bun, 'Let's get out of here. He doesn't like me.'

Because I was staring, as I had always done in Medford – standing there, seeing everything; listening, hearing everything; saying nothing.

'Vinny Dogs Dogano,' Bun-Bun said. 'He's with the Angiullo mob.'

I glanced back, through the window. He was eating a donut, and had sugar on his cheeks, but before he saw me I turned away.

'We just saw Vinny Dogs at Dunkin Donuts,' Bun-Bun said to Weechie when she arrived.

Weechie, snapping her chewing gum, looked at the little man in the bright window. She said nothing but her expression was one of fear, awe, curiosity.

'So where's this tattoo party?' I asked.

'Riverside Avenue.'

On our way, while I negotiated the icy road, Bun-Bun said, 'But I never think of writers when I read books. I don't care who wrote them. Hey, like I never noticed. You gave me something to think about.'

I asked, 'How do you know that little mobster back there?'

'We used to dance at one of his bars, Weechie and me,' Bun-Bun said. 'I know what you're thinking, but I wasn't heavy then. Exotic dancing.'

'He owns bars?'

'Nah. He's an enforcer.'

In conversations with people who asked me about my past I always told people I came from Boston. I talked about the woods, the library, my rifle. But this was nearer to what I had known: the ignorance, the mob, the small town fame of bullies, all this ice. It was what I had chosen to forget. The truth was always more interesting. I had come from nowhere.

Riverside Avenue was another street that had been cut in two by the interstate, but the number we went to, near Medford City Hall, was a house I had delivered Sunday newspapers to one school year, pushing a cart with big rusting wheels through the slush and the rain.

There was no bell. We went into the front room on the first floor of the wooden house, and I could see at once that except for the tattooist it was all young women and girls, fifteen or so. The tattooist was bearded and wore a blood-spattered apron. His own tattoos were elaborate, Japanese designs up and down his arms, and on the back of his neck. He was sitting at the edge of a chair while a woman on a hassock was having a blown-open rose tattooed on her shoulder.

'I want one of them,' Weechie said, breathing hard, so eager.

A woman approached Bun-Bun and kissed her on the mouth.

Bun-Bun said, 'This is the guy I was telling you about.'

The woman shook my hand and said, 'So you know River Phoenix?'

'I guess so.'

'Janie read your book. Hey, Janie.'

And a young woman in an oversize sweater approached, carrying a thick paperback. And she handed it over, *Presumed Innocent*.

'So how about a signature?'

'I didn't write it.'

'Aren't you Scott Turow?'

'No. I'm – '

'Forget it,' she said, sweetly, 'I didn't really read it. I started it, but it kind of sucked.'

'I am so pumped!' Weechie said, seeing the tattooist. She crouched and watched him work, drilling, wiping blood, drilling again.

'Get in line,' he said. He looked at me and said, 'You here for a tattoo?'

'I don't think so.'

He smiled at me and drilled his needle gun against the woman's shoulder. He said, 'You look like you just got shot out of a cannon.'

It was a pleasant scene. There were women drinking and talking, passing plates of snacks, listening to music.

I said hello to a black girl.

'Do I know you?'

I shook my head: no. 'You from Medford?'

'West Medford,' she said. 'Jerome Street.'

'One of my high school friends lived on Jerome Street. George Davis.'

'I've heard of him,' she said. 'You getting a tattoo?'

'No. I'm just visiting. I came with Weechie and Bun-Bun.'

'You're the guy who knows River Phoenix?'

'That's right. I used to deliver papers around here.'

'What kind of papers?'

'Newspapers.'

'Oh, yeah,' she said. 'Look, will you excuse me? I am out of cigarettes. There's a store down the street where I can get some.'

Watching her cross the room, I saw that the tattooist was kneeling before Weechie. He had finished the rose, and was preparing her. She lay limp and drooping like a pietà, her face glowing in ecstasy, Bun-Bun cradling her head, while the tattooist shaved an area near the knob of her hip bone. He scraped away foam, readying her for the tattoo. Two girls watched, holding hands, and two more on the sofa were kissing. Several couples danced in the shadows at the far end of the room. Some others were grouped around the table of snacks, as a girl in fur-trimmed shortie pajamas dealt snapshots for them like playing cards. Nipple rings, she was saying.

I hurried to the door where the black girl was putting on her gloves.

'Mind if I go with you?'

'Up to you.'

Then we were outside, in the snow. I said, 'My name's Paul.'

'I'm Peaches.'

'Listen, Peaches, this used to be a deli – a really good one, called Savage's,' I said as we walked along Riverside Avenue. I bought her the pack of Marlboros and, on our way back, passing behind the city hall, I said, 'See up there. That's where I used to go after school in the second grade.'

'I'm too stoned to climb that thing,' she said.

'Take my hand,' I said, and I tugged her up the path. 'Over there used to be Fountain Street, and that exit sign was the Washington School.'

At the shoulder of the road, we sat on a log, the vandalized trunk of an old fallen tree, the traffic passing above us.

'My Uncle Hal used to live where that off-ramp curls around. It was a really old house, full of treasures, with a chimney in the middle. The story was that Paul Revere stopped there on his midnight ride. He came right down Salem Street on his horse.'

'Your uncle had a horse?'

'Paul Revere,' I said.

The lights of Medford Square were dim in the scorching lamps of the interstate. The river, all ice, was flat and pale. When I was seven years old, in 1948, on this spot, or very near to it, I had kissed Linda Palmer and told her I loved her.

I wanted to kiss this black girl, Peaches. I imagined having her as a girlfriend – a Medford romance. I put my arm around her and my face near to hers. Then I sensed her whole body recoil and contract, as though getting smaller with fear, as though I were a slavering dog about to lick her face.

'No,' she said.

'I just want to kiss you. Nothing serious.'

'That's more serious than anything. I haven't like kissed a guy for maybe two years.'

'Maybe you could get used to it.'

She made a raspy little sniff of disgust and said, 'Sometimes when I'm doing my girlfriend her husband watches, but we don't let him touch us. Anyway, he doesn't care.'

She lit a cigarette. She said she was cold.

'Now I remember what this used to be, before the road went through.'

'Yeah?'

And I saw it, the slate stones, all of them chipped, some of them ancient, and incised with names and dates and simple skulls at the top. They were the first gravestones I had ever seen, on my way home from school right here on the bluff above the tracks – where the railway tracks used to be, and the tadpoles in the ditches, where Exit 32 now led off the interstate. I was seven or eight, holding Linda Palmer by the hand, and for a long time after had thought that all gravestones were flat gray slabs carved with grinning skulls.

'A graveyard.'

She screamed and said, 'I know what you're trying to do to me – just quit it!'

She was hysterical. I could not calm her. She would not let me touch her. She hurried away, walking in the street, which was clear of snow, heading back to the tattoo party. I was afraid to follow her, afraid that this misunderstanding would mean they would confront me. They might be very angry. But this was Medford, my old home, and they did not know me; no one knew me.

Better just to leave, to slip away. I got into my car and drove down Riverside Avenue, then changed my mind and headed to the on-ramp for the interstate. It was so simple to leave Medford now. In seconds it seemed I was out of there, within minutes I was in Boston, and Medford was darkness and a few blurred lights in the rear-view mirror.

FOURTEEN

The Queen's Touch

I

The short-cut through Boston that night was a mistake – I could not drive fast enough to escape my feeling of failure. Winter tramps and homeless veterans lurking in these narrow back streets looked like Arctic explorers in old engravings and blurred photographs – over-dressed, shrouded in lumpy clothes, frostbitten and doomed. They walked stiff-legged like homemade monsters. It was face-freezing weather, and the plowed streets were lined by barriers of dumped snow. The sidewalks glittered with crystals of black frost. I was in a car, yet I was one of these men. Failure is a sort of funeral, and a person fleeing a collapsed marriage is both the corpse and the mourner.

A croaky-voiced yokel on my car radio said, 'If you don't care where you are, you're not lost,' and I laughed angrily.

Like the other wandering men I saw, I was anonymous – or rather, most of them looked like me, hunched over, kicking the dirty snow and wearing misshapen caps, their hands in their pockets. They were lost explorers, waiting to be rescued. We were ignorant and il-literate and sick; we had a vague sense of needing another life. The only cure for my disorientation was to go far away and start again. There was no rescue for me here.

Arriving at midnight at my own house on the Cape, I was not con-soled. It was chilly inside and the low temperature made the damp air greasy. I switched on the lights and turned the thermostat up. Just then I heard the ping of my answering machine indicating that it had taken a message. Two messages, so the window blinked to me in a yellow number. After almost three days away from here, only two messages, and the first one began, *'You bastard, don't you dare'* – at which point I hit the *Skip* button, making it quacky and meaningless.

The second message was strangely formal after the sudden abuse of the first one. It was like hearing a different language. I could tell from its hesitation and twittering and the howling wires that it was probably transatlantic.

'*This is a message for Paul Theroux from Mr and Mrs Laird Birdwood,*' it began – a female voice, submissive and secretarial. '*They wonder whether you are free for dinner at their house in London on February twelfth. A few details. Black tie. Arrival at seven-thirty sharp – the timing is rather important, I'm afraid. We'll fax an invitation when you've confirmed that you can make it. We very much hope you can. Please ring back when you have a chance.*'

It was a complete statement – precise, confident, efficient and clearly enunciated.

I listened to the message again, looking into the mirror of my bedroom. I was pale, unshaven, the tip of my nose was pink, a scab of snot clung to one nostril, my hair was twisted into spikes from my wearing an Arctic explorer's wool hat. I had not changed my clothes for three days; I had slept in them.

'*Black tie. Arrival at seven-thirty sharp . . .*'

Another certainty in my condition was knowing what was possible and what was not. Dinner in London was out of the question. I could not think of a single reason for going. It would simply be a matter of working out the time difference between the Cape and London and then calling during office hours to convey my regrets.

I had a bath. I shaved. I drank green tea. I got into bed and read some pages of Malinowski's *Coral Gardens and their Magic*. Sleety rain had started to patter like sand grains against the window. I fantasized about disappearing in New Guinea – no lumpy clothes, no gloves, no frostbite. I warmed myself with my tea and my reading and, warmer, I was soon asleep.

In the morning I called Birdwood's number in London to say I could not make it. I got his secretary, the polite woman who had left the message.

'I am so sorry,' she said. 'I know Mr and Mrs Birdwood will be disappointed. They were very keen for you to come. Whatever is that noise?'

'The wind,' I said. It was last night's storm, still blowing, tearing at the shingles. 'It's just that it's quite a trip from here to London for dinner. And it's rather soon.'

'Quite. But it's going to be a special occasion.'

'Oh, I'm sure. But –'

'I think that you ought to know that the guest of honor is Her Majesty the Queen.'

'Yes,' I said. I could not look at my face in the mirror and still make sense of these words. The Queen?

'And Prince Philip of course. They've never visited Mr Birdwood's home before. Everyone's very excited, as you might imagine.'

'The Queen,' I said. I was smiling, standing naked in my room, yesterday's clothes in a pile, looking like the carcass of a large animal. The word 'queen' called up her portrait on the postage stamps, her slender neck, her dainty chin, her perky nose, her crown prettily tipped on the back of her head.

'For security reasons we have to have our final guest list fairly soon.'

'I'll be coming alone,' I said.

Flying into London on my low-season fare using Frequent Flyer miles, my only luggage my tux in a bag, I reflected that what I needed was the solace of anonymity in a place where no one knew me. In the meantime, feeling like someone on the graveyard shift on his way to work, Mr Half-a-Life carrying his shabby uniform, I was setting off to meet Her Majesty, Elizabeth II, Queen of Great Britain and Northern Ireland, Defender of the Faith.

I was in Coach. Carl Lewis was in First. A bossy, buttocky flight attendant – male, wet-eyed, twitching to be noticed – blocked my way, allowing the Olympic runner off the plane. From my humble place in the steerage line I noticed that Lewis had the smallest ears I had ever seen on a human being.

In the Underground, I realized that having left a year before, and with no good news to report, there was no one I wished to see in London. I did not want to be asked how I was doing. Or what was I working on? I had no answers. I craved the company of strangers. The teenagers in Medford had not worked. I liked the idea of naked illiterate islanders grinning in my direction and seeing me (so Malinowski had said) as someone who did not belong to the human race.

The Birdwoods were almost strangers to me. Charmian was English, 'the queen's cousin,' people said, as they said about many people, from one of those families – but perhaps this royal visit was the proof. Laird was a wealthy American, a breeder of horses who needed to be near Newmarket. He prided himself on his stables (he had twice won the Grand National) and his library of first editions – look under *T* and you would find editions of mine that even I did not own. Years before, in Ascot Week, he had invited me to dinner with Princess Anne, and he had sat me next to her. 'Daddy had a go at the *Daily Express*,' the Princess Royal had said. After dinner, her husband, 'the Captain,' as she called him, had complained about her trips to Africa to visit hungry villagers. 'What I say is, charity begins at home.' He had broken his leg in a riding accident. It had not stopped him from attempting a foolish little jig as he wearily kicked his plaster cast while the Princess Royal sighed and suffered. They were separated now.

The seating arrangement had worked. I was American, a writer, the soul of gratitude and politeness; and I was harmless. Being socially unclassifiable helped solve the problem of a royal seating arrangement. A presentable American created no class conflict. It was much better that I was obscure, that we were all strangers to each other, even the hosts. And it was easier returning to London this way, a visit as parody, the guest dressed as a waiter.

In eighteen years of living in London I had never stayed in a London hotel. Only the out-of-towners truly understand a city's hotels. It did not matter – I had lost my money and so I no longer had any choices. I got off the Underground at Earl's Court and found a 'vacancy' sign in the window of the Sandringham House Hotel. It was as cold and dirty and poorly lighted as the house I had just left.

Eight o'clock on a winter morning in London, the forty-watt bulbs burning so feebly in the foyer they cast no shadows. An Indian in a sort of teller's cage signed me in, took my money in advance and welcomed me. A plastic name-plate gave his name as R. G. Pillai.

Then he said, 'Room 22. It is not ready.'

'Do you have any that are ready?'

'Not available.'

'I've just flown all night.'

'Check-out time is noon. Maybe then.'

Interrupting me in my protest he said, 'Take breakfast in lounge.'

It was not a lounge. It was a drafty rear room on the second floor, colder than the foyer, with velvet drapes, tables too close together and an electric heater in the fireplace. A flickering red light on the plastic ornamental log had been switched on but not its burners.

The waiters were Indians in stained white jackets. I sat for a while, watching people at other tables being served. Soon the paraphernalia was brought to my table – an empty jam jar with a dusty lid, a saucer of two butter pats, a toast rack (two slices), a sugar bowl, milk jug, tea pot, pot of hot water, tea strainer and tea-strainer holder, spoons, forks, tongs for sugar cubes. They had the look of what was left of the family silver and the last cracked crockery in the family, and filled the table like the clumsy old tools of a barber surgeon. The waiter apologized as he set this stuff out, and by the time he had finished the tea had gone lukewarm and the toast was cold and damp. Elsewhere in the room the rattle-clink of silver and porcelain took the place of conversation.

A heavy-faced Englishwoman scowled at me as she walked past. This was Betty – Mr Pillai's wife. Her false teeth were very white and slightly crooked in her mouth. She wore a hair-net and when she saw me she chewed and worked her doggy jowls.

'Yes?'

'Is there any jam?'

'If you don't see it we don't have it.'

That was the commonest catch-phrase in shopkeeping England, yet I knew it to be untrue of English life: what you did not see ex-isted profoundly in the society, the whole culture was its invisible es-sence. Nothing showed – not attitudes, nor texture, nor feeling. It was enigmatic in an almost oriental way. In other words, there was raspberry jam but you had to know how to ask for it, in the English world, where everything important was hidden.

I envied the people at the other tables, the way they sat, quiet couples, man and woman together, reading the morning papers or silently communicating – smiling, that wordless intimacy of mar-riage that was mine no longer. This subtle affection depressed me, the hand-holding, the meaningful looks, the familiarity. I did not want that. I wanted savages and strangers.

I sat alone, nibbling at my awful breakfast, regretting the life I had lost, hating the effort I had made in coming all this way, on a fatuous errand, just another desperate remedy for my loneliness.

At last, I was led to my room by a wordless Indian, up a stinking staircase, down a passageway. Every footfall squeezed a creak from the loose floorboards under the worn carpet. Passing a bedroom door I heard a furious accusatory woman's voice:

'I don't want you here!'

After that was a man's inaudible murmur; then the woman again.

'You've done nothing but complain since the minute I entered this room!'

It startled me, but the Indian leading me showed no sign of having heard it. Five doors on, he slotted the latch-key into an old lock, played with it a bit and pushed the door into a narrow room. He gestured, he did not enter, he was like a guard showing a new prisoner to his cell. I drew the drapes and lay in the semi-darkness, and fell asleep.

My reverie was shattered by a sudden shouting from the next room, so loud it penetrated the plaster.

'I don't want to hear any more of this!'

A woman's voice, shrill and almost hysterical.

A man's voice said, *'If you'd only let me explain . . .'* and he was quieter, even reasonable-sounding.

Was it that women in such arguments yelled because they faced the physical threat of a man? In these walls, women screamed, men grunted. Neither of these voices matched the voice I had heard down the corridor.

'I don't want that bitch in our marriage! You wouldn't have done it if you cared for me. And her, of all people!'

'She's not the problem. Don't you see it reveals a deeper –'

'That's all ballocks! Go get your little whore. You'll be sorry. You'll see that it's the biggest mistake you've ever made.'

The man murmured. It was not audible, he was hushing her.

The woman then cried out, *'Don't touch me!'*

In a low severe voice the man said, *'Pack it in.'*

'Leave me alone, you bastard!'

The rest was murmurs, then tears, and a slammed door. I was fully awake now, but I soon subsided into sleep, until I was woken by voices from the other wall, egging each other on.

'You're always doing that. Well, two can play that game.'

I thought: Apologize and this will end. Say, 'Yes, I am sorry I hurt you. I will never do it again.'

But the man said, *'You're pathetic. Look at yourself. You don't know what you're talking about.'*

I thought: Say, 'I've suffered. It made me miserable. But we can overcome this.'

But the woman said, *'I hate you. God, do I hate you.'*

I covered my ears and shut my eyes. There was a quality in the darkness which gave the room a terrible smell – of fur and flesh, and not feet but hooves. It was like being in hell. I slept again. There was more of it in the night – shouts, accusations, a struggle, a man on the phone, thumps and pleading; but by morning – I woke early, remembering that this was the day of my dinner with the Queen – there was silence.

Morning again, the lounge again, breakfast again. But these words were all approximations; they did not really describe the day, the room, or the meal. The gray sky seemed to hover a few feet from the chimneys on the next roof, and electric lights in obsolete wall fixtures burned yellow in the shabby dining room, casting unhelpful shadows. There was jam today but the light was so poor it was impossible to tell what flavor it was. In this bad light all the jam was black.

The same tea ritual, the same paraphernalia looking like old science, the cluttered table, the lukewarm tea, the damp toast.

Betty served. She carried a bowl on a brown plastic tray. She said, 'Fruit compote?'

I said yes. The answer was prunes.

The silent couples in the room ate neatly, and their silence was like hunger and gratitude and obedience. Two read newspapers, no one spoke. The night-time darkness had been full of voices, mumbled accusations, obscenities, the closets shrieked, the pipes gushed with collapsing water. When I switched on the dim bulb beside my bed, my room was lit and the picture on the wall spoke: it was the Yorkshire Dales, a rushing stream, a bare mountain, some pines, a glorious landscape inhabited by an angry, quarreling couple. But here in the pale light of day the spectral residents of Sandringham House ate in silence and read the papers, and once again it was like being in hell – not a Catholic hell of bonfires and molten lava and cackling devils, but the secular English hell of stinks and shame and narrow, clammy rooms. Rattle-clink.

Walking to the bus stop after breakfast, I was almost run down by a large green Range Rover.

It was her again, the bony-faced woman I had always encountered in London traffic – lovely hair, neck scarf, sleeveless quilted Barbour jacket. Dressed for the country, impatient in the West End, she did not glance at me, didn't have to, she knew I was stepping off the curb. It was not merely that she was in a hurry to get to the motorway; the point was that she was on the phone, the thing clapped to the side of her face, while she steered the vehicle with her other hand. She had been doing this to me for years. She muttered under her breath, she drove on, still talking on the car phone. She missed but managed to splash me.

I took a bus to the King's Road, then walked down Beaufort Street to the river. I was heading for Clapham but halfway across Battersea Bridge I realized I did not dare to look at the family house. I knew in advance there was no one home, but more than that I did not belong there. I could not go in; I would be on the sidewalk staring at the bricks, my old windows. My London had been my house and my family; I'd had nothing else. And now, an unwelcome ghost, haunting this place, I had no friends, and no longer a family. I had never really lived here. I had pitched my tent in London, and now it was folded, and I had stolen away.

So, walking in the rain, I lost my nerve, but out of curiosity I went to the Fishmonger's Arms for a drink. The licensing hours had changed, and pubs in London were now open all day. Cigarette smoke, a damp carpet, the gluey smell of spilled beer, the underwater honks of a spinning fruit machine. A man sat at the bar, smoking over his pint of beer. A boy stood next to him in a school uniform, probably his son.

It pleased me that I knew the barman's name – Dermot. He smiled at me.

'You've been scarce.'

'Been away.'

'Good trip?'

'Some hassles.'

'Fuss is better than loneliness,' Dermot said.

That was all, after my year's absence. It was an Irish pub, everyone was friendly, but it was no more than alcoholic bonhomie. He didn't know me well enough to ask me anything else. I ordered a half-pint of draft Guinness.

'Let's go, Dad,' the boy said to the man drinking next to me.

'Can't you bloody wait, Kevin?' the man said. He was drunk and irritable. He sipped at his beer – the sipping was his way of showing that he would not be hurried.

I said to the boy, Kevin, 'Where do you go to school?'

'Emmanuel.'

'Studying for exams?'

'A-levels are next year,' he said, sounding weary.

'What subjects are you doing?'

'English, history and French.'

As he spoke, his father squinted at me, sizing me up.

'I've got a history question,' I said. 'What do you know about the divine right of kings?'

'It's Jacobean – well, James the First wrote about it. The French monarchy had more developed ideas of it than the English, but the English believed it. You know about "the king's touch"?'

'Tell me.'

'The king could cure certain diseases,' Kevin said. 'Scrofula. That's the one they always talk about.'

'Whatever that's supposed to be,' his father said.

'It's inflammations.' Kevin smirked. 'Also it means degenerate.'

'I was just wondering – say, the present Queen. Isn't she supposed to have a little bit of divinity?'

'She's head of the Church,' Kevin said.

'Bloody black Protestant Church of Anglican bloody England,' the man said, and spat on the floor.

Kevin went on, 'The idea is that she does have a touch of divinity. Look at the Book of Common Prayer, there are prayers for the king and prayers for the royal family. "King of Kings, Lord of Lords, the only ruler of princes." That sort of thing. It's an aspect of monarchy.'

'It's an aspect of bollocks,' his father said.

'Does anyone ever say those prayers?' I asked.

'We were saying one at chapel last week.'

'Don't let me bloody catch you,' his father said. He was drunken and ineffectual.

'Come on, Dad. Let's go.'

Kevin winked at me as his father went on resisting.

What there was left of the drizzling day I spent walking through Clapham Junction. I bought a pair of black socks and a black bow tie at Marks and Spencer, then walked down to the river again, through the churchyard of St Mary's in Battersea. Hunched over, bent against the bad weather, I spotted a bus at the Fulham Road and caught it back to Earl's Court and the Sandringham House. There had been no dawn, only a porridgey sky that had lain low and gray across the rooftops. The day that had begun late in darkness, now ended early in quickening dusk like a dropping curtain of blackness that became cold, slimy streets and wet pavements and drizzling bricks and roof slates shining in the glare of street lamps. The dim lights had burned all day, less as illumination than a reminder of the undefeated dark.

Passing through the hall again I heard new voices.

'I don't know why you love me. I'm awful.'

'Don't start that!'

I had preserved my dress shirt and tuxedo in a box that was bound with string. I had bought the socks and tie that I had forgotten, but when I put on the shirt I realized I had no cufflinks. I called downstairs.

'Executive offices.'

'Mr Pillai, I seem to have left my cufflinks at home. Do you have any I might borrow?'

'You looked in room?'

'No.'

'If you don't see them in room, we don't have.'

'Do you know what I mean by cufflinks?'

'No. Not knowing.'

'Then why do you say you don't have any?'

'Not available,' he said, and then I heard Betty shriek, and he hung up.

A female voice in the next room said, *'I don't want to have this conversation. I don't want to see you. Do you understand? I want you out of my life.'*

She wasn't interrupted, she must have been on the phone.

'And yes, I want you to fail. I want you to be as miserable as I have been. I want you to know what it's like.'

It was too late to buy any cufflinks. I managed to fasten my cuffs with paper clips from a drawer. That held them, and poked into my sleeves they were invisible.

My tux made me look seedier not better. I could see that in the foyer mirror. A woman walked past me, smiling. Was she the one who had screamed in the phone upstairs? Setting out from the Sandringham House to hail a taxi I had a feeling this was not going to work – and why should it? I was obviously posturing. I had flown from Boston to London to have dinner with the Queen, and I had agreed on the desperate pretext that it might cheer me up and give me something to write.

No. My hotel was awful. It was inhabited by angry and treacherous people – their accusations came out of the walls. I was sick with jet lag. You could not see that my shoes were wet, but they were, from my walking. Dinner was not going to happen, and even if I got to Birdwood's house in time there would be no dinner and no Queen. This was all paranoia and misunderstanding, not a bad dream but the average dream of humiliation and pursuit. At any moment I would wake up in my bed on Cape Cod, and I would groan and listen to the wind lisping on the cedar shingles and making sounds of a push-broom in the juniper boughs.

The taxi sped me to Chelsea Embankment, where just off Swan Walk, the porch and its pillars were floodlit, a whole house protected by a high wall. Then, ahead, through the flap of the taxi's windshield wipers, I saw the flashing lights, the police cars, the policemen themselves.

Sliding the glass partition, the taxi driver called back to me, 'You sure this is the right address?'

'This is it.'

'Flaming circus – what's this all about?'

'The Queen's coming to dinner.'

'God bless her,' he said. 'That'll be six pounds even.' I tipped him and he was chastened. 'Ta, guv. Mind how you go.'

2

From the first it was like a seance, but of a very classy kind. There was a tremor of nervousness in the house – everyone a little too ready to respond, no one quite listening to anything that was being said. I was greeted by a doorman, perhaps hired for the occasion, then Birdwood and his wife said their tense hellos. The others were shiny and dressed up and alert. I was handed a card. Four circles on it represented tables. A red dot indicated my place. There was an intense watchfulness, guests listening hard but too edgy to hear clearly. A mostly American gathering, it was first names and fixed smiles and bright, anxious eyes.

In the mirror of the reception room I saw that I did not look the way I felt, and that I could pass for a guest at a dinner party. Apart from Laird Birdwood and Charmian, there was no one in the room whom I recognized. A man standing next to me smiled. I spoke to him. Deaf with anxiety, he did not hear me. Another man began talking as I approached him, possessed by an almost hysterical garrulity, a talking jag brought on by the suspense. I could imagine all these reactions in passengers in a jammed elevator – claustrophobia, insecurity, fear. No one mentioned the Queen.

'What are you working on?' a man asked me.

I began to give him my tentative answer and was relieved to see that he was not listening.

Birdwood was saying, 'Actually very unexpected,' to a woman who replied, 'Perhaps better not to speculate.'

Were they talking about the royal visit? If so, there was nothing more, and yet I was sure this was on every guest's mind. We were participants in a seance that was about to begin, too nervous anticipating what was to come to mention anything so obvious as the object of the seance, the apparition we were about to conjure into existence. The drama of the moment made for the most frenetic and banal chit-chat. We were desperate to see royal ectoplasm, yet we pretended otherwise. The English guests were the most talkative.

'I think the sun was trying to come out today.'

'We've been extraordinarily lucky this winter.'

'The going at Goodwood was uniquely horrible.'

Drinks were brought around by flunkies who, less nervous and better dressed than the guests, seemed slightly superior and almost mocking in the way they offered the wine.

A guest with a cadaverous face and a tight collar was saying in a high, insincere voice, 'Made an absolute pig of myself eating and drinking.'

'I say, what are you working on?' I was asked again by someone else.

The idea was that we had to remain upbeat. It was extreme bad manners to have any bad news, with the idea of the Queen looming. We were anxious but we were also very lucky to have the privilege of meeting the Queen in a private house.

'What are you working on these days?'

We stood, the men in black, the women in pretty gowns under the chandeliers, as the time of the seance drew on, and we were helpless, waiting for any sign that something definite was stirring. Our eyes were averted from the large door that was the entrance to the room: no one wanted to be caught peeking.

'Not much,' I said.

No one listened, no one heard me.

A man was saying, 'It's always that way, isn't it?' and I had no idea what he was talking about. He was faced in my direction, still talking obscurely, still making no sense to me, nor was he looking at me.

The room had gone very quiet.

I turned to look at what the man was looking at and got a glimpse of a woman being introduced to a group of guests and I knew from her diamonds and the size of her head that she was the Queen.

'That reminds me, I must buy some stamps,' I said.

It did not matter. No one heard anything that was said.

But she was not the portrait on the postage stamp; she was a small muffin-faced woman in a blue gown of stiff gauze. She had a shy but warm smile, not the fixed grin of the politician. Diamonds were clamped to her hair in a tiara, and more diamonds around her neck. On one wrist was a diamond bracelet and on the other a diamond-studded watch. They were dazzling stones, small in size but so many of them, and in such clusters, they made you think of electric circuits. The queen's wire-frame eyeglasses looked banal on the royal face. The room was hushed, as though no one dared speak while the Queen was present, yet she was saying little.

Behind her the Duke of Edinburgh straightened himself. So far this royal entrance was all about silences. She was Her Highness, he was His Royal Majesty. He was taller than I had expected – taller than me – and he nodded when he was introduced, keeping his hands behind his back. No hands were extended, none were shaken, no one was touched: a seance would progress like this, too. The royal creature had been conjured out of thin air. One would never be sure whether the ectoplasm was real or imagined.

I glanced again at my diagram of the dining room and my red dot. I made sure my cuffs were tucked into my sleeves. I saw that my shoes were not obviously wet. I was an absurd and flagrant fraud, and began to dislike Birdwood for believing in me, giving himself and me the illusion that I mattered. I was a deserter and a bad husband who had used his last Frequent Flyer miles to get his hand on a glass of wine here in the royal presence. I had holes in my shoes and paper clips in my cuffs, and an aching heart. I had not done any work for seven months. I stayed in a hotel run by a nasty negligent couple, where antagonistic conversations came out of the walls. The shouts had kept me from sleeping. I dreamed of going to New Guinea, of parting some huge plumes of greenery, curtains of palm fronds, in a place where cockatoos screamed; of walking into the darkness of the jungle; of vanishing and taking my failure with it.

'And this is Paul Theroux, the writer.'

I was at last the miserable person I had always feared I might become – destitute and shallow. That was the ultimate failure – not obscurity but the paradox that I was known to the world, revealed as a selfish man who had run off, who in trying to be right had become an old bore. It was not a question of being forgiven. I had to go away, yet here I was, a faker in a drawing room, in my waiter's costume. Flustered and tense, I farted, and quickly covered this bugle note by raising my voice.

'Very pleased to meet you, Your Majesty.'

The Queen smiled, she seemed to murmur something. Beneath all that glitter was a muffin-faced granny and I realized that I had nothing to say to her. It did not matter. She was being led onward, still smiling. She had a lovely smile.

There were more in the royal party – the Earl and Countess of Airlie, and some others.

No drinks for the royals. They were greeted and introduced and they passed into the dining room, a slow procession of swishing gowns and murmuring men. I hid myself among the shufflers, realizing that I liked this, for everyone in the room was humbled. At any dinner party people contended to be noticed, usually the worst people. But here were no upstarts. It was not my imagination. We filed in like children, fearful of making a wrong move. Ahead of us were the Queen and the Duke, so we were obedient and deferential, showing respect, more than I had ever sensed in a room, and such reverence seemed to generate heat and light.

I consulted my dining-room diagram again and saw that my dot put me at the Queen's table. She was being seated next to Laird Birdwood. There was another man on her right, and a woman on either side of me, six of us, including Her Majesty.

Our food was brought promptly, the first course was (I identified it from the menu) roulade of sea bass with champagne and caviar sauce.

The woman on my right smiled at me.

'What are you working on?'

'Not much.'

'Sounds super,' she said. 'I wish I could write.'

'So do I,' I said.

Then she turned away, to listen to Laird Birdwood talking to the Queen. What he said was inaudible, but at such close quarters it did not seem improper to stare at the Queen – in fact, this unembarrassed goggling could have passed for politeness.

After a while it seemed almost normal to be seated at the same table as the Queen. She hardly ate, she hardly drank, it was all like a ceremonial – ritual talking, ritual tasting – and so she appeared to be going through the motions, slightly bored. Standing, she had seemed the wrong shape and size; seated, she seemed slightly hemorrhoidal, but you could see that she was trustworthy.

'Quite,' Her Majesty said.

Birdwood talked energetically for a while. The subject was horses.

'Oh?' Her Majesty said.

Because she was so grand, not to say blessed with a hint of divinity, she gave the impression of foreignness, of speaking a language that no one knew very well – not us, nor anyone in the world. Birdwood was doing his best to be understood.

'Yes,' Her Majesty said.

It is said that everyone in Britain dreams of the Queen. It is another standard dream, like the desperate one about being naked in a public place or the reckless one about flying over treetops by flapping your arms. In my Queen dream, which I had used in a novel, the Queen and I were alone in a palace room on a royal sofa. She was the young, thin-faced Queen whose profile appeared on the British stamps – a simple enough portrait to impose any fantasy upon. 'You seem dreadfully unhappy,' Her Majesty said. Her face was pale as on the stamp. I was too shy to admit that I was miserable. She was wearing a stiff dress of green brocade, with deep cleavage. Her rings sparkled as, using both her hands, she pulled apart the bodice of her gown, and as her breasts tumbled out I put my head between them, feeling her cool nipples at my ears.

'Isn't that better?' said the Queen in my dream.

I was sobbing between her breasts and could not reply.

'What are you working on at the moment,' the woman on my left asked.

I propped up the menu and read from it: *Fillet of lamb, lemon thyme sauce. Fresh garden vegetables. Broccoli timbale. Gratin of potatoes.*

'Yes, I imagine so,' Her Majesty was saying.

I could not suppress the devilish voices in my head that were cackling and gossiping, reminding me of the scandalous stories about Prince Philip who was said to have had a fling with Princess Margaret when the Queen was pregnant with Anne; that Prince Andrew had been fathered by one of the Queen's lovers – which was why Andrew looked physically different from all the other children; that the Queen still had a lover, and that Prince Philip had had a succession of actress mistresses who regularly appeared on television, prompting viewers in the know to smile and say, 'She's one of his.'

Never mind. As Kevin had told me in the Fish, the Queen is holy – not godlike, but godly and quasi-divine, a descendant of the Creator. And this ancestor was not a funny-featured pagan idol from the polytheistic pantheon but the capitalized and bearded God, the Father Himself in a white robe, the Santa Claus with a halo, that we all believed in. That was the English dilemma. Of course, the Queen was good for the tourist industry, but if you were English and believed in God you had to believe in your monarch, who was a distant relation of God.

Her Majesty was patting her lips with a small square of lace.

'Yes, it must be so pleasant,' she was saying.

She was looking straight ahead – not at me, but into the middle distance. Laird Birdwood was still speaking in a gentle yet earnest way. The man to her left was attentive, yet he had not so far succeeded in saying anything. He smiled at me. He made a scribbling motion with his hand, a gesture that was unambiguous; it meant, Are you working on anything at the moment?

I smiled hopelessly back at him, as dessert was served: Chocolate mousse royal, with fresh raspberries. For this (again I was reading) our glasses were filled with Schramsberg blanc de noir.

We smiled, we ate, we sipped. This was not an occasion for conversation; this was an experience. The idea was to get through it successfully and not be noticed, to avoid calling attention to yourself. There were so many possible pitfalls that it was better to say as little as possible. At such a dinner, with the God-Queen four feet away, no one could be faulted for saying nothing; one could only commit a gaffe by being a bore. My crack about seeing the Queen being a reminder that I had to buy postage stamps had been unwise. It was a good thing no one had heard me.

There was movement, the Queen was rising, and everyone in the room with her. Moments later we were milling around in the drawing room, being polite again and trying not to think about Her Majesty seated on Laird Birdwood's toilet. I needed to think of that, to be reassured that she was human.

She returned, more relaxed and cheerier, breathing more deeply, as people do after an evacuation. But she was across the room. I was talking to her Lady in Waiting, Lady Airlie, who had just asked me what I was working on at the moment.

'I was thinking of going to the Pacific,' I said, and thought: To vanish.

'Her Majesty had a most successful visit there a few years back. I was fortunate to be included. So many fascinating places. Most amusing in New Guinea.' She had a bright smile and impish eyes. 'She gave a speech, almost. Ha!'

'Tell me,' I said.

Across the room the Queen was surrounded by four or five people – taller than she was, so I saw just the piercing flashes of the royal tiara.

'Her Majesty can tell the story far better than I could.'

I drifted over to the Queen's group. Her Majesty was listening intently to someone speaking; she had obviously perfected the art of seeming fascinated, one of her most Godly attributes. She was formal, certainly, but more than that she was polite. Nothing improper, contentious or untoward occurred in her presence. All was order and harmony. She was God the Mother.

But the strain of being Queen at such close quarters was beginning to show.

'. . . lifted his entire body,' a man was saying haltingly, 'but before he could clear the fence the band began to play and it spooked him and then – '

'Quite,' Her Majesty said, with feeling.

'He wasn't seriously injured,' the man said.

'That does happen,' Her Majesty said. 'Yes.'

What was this, horses again? Even with Her Majesty's famous love for the creatures she displayed just the slightest tic of impatience. And why not? Throughout this evening I had seen no evidence of the Queen being told something that she did not already know.

'Your Majesty,' I said. 'I have been planning a trip to New Guinea. I understand you visited some years ago.'

'Papua New Guinea,' she said, giving the country its correct name. 'Marvelous country. The prime minister visited the palace just last week. He had splendid hair. Fuzzy wuzzy hair!'

There was a scream of laughter from us at hearing this description – we were nervous, eager to approve; it jarred the room.

'Yes,' Her Majesty said, looking solemn yet knowing she had our complete attention. 'There is no other way to describe it. And his wife. Didn't speak a word of English. Just sat next to him, smiling away, in her splendid gown. And she had fuzzy wuzzy hair too.'

'This would be Rabbie Namaliu,' a man said.

'Yes,' Her Majesty said.

'The Scottish name is so reassuring,' I said.

She shrugged. She said, 'Perhaps there was some Scottish missionary in the picture.'

Over the disbelieving laughter, I said, 'But your speech –'

She glanced at me in a suddenly wintry way – was it because in my haste I had left off 'Your Majesty'? The way a child playing a game who forgets to say 'Simon says' is sent to the back of the line? But perhaps not. I saw that her normal mode of discourse was the monologue: you did not converse, you did not give Her Majesty information, you did not hurry Her Majesty. My cuffs were showing, my shoes were still damp.

'The state visit took us to the Highlands,' she said. 'We drove to a clearing some distance from the town. And there were the people – several thousand of them. Some of them had walked three or four days to be there. They had feathers in their hair, and lovely costumes. They wore paint on their faces. They came in families. I stood on a platform to make my speech.'

'When you were introduced, Your Majesty, did they refer to you as "Missis Kwin"?'

And you certainly did not interrupt Her Majesty. She blinked at me, ignoring what I said, and went on, 'I saw all the families. Mud family. Feather family. Shell family. Children, wives, old grannies, with marvelous painted faces.'

We smiled, imagining the families looking up at their Queen.

'When I opened my mouth there was a great clap of thunder. At once all the people ran under the trees. I had hardly said one word. The rain was next. I imagine they didn't want to spoil their feathers. They wore such lovely costumes, you see. There was no point in continuing. Somehow we got back to the car and that was when the hail came down. Hailstones so large they crashed against the windows – actually cracked the glass. It was amazing. We didn't get far. The car was a huge Rolls not made for those conditions and it quickly got stuck in the mud. The driver tried to move it but it skidded and tilted on to its side. And there we were – couldn't go forward or back, with the hail smashing into it.'

'I would have been absolutely terrified, Your Majesty,' a woman said with actressy passion.

'One wasn't, actually. But it was a bother.'

She savored our reaction to this, while we waited for her to tell us what happened next.

'A man came towards us, an Australian by the look of him, soaking wet and smiling. He was wearing one of those funny Australian hats. He had obviously had a bit to drink. He leaned over and put his face against the window and looked in at me.' She hesitated a moment, then pursed her lips and in a suddenly vulgar Australian accent said loudly, ' "Hile to the Quoin!" '

The unexpected accent, the shock of it from Her Majesty in diamonds, caused another howl of pleasure.

'I could have strangled him,' Her Majesty said.

I was thinking: Yes, God the Mother would look something like this – muffin-faced, crinkly, twinkling, small and dumpy, but also diamond-studded, bossy and appreciative and willing to please. She could not control everything – there was such a thing as Free Will. Take her diamonds away and she was Old Auntie Beth. You didn't converse with her and yet she gave good advice.

I said, 'Your Majesty seems to have visited most of the Pacific.'

She did not reply directly, but I had succeeded in prompting her. You didn't converse, you gave her cues.

'I was at one of these Commonwealth prime ministers' conferences in London and I looked at the menu. On the back cover it listed all the Commonwealth countries. I got a pen. I ticked them off.' Using both hands, one holding an imaginary menu, the other gripping an imaginary pen, she flicked with the pen and said, ' "Been there. Been there. Been there. Haven't been there. Been there. Haven't been there. Haven't been there." Went through the whole list. I gave the list to my secretary and said, "I want to go to all the places I haven't been." That's how it happened.'

'It's much the best way to keep up,' a man said.

Her Majesty did not agree, though she did not say so directly. She said, 'There was a very bad hurricane in Samoa.'

'When you were there, Your Majesty?'

'No, yesterday!' she said with force. It was the nearest she had come to being impatient. She added, 'Western Samoa has all the bad luck. Your chaps in American Samoa always miss those terrible storms.'

'I want to go to the Pacific,' I said.

Her Majesty said, 'But you must go.'

I wanted more. A voice in my ear – it was Birdwood – said, 'No one's talking to Prince Philip. Will you go over and talk to him?'

Birdwood introduced me to the tall man who stood aloof, his hands behind his back, and then withdrew. The Duke did not ask me what I was working on. He did not say anything. His smile was that of a man who is not comfortable. Now he was the one looking hemorrhoidal.

'The Queen was just telling us a story about her speech in New Guinea,' I said. The Duke said nothing. 'When it rained,' I said. Still nothing. 'And those hailstones,' I said. ' "Hail to the Queen." So amusing.'

He looked unbelieving. With the deepest skepticism he said, 'Do you really think so?'

'I imagine you were there,' I said.

'Nowhere near it,' he said, in a tone of tetchy surprise.

'But you've been to New Guinea, Your Highness?'

He shrugged and his deliberate snort, using both nostrils, meant, 'Of course.'

'Fascinating place.'

He shrugged again. This was a man who knew how to express boredom. In order to show me how utterly uninterested he was he worked his mouth, savoring, tasted something foul, pulled a face, then made an effort of swallowing.

He said with a show of reluctance, 'First time. I was in a village. Young girls got up to dance. Bare-breasted, of course – all smiles. Splendid. Next time – went back. Same village. And they all had these ridiculous ruffles and silly dresses. Appalling.'

'You didn't approve, Your Highness?'

'It's a hot country!' he said. 'Missionaries covered them up.'

'I'm told Vanuatu is an interesting place.'

'Do you think so?' he said, accusing me.

'I don't know,' I said. 'But apparently there's a group of people in Vanuatu who keep portraits of you in their huts.'

'I don't want to hear about it,' the Duke said.

'It seems they admire you.'

'I don't want to know this,' he said. He was not smiling. Another sound came out of his mouth.

He had a mirthless, barking laugh that seemed intended to threaten me. He continued to stand, looking away from me, and so I never got his gaze but only his profile, that nose that looked like a handle on the front of his face.

'I was thinking of going there, Your Highness.'

'Well, what's stopping you?' he demanded.

'It seems far.'

He said, disbelieving again, 'You think so?'

'Something like ten thousand miles away.'

'Don't be silly,' he muttered, still giving me his profile.

I wanted to twist his nose.

'You think I should go, then?'

'Why in heaven would you want to go all that way?'

His relentless negativity and unhelpfulness baffled me. I could not say anything without his raising an objection in the form of a rude reply or a dismissal.

'Where do you suggest I go, Your Highness?'

'How should I know?'

'I was just asking, sir. I thought you might be a wealth of information.'

'You did, did you?'

He frowned, and more negative noises came out of his nostrils. It was very clear to me why no one had been talking to him and why Birdwood had ushered me over here.

'I've got one of these computers,' he said. 'I generally ask my computer questions like that.'

'Does that work?'

'Of course not. They're useless. Can hardly get the damned thing to work. Better off with a pencil.'

'I've never used a computer.'

'So you don't have the slightest idea, do you?'

I let this pass. I wanted to walk away. I remembered that he was President of the World Wildlife Fund.

'The World Wildlife Fund must take you to some wonderful places.'

'First I've heard of it.'

'You're the President of it, sir.'

'Are you telling me that?'

'Isn't it true?'

'Who told you that?'

Still he was asking questions without looking at me.

'I think I read it somewhere,' I said. 'Weren't you on a tour of Africa? Looking at animals?'

'I haven't the slightest idea.'

'So you're not the President?'

'If you say I am,' he said.

Saying so, he turned away entirely and seemed to signal, sema-phoring with his nose across the room. But Her Majesty no longer stood in the center of a congenial group.

The Duke's height helped him – his signal was seen by Laird Birdwood who approached and began effusively to thank the Duke for coming. The Duke only smiled in that negative disbelieving way of his. I slipped aside and was so eager to get away from that maddening man I stepped into another room, and came face to face with the Queen who was adjusting her dress. She looked up at me, surprised in her plucking, then raised her chin in the postage stamp pose, and seemed to remember me.

'You're in a frightful muddle, aren't you?' she said.

'Yes,' I said, because what use was there in denying it? She obviously knew.

I was afraid, I did not know why, and as she stepped closer to me I felt even more trembly.

'You will get nowhere if you simply moon around, feeling sorry for yourself.' She tilted her head to scowl at me and as she did so her defiant bosom swelled against the stiff gauze of her beaded dress, offering me a wink of cleavage. 'What you want, young man, is purpose.'

'Yes, Mum,' I said, catching my breath. I was afraid that I was on the point of recklessly touching her.

'What is happening to you happens to many people. I ought to know!' she said. 'Don't think you're special just because of your muddle.'

I could not look her in the face and yet I was more afraid, with my eyes on her full bosom.

'You're in books, aren't you?'

'Yes, Mum.'

'Go back to books, then.'

Moving her hand to where mine trembled clawlike near her dress she touched me, no more than that, and something like a bee sting made me involuntarily splay my fingers.

'Yes, Mum.'

The door swung open, the Duke's hand on the knob. He was followed by Lord and Lady Airlie, and behind them the Birdwoods.

'Oh, Lord,' the Duke said.

'I was just saying goodbye,' I said.

'He's in books,' Her Majesty said.

'Good night, Your Majesty,' I said. 'Good night, Your Highness.'

'What earthly good is that?' the Duke demanded. I did not know what to say. He smiled his dreadful smile. 'You're in the way!'

Passing me, the Queen said, 'Don't put it off' – *orf* – 'you must see the Pacific.'

I promised I would. To myself I said: Keep this promise.

'You might never come back,' Her Majesty said.

Then, as though a valve had been twisted in the ceiling, the air pressure in the room began to diminish, finally returning to normal, as side by side the royal couple became a procession of two. Little Mrs God and her tall consort. They seemed a bit foolish and vulnerable walking away, their backs to me. They were very powerful and yet brittle; if you were not gentle with them they might shatter, like antiques. I liked her and felt superior to him.

There were no other goodbyes. The Birdwoods thanked me for coming. I went out and looked for a bus, but the drizzle defeated me again. I hailed a taxi to Earl's Court and Buckingham House, where there were voices in the corridor, every door had a complaint tonight. And inside my room the walls were speaking.

'*But don't you see? It's too late. I don't want you back now,*' from one room.

'*Because you make me sick, that's why,*' from another.

Lying in bed I heard a familiar voice.

'*I don't want it to end this way.*'

'*Oh, shut up. Get out of my life. See how you like it. You'll be sorry.*'

'*I'll manage.*'

Behind the other wall there was a woman on the telephone. I recognized this voice too.

'*You bastard, don't you ever call me again.*'

She hung up. There was a chuckle of laughter – a man. So she had someone with her. She was confident, but I could tell from the rest of the murmurs that she was uneasy with this man.

The walls were soon silent. There was a finality in the silence. I left the next morning, hurrying to the airport. And there remained a warm spot where the Queen had put her hand on my pen-holding fingers. It was the cauterizing pinch of a recent bee sting. It did not hurt yet it was tender. It was also as though she had made my fingers sentient, and given them a memory; as though flesh could not forget.

FIFTEEN

George and Me

I

The Medford shipbuilder Thatcher Magoun (his more famous father and namesake, started the firm) gave the family mansion on Main Street to the town in 1875, two years after his last Medford ship was launched. This magnificent old house, 'with all the expensive bronze gas fixtures, marble statues and vases' (as Magoun described the furnishings in his presentation letter), became the Medford Public Library.

When I was in high school, I did all my homework, all my writing, and most of my reading there. Shelves and stacks had been put up in the mansion, but the rooms were preserved; no remodeling, no walls torn down, no moldings removed; all the grandeur, including the fireplaces, the gas fixtures, the statues, the vases, the paintings, the french windows, the communicating doors, the window seats, the enormous columns and portico in front – it was all kept.

And it can only have been the same Magoun floor, because one of the things I remember best about the library was the sound of the floorboards, a creaking in sudden distinct phrases. A walk from the stacks to your chair – and it was usually a venerable wing chair – uttered a whole tortured statement. My own feet on the creaking floors made me anxious, because the sound of my footsteps seemed out of all proportion to my size, and I feared it called attention to my puny body and my restlessness.

The fireplaces were an agreeable feature. It was not until after I left Medford that I realized that libraries seldom had fireplaces. I had never seen fireplaces this big – they had cavernous hearth-openings, with fire dogs inside, and a mantelpiece, and wood surrounds. There was a fireplace in each room and comfortable armchairs on either side of each one.

I did not know the name Thatcher Magoun – did not hear it until years later; although the family was one of the town's most celebrated, this benefactor's name was unknown to most people in Medford. Yet I felt a sense of comfort in this building, of space and warmth, and a benign silence that went beyond books. I loved my family, I needed their approval, but a large family made jostling inevitable. And so I was happier and more contented there in the library than I had felt at home.

One winter afternoon in 1957 I sat with my friend George Davis at one of those fireplaces under a loudly ticking clock. George used the library for the same reasons I did – big family, busy household, no room. He was also one of my best friends. We were tenth graders at Medford High School. We had been assigned a book report. My book was *The White Tower*, by James Ramsey Ullman – mountain climbing, and danger, and love, and even some sex.

I looked up from my writing. 'What's your book, George?'

He took a long breath, and nodded, and looked into the middle distance, as though remembering.

He said, 'It's about this guy, who goes to Mexico to sell cats, because,' he paused, 'they got mice in the village. And they call him the Cat Man. A woman there, she falls in love with him. She's like a mouse, see, and he's the cat. He cures the village of mice and they get married and, um,' he laughed, 'that's as far as I got.'

'What's the name of it?'

He compressed his face into Don't Know.

'Is this a novel or what?'

'I think I'll call it just *The Cat Man*.'

It seemed bold and dangerous to invent a book, a title, a whole book report. I said, 'Why don't you just read one?'

'What's wrong with my story?'

It was a good story. But this was such a sideways method for doing a book report. I said, 'What if he asks to see the book?'

George had not thought of that. He frowned.

'Here's one you could read.'

The shelf was nearby. The book was *The Scarlet Pimpernel*, by Baroness Orczy.

'You think so?'

Because he had spent so much time inventing his own story he did not have time to read *The Scarlet Pimpernel*. And so he claimed in his book report that it was a fairly boring story. *The Scarlet Pimpernel* was one of the teacher's favorite books. George got a C for his book report. He angrily showed me the mark on his paper. It was all my fault. If I had left him to use his made-up story he would probably have earned an A.

He forgave me – he did not bear grudges. He was a very funny and confident person. Inventing a fascinating story rather than reading a dull one was typical of him. He seemed to get anything he wanted. He thought for himself, often saying unexpected things, and his skepticism made him seem rebellious. He had his own car; few others did. Never mind that his car was a small misshapen vehicle, which George himself had painted purple – he had wheels. This made it possible to go out on a date and, double-dating with George and his girl, not be humiliated by having to take the bus. We went to jazz clubs, we were sixteen and then seventeen, we were served soft drinks while everyone else was drinking alcohol in the smoky room; we listened to Thelonius Monk and Maynard Ferguson and the Four Freshmen.

George and I were on the Medford High soccer team and track team. I was a second stringer, George started and was a brilliant, deft, almost balletic soccer player. Few public schools offered soccer and so we played Andover and Exeter, the exclusive private schools. We envied and hated most of those players – they were privileged, they had money. We figured their parents had gotten them into these schools to save them the embarrassment and challenge of public schools. We played Tufts freshmen and MIT freshmen. They always had foreign students, good at soccer, but even so, with George's great playing, we often won. On the team bus back from one of the Andover matches we recounted with exquisite joy how one Medford player or another had kicked the ball straight into an Andover boy's face, sending him bruised and weeping off the field. But strangely one year, one of the Andover boys had been black. George, curious to see this black boy at such an affluent place, had talked with him.

I ran the 220. I was slow, I never won, I hardly ever placed. In those days, and perhaps now, no time was set aside in any practice to help someone learn a sport or even a skill. If you had it you were on the team, and if you didn't you were merely tolerated. There was no training. The emphasis on winning meant that it was a waste of any coach's time to teach technique to a poor athlete.

George had trained on his own. He wanted to run cross-country, but the coach insisted he was a sprinter and put him into the 220. George had an intensity in his running that I had only ever seen before in someone solving an intellectual problem; it was silence and concentrated thought and total absorption – strange, almost shocking, in someone who was usually so outgoing and relaxed. It was a sort of controlled fury that had made him a superior athlete.

The passage from boyhood to adulthood was made emphatic on the sports field. An average boy who proved himself an athlete became someone to reckon with. George became a man, and was respected by the rest of us. I was a poor athlete – no team wanted me. George gave me advice – 'Turn your foot this way,' 'Lean more,' that sort of thing – but I knew that I was hopeless.

He was the fastest boy in the school, everyone knew that; and one of the happiest, the brightest, the most accomplished. He could sing – sometimes a small group would form in a corridor and I would hear George singing in a falsetto, 'Oh, yeeehh.'

Singing got George into trouble one time. And it was characteristic of George that he could get out of trouble as quickly as he got into it. The singing incident is typical. He was in a corridor with two other students, extemporizing – 'doo wop' was in vogue. A teacher nearby objected and, more than that, spoke crudely to the students, using abusive language. When the teacher tried to grab him, 'This is it,' George said, and hit back. There was a fight and later all three students were brought to the headmaster, Henry Hormel.

Hitting a teacher was grounds for expulsion. But George's case involved the sort of paradox that compelled me to admire him. About a month earlier George had become a local hero by rescuing a boy from drowning. The boy had fallen into a water-filled hole near the excavation for Route 93, the interstate which accounted for Medford's eventual division and decline, and George had happened by and saved the boy. The rescue was an item in the *Medford Mercury* – the boy was the son of a policeman. For his bravery and quick thinking, George was to be awarded a medal. George the brawler was George the hero. Mr Hormel expelled the other boys and allowed George to stay in school.

George joked about his survival. He could be a clown. Studying lenses in physics we learned the meaning of the word 'concave.'

Turning to a huge Italian boy, George said, 'Mess with me, and I will concave your chest.'

George and I took our girlfriends to the prom together. We worked in the library. In spite of our different abilities, we were friends on the teams – the fall soccer, the spring field sports. I lived in North Medford, at the edge of the Fellsway, the woods. George lived near the Mystic River in West Medford, three houses from where my mother had grown up. George and my mother had gone through the same schools, thirty years apart, but the neighborhood had not changed, nor had the schools. That was another link. And my widowed grandmother still lived in George's neighborhood. I stayed with her on Friday nights when I worked late at the Stop and Shop supermarket.

At graduation George looked dapper, as ever, and proud. He was off to a prep school and was confident of winning a full scholarship to the University of Rhode Island. I was pleased to be leaving Medford High, not realizing that I was starting what would prove a two-semester stay at the University of Maine.

After the ceremony my Italian teacher, Miss Pietrangelo, said, 'I saw you and George Davis walking down the steps. You looked like you owned the world.'

That was 1959. In the three long years of high school, we had never discussed or even remarked on the fact that George was black and I was white.

Thirty-two years passed. In that time I did not see George, though I often thought of him. In high school we had done everything together and so it seemed natural to think: Where is George while I am here? I had the feeling that I would run into him – not in Medford, but in the places where I lived or traveled, Uganda, Singapore, Europe, Mexico, South America. I looked for him at our 20th high school reunion. He was not there. I never went to another one. I thought about him a great deal because no one I had grown up with had seemed more alive, more eager for experience.

One day, out of the blue, George wrote me a letter. He said he had read some of my books and that he had thought about me over the years. He suggested we meet. *I've been on a hellified trip,* he wrote. George seldom exaggerated.

2

I called him that same day and I understood that when George said that he had been on a hellified trip he did not mean a recent trip or any single journey. He meant his life since high school, all those years.

Soon after, we met at his house – the old family house on Jerome Street in West Medford, where we had met on high school afternoons and weekends. George was back home. He even looked his old self. Apart from his hair, which was profoundly white, and as dense as a ball of cotton – with a startling whiteness that comes from the shock of experience rather than age – he was exactly as he had been in high school. The same smile, the same weight, the same build, the slightness so deceiving, because he was an athlete, a whip. He had begun running cross-country again, two miles around the Tufts track.

He said, 'I'm training for a masters' in January.'

'You look the same,' I said.

'That's good and that's bad,' he said, and hardly parted his lips to laugh, a heh-heh scraping deep in his throat, the George Davis laugh.

We went up the road and found a spot under the trees on the rocky shore of the Upper Mystic Lake, and talked.

After graduation from Medford High, while I passed a futile year in Orono, Maine, George attended Huntington Prep in Boston. The next year I switched to the University of Massachusetts in Amherst – it was $100 a semester – and George won a full scholarship to the University of Rhode Island, a track scholarship. There were seven black men in the university, hardly enough to form a fraternity. George was rushed by Tau Epsilon Pi and considered joining.

This mainly Jewish fraternity employed two black women who cooked and cleaned the frat house. George was insulted by the way the fraternity brothers treated the older women with casual rudeness, or demeaned them in an off-hand way when their backs were turned. Actively offensive, they seemed oblivious of the fact that George was black – or perhaps they didn't care? George got to know the women. They were sisters whose roots in Providence went back to before the Civil War, when their families had been smuggled north by abolitionists on the underground railroad.

These sisters, unknown to the members of this Jewish fraternity –

who had clearly not inquired – were also members of the Nation of Islam. They were scrupulously clean. They studied the Koran. They observed the Muslim diet. George moved in with them as a lodger and discovered them to be energetic proselytizers. They told him about Elijah Muhammad, they preached him the doctrine that whites cannot offer salvation to blacks; that blacks have to find their own way. George was fascinated, but he was uncomfortable at the university.

One day, as a freshman runner at Rhode Island, George ran past the track coach, who urged him to run faster and – comparing his times with another team mate – said, 'Come on, George, you can run faster than that Jew.'

Afterwards, George began pacing. 'When I get really agitated I walk.' He spent hours pondering the coach's remark. His first thought was, 'If he said that to me, what's he saying to the guy behind me?' The man behind him was white.

'Something in me broke that day – confidence in the school, in the team, in the coach. Field sports are great for having no rah-rah. Everyone's running for himself and interested in what the other guys are doing. There's real spirit in running.' He guessed what was being said behind his back in Rhode Island. And he felt lost in the sea of white students. 'I knew I had to go.'

He quit, went home, back to Medford and applied for jobs through an employment agency. While George sat in front of the desk the middle-aged white clerk made a phone call to a Boston bank.

The man said, 'I have a Negro here.' There was a pause. The employment agency clerk listened and then added, 'He is not hard to look at.'

George got the job, at the First National Bank of Boston, and was the only black person employed there. It was 1962. In his spare time he went to the Boston Public Library – to meet girls; and to jazz clubs. He bought expensive clothes. His job as a credit adjuster was good. Promotions were hinted at. George was clever and personable, and good with numbers. He made plans, one of which was to buy an Austin-Healey 3000, using a bank loan. He saw himself in this very cool car, tooling through Medford, into Boston, with the top down.

In the spring of that year, I helped organize a student protest, picketing in front of the White House. We had a convoy of buses from Amherst to Washington. But although we were aware that civil rights was an issue, the protest was about nuclear disarmament. It was the early anti-war movement, and the next month, back in Amherst, we vandalized a Sherman tank that had been parked in front of the Student Union for the ROTC Military Ball. I alone was arrested, held for six hours and released. It continued to be a great thrill recalling how my group had shouted, *'They got Paul!'*

George had paid no attention to the anti-war pickets. The notion of race had been on his mind, but it puzzled him rather than vexed him. As a bank clerk in Boston in 1962, earning a good salary, 'I couldn't go to some places – certain clubs. They don't let you in. They don't say why.'

'Didn't that make you militant?'

'At that time I wasn't thinking. I didn't give a shit about it. All I wanted to do was go in there.'

He had a girlfriend by now – she was not black. It annoyed him that he could not follow her into the club.

'I came up with the idea of starting school all over, so I contacted my friend who had been to Tuskegee. Tom Poole.'

And he explained that Tom Poole had been the black boy, the only one on the soccer team, at Philips Academy, whom he had chatted with after one of our matches at the school. Unknown to me, they had become friends.

'He was from a respected Tuskegee family. I got hold of him and some other people. It was kind of a rushed thing. I got accepted and went to Tuskegee.'

When George wanted something badly, he always got it.

'My plane landed in Birmingham, I took a taxi to the bus station. It was segregated, and I went into the wrong waiting room. I saw all the white people and says to myself, "This is testing, I'm testing them," but nothing happened. Then I went into the other side, the black waiting room. That side, the black side, was fantastic. It was a party!'

In the black waiting room people were talking and singing and circulating, and they greeted George with warmth. George, from the North, was won over.

'I took the long bus ride to Tuskegee. I arrived in the rain. Going to the cafeteria, I saw a pretty girl walk off the porch with an umbrella. She held it over my head, and walked me all the way. She was smiling. I was smiling. That was a great moment. I said to myself "I belong here."'

In that same month, September 1963, newly graduated from the University of Massachusetts in Amherst, I was being told that as I had been disruptive and discrepancies had been found in my record, I could not join the Peace Corps. In desperation, I wrote a long letter to the selection board and said in effect: Give me a chance and I will be a model Peace Corps Volunteer. When I got word that I was being sent to Central Africa, I wanted to tell George, but he was in Tuskegee, in Alabama. I thought: George is still in school?

George got into the student movement and was immediately an activist. After a demonstration insisting on freedom of speech, he invited Malcolm X to Tuskegee to speak. By the time Malcolm X arrived, George was in jail in Selma with Dr King. 'We called Dr King the Lord: The Lord says we've got to do this or that.' The Tuskegee students brought Malcolm to meet Dr King in Selma. In the jail George and others formed the Tuskegee Institute of Advancement League.

This was 1964 and 1965. This whole time I was in Malawi, Central Africa, teaching English.

George was in Alabama, organizing. 'We went out into the country and helped people with reading and writing and voter registration – we were like infiltrating, right? That was my word for it.'

I lived in a hut in Kanjedza, an African location outside Limbe, and rode my bike uphill to Soche Hill every morning at dawn to teach my students. On school vacations I worked in the bush, and for one long period at Moyo leprosarium near the lakeshore

George, in farmer's overalls, was in the Alabama countryside, 'blending in.' 'We were anti-prominent. We were against suits. Jesse Jackson was a suit. We always thought he was CIA – we never trusted him. We didn't trust suits.'

Tuskegee was still home for him. Built on a hill to protect it from the Klan, it was solitary and safe. George was admitted as a brother in Omega Psi Phi, regarded as the most powerful of the black fraternities in the United States. He was tattooed with the Omega horseshoe. One of the pledge rituals of Omega was learning 'the Pearls' (of wisdom). Unfamiliar with the George Davis smile and the deep-throated heh-heh, and feeling that George did not take the Pearls seriously, one of the fraternity brothers said to him solemnly, 'Some day you will need these Pearls.'

At Omega his nickname was 'Vulture.'

There were more marches, more arrests. George and some others, trying to present a petition to George Wallace, the governor, were arrested in Montgomery for refusing to obey police officers – they had been protesting the beatings of marchers by state troopers. For the next several days they filled the jails. 'That meant Wallace couldn't put Dr King and the marchers in them.' After the jails were filled, Wallace had no choice but to allow Dr King and the marchers, who had been waiting with him after their trek from Selma, to enter Montgomery, where by then George was in a maximum security prison, charged with obstruction.

At that time, late in 1965, I agreed to do a favor for an African friend who had been a member of the Malawi government. I passed a message, I drove his car out of the country. I did not know that it was the intention of his group to assassinate the Prime Minister Dr Hastings Banda. I was found out, and deported from the country, and – after almost two years of bush living – kicked out of the Peace Corps. 'Terminated early,' 'deselected' were the expressions.

Fearful of being drafted to fight in Vietnam, I immediately went back to Africa, as a lecturer in English at Makerere University in Uganda. Makerere was one of the great universities in Africa, and many American blacks paid visits. Several said they had heard of George Davis, but I gathered that George while being very active in the civil rights movement was also very elusive, working behind the scenes, a furious shadow in Alabama.

George said, 'In January 1966, Sammy was killed. That was terrible.'

Sammy Young, a charismatic activist, was shot in Tuskegee by white racists who put a golf club in his hand when he was on the ground dead, claiming he had attacked them with it. When the killers got off in 1967, 'we burned downtown Tuskegee. It wasn't spontaneous, it was carefully planned. We burned down gas stations, we tore down some buildings. Tuskegee was a black town but all the money was made by white folks.'

In Uganda, we had riots and demonstrations – students against Rhodesia, Vietnam and whites generally. I was caught in a demonstration that turned into a riot. I was beaten and my car demolished, a frightening experience. I realized that for most Africans, even ones I knew well, I had no name, no identity. I was a bwana, a white man. That made me feel deeply insecure in Uganda.

George got married in the town hall in Tuskegee in 1967. So did I, in the registry office in Kampala, Uganda. George's wife, Tunie, was the same age as Alison.

By the time George graduated from Tuskegee in 1967, there was a lot of infighting in the movement. All these civil rights years he knew that he had been breaking the law, and was regarded as an outlaw. Prison held no terror for him. He had contempt for the police. He had already been arrested and imprisoned four times in Alabama.

'I got more and more with the renegade crowd,' George said. He and what he called his 'core group' had some reefer with them at the famous SNCC convention in Atlanta where Stokely became chairman. Whites (and 'northern-educated college Negroes' – white-influenced blacks) were disallowed from holding office. 'I had mixed feelings about it, but it made a profound impression on me,' George said. 'I remembered what I had been told by those women from Providence, who were in the Nation of Islam, about the lie that our salvation could come from white people and not ourselves.'

My African students in Uganda had reached a similar conclusion, and the feeling against whites and Indians, any non-Africans, was strong. Like George, I now had a wife and child. I had published my first novel and had finished another and was writing a third. I applied for a job at the University of Singapore. At first there was a problem. A security check was done on me by the Singapore government. They used FBI files, where my record showed that I had been a student activist and had been arrested in Amherst, that I had initially been refused entry to the Peace Corps for these transgressions, and at last had been kicked out for covert political acts that placed the Peace Corps in jeopardy. All this was relayed to me by my brother in Washington, who had been phoned by a friend at the FBI. My brother assured him that I was not dangerous or a security risk, and I got the Singapore job.

The FBI was also watching George Davis. It was years before he was aware of the thickness of his file, but it dated from his first civil rights arrests in 1964. Three years later at the SNCC convention, George was more consciously an outlaw and identified with the renegades – the reefer smokers – not with the suits.

Even in this rebellious mood George decided to go to law school. He applied to a number of schools. 'I was a high black recruit, one of the top recruits in the nation. All the schools accepted me – they all accepted the same blacks.' George won a full scholarship to UCLA, and became UCLA's advisor to the Black Student Movement. 'I got very political. I worked with the Panthers.' And with prominent black athletes, and student leaders. 'I got to practice my smile.' He did no studying. 'I passed one course, I think.'

Then, in 1968, with so much happening, the murders of Dr King and Robert Kennedy, and George hugely successful, 'I went utterly wild. Using his considerable mathematical skills, George worked a scam with credit cards and airline tickets. He soon had a stack of both. He had now also a taste for cocaine and a confidence that there was profit in the drug. 'At the end of the second semester, 1968, I was living in Frank Zappa's house in Laurel Canyon, and I started doing some business. One of our runners from Panama got busted.'

Although George had never been out of the United States, he decided to go to Panama alone and buy as much cocaine as he could afford. He heard fireworks on his arrival at Panama Airport. But no planes were taking off and the streets were empty. It was, he was told, a revolution: Omar Torrijos was taking over.

Very soon he met a Panamanian drug dealer, Little Tito.

'He became my teacher. From him I learned the true art of smuggling.'

'Did you smoke dope in high school?'

'Yup. I had met a fellow from New York at the Newport Jazz Festival my junior year.'

'You were probably the only person in high school doing it.'

'I was the first to do a whole lot of things.'

3

I understood George's divided mind. I shared it. There was placid George, intelligent, rational, cool, orderly and philosophical, considering his options; and there was urgent George, the fastest man in Medford, the dreamer, spinning yarns, trying everything, the risk-taker, the vulture. I was similar, but I had devised a use for all my experience and everything in my mind. At the point where George became imaginative, and restless and active, I shut the door and turned to fiction. George left the house and lived his fantasies.

It was some months before I saw George again, but I had become fascinated by our stories, our parallel lives. We were Medford boys. We were exactly the same age. Our family circumstances were comparable, we had gone to the same high school, and had been close friends. Academically we were about equal; George was my superior as an athlete, and he was socially far more gregarious. We had grown up at the edges of the city, he by the Mystic River, I by the woods of the Middlesex Fells. Our earliest memories, we agreed, had been the same – to leave Medford, to experience the world, to take risks.

I picked up George in Medford and we drove to Boston, to find a place to talk.

'Take a left here,' he said.

'That's not the way, George.'

'Listen to me. That is a freakin' short cut!'

And it was. George knew every back street, every connecting road. I had grown up here and had never gone this way to Boston, through Somerville, down these side streets. It amazed me that he had his own map of the city, and when I told him, he said that he had always used these back roads to Boston. Coming home from downtown late at night, or after a football game in Somerville or Malden, he had to stay off the beaten track where uproarious white youths might confront him and challenge him to fight. In his mind he had a black map of the city, full of safe zones.

Driving down these streets, I turned on the radio, having forgotten that my son's tape was in the tape machine. It was 'The Chronic' that blared from the speakers, a Dr Dre and Snoop Doggy-Dogg rap tape about a 'nigger' with a 'mother fuckin'' gun.

'Heh-heh.'

But he made a face.

'That's not my thing,' George said. 'I still like Coltrane and Miles and Monk.'

He was doing his master's degree in drug counseling, and being counseled himself in Boston. Still living at home in an almost monastic way – studying, exercising, avoiding risky friends. And confined, and solitary, he began to write. Sometimes he wrote about his past, vivid stories, one about a gun fight, one about a robbery. A long story about two friends whose lives are interlinked he called 'Tight Partners.' The stories gave some coherence to his past, but there was so much incident in his life that these few episodes did not help much. Looking back, everything was chaos. He had trouble connecting one incident with another, one place to the next. He lost his wife, he found her again, he changed countries, he got money or drugs, and often he lost the money or flushed the drugs down the toilet. He smuggled; sometimes he got caught, more often he succeeded.

'After a while smuggling became a high. It became a tremendous rush. It wasn't the money or the coke – it was beating them, being able to think on my feet.'

George smuggled the coke by filling condoms and inserting them in cans of talcum powder. In the tropics everyone used talcum and deodorant. Everyone carried it. George doctored his containers – replacing the tops and bottoms.

'I remember one time I had some material in some deodorant and the agent had it open and was about to stick his finger in. Golden rule – you never break rhythm. So I continued my conversation and I said, "By the way, where can I get my money changed?" He thought for a moment and used that same finger to point and give me directions. Then he gave me a "Now what was I doing?" expression, and looked at the deodorant, and screwed the top back on. Now that was a rush.'

To learn the drug business properly, George worked part time in a cutting house in Los Angeles owned and operated by infamous drug dealers, the Huggins family from New Orleans. There was not much money in it for him, but it was an important apprenticeship.

'Processing cocaine is very involved,' George said. It is first pasta or paste, from the leaves. That is made into base, commonly known. Base is then crystallized into a rock form that you might term early rock. That can be reprocessed one more time into flake. If all the hydrochloric acid is removed it becomes crystal or pharmaceutical cocaine.

The rock, which might range from a bundle of lumps to a solid kilo, is chopped small with knives, and chopped again. This is then sifted through nylon stockings. The resulting powder is blended evenly – this is then cut with milk sugar to increase the amount of salable coke.

If it is strong pure coke it is cut continuously, always with reference to a 'pig' who tests it by shooting the provisional cut and commenting on the high he gets from it. The profit derives from the strength of it – for the distance it can be stretched and still retain its strength and the thoroughness with which it is mixed. Finding the perfect homogenous blend requires experience and fine tuning, because no cocaine is exactly the same in purity or composition.

George was at this for months, starting as a chopper – carefully hacking the sometimes two-pound rocks, and progressing to a blender, a more demanding skill. He also helped sell the drug. Each person in this operation had his own customers. George and his colleagues were the exclusive suppliers to high-profile people – 'beautiful people,' George said. Basketball players, entertainers, singers, celebrities.

'Is it possible to be a serious basketball player and have a coke habit?' I asked.

'It wasn't a habit with them. They were very serious about their thing, and they were also very serious about their party time. But no angel dust, no acid. They would snort cocaine and smoke reefer, but they wouldn't fire.'

Wouldn't inject it.

One day in LA he and Gene, a Tuskegee friend from the civil rights years, had a pound of coke to sell.

'Gene and I were playing gangsters. I even had a little gun. We had a deal and got a hotel room to meet the buyers. One of the buyers said he didn't want it and they left. Later on that night there was a knock at Gene's door. We had adjoining rooms.

' "Police," I heard and shut the door to the room where the cocaine was. There were three men – black. One, the gorilla, had red eyes. I'll never forget that. They threw us to the floor and because we didn't move fast enough, they smacked us on the head with the pistols. They tied our hands and feet, put pillow cases over our heads. "Get on your knees. Where's the cocaine?" "What cocaine?" All that. One of them said, "I'm going to make this real simple. The one that's alive is going to tell me where it is." '

I was in Singapore, writing, teaching, living on the margin. I earned a salary that was low even by Singapore standards – fifty American dollars a week. We were in debt. We had two children now, and lived in a tiny house that stank of bus fumes and the monsoon drain that ran by the front door. I had finished my fourth novel, *Jungle Lovers*, and was working on *Saint Jack*. Now and then my short stories were published in *Playboy*. George saw my name in the magazine and read them. *I went to high school with this dude. Heh-heh.*

'Why didn't you get into the drug thing, Paul?'

'I did get into the drug thing. But it didn't last.' And I explained.

Now and then I smoked ganja, buying it from a Chinese waiter at the Staff Club or a Malay in a bar on Arab Street. One Saturday in Singapore I bought a joint from the Malay and went home and smoked it. I had the sense that my arms and legs had inflated, that my brain was blazing, my eyeballs boiling in their sockets. Out of control, I clawed my clothes off and rolled on the floor, gasping with pleasure, feeling airborne, and at times twisting in a horrific frenzy of vertigo. The joint was not ganja. It was my first experience of smoking heroin, and it was the last drug I took.

George, at that time, 'took a fall in Atlanta. My first big bust. I was still new at the business. It was during the Muhammad Ali fight, all the gangsters and players were in town.'

He was at the house of a man the police had under surveillance. And the drug deal that afternoon, the day of the fight, was going slowly – the customers were doubtful, and they stalled. The police moved in, and they found George, who had agreed to carry his friend's wallet. There were drugs in the wallet.

'I was in jail in Atlanta for a month, and then out on bail.'

While on bail, preparing his case, George wrote a letter to a university up north. It was another inspired George Davis strategy. When he was truly desperate he became ingenious, fluent, even eloquent.

'I wrote them about what the problem is with going to graduate school today. Universities are basically hostile environments' – few or no blacks at these institutions – 'yet they invited blacks to come. I said I wanted to attend, but the only way I could do it was if Gene and his wife came. I got a scholarship, the Martin Luther King scholarship. I was made a teaching fellow. "Negro history." I changed it to Black history – American Domestic Policy.'

'What about your drug bust in Atlanta? Wasn't that on your mind?'

'I won the case. And things were all right. But then I do the flip side. I get in trouble up there. I did something horrible. I don't want to tell you.'

'I need to know, George.'

'Heh-heh. You got all the questions,' George said. 'I cut a dude with a buck knife. He was calling me names. It was bad.'

'Did he die?'

'No, no. But it was trouble, and I had to leave. That was the end of American Domestic Policy.' George's alternative to teaching history was to return to his other passion – smuggling cocaine. 'I got back into business again. And then Tito took a fall in Panama. So I started looking for new sources for the product.'

'Different dealers?'

'Different countries. I went to Harvard, to the Peabody Museum. That place has some of the world's greatest work on cocaine. And I got the major book on the subject, *Peru: History of Coca, the Divine Plant of the Incas*, by W. Golden Mortimer, MD, 1901.'

That was the George I recognized from high school, from the Magoun mansion of the Medford Public Library, pacing the stacks, rifling the shelves, and ending up with the unlikeliest books.

'I did a lot of reading. I found out there are coca plants that grow in Ghana – wherever there's coffee, and if you've got 9,000 feet, you've got coca. There's four areas of the world where we get the species that produces what we want. An area crossing South America, an area in Africa, an area in the Golden Triangle, and an area in Indonesia – in Java. There are about 100 different varieties of the plant. The one that produces the most echocaine is in Africa. So I went to Ghana and the Ivory Coast.'

It was August 1969. 'I was hanging out with Africans, thinking of giving up cocaine, thinking about staying. I had never been around so many black people that walked the street. You know, like they don't have to stoop.'

But he had a wife and child and responsibilities. This trip had cost a lot, and he had not found any cocaine. So ('in order to salvage the trip') in his search for product, he went back to the States and left almost immediately for Peru. He brought back a package, which he sold at a profit. And then he set his sights on Ecuador.

'How did you find out about Ecuador?'

'Gene had read a *National Geographic*, and from my research at the Peabody Museum.'

'Was this drug thing profitable?'

'Oh, yeah.'

'I was getting fifty bucks a week at the University of Singapore.'

All went well with George until, in 1970, on one trip, his plane made an unscheduled landing in St Croix, which entailed George unexpectedly having to pass through St Croix Customs and Immigration. He had pioneered a route from Ecuador through Venezuela and Trinidad to Canada. The key was that you had to lose your passport and get rid of your ticket in Trinidad, and get a new ticket and use your driver's license as an ID – all of this to obscure the fact that you had ever been in South America.

Life has no apparent plot, and so it seems messier than fiction, but if you have the stomach for it, this raw ingredient of art in its pure form is dense and fascinating, as different (to use the cocaine image that George had given me) as the rock is to the crystal. So many things happen in a person's life without warning, contradictory, seemingly unrelated and without a pattern; and so without discernible unity it seems as though in all these incidents a single person is leading separate lives. In one long life, so many people, so many other lives. Yet because they happen to that one person, a pattern is established, so large and elaborate that it cannot be read from the little we are able to see. Who can tell from a few hundred yards of road that this is a highway that goes from coast to coast? There is, in any long life of a person, the logic and harmony that is crystallized in fiction.

An old black woman ahead of him in the Customs and Immigration line at St Croix Airport was confused. Like George, she had not expected to be here, and she was disoriented, slow with her responses when the St Croix official demanded explanations. And then the man began to intimidate the woman with his repeated questions. The old woman, frightened into silence, roused the man's fury. 'He was a cracker, a southern dude. It was white against black, young against old, and he didn't understand about the plane.'

'I'm tired of you people trying to sneak in,' the immigration official said to this woman whose trip to Montreal had been interrupted.

George stepped forward. He said, 'Mister, have you got a grandmother?'

The man eyed him.

'Well, how would you like her to be treated the way you are treating this woman?'

The man said sharply, 'Get over there, mister wise guy.'

For his supposed insolence, George was interrogated and then searched. 'They were just elated.'

They found three ounces of cocaine in a can of talcum. 'We got your black ass now.'

For this offense, George spent three months in the fort – 'an historic place, where they had put slaves' – in St Croix.

After another arrest, this time in San Francisco, George decided that he might be safer if he relocated to Ecuador. And so he went to Quito and fell in love with the place – the Sun Festival, Viva Quito was in full swing – and also fell in love with an Ecuadorian woman from a prominent family. Her parents approved of George, whom they took to be an American businessman.

'I had moved up. No more smuggling. I became a packaging expert. I brought in sealing machines.'

And throughout the year 1971 he stayed put in Quito, packaging and sending cocaine out of Ecuador. He had a car and a house; expatriate life had its nuisances but it was safe.

In November 1971 I quit my job in Singapore and went to England. I lived in Dorset, in a cottage, paying five pounds a week rent, less than ten dollars. I had not saved much from my Singapore job but even the little I had would allow me to live there for a long time. That was what I needed: security, monotony, life in the bosom of my family. After nine years in the tropics I was in retreat from experience.

I asked George what he was doing that month and year.

'Living large,' he said.

4

On those summer weekdays in Medford and Boston that George and I talked, catching up, I sometimes saw people glance at us and look away with a kind of sour disapproval, muttering the way they do when they are baffled by the threat of unfamiliar men who don't seem to fit into the foreground.

We were two older fellows, one black, one white, sharing a park bench in the middle of a working day, laughing too loud, and not dressed particularly well. Probably out of work, or procrastinating, looking reckless and marginal. What probably roused the fury of many passersby was our undefinable air of conspiracy and, worst of all, an obvious disregard, like those motionless and apparently unemployed figures in a landscape who seem as though they have not earned the right to be so idle.

Sensing this scrutiny from car passengers and pedestrians, George said, 'Watch this,' and smiled at the strangers, giving them his irresistible George Davis smile. He never failed to provoke a smile in return.

What the strangers saw was partly true. We were men in suspension, performing hard-to-describe jobs, keeping odd hours – high school buddies thirty-four years after graduation, grizzled but still fit, the runner and the rower, crowding the bench by the Mystic River, or near the Admiral Morison statue on Commonwealth Avenue, single again, back home.

All the pain, and the pleasure, all the difficulty of living, were in the past, with the risks, the compromises, the friendships, the failures. Now our lives were just talk. And it was random. We would launch on a theme – drugs, civil rights, school – and end up talking about our ex-wives, or injuries, or children, or music, or baseball.

'Back home' said it all. George was living at his parents' house on 148 Jerome Street; I was alone on the Cape. My wife and I had split up – I accepted it now; George and Tunie had done the same. George was not working, I was not writing. But no matter what had happened in all the eventful intervening years, still we had started off together, white boy, black boy. Now we were back where we had started, living outside Boston, not needing to be hopeful, because although no miracle would happen to us, the danger was in the past, with the sorrow, the risk, the great anger that comes from impatience and ambition. What we felt was not resignation but a kind of enlightenment, even wisdom. No bitterness, only mercy and gratitude for being still alive. As George said: Smile back at them.

Being here on the bench, whole and healthy, was a kind of victory. The place itself was important. The bench might have seemed to those passersby like a featureless prop on a bleak stage. But this was home for us. No one could question our right to be here, nor send us away. We had survived to tell the tale.

Somehow we had arrived back at the same place, in the same mood. George had not changed; he was as kind, as generous as ever;

as watchful and alert, as funny, and still the athlete, still fast. But George's suffering had been far worse than mine.

'I don't know how I didn't die,' he said.

I invited him to the Cape. He brought the new woman in his life, and her two children. 'Yup,' George said, looking around, and he walked across the grass. 'Yup,' he said again, nodding and sizing up my house. He was pacing again, not agitated but reflecting. 'This is cool. This is a long way from Mess Dedford.'

We were soon back on our benches, in Boston, in Medford, under the leafy maples, and sun-heated and resinous pitch pines, talking. How far had we got? I wondered. Oh, yes, George living large in Ecuador, a house in Quito, someone to be reckoned with in Esmeraldas.

One day at his house in Quito, at the beginning of 1972, George was making a package to send to some friends in the States. 'And I just felt it – you know how you just get the feeling?'

He went outside the house and saw two plain-clothesmen asking for Señor Davis at the next house. He walked off and as soon as he turned the corner he ran – the fastest man at Medford High was sprinting through Quito. He was seen, and stopped by police, and he realized that he had been turned in by one of his runners who had been caught and beaten.

'Where's the cocaine?' the police asked George.

At first he stalled, to give another runner time to leave the house, but the police were suspicious and impatient. He was arrested, not formally, just taken to the basement of the police station. There were five men on him, trying to get him to talk about drugs.

'They kept me awake all night. They hauled me up, and they stretched me, pulling my arms and legs apart – pulling hard.'

One of the men held a bayonet to his face. Three other men were still pulling on his arms and legs, stretching him. Later, as a result of this Ecuadorian version of the rack, George developed a hernia and underwent a serious operation.

'Which eye do you want?' the man with the bayonet said. 'Left or right?'

And when George remained silent the man made the motions of beginning to cut his left eye from the socket.

I said, 'At this point weren't you terrified?'

'I was numb. Everything in me closed down. My mind was gone,' he said. 'And somehow I know that they're threatening me but what they really want is money.'

And giving him confidence was the knowledge that at this point the men had found no drugs at all.

'I took the beef,' George said. 'And that stopped the case.'

While everyone he had ever known or associated with in Quito was arrested (taxi drivers, hotel managers, and 'all my field associates'), George was put into a prison in Quito, a dungeon. 'It was horrible, a hole, rats crawling over me – terror, terror. And after three days they took me down to Guayaquil, to put together a major case.'

The more people involved in the case the greater the likelihood for bribes.

George was taken to Penitentiary Littoral, first in isolation in Guayaquil, while his case was being prepared; and then in what they called *casal*, with the general population, in a large prison hall, an enormous open cell, the size of two basketball courts, with at times as many as three hundred men. Each man had marked out his own space on the floor – some had put a sheet or curtain around – which was not much larger than his sleeping area. They were locked up all day.

This was January 1972. I was still living with my wife and children in a cottage in West Dorset, outside a tiny village of xenophobic and underpaid farm laborers. They wanted to know when I was leaving. I told them I could not leave until I finished my book.

Guayaquil, on the coast, by the muddy Guayas River, is one of the hottest and most humid places in Ecuador. I passed through Guayaquil in the late Seventies and in my room in the best hotel there were rats. Their squalling inside the dropped ceiling was so loud it kept me awake. It was a city of rats. They were fearless, like a protected species, and always underfoot.

'Oh, yeah we had them,' George said. But rats were the least of his worries in the prison. 'Anything you get is what you fight for. And the prisoners – some of them – were messing with me. Trying to intimidate me, threatening me, throwing scorpions at me.

'I was rich. I had clothes. They thought I had money. They wanted me to get them reefer or give them money. Give them clothes, give them shoes. When the guards left they jammed my food slot from the outside so that I couldn't open it.

'And then I'm caught smoking reefer. The guard had supplied it. And I'm caught. The other guards threatened to torture me, to find out where I got it. A crew of reefer smokers showed up at my cell, and one guy gave me a razor blade. He told me to cut myself – deep cuts in my stomach and arms, so I'll bleed. If I do that the prison guards won't hang me up by my thumbs and beat me, or I will bleed to death. But I didn't slash myself. I bribed my way out of it with a fifty-sucre note.'

George signed a confession and soon after was admitted to the prison clinic for his hernia operation. The hernia was a result of the stretching and pulling that first night when the guards tortured him to get information. The doctor told him that if he paid enough money he could buy his way out. But the sum was more than George had – and in that first year, everyone was hitting George for money.

After the operation George was assigned to Pavilion C and there began another year of Ecuadorian prison life. By now his money was diminished. Instead of giving other prisoners food, he was himself begging. The prisoners who had been rapacious when George had been new and flush, proved unexpectedly sympathetic when he was needy.

George joined the volleyball team and, as always, a fast learner, developed his skill to the point where he led his cell block to the prison volleyball championships.

Still, everything was available somehow to the prisoners, food, alcohol, reefer, 'red devils' (a type of Seconal); but it all cost money. As a star volleyball player George was allowed the occasional phone call home. He had the respect of the other prisoners as well as the prison administrators. Now George had become a habituated inmate. 'I've got a new walk – I'm a prisoner, I'm a person and I'm not a gringo. I'm an old-timer. '

And on Tuesdays there was 'visita intima' when girlfriends or wives came. Whores were provided for the single inmates.

'What did they look like?'

'That was the problem. They were old, they were fat. They were the ones that couldn't make it out on the street. Pavilion C was a poor cell block so we only had one whore. B and A were a little more upscale. On Tuesdays they had lots of whores and music and dancing. The best block was *Pabellón Político*, where the political prisoners were kept. The former mayor of Guayaquil was in there –

the governor of the province used to visit him to pay his respects to Don Jaime.'

An incident on New Year's Eve almost resulted in George's death. George met Indiano, a psychopath, on the stairs. Indiano had already killed three men in prison with a sharpened bicycle spoke. He moved aside to give him room, and the insane man rose up and thrust at him with his hand, gesturing *I can kill you*. George went backwards over the side of the stairs and fell eight feet but somehow managed to land without breaking any bones.

'But I was so shaken up I asked the guard if I could see Dr Castello, the former mayor of Guayaquil. He was a big shot drug man – he did 100 or 200 keys at a time. I told him what happened. And that night I moved to *Pabellón Político*.'

That was the third stage of George's prison life. From fighting for his existence in the mob of inmates, to excelling at volleyball and making his way in the cell block, he had now arrived at the most exclusive area of the prison, where the prisoners were men who had influence on the outside and still had rights and privileges and a sense of power. This gave George hope, not of being released and going home, but of having status and a future in the prison, of 'being a pure prisoner.'

Although George had written many letters to the consul in Guayaquil, nothing had come of them, yet the consular officials visited other Americans. Once George noticed an American man visiting Frankie Diaz, who had worked for the mafioso Joseph ('Crazy Joe') Gallo. This man from the consulate kept looking over at him, and in spite of his pale skin George said to himself: He's black. 'I just knew it. It was from having lived in the South and knowing about black people who pass.'

The man, who was the vice-consul, came up to George and said a secret word that is known to all brothers in Omega Psi Phi, an affirmation of friendship and brotherhood. In his letters to the consulate George had said that he had been chosen Omega Psi Phi Man of the Year. The vice-consul had obviously seen the letters. His name was Wyatt T. Johnson and he had been an Omega at Lincoln University. The motto of Omega is, 'We are Omega Psi Phi until the day we die.'

'How many friends have you got?' Johnson asked.

George, recognizing the secret formula from Omega, one of the

Pearls of Wisdom, gave the correct answer, and showed his Omega tattoo. And he whispered, 'I'm going to shake your Pearls,' meaning that he was asking the man to do him a favor.

Johnson began visiting, he brought George food that his wife had cooked, and the two Omegas sang fraternity songs and talked, and became friends. When this trust was established, George explained the favor he needed.

No case had ever been made against George. He had never been formally charged with any crime, no drugs had been found; there had been no trial, only the interrogation and torture; all that was on file was a signed confession that had been forced on him the night he was stretched. He had not been sentenced. He had made one attempt to escape by offering a guard a drink spiked with Seconal. But the guard had urged George to join him, and that was George's undoing; in the morning both George and the guard were found asleep.

There was a judge who had the power to release George. Earlier in the year George had sent some money to this judge, but instead of passing it on, the judge's secretary had stolen it. George asked Wyatt T. Johnson to be present when George gave the judge's money to the secretary. George knew that no underling would dare to steal money that an American official had witnessed being handed over. Johnson agreed and the money changed hands.

'The secretary don't want to jam him because he has to go to him to get his visa to the United States,' George said. 'The doors opened up, and they sang, I'm telling you. The brothers in the penitentiary sang that day. Oh, it was one of the most beautiful days, you know, and the doors flew open.'

This was November 1974. In the period that George had been in prison I conceived the idea of taking a trip deliberately to write a travel book, and wrote it. Soon after George was arrested, I set out on a series of linked railway journeys from London to Tokyo and back. I had returned to London in a state of shock; nothing after that was ever the same in my marriage. I had gone too far, I had been away too long. By the time he was released, I had finished *The Great Railway Bazaar*.

'I was not supposed to leave the country until my release was confirmed,' George said. 'That meant somebody else wanted money. So I sneaked to the bus station and slipped out of Guayaquil, and went to Quito, and took a bus to the border, Tulcán. Took a taxi across, like I'm visiting for the day. And off I went.'

By January 1975, George was back in Medford, after two years in an Ecuadorian jail and more travel. Apart from his wife, Tunie, with whom he was now reconciled, he told no one about the prison, only that he had been away. He got a job first as a substitute teacher, and then – never more effective than when writing a letter – writing proposals for grants on behalf of the Alma Lewis School of Fine Arts in Boston. Soon he was promoted to head accountant.

Jimmy Carter, in his presidential campaign, visited the school and spoke to George in September 1979. Discovering that George had been to Tuskegee, they talked about peanut farming. And in the foyer afterwards, just to make a point, 'I stabbed him.' That was the way he thought of it. Carter walked by him, and to prove that the secret service were inattentive, George reached out and touched him. If George's finger had been a knife, Carter would have been a dead man.

It was around this time that George began reading my books. He read *The Black House*, which had been published in 1974. He read *The Great Railway Bazaar*. He thought of getting in touch. He had stories. He wanted to tell me one especially from prison, about the black prisoner they called Cabeza Radio – Radio Head – because of his huge head – how after one Tuesday and the *visita íntima*, he had walked out of the prison dressed as a woman, in clothes that had been smuggled in by a whore. And he had been caught and killed, and then his corpse, his dress soaked with blood, was brought back in a jeep and parked in a place where prisoners would see it and be suitably warned.

George inquired and found out that I was in London. George was wishing for a friend. 'Because one day I came home for lunch and the removal van was there. She took the cat and the dog and everything. Goodbye, Tunie.'

Now he was alone again.

'I decided to do my masters'.' He went to Atlanta, scene of so many Sixties dramas – civil rights struggles, the SNCC convention, his drug bust. But now Atlanta represented law school; this time George lasted into his second year.

Dropping out was not the disaster it had been ten years earlier in Los Angeles. He was older, tempered by two years in an Ecuadorian prison; he had learned patience. How many times had his world turned upside down? A friend recommended him to the head dermatologist in a research unit at Morehouse. 'George can learn anything,' the friend said. George was hired and ended up running a lab, setting up experiments and recording them. His boss was Dr Louis Sullivan, now Surgeon General. George's research was testing sunscreens on white mice.

This job lasted into 1984. George had joined the Atlanta Track Club and was running again.

'And I started chipping a little bit' – for a reason he cannot fathom George began snorting cocaine. 'Maybe I did it for the reason I did most things – that I feel I can do anything. I don't ask why. I don't realize that if I am not careful I will screw up real bad and sabotage my own shit.'

The first sign of self-sabotage was that he started losing animals. He got sloppy. George would go to sleep in the lab, while the mice were being radiated, and he would end up cooking them. He could not explain all those dead mice. And so he was fired.

Feeling lost, he was drawn back to Tuskegee. He had strong memories of the place, of the civil rights struggle, of the singing and the friendships. He had considered it a place he could always return to. So he loaded a van and drove there, became a counselor, a dorm director and faculty member. He began running again.

Visiting Medford in the summer of 1987, George decided to stay. And that had its consequences. 'I got back into the business, handling big weight' – kilos of cocaine. It had been years since he had been in the drug business, and it seemed so simple now. He was making money again. He worked in a straight job and used it as a cover for selling drugs and within a year he had resumed snorting cocaine.

'Dope cocaine took me,' he said. 'I've had it good, but I get weak. And then I end up sabotaging my own shit.'

George was now using so heavily it made him physically ill, or at least seemed to. He decided to go to a detox center, but the problem with his health was not related to his use of drugs. He gave up drugs, he was clean, but he still felt ill. He was diagnosed as having tuberculosis – the result of the prison years in Ecuador. When he was released from the hospital in 1991, he wrote me the letter, saying, *It's been a hellified trip.*

I was inexpressibly grateful to George for his company and his good mood. At the end of a twenty-year marriage it was hard for me to be alone all the time. A door had slammed; then silence. Only another estranged man can understand that exile. Families don't know what to say, and their eagerness to reassure with platitudes is the coldest comfort. No emptiness on earth can compare with the loss of love – and, after all that struggle and expense, the shameful hardship of being alone. Nothing mitigated my sense of misery, and when people – family members mostly – said, 'It's for the best,' I knew I had failed. George was monkish, resigned, unassailable, and still funny. It was a good thing that I had met him now. We were both alone – we offered each other sympathy, not advice. We took turns listening. No one else understood. Our talks were friendly and affirmative.

He was now completely clean and sober, studying for his doctorate, running every day, working part time in Boston, still seeing a counselor, living quietly, reading voraciously. And after a long period of sadness and brain ache I had begun to write again. I had something to write.

'You took risks,' I said, the last time I saw him. 'And yet you seem the same person you always were.'

'You told me that before,' George said. 'But, like I said, that's good and bad. You've got to move. I wasn't caring about money. It was about being in the world. And the story isn't over. We're not at the end. Me, I'm not laying down. I'm putting some order in my life – enjoying whatever this thing is. I know I'm going to move on to something pretty soon.'

'I've got the same feeling,' I said.

'Yeah. Some people are meant to do things – not watch or write, but do things. This is what we do. A lot of people live through us.'

He was thinking hard.

At last he said, 'I'm a vehicle.'

SIXTEEN

My Other Wife

I

Just after my miserable drifting period, I received a postcard at my house on the Cape saying, *I found this picture of our old stomping ground. I think of you often. My life has changed quite a bit. I imagine yours is as serene as ever*. And at the bottom, the initial W.

W stood for Wanda Fagan.

'*I hate my name,*' she had said. '*Probably because I hate my father.*'

'*Use your mother's,*' I said.

'*That's worse,*' she said. '*Feskowitz. And I hate her too.*'

Another woman – not The Other Woman. If I had told her story earlier it would have seemed like the reason Alison and I split up. But I did not want to exaggerate its importance. A single instance of infidelity was not the reason. Marriages end when love and hope are gone; a period of obsession and fantasy is not the end of love.

It was not a long story. I was needy, I was unfaithful, I was found out; there was a spell of upheaval – anger, misunderstanding, tears. It ended and life went on, our marriage continued, and I was inexpressibly grateful. I looked at Alison and thought: *How could I have ever thought of leaving you?* and sometimes I said this to her.

'Maybe you would have been happier if you had left,' she said.

'No, no,' I said, and I meant it.

I was allowed back home, I never speculated on what life might have been like with Wanda Fagan. I told myself that we had had our love affair – and didn't it have the odd mimicry of a marriage, the same shape, except shallower and shorter? Somehow, Alison forgave me. She had always said, 'These things don't matter. What matters is where you are in the end. I feel you do love me. But don't push me too far.'

Years later, when Alison and I were apart, instead of all the vivid

411

memories of marriage it seemed strange to me that my mind went back to its satisfying monotonies, returned again and again to revisit its most prosaic routines. I was moved more by remembering shopping trips to the supermarket than the weekends in Paris. It was something about sharing the burden, solving the problems, performing tasks together – painting shelves, or wallpapering, or putting down a carpet, cleaning the attic. Not any particular voyage but rather our bobbing at our mooring.

The memories of the long hours we had spent this way moved me most because they ought to have been a kind of hardship, and yet I treasured them because they were precious in their difficulty. Taking pleasure in them was the evidence of love. The home we had made like two busy birds, taking scraps of dead grass and bits of old string and turning this into the rough symmetry of an unshakable nest. All the time we had spent in this apparently unromantic work amounted over the long term to devotion, almost to passion.

In the course of our break-up I never thought of calling Wanda Fagan and saying 'Let's get together' – or rather, I thought of it but immediately rejected it as unwise. The broken marriage was on my mind. I felt awful. I knew that Wanda Fagan was ill-equipped to share my misery. Long before, her attitude to Alison had put me off her. She had called me at home, she had threatened suicide, she and Alison had had several acrimonious conversations. And the whole terrible mess was all my fault. On one of the worst times, at a family dinner – Alison carving a turkey, the boys serving hors d'oeuvres, everyone merry and bright, so festive, it must have been Christmas or Thanksgiving – the phone rang.

'It's for you, Paul.'

I said, 'Hello?'

And a woeful voice said, 'I'm coming apart.'

'I'll have to get back to you –'

'Don't hang up!'

'Thanks very much.'

'Don't do this to me!'

'Listen, we're just sitting down to eat.'

'What about me? I can't take this. I'm losing my mind. Didn't you hear what I said? I'm coming apart!'

Somehow, I managed to end the call without revealing my fear, and I sat in terror the rest of the day, expecting another call. No love affair can survive threats and pleas of that kind. Humiliation kills desire by scorching the heart, and a call like that made us both ashamed and afraid. On another day she shrieked into the phone, *'I can't deal with this!'* and it bothered me and made me cross because I imagined that she had heard someone else say it just that way.

Anyone with sense who has been through this once never ventures upon it again, or if they do, deserves to be destroyed. I had learned how close I had come to losing my life.

Unhappy, sniffing and blinking like a bunny, she would say things like, 'I hated my body when I was growing up,' or 'I had to come to terms with my sexuality.'

'How are you?' I would ask at the beginning of one of our many lengthy phone calls.

'If you had asked me that question this morning I would have said, "Fine,"' she said. 'This afternoon I was very low.' There would be a pause, and then a doom-laden, 'Now, I don't know whether I can handle it.'

And of course there was more. I should have guessed, when I noticed that our phone calls always lasted one full hour, that she was used to talking, usually in a monologue, to her psychiatrist.

She hated her name more than I could understand. 'A name is just a name,' I told her. I mentioned some of the names in the news, Walter Tkach, Ed Custard, Robert Abplanalp, Murray McAdoo, Sherman Pinsker, Lech Walesa, Lawrence Eagleburger. I said, 'Fagan's probably Irish.'

'I don't want to talk about it.'

But all she did was talk. This was some months after the phantom offer of a part in a movie. I understood the meaning of illusions and the importance of my work to my sanity.

As time passed I wondered what had become of Wanda Fagan. Strangely, when Alison and I split up, I stopped wondering – didn't dare to. Being single made me feel vulnerable. I felt weak. Perhaps some desire still remained but it was a haggard and desperate fugitive, a nocturnal creature – why stir it and rouse it and drag it into the daylight to show all its nervous yearnings? Better to let it slumber and dream and drool – let it die in its sleep.

Alive, it was lust like a pile of greasy rags which, left in the darkness to stink, begin to heat as though from the growing density of their very gases and smells, and without warning burst into an orange flame, throwing off soot. As an affair with a beginning, a middle and end, it may have been like a marriage, but a bad marriage. Ours was. Perhaps less bitter than most bad marriages – perhaps longer than many marriages. She knew that, too: in graduate school she had been briefly married to a man named Harry Cole, a graduate student. I heard about his beard, his old car, his debts. I had a Philip Glass tape in my car. 'Harry liked him, too,' she said. I knew little else. His mounting debts ended the marriage.

Of the great deal I learned from our affair, the most worrying was how easy it is to underestimate a lover's ambition. For me it was an indulgence in fantasy. I was hardly aware of time passing. But Wanda Fagan – like most other women, perhaps – thought constantly about her age. Such women's frequent reference to aging, to their looks, to the passage of time is an unsettling challenge, as distracting as the tick of a loud clock with a wagging pendulum. Not long after I met her she was talking about our old age. She saw us retired, two oldies holding hands, rocking on the porch. She was looking for another life.

She was disgusted and maddened by her own life – saw it as negligible – hated her name, disliked her body, had no money. In her terms she did not exist. Her attaching her half-life to mine would, she felt, totally redeem her.

'It's not your writing – you're much more than that,' she said.

She was mistaken. But I could not interrupt. She was still talking.

'I love who you are – you're a good man,' she said. 'You're rational and generous and compassionate.'

Wrong again, Wanda. Why would a person with those qualities, so complete and good and loved, have any pressing need to become a writer of the things I wrote?

She did not know that. She did not know me. Only an irrational or desperate person would see matters her way. So as we took a turn into the short furious cul-de-sac of desire, it was obvious that this affair could only have one conclusion. Afterwards, Alison and I shared a grim celebratory mood, as though after a painful illness a difficult friend has gone away, into the unknown. Or a house guest leaves, and the house is again large and liberated. Now she did not have to think of Wanda Fagan, and as my shame and guilt diminished I thought: Never again.

*

Then Alison and I separated. I fled. I suffered my own half-life. That cold winter and its sorrows and its signs: *Medford – Next 3 Exits*. George.

But when the postcard came I was better – more than better. I was about to embark on a long Pacific journey. Travel is only possible in a mood of optimism – I knew I was well. I was going away intending to come back, not looking for a new life. It was a realm of travel I hardly knew.

I had never been happy about Wanda Fagan's handwriting, the way it was so uncertain in its form, always looking as though it had been done in a hurry. People wrote like that on moving buses, children wrote that way, unhappy people. It lacked design, it seemed to reveal everything – uncertainty, unhappiness, haste. It was not intelligent script. You would never have known you were dealing with a PhD in computer science, and yet that was the degree that Wanda Fagan had earned, and she had tenure in a large state university, NYU to be precise.

How I hated that expression 'our old stomping ground,' referring to the postcard picture, a windmill on the Cape, the one in Brewster. It showed that her memory was as wobbly as her handwriting. Hadn't she remembered that we had had a furious argument on the way back to my house? It was her old eternal subject: *What about me?*

If I surrendered everything and she had my life, she would be happy. Then, what would I have? In true romantic love such questions are seldom asked – it is all delirious risk, and often, as in the case of Alison and me, it blossoms, and only withers after a long time. I was too old to take that risk. She was young enough to take any risk at all. And so I felt we would not last. I recognized our condition from the extensive and self-serving literature of men gloomily betraying their wives by taking a mistress: there were some few moments of peace, but the rest was fatigue and anxiety.

I sensed a great apprehension in realizing that I liked her a bit less after we made love, and sometimes did not like her at all. At times I did not know her afterwards. Who was she and what was I doing with her? I was sure she had the same ridiculous questions about me. So we were both disgusted strangers until the next fever made us lovers again. So much for the self-serving literature of betrayal.

Looking back, our affair seemed hardly significant. I suspected that it meant more to her, or that she wanted it to mean more. Yet she was all right now. The postcard said that much. She had wrongly felt that I was my old self – still married, regarding the marriage as indestructible because, as she had not managed to destroy it with her tears and her threats, who could?

My pain had liberated me. I now felt strong enough to reply to her postcard.

> *Dear Wanda,*
> *What a surprise to hear from you! I can't imagine*
> *where you got that old postcard, but I'm sure that –*

And then I faltered and stopped. It occurred to me that there was no return address on the postcard. I had no idea where she was. Seven years later was she still in New York City? I looked at the postmark: *Danbury CONN.*

I could not continue writing this letter to her until I knew her address. I called her at her home number, the only number I knew and was told by the recording office woman with the disciplinarian's voice at the telephone company that the number was no longer in service. Information for Manhattan said there was no listing for her name.

Her old secretary said, 'Dr Fagan is no longer a member of this department.'

'Do you have a number where she can be reached?'

'Just a minute.' She sighed; she had wanted to hang up on me. When she returned to the phone she said, 'Who is calling?'

I said I was a book dealer; that I had found a book order that had been mislaid; that I wished to send it to her.

'But you asked me for her telephone number.'

This was a very shrewd secretary.

'Her street address will be fine. I'll just pop this in the mail.'

'She is not Wanda Fagan anymore. She is Wanda Falkenberg.'

Her new name was spelled slowly by this cranky woman, and her new address was in the New York City area. I called information and got the number. I tried this over several days, at different times. Finally, a man's voice: 'She doesn't live here anymore.'

But that voice said everything: this might be her ex-husband, he was glum and defeated-sounding, wondering who I was. I wanted to talk to him much more than I wanted to find her. But I knew I had to talk to her first.

'I have a parcel for her' – I gave him my bookdealer's spiel.

Rather crossly – annoyed that he had to bother – he gave me her street address. It was in Danbury, Connecticut. That explained the postmark.

'I am sending this Fed Ex, so it would help to have her phone number.'

He rattled it off – only an ex-husband would know it that well and say it so disgustedly. I put the phone down, then picked it up and dialed the number.

'Hello.'

It was that small old tentative voice of a person who was accustomed to receiving unwelcome telephone calls. Wanda Feskowitz Fagan Cole Falkenberg. What a lot of names even a young woman can pick up.

'It's me.'

'Paul?'

And then the sparring began.

2

'How did you get this number?'

'One of your old friends.'

I had never known many of her friends. That was another problem with the affair – just the two of us. Or maybe it was not a problem. It exposed and isolated us and so we got to know each other quickly. The few friends I knew were so much like Wanda they frightened me.

'Who was it?'

'I don't want to get her into trouble, so I don't think I'll reveal her name.'

It seemed the right thing to say, and it worked.

'What do you want?'

'I thought I'd send you a note in reply to your postcard, but I didn't have your address.'

'Where are you?'

She had always been anxious but these questions revealed an even deeper intensity.

'Oh, I'm just traveling.'

If she knew where I was she would call me back; selfishly, I wanted to control the situation.

'Are you still married?'

'You seemed to think so when you sent me that postcard.'

'I think you're divorced – or else why would you be calling me?'

In her logic a person who made a call like this out of the blue was weak or desperate.

'I am separated. But that's not why I called. I was just wondering how you are.'

There was a long silence.

'I wish you hadn't called.'

'Are you married?'

There was another long silence which was like the weariest sigh imaginable.

'I don't want to talk about it.'

That said everything: she had been married, she was now either separated or divorced. She was easier to read than my wife of twenty years.

'I just want to get on with my life.'

That was the title of yet another of her insincere and muddled marching songs. It was not that I objected to her clichés, it was that she did not really mean them. She still had no life, she was still on the look-out for someone else's.

'I was glad to get your postcard. That windmill.'

'I thought you'd like it.'

Having a poor memory helped lessen a person's woe. Everything connected with the windmill had been miserable. If she had remembered anything, she would never have sent that picture.

'It was nice of you.'

'I have my points.'

'You sure do. You sound well.'

'So do you.'

'It's great to think that after all these years we're still strong.'

'I manage.'

'Do you have any children?'

Silence again. But it was a direct question, and she had to answer or be found out. She hesitated a fraction too long, her silence meaning yes.

'How many?'

'A little girl.'

Her voice was pride, defiance, anger that I had asked, irritation that she had replied, a kind of sorrow, and great confusion. This was not a troubled young woman anymore. This was the troubled mother of a tiny and probably demanding daughter. God help the man who became involved with the daughter of this woman.

She was a new woman; she had a new name and a new life. She did not want to be associated with her past. This was a woman I did not know.

'How long have you been separated?' she asked.

She could not resist, she really wanted to know. My marriage in her view was the one thing that had kept us apart; yet I knew better. It was my only excuse for keeping her at arm's length. I had used my marriage in order to be irresponsible. After I was separated I didn't dare. So I was the coward. My love for Alison had gone beyond the marriage, and that was why when the marriage ended I was so bereft, because I wanted to remain friends with her.

'I'll tell you how long I've been separated if you tell me the same thing.'

'I don't want to play games.'

Another of her feeble clichés, and one of her most insincere, since all we had ever done was play games; and what was this conversation except a game, in which each player was lying in order to extract the maximum amount of information, while revealing the minimum?

'You don't have to tell me anything. But I've been separated for about a year. It was sad and I'm sorry. If you've been through the same thing I know how painful it was, especially with a little child.'

A milder, less reproachful silence had no sigh in it, only sadness.

'We weren't getting along.'

Why did this statement irritate me so much? It was her tone of voice, uninvolved and dull and dismissive, and it was the ready-made expression. Even if she had met this man soon after she and I had split up she still could not have known him long, or been married more than – what? Allow a year for courtship, take away a year

419

or so since she left him, and what would you have? Maybe three or four years of marriage. I thought mainly about her child.

'But it's so hard – it shouldn't happen,' I said.

I kept on in this sorrowful and sentimental way until she interrupted sharply.

'I didn't love him anymore.'

It was her dismissive tone again and when I heard this trite expression as a summary of the marriage a chill went through me. Yes, my fears of her shallowness were justified. I had always been suspicious of her, fearful of her dependency and her moods. Yes, if I had left Alison for her it would not have lasted. But would it have been a disaster?

Perhaps, with that child, but I did not know.

Her dumb, perfunctory *I didn't love him anymore* sounded to me like, *I changed my mind.*

It was what I had disliked most in her, the very argument that day on the Cape when we had been heading for Provincetown and she got suddenly bored and irritably said, 'Isn't there anywhere nearer we could go?'

'You said you wanted to go to Provincetown.'

She had seen a restaurant review. Single women are tremendous readers of such reviews. It had less to do with food or eating than their fantasizing about a safe and stable world where, dressed up, they might allow themselves to be chaperoned.

'It's too far.'

'But I've already made the reservations at the restaurant.'

'You can unmake them.'

'I was looking forward to going.'

'See? Now it's all about you.'

'This trip was your idea. The restaurant that was mentioned in *Bon Appetit.*'

'I changed my mind.'

I got angry. She got upset. My anger proved I didn't love her – so she said. She began to cry. She seemed physically very small, like an ugly dwarf, when she cried. I thought: Leave her. I felt like dumping her by the side of the road. I was also afraid and had the distinct sense that she would grab the wheel and wrench it and send us into the path of an oncoming car.

For about ten minutes, overwhelmed by this hysteria, we said nothing. Then we came to Brewster and I pulled off the road, fearing that my ability to drive had deteriorated. It was just a tourist attraction – the real windmills of the Cape were gone. But she believed in it.

'I wish I had a camera.'

So she was gullible as well. Unreasonably, I held that against her.

And here was her windmill again on her postcard. She had forgotten the argument that had led to my wanting to leave her. Her saying 'I changed my mind' was something I feared; that she would tell me one day, 'I don't love you anymore.' I knew that now.

This whole recollection was a silence that had frozen our telephone conversation.

'Are you still there?'

How long had she been saying that?

'I'm here. Just thinking.'

'I thought we got cut off.'

She had forgotten the cause of my reverie, that she had said, *I didn't love him anymore.*

'What you said sounded perfunctory,' I told her.

'You know all the put-down words.'

'That you didn't love him anymore.'

'He was in denial. He had been co-dependent. You can be such an asshole.'

'So that was that. "Guess I'll move on."'

'I didn't have to process that relationship.'

'Time for me to move on.'

'So you just called me up to torment me with all your sick writer's questions.'

'No. I wanted to thank you for the postcard.'

'Oh, that. So where are you traveling to?'

'Maybe New York.'

'I'm not that far away.'

'What's your area code?'

An idle question – nothing on earth would induce me to see her. It was first the idea in her mind that I was separated, and that there might be a resumption of our affair. But more than anything our little affair had been a lesson in the danger of trifling with someone's emotions.

And she had a life now – perhaps the one she had always wanted.

She was a single parent, had a child. She had not wanted to be denied anything. In those years since we had split up she'd had it all – she was a fiancée, a bride, a wife, a mother, a divorcee, and an employee. All that! It was an elaborate form of conquest – total transformation. I guessed her ex-husband had filled her with the confidence and given her the money she needed in order to leave him. That was what fascinated me: she really was different from the young woman I had known.

My life has changed quite a bit.

She had truly found a new life. It obliquely gave me hope, but perhaps you had to be very shallow or calculating or greedy to make it work.

Now she and the child remained, and she was back to earth. She had gotten what she had asked for, even if it was not what she wanted. It was hard for her to be needy now – the child came first, and life could not have been easy. She was not young anymore and, as for her beauty, you had to subtract the child from her looks.

I was glad I had called her, because now I knew I never wanted to see her again. She sensed this. She had the instincts of an intrusive animal, the reflexes of a rat, always sniffing, always looking up, always alert and twitching.

'I have to go. I'm having a drink with someone.'

'You're such a fucking snob.'

Believing that I was rejecting her, she had to insult me – her pride demanded it. I let it pass.

'Sorry I intruded.'

'You're so insincere.'

'Do you really want to know what I have to do?'

'No, because you're too fucking anecdotal.'

I pitied her, I pitied all people who helplessly raged at life and its injustice, never guessing that, however unfair it seemed, it was justly deserved. If her nose was in a trap it was because she had been sniffing greedily for more cheese. That was the piteous part.

'See you later.'

'Not if I can help it.'

That was my reward for calling when I shouldn't have. It had been a mistake. I deserved her clumsy insults.

3

Who was he, this man she had married and divorced, the father of her child? I told myself it did not matter. But the longer I thought of it the more profound my feeling that he mattered. In the end I was preoccupied by him, because whoever he might be he was the man I would have become; whatever life he was leading would have been mine.

And though I did not know Wanda anymore, I understood that she had not merely been married and borne a child but that she had gotten a life. Yet what had happened to the man who had supplied that life? What she had left him with was what she would have left me with. Had she been my other wife, I would have been that man, and his life would have been mine.

In my speculative frame of mind the only way I could determine the caliber of the bullet I had dodged was to see the man it had hit.

The secretary of a lawyer friend of mine once told me, 'I can find anyone,' and it seemed to me an absurd boast. That was naive of me. One of the greatest skills a person can have in the commercial world, and not only commercial, is the ability to locate the where-abouts of a particular person – a debtor, a patron, a client, a cus-tomer, a felon, a friend. Your whole working life depends on such people. Only writers, dealing in the realm of the imagination, are content to find people in their heads. That is the writer's boast. We invent them. Everyone else goes looking.

But in the active search for my other life I was operating in the world of reality. I needed to find this man in order to finish my story. I realized that the ability to find someone – to locate a stranger lost in the darkness – approaches an art, since its nearest analog is in the writer searching his imagination for a character.

I strongly suspected that the man I had spoken to when I was trying to find out Wanda's address was her ex-husband. But I needed to be sure. So I called my friend's secretary and reminded her what she had told me.

'I think I can find the guy,' she said. 'Tell me everything you know.'

'Just his last name and his telephone number.'

'Area code?'

'Nine one four.'

'Does he work in New York City?'

'Why do you ask?'

'Because that's White Plains,' she said. 'What else do you know?'

'He might be in computers.' Wanda certainly was. And these computer nerds – 'tech weenie' was her expression – tended to gravitate to each other.

'That helps. There are directories.'

'And I think he used to live in Danbury.' Surely if she got his life, she got the house.

'Tell me where he used to be and I'll tell you where he went.'

I liked that, because that had its literary parallels, too.

His name was Todd Falkenberg. He worked for Global Teletronics in the Sales and Marketing Division. He was just a year older than me. The company was one of the leaders in telecommunications and had developed a range of portable satellite telephones. The Global brochure depicted these phones as convenient as luggage – one was a suitcase, another a briefcase, the last the size of a laptop computer.

I decided to ask Mr Falkenberg for a demonstration. I called him, but – worried that Wanda might have told him about me – said that my name was Edward Medford and that I was coming to New York.

He said, 'I'm in the city Tuesdays and Thursdays. How about next week? I can do Tuesday afternoon. Let me make a suggestion.'

That voice was almost certainly the one that had given me the Danbury number.

He was accommodating, he was manipulative, he was a sales-man, and when I met him I was pleased to see that not only was he talkative, he was also informative and observant – brand-name con-scious in the way that competitive people are; not necessarily accur-ate, but I could do the subtraction. He was smiling at my briefcase.

'That an Orvis bag? I buy their stuff all the time. Our newest model satellite phone will fit inside that puppy.'

'Is it on the market?'

'I'll lay it all out for you.'

Salesmen never gave a straight answer, and the words yes or no were not in their vocabulary.

We were in his office on Lexington Avenue in the Seventies, a busy neighborhood, because of the large hospital nearby, and in spite of the hospital, very noisy. The office he said was temporary – he was in the process of moving. True, there were cartons stacked at the side of the room, but I had the feeling he was not going anywhere.

In contrast to the provisional look of the office, he was careful about his appearance, very tidy. Everything about him was studied – the shoes, the belt, the tie, the suit; he knew how to make an impression, though it was lost on me. I saw only a man who wanted to be regarded for the way he was dressed; this was not something I valued at all. He was a bit older than me, but he was in much better shape. That did impress me. I wanted to know more about that.

I was on the verge of asking this when I was distracted by the framed photographs of the little girl on his desk. Three photographs – in a pink blanket an even pinker infant; on all fours, like a wind-up toy; a portrait of a woman as a little girl. She had Wanda's looks – the pale eyes, the willful mouth and there was something of the diet-prone Wanda in the little girl's chubby cheeks.

'Hey, welcome to Global,' he said, full of salesman's poise, and he shook my hand and showed me a chair, all the while apologizing for the state of the office.

There was a great deal in his handshake. It was of course a deliberate grip, a bit overprecise. But his fingerpads were hard, the heel of his hand was hard. He did not have to squeeze hard for me to know that he had a powerful grip. I guessed that he probably rowed or biked. Realizing that he had a sport, at his age, and probably a sport he excelled at, made me judge him differently, as much more complex than the salesman stereotype I had first seen.

His face was blotchy and burned. He was not sleek in the vain way of someone who worked out, but rather, seriously healthy in the manner of a solitary athlete – his muscles knotted and bunched, his neck thick, his knuckles skinned. You noticed his strength because it made his clothes fit awkwardly; he had sturdy shoulders and patches on the balding top of his head were sunburned and peeling, as were the backs of his hands.

He conveyed the restless impression of an athlete confined indoors, for he had a slight clumsiness, checking himself as he moved in the small space of his office. In this setting his good health was incongruous. He was a big man, and when he squatted to show me the smallest model of the satellite phone, he hitched up his trousers; a guess told me he might be a cyclist. Two solid blocks of muscles were his calves, and the rest was whipcord.

'You ride a bike?'

'How'd you know?'

I was sorry for being so impulsive in my curiosity. But cycling was a generally solitary business. It had little to do with teams and companionship. It was another and almost unknowable life, a kind of monasticism – that was what made me see him differently. I was more respectful but also warier.

'Just guessed.'

'You know bikes?'

'I have a Merlin.'

He smiled. 'You know bikes.' He looked aside and said, 'I had a Kestrel until a little over a year ago. Carbon fiber. It had a few dings but it was incredibly light. A beautiful machine. I had to sell it.'

I filled in the rest. It was a $3,000 bike. He needed the money because of the divorce.

'Now I'm just riding an old Fuji I had in the garage.'

'You cycle in Manhattan?'

'I cycle to work from Westchester. I've got an apartment there.'

'I can't imagine many people do that.'

That pleased him. He told me how long it took, the route; how he changed his clothes and got a shower in this office. And with all this talk about cycling I liked him a bit better and he saw me as something other than a customer.

'I drove in today, because I've got an errand to run in Connecticut.'

Where Wanda lived; he was probably going to make a visit, his once-a-week chance to see his little girl. I was thinking of this, seeing him with the child when his voice broke the spell.

'Where's this going?'

'Excuse me?'

'You want to talk bikes or you want to talk satellite phones?'

He said it pleasantly in the bantering manner of a friend, and as he spoke I saw another picture of his little girl: another shrine, Wanda's face distorted and miniaturized. It made me more curious about him.

To satisfy and detain him, I talked phones. 'It's a niche market,' he was saying. I found it hard to listen, because I was distracted by his athlete's health and focus. He was two men, the sportsman and the salesman, and they were so different he appeared divided and somewhat clumsy.

'We're a small company, we started in semi-conductors' – Wanda's field, as it happened – 'but we began to concentrate on telecommunications. We sold the semi-conductor division and – hey, can I give you an analogy? The big companies are like elephants. Ever see an elephant's foot? Big round thing, but if you imagine it in a room it doesn't get into the corners. That's where we are, in the corners, where the elephant's feet of your IBMs and your Toshibas and your Microsofts can't go.'

I complimented him on his elephant-foot illustration and said, 'I'd like to know more about the satellite phone.'

'I can give you the specs. I'll find a spec sheet.'

'I just wanted to see how the phone works.'

'Right. Why should you be interested in tolerances? Here, let's get someone on the phone.'

'Shall we call your wife?'

'Ex-wife. No thanks.'

He was hurt. He remembered.

'I'll try the head office. It's on Long Island.'

We tried three times, and failed.

'It's not locking on to the satellite. I keyed in the right coordinates.' He frowned at the window. 'The hospital might be in the way.'

'That must be very frustrating,' I said.

But he smiled. 'No problem. I've been in anger management.'

I was so fascinated by this expression 'anger management' I was unaware of his re-positioning the phone on the window sill. He had aimed its lid – which contained the antenna – past the upper corner of the hospital. He handed the receiver to me. I heard it ring and then, 'Good afternoon, Global.'

It was better, smaller, more efficient than I could possibly have imagined. The fact that I had no use for it, that I had only come here to see the man Wanda had married and divorced, did not keep me from admiring the product he was trying to sell me.

'Help me with this,' he said. 'You want one of these phones for what reason? Remote places? Construction site? Secure line? You know, a cellular phone works in so many places.'

'I'm planning to do a lot of foreign travel. I think "remote places" is probably the best description.'

'I'm not asking you what you do,' he said – and it seemed slightly arch. 'Only where you do it.'

'New Guinea is one of my destinations.'

'There's some microwave technology out there because of the mining, but you're right – this phone would be very useful.'

'What do these things cost?'

'I can get you a price on it.'

That was salesman-speak for a lot of money.

'I'll need to know that, because' – and here I was freewheeling – 'I'm relocating to Manhattan and I've obviously got to factor in that expense. I know these phones cost quite a bit.'

He did not hear me say that. He said, 'You looking for office space?'

'I'm looking for everything, but office space is my priority.'

He became even more alert – friendlier, more companionable.

'I might be able to help. You got some time?'

'I don't want to monopolize your day. You said you had an errand to run.'

'If you want to go for a ride I could show you some locations. It'll only take an hour. How many square feet are you looking for?'

That seemed an accurate question, though I had no idea of the answer.

In desperation, I made conjuring gestures with my hands and said, 'About this size.'

'This is just under three hundred. Let me show you two places.'

I was glad for a chance to spend a little more time with him, even though it was under false pretenses. But it was no greater a charade than my proposing to buy one of his $20,000 phones. His car, which we retrieved from an underground parking garage on Seventy-seventh Street, was an old Volvo station wagon, with a bike rack mounted on the rear. Stacked on the back seat were Global brochures showing the various satellite phones.

'I'd rather be on a bike,' he said, in the crush of the Lexington Avenue traffic.

'I don't think I could handle this,' I said.

'After my marriage broke up I was not about to compromise my immune system with casual dating,' he said. 'The biking was a necessity. And I worked more – for the money, and for the distraction.'

Crossing over to Third Avenue, we became caught in the middle of a block behind a delivery van. Falkenberg shook his head, he smiled sourly; and I remembered what he had said about having been in anger management.

'That's how I came to be moonlighting in real estate,' he said. 'Funny, I didn't start out in sales.'

On the dashboard of his car was another shrine to his daughter: a snapshot in a plastic frame was magnetized to the dash, and a ribbon tied in a bow to it – probably a hair ribbon, definitely a relic. I thought how estrangement from your children can turn that desperate love into a religious frenzy.

'Cute kid,' I said.

'Yeah,' he said hoarsely. He was too moved to say more.

When I saw that he was trying to hide his pain – that he felt pain, that he had been hurt, and undermined by it, I saw myself in him. He was like a weak and susceptible part of myself, someone I pitied and partly loathed.

The compassion I felt was useful, because his sadness, his depression perhaps, made him reactive and strange. Heading for a parking lot he saw a car pulling away from a meter and he shouted so loudly in a mirthless parody of glee that he startled me.

Walking from there to the first office he wanted to show me, he pointed to a tree inside an iron-work fence in front of a brownstone and said, 'I used to have one of those trees. It's a Japanese maple. I had a fence like that, too. They look nice but they're hell to fix. Sometimes the cold gets to them and they crack.'

It was a bonus to have him outside his office, in the world. By way of being competitive and impressive he volunteered a lot of information. The tree was not in White Plains – that was just a temporary situation. No, he had planted the tree himself at his house in Danbury, where he had raised a family. He had two older children, a boy and a girl. They were out of college – they were in jobs now, in their late twenties.

He even spoke of Wanda, though obliquely.

'I said to them, "You're glad I'm here?" ' – he was referring to one of his employers, I had missed the prologue – "Thank my ex-wife for that," I says. I could have put in for early retirement. Now I'll probably be doing another fifteen years.'

This thought was so dismal all I could manage was a platitude to the effect that work was one of man's driving instincts.

'And sex is the other. My shrink told me that,' he said. 'But this isn't work. I was doing the real thing before. I'm not a salesman – I'm just trying to turn a buck.'

'You're succeeding,' I said, hoping he would tell me more.

He made a face, meaning that he was struggling, and he said, 'I don't want to succeed at this. I was in development. I was creating programs – software for satellite phones. I was my own boss. I was free.'

I wondered whether I wanted to hear the rest of this painful story.

He said, 'I lost everything.'

At the moment his life had become simpler he had fallen in love and left his wife, he said. 'It was one of those things.' He was not in despair. That was the worst of it. He said that he had payments to make – alimony, maintenance – a job to do, a daughter he adored. He had not expected any of it. He had lost his job, his house, his wife, his child, his peace of mind, his money; he feared for his health or he would not have been biking so furiously. He was saying, *Hey, you don't plan these things.*

'My second marriage didn't work out,' he said. 'But I have a lovely daughter.'

He saw her every week, he said. He was going there this afternoon, after he showed me this office space. He didn't want to leave it too late, because of the traffic.

'Why today? Isn't seeing your kid kind of a weekend thing?'

'Tell that to my ex-wife.' There was emotion in his eyes. 'It doesn't matter what day it is. I'd go anytime. But, God, these visits break my heart.'

He did not say a bad word about her, nor did he praise her. All he said when I asked him a direct question about her was, 'I think I know her a lot better now than I did when I married her.'

He had resigned himself to this. He was like a mountain climber who for the sake of making it to the summit had lost all his toes to frostbite. But he did not contemplate his loss. That was the hardest part for me to bear, that I knew what he had lost and he didn't; and I began to understand that I was a free man.

I went through the motions of seeing the office space. It was two shabby rooms, dirty windows, newspapers spread on the bare floors. Commenting about it was a bit like talking about abstract paintings at an exhibition. Was I vague and uninformed and obtuse, or were the pictures bad? Now the very term 'office space' would make me think of a rathole.

Falkenberg had gone to the window, and with his back to the room, and to me, he began speaking in a low voice.

'I haven't talked about this at all, with anyone,' he said. 'I think I should do it more often. Are you married?'

He addressed this question to the window, though I knew he was speaking to me. That was awkward. Because his back was turned, and he could not see me, I was unable to give him a simple nod. I had to make a whole sentence.

'My wife and I split up over a year ago.'

That was when he turned and looked at me. His eyes were like an exile's – wounded and wary; everything looked strange to those eyes. He said, as though to another exile, 'I'm so glad I met you.'

He approached me. I dreaded that he was going to embrace me – hug me, saying something that would make me feel even worse. But he shook my hand. He apologized for his hurry, he urged me to stay in touch. I had the feeling he wanted to be my friend.

'I hope to see you real soon!' he called out, just before he drove away.

But time passed, like mist lifting from a marsh and revealing the ditches and bones and the tidemark and the broken shells on the mud banks; more light, more detail, and it was the detail that shocked me and made me sad.

SEVENTEEN

My Other Life

One of the delusions of travel is that you can be a new person in a distant land. I was in Honolulu, and Christmas was coming, and I should have been happy. But putting out the trash barrels or carrying groceries up the driveway – whenever I was exposed to the gaze of neighbors or just their twitching curtains – I felt like Adolf Eichmann on Garibaldi Street in Buenos Aires. I was another fugitive hiding in a far-off bungalow. What about the notion that being far from home meant the past was erased? My hedges, my flowers, the barrels I dragged made me seem like just a harmless householder, yet every move I made on this prim suburban street was furtive, and in my mind I was a monster.

This feeling persisted, a memory of that book about Eichmann's capture by the Israelis. What I remembered best about it was not the commando operation, but rather the routine of that awful man shuffling anonymously in the suburbs, doing ordinary things, but always looking over his shoulder. I could not explain my feeling. I was not a murderer or a criminal. Hadn't I a right to be happy? Yet I had an obscure sense not of guilt but of danger, as though I was a victim being stalked in a case of mistaken identity. Nothing I did prevented me from thinking of myself as a hunted man.

I had stopped dreaming. Dreams had always stirred me, given me ideas, and I woke with my imagination going, as though my dreams had given it a spin and it was still turning when I opened my eyes. I thought of dreams as my other life. Without them I could not write and, because writing vitalized me, I was less than half alive without it. My work had come to a stop. I felt slow and stupid, my mind was muddy. I found the sunshine unbearable, and my nights were worse. Instead of dreams I had nightmares. I had no memory of them in the morning, only a sense of terror that took away my wit. Each dream is different, but every nightmare is the same, because fear is monotonous, like something spilled in the mind, ruining the imagination.

One night in Honolulu, there was a phone call, a calm voice that said, 'I have some news.'

'Who is this?'

The voice was uneducated, with a hint of an accent and yet it was mellifluous. It combined politeness with a kind of insult, the way English people are often rude.

'Never mind, listen,' the voice said. 'Paul Theroux is dead.'

I said, 'I'm Paul Theroux.'

'No, you're not. I know who you are.'

This shook me. I wanted to say, Ask my wife! But that very thought upset me. The word 'wife' or the word 'marriage' I could not even pronounce without stammering. This was a delicate matter and it was so painful I preferred not to think about it. I had not seen Alison for four years. I had been separated from her for that long – 'Semi-detached,' I explained to the few people who asked, and I hated my glibness. But semi-detached was what we were. I felt it was helpful to her, my resisting the finality of petitioning for divorce. Divorce would be like shoving her out of the window. This way neither of us was alone. Being alone seemed to me like the worst fate – like not existing at all, and although I had never asked her I was sure she felt the same. On any official form I had to fill out I always swallowed hard and checked the box marked 'Married' and felt that this was a favor to her.

That phone call ('Paul Theroux is dead') gave me a reason to call her, but I put it off. Because of the time difference between Hawaii and London, I was never able to call her. Anyway, I had something else on my mind.

I needed a break; I had to get away from this bungalow that made me feel like Eichmann. The weather was perfect for paddling off the coast of Molokai. Paddling, and camping on a beach, and moving down the coast, from bay to bay of a tropical island, would be a tremendous restorative, and these south winds meant that this normally dangerous coast would be safe: calm seas, low surf, a light following breeze to give me a tail wind. No let-up in this sticky Kona weather, the weatherman said on TV, but the trade winds would be back next week.

So I had four days of perfect weather. I made my arrangements quickly: packed my camping gear and collapsible kayak, bought some food to take with me, and a plane ticket to Molokai.

The night before I left I had another call, and I could almost see the gloating face when I heard, 'Paul Theroux is dead . . .'

I hung up and set off in the morning, having hardly slept. I got an early flight to Molokai, rented a car at the airport at Hoolehua and had lunch in Kaunakakai, bought some bottled water, and drove the twenty-odd miles to the Halawa Valley. My idea was to leave my rental car there, paddle along the north shore to Kalaupapa, and then get a lift back to pick up the car. My only worry was the weather and the sea conditions: would the winds remain light, would it be calm enough to launch the boat in the notoriously surfy Halawa Bay?

Conditions were so good that I was able to make camp, set up my boat and go for an evening paddle to the outer cliffs of the bay. I looked west along the shore, where the high cliffs loomed, the same blackish hue and shape as the turrets on a gothic cathedral: towers, spires, belfries and buttresses. It seemed more appropriate and precise to describe these cliffs in terms of architecture than as geological formations since they seemed more orderly and glorious and dignified than any amorphous rock walls.

These were the cliffs I paddled past the next day. I struggled in my small boat, in spite of the calm sea. I had slept badly in my tent on the dark sand beach. Every sound in a distant place to me these days was like a reproachful voice.

It helped that almost from the moment I set out I could see my destination, Kalaupapa Peninsula, twenty miles off. That first night, as the sun set behind it, I steered myself into a bay – Pelekunu Bay, I reckoned, from my chart – and landed my boat almost without getting my feet wet. I set up camp quickly, and made noodles and tea while the sky was still light. The gothic cliffs of the bay enclosed me, and when darkness fell it was as though I had fallen into a cellar of that same cathedral I had imagined – but a damp, unholy dungeon, strangely hot and airless.

I had a nightmare that a specter had appeared to me and was standing before me and stinking. But it was not a nightmare. When I woke, and crawled out of the tent, I saw it – dark and hooded, the same shape as the looming cliffs. Much worse than an angry apparition, the thing seemed to be gloating in silence because I had done something wrong. And it was not a ghost; it was an actual shape, with a shadow, and real smell hanging about it. I got back into my tent with the full knowledge that the thing was outside, casually haunting me, as though I had already died. I did not sleep that night either.

In the morning I left the bay and paddled on, with the smell of that hooded figure still clinging to me. I was so determined now to end this trip that I hardly took any notice of the cliffs beside me. The waves reflected by hitting the foot of the cliff made the water so turbulent that I paddled a mile or so offshore to where the water was calmer. Unable to land, I ate lunch – a sandwich, a swig of water – in my boat and paddled on slowly until the late afternoon. Towards noon I passed the lighthouse just above Kahi'u Point, at the tip of the Kalaupapa Peninsula, and around five I was just off Kalaupapa.

It seemed to me that this trip had been worth it. I could now see the leper settlement, my destination, and I had a sense that though I had been spooked the night before, I had overcome my feeling of persecution, or at least had managed to diminish it. Yes, the fear still straggled after me, but it was a threadbare remnant and at this rate I would soon outdistance it.

Just inside the harbor there was a jetty, and a man standing on it, watching me, the sun setting behind the cliffs casting a shadow over my approach. He said nothing, although I called out hello. His face was dark, and I took him to be one of the few lepers still remaining.

I decided to take my boat apart while there was still some day-light, because I wanted to get an early start on the mule track in the morning. I removed my gear from the boat, unfastened the frame and stripped off the hull, working quickly in the fading light. As I broke down the frame and began packing it, making it into bundles and slipping them into my carrying bag, I noticed that the man – the leper – was crouched a short distance away. He had withered fingers and a sunken face, his skull clearly showing through his skin.

'Still here?' I said, trying to be friendly.

He did not reply. His silence threatened me, and at last he spoke up and froze me.

'We are better off knowing that we belong here, alone in our own world. No one is waiting for us somewhere else.'

I wanted to say: I didn't ask you that. No sooner had he stopped speaking than a shadow covered him, a moving darkness with a black edge, the mountain slipping over him as the sun sank behind it. I could not think of a reply to what he had said, and I thought he had gone, when from the darkness he spoke again.

'You have a telephone call.'

'How do you know who I am?'

But he simply pointed to the office in the small frame house on the pier. When I entered it I could hardly see, and it was only by fumbling on the desk that I discovered that the phone was off the hook. Standing in the darkness, I held it to my ear, and heard a familiar voice.

'Paul Theroux is dead . . .'

I put down the phone and went outside to look for the leper. He had gone. There was no light at all, no moon, and not even the lamps of the small settlement reached the jetty. I was too upset by the phone call to introduce myself at the mission, and I was too tired to eat. I picked up my sleeping bag and water bottle and, leaving my boat, walked to the edge of the beach I later discovered was called Papaloa, and I slept there, miserably, fighting demons, thinking: We are better off knowing that we belong here, alone in our own world. No one is waiting for us somewhere else.

At first light I went back to the jetty for my food bag and ate a grapefruit and some cheese and bread, and looked for a way out of the valley. I knew that there were fewer than fifty lepers left in Kalaupapa, but even so I saw no people at all. The valley was famous for its zigzag mule track up to the ridge. I thought of hiring two mules, one for me, the other for my gear, but how to arrange it?

I was debating this when a pickup truck appeared on the jetty.

'You can get in,' the driver said. He was the man I had seen the night before.

'I want to go to the airport,' I said.

'I know.' He smiled and, before I could ask him how, went on, 'I know who you are.'

It was not the voice but rather the statement that seemed familiar. Where had I heard it? Then I remembered – on the phone. And I recognized the voice, the same voice.

'Do you live at Kalaupapa?' I asked.

'You're wondering if I am a patient here,' he said. 'No. I'm cured.

These are harmless scars,' and he raised his withered fingers, saying goodbye.

I dreaded going back to Honolulu because now I knew my nights would be terrible and that the phone would ring and the leper's voice would tell me that I was dead. And so it happened that very night, but I let it ring. Its ringing was worse than any words could be, because I imagined the ringing to be the words, jangling and repeating my death sentence.

The middle of the night in Honolulu is morning in London. I picked up the receiver and stabbed at it until I got a dial tone, and I made my call. I knew the number so well I could dial it in the dark, and was sad as soon as I heard the familiar musical phrase of the seven notes of the touch tone.

I had dreaded this day, but I went ahead and said it: 'I'm divorcing you.'

It was a short conversation, and afterwards I was alone. I had never felt so solitary. The sun came up, but I was so tired I dozed off and overslept and began to dream. They were dreams of great happiness, that I had never had before, and they were tinted by the color and light of the dawn.

EIGHTEEN

EPILOGUE:

Personal Effects

The boxes had been sent from London, marked *Personal Effects*, and I opened them at random, unwrapping the bandaged and wadded contents and setting each item down on the sunny lawn.

One large brass samovar, Moscow, 1968, with a dent from my having kicked it under my seat as I flew to Delhi on my way to Singapore. I had been worried that the Soviet customs official would ask me where I had changed my money to buy it. I had done so illegally on the black market, eight rubles to the dollar. The samovar had cost ten dollars. The Soviet official tore open the paper wrapper, and saw it was a samovar. He smiled and said: 'You like tea!'

A wooden teapot in red lacquer, a present from my Japanese hosts in Tokyo, 1976. I had admired one in a noodle shop, just lingered over it, saying, 'That's nice,' and this was given to me the next day without explanation.

A thick ceramic mug penciled on the bottom in Will's writing: *To Dad. Will made this the Summer Term 1984 under the stern vigil of Mrs Whalen.*

A meerschaum pipe bowl of a bearded and turbaned Turk: Istanbul, 1973, *Railway Bazaar* trip. An English-made silver tankard – Whitbread Literary Award, 1978, for *Picture Palace*. A medal encased in lucite, inscribed: *Playboy Magazine Best Short Story 1975.* Associate Alumni Award plaque, 1984, University of Massachusetts, *For Distinguished Professional Service,* handed to me by Michael Dukakis, Governor of Massachusetts, and unsuccessful presidential candidate, 1990.

A gunmetal box made in India, inlaid with silver and inscribed on the bottom: *To Alison and Paul with much Love on your marriage, Barbara and Rajat, Dec 1967, Kampala.*

A split rock half of purple crystal – given to me in London, 1972, by a woman who said, 'It's a geode. You mean you didn't know that?'

A dog-tooth necklace: New Guinea. 'Please come back, Mister Paul. We go fishing catch too mas this time.' A brass turtle incense burner from South India, bought when Anton was working at SOS Children's Village outside Madras, 1986, the year he went to Cambridge.

A human skull, with a latched lift-up cranium, sold to me by a former Singapore student Chung Yee Chong for £150. Her name for the skull was 'Henry.'

A Chinese pale jade bowl, a small rock-crystal fish from a shop in Chengdu, Sichuan. A large antique brass temple pitcher from the market in Lhasa, Tibet. A gold Tara, Tibetan. A bowl made of a human skull, lined with silver. A set of wooden bowls lined with silver, *Iron Rooster* trip, 1986–7. Tibetan guide: 'I am obliged to tell you that you are forbidden to take these objects out of China. You can try, but you understand that I have to tell you this.'

A collection of walking sticks: one made from the spine of a shark (an iron rod running through it), the handle a dodo's beak; another of ebony, the handle a tiger's tooth – from Wales, *Kingdom by the Sea* trip, 1982; two Malacca canes, one with a silver handle; a bamboo cane, a sword stick.

A leather box from Florence, present from Mother, 1976, with a Florida seashell inside. A brass oil lamp bought in the Singapore flea market in 1969. A baby crocodile skull from Zimbabwe, bought on a visit to Will, who was teaching at Guruve, 1988, the year he went to Oxford. A jawbone of a cow found in a field near Eddleston, Scotland, 1982, on a family walking holiday. That same day we found a sheep so heavy with wool that it had tipped over and could not right itself, like a turtle on its back.

A high-powered microscope bought at an auction in Putney, southwest London, 1975. I bought my first microscope when I was in the sixth grade, and planned to be a doctor; one of the regrets of my life is that I did not become a medical doctor. I have owned and used microscopes ever since I was twelve years old.

A porcupine quill from Malawi, 1964. The quill, regarded as a good luck charm, was sold to me by a doctor at the market in Lilongwe. He was a *mganga*, a witch doctor, not because he was a witch but because he cured people of witchcraft and possession. He said, 'It is sixty shillings.' I said, 'I will give you two.' He said, 'That is all right,' and handed the quill over.

A dagger with a horn handle carved in the shape of a lion, bought in Colombo, Sri Lanka, 1973, used by me as a letter opener. The toothy hinged jaws of a barracuda, from Mombasa, 1985.

One kudu horn, found in a London junk shop, 1974. A rectangular marble paperweight, London, 1978. A large ceramic glazed disc depicting a phoenix perched on a stump, Kunming, China, 1986.

A small pewter teapot with a jade handle, Suchow, China; a large carved and lacquered fish, from a trip down the Yangtze, 1979. A metal inkpot in the shape of a frog, from Hong Kong, 1987.

A small wooden mortar and pestle for mixing betel nut and lime; two carved canoe splash boards, two carved canoe prows in the shape of crocodiles: New Guinea, 1991.

Two bronze Buddhist Taras, Darjeeling, 1984. A Chinese puppet head of a demon, Yangguo, 1986. A pair of binoculars. An opium pipe, Singapore, 1970. A large glazed fish bowl, decorated with carp motif, eighteenth century, from Shanghai. An African hand ax, from Malawi, 1965. A wood-panel painting, depicting a mandarin with two attendants, torn from a Vietnamese temple that had been partially destroyed in a rocket attack, and bought from a Chinese antique dealer who ran his business from an attic in Saigon, 1973.

A wooden armchair bought in Fulham, London, 1976, with two large worn velvet cushions. A hand-woven square yard of cloth, from Guatemala, an eighteenth-century painting of Saint Dominic, from Peru – *Old Patagonian* trip, 1978. A topographical map of coastal Honduras. A small carpet, woven in Iran, with a motif of men carrying machine guns. A Victorian garden statue, cast in lead, based on Michelangelo's *The Freed Slave*. A copy of *In the Clearing*, by Robert Frost, inscribed: *To Paul Theroux from Robert Frost,* *1962.*

One teak writing desk, with large, ingeniously designed detachable legs, one teak armchair, both made to order by a Chinese carpenter in Singapore. I drew a picture of the ideal desk and had it made because I was having trouble with my novel *Jungle Lovers* – working on a wobbly table.

Some pictures, some books, some files, a trunk of manuscripts, a sum of money.

And a large glass mixing bowl, stamped on the base *Made in Poland* and bought in Nyasaland at the Limbe Trading Company in 1964. Somehow this inexpensive and ordinary household object, perhaps the first I had ever bought, had survived almost thirty years. But that was only part of its fascination. This was the bowl that my African cook, Julius Magoya, had used to hold fruit salad.

He had asked me to buy it, and he had filled it that first day with cut-up fruit: pawpaws, bananas, apples, oranges, grapes, and tangerines for which he used the Afrikaans word *naartjies*. There was far too much fruit salad. After a week half a bowl of it was left. Julius did not throw it away. He cut up more fruit and added it, filling the bowl again, giving it a stir. A week later, though I had not finished the fruit salad, he added more, and the bowl brimmed again. He repeated this every week, mixing the new with the old, the sweet with the sour, the crisp with the sodden. He never tossed out what was in the bowl, no matter how small the amount. It was replenished every week; years later I was still eating fruit salad, out of the same bowl, which had never been emptied.

At the age of fifty, I was glad to have that bowl back. Now I saw the point of it: Julius's endless fruit salad represented for me the meaning of life and the source of all art.